EDENLAND

EDENLAND

WALLACE KING

This is a work of fiction. Names, characters, organizations, places, events, and incidents are either products of the author's imagination or are used fictitiously.

Published by Lake Union Publishing, Seattle

www.apub.com

Amazon, the Amazon logo, and Lake Union Publishing are trademarks of Amazon.com, Inc., or its affiliates.

ISBN-13: 9781503934948
ISBN-10: 1503934942

Cover design by Mumtaz Mustafa

Printed in the United States of America

That love is all there is,
Is all we know of love

—Emily Dickinson

ONE

It was the light that pulled him from the Great Dismal. At first he thought it was his imagination, for he'd seen other things that weren't really there in the three days since he'd entered the awful swamp. For nearly one day and one whole night he was certain he'd never again see another human being, for the swamp was dark and endless and full of horrors beyond any of his expectations. But the light was still there after he'd shut his eyes tight and opened them again. It burned bright and steady. A nightbird sang its lonely little heart out as he crossed a crude footbridge but the song was swallowed by the wind. It was whipping up a frenzy and he had to grab a worn rope to keep from falling into the thick sludge beneath. A lantern flickered in the window of a one-room shack. A stringy wisp of white smoke hovered over the slapped-on roof. For a moment the light disappeared as the trees around the place hid it from view. A gust nearly lifted him off his feet and the trees blew wild and frenzied, almost like they were trying to rip themselves free and flee. When the trees parted, the light beckoned once more. Something inside whispered, *No, no, get away,* but he hadn't eaten and he was more scared of the Dismal than the voice in his head. He hunched down low and snuck up on the rickety porch. He lifted himself just high enough to peep inside the lighted window.

He nearly fell off the porch when he saw her, for it certainly was nothing he was expecting, but then again, nothing he'd expected had happened in the three days that now seemed like three years, so he sucked down his surprise at seeing the woman inside. Black hair hung long down her back, crazed in matted curls. Her threadbare calico dress was three inches too short and her feet were filthy. She was dancing though there was no music. Around and around she whirled, her skirt belling with air. In the glow of the lantern she held a crockery bowl with two hands in front of her as if it were a partner. Every couple of spins she'd pause, dip a wooden spoon, lick it clean, then recommence her twirling. The spin and whirl mesmerized him but for only a moment. His focus was on how to get whatever was in the bowl. He squinted through the window trying to make out her face, but the matted black hair kept swinging in front of it. He ran a series of lies through his head quick as lightning and was getting ready to knock on the door when he saw the fat old woman asleep on the sagging bed in the back of the room. The other woman stopped her dancing in midwhirl. With a shriek she held the bowl over her head and threw it across the room. He heard the bowl shatter with a mighty crash. He ducked down, blood pounding, unsure what would happen next. When he finally drew a breath, all was silent, except for the wind.

He peered inside, surprised to see the racket hadn't woken the old woman. She was still asleep on the bed, but the black-haired one was throwing a shawl around her shoulders. She picked up a battered little portmanteau in one hand and the lantern in the other. She bent over the sleeping woman as if to kiss her goodbye. But she didn't. Instead she lifted the glass bell and turned the wick up. The freed flame shot up a foot high. Then she dropped the lantern on the bed, right beside the old woman. He watched speechless with shock as the fire licked the bedclothes teasingly at first, only to explode when the camphene in the lantern ignited. The bed, and the old woman, disappeared in flames.

He was backing off the porch when the door flew open and the woman with the wild black hair ran past. She was screaming, her dress was on fire. Without thinking he tackled her and rolled her over and over in the muddy yard. When the flames were smothered she lay there, facedown, the calico of her gown smoking, the little suitcase flung to one side, her hair spread out around her like a black stain. He could smell the singed ends of it. Maybe she was dead, but he didn't want to wait to find out. The fire had already spread to the roof of the shack and in moments it would ignite a sorry excuse for a chicken coop. Branches of an oak exploded in arcs, lighting up the night sky. In the distance he heard the thrumming pound of horses approaching.

Just then the woman rolled over and sat up. Her face was caked with mud. Only her eyes shone in the light of the fire; they gleamed like polished stones. She looked at the burning shack, the flaming trees, and began to laugh. As he backed away she shouted, "Take me with you."

He turned and ran, leaping clear across the swaying footbridge back into the Great Dismal Swamp. If the men on those horses even glimpsed him they'd be after him with dogs and howls. He ran deeper into the darkness. No one would believe him if he told them she was the one who'd done it, set the place on fire, murdered the old woman. *Crazy. Murderer.*

He ran in the moonlight, branches slapping, muddy water splashing up to his knees. At last he knew he had to stop or be sucked down to death. He paused to catch some wind back, holding on to the branch of a sassafras tree. He could see the fire's bright glow through the Dismal's tangle but there was no light in the swamp. It was black as the inside of a box. The moon had now hid itself behind clouds threatening to drop even more misery on him. He was shivering, so cold, so hungry there was nothing for his stomach to growl over. This wasn't supposed to happen. This wasn't the way it was supposed to be.

TWO

When he'd fled from Our Joy he'd thought he'd track his way to the runaway slave colonies he'd been told were hidden deep in the swamp. Track his way like an Indian to where slaves lived off the land like the red man, so deep in the Dismal no slave catchers could find them. But he'd never been away from Our Joy. Not once. His whole young life had been lived on three thousand acres, and of those he'd actually seen less than one hundred. As for tracking like an Indian, he'd never so much as trailed a squirrel. His experience was limited to following the path of silverware and bone china from the pantry to the long mahogany dining table that countless hands had polished to a gleaming shine. That table had outlasted most of those hands, and the table didn't give a damn about it either. The dining table was bound to outlast him too, and he was determined to get as far from it as he could. Not just the dining table, all and everything about the place he'd been born and the place where he was determined never to die.

He knew Our Joy wasn't the only world. Not even the real true world. He knew things about that true world. There was a set of books in the study bound in brown calfskin, their spines lettered in gold: *The*

Encyclopedia Britannica, Fifth Edition. When he was certain he was alone, he'd open a volume at random:

> *CATALEPSY, a term applied to a nervous affection characterized by the sudden suspension of sensation and volition, accompanied with a peculiar rigidity of the whole or of certain muscles of the body.*

He read frantically for fear of being caught. But he had a remarkable memory. Words seemed to stick inside his head as if glued. But there was a problem. Since he had to grab whatever volume was closest and scan fast, he could rarely find the same page again. So the things he knew were in unsorted snippets and bits: *The great natural and economical centre of Siam is the delta of the Me-nam river, which is annually flooded between June and November,*

or,

For a month Alexander allowed his main army to rest near Persepolis; for himself there could be no repose, resulting in something like only a few pieces of an enormous jigsaw puzzle. He had no idea what the finished puzzle would look like. All he knew was these snatched bits were part of the world beyond Our Joy. And after what had happened? There were no more reasons to put it off. It was time even if it wasn't the time he'd hoped for.

He would find one of the slave colonies he'd heard were in the Dismal. The former slaves would help him get to freedom. But these colonies were hidden deep in the swamp to avoid capture. He'd have to track them like the hero of his favorite book—that stolen novel he'd treasured till it was ruined. Yes, that was what he'd do: look for footprints, broken branches. That's how he'd find the runaways in the swamp. Maybe they'd even be expecting him. They must have scouts too. Why, perhaps they'd embrace him, saying, *Welcome, brother!*

But he soon discovered this horror, this Great Dismal, was a place that would give even his hero, Hawkeye, great pause. In *The Last of the Mohicans*, Hawkeye, Uncas, and Chingachgook stalked their prey or tracked their enemy on solid ground, not sucking mud or slithering black water with terrifying things you couldn't see splashing around in it. This was thorns that tore and bugs that bit. All he'd eaten was a handful of berries, so bitter he'd had to spit them out.

He sank down onto the soggy earth and damp bracken. He was too tired and too miserable to cry, to care. When he felt the strike he cried out, more in shock than pain. It was too dark to see and he batted out with his other hand, feeling the thing's foreign roughness, the coldness of the thick muscle of a body, before the jaws unhinged and released him. In seconds his arm felt dipped in red-hot lead and he began to shake uncontrollably.

"Cottonmouth," shined a voice. "Give your hand here so I kin bind it."

Something flapped in the cage of his ribs. He peered toward the voice but saw only a shadow. He barely felt the red scarf as it was tied tight at his wrist. "Coneflower potion," rang the voice, reminding him of fork tines on china plates. His stomach rose and he threw up bitter bile.

"Snake poisin gits all through you. Drink this."

Something small as a thimble was pushed to his lips.

"Open your damn mouth afore you die."

Whatever was poured in was bitter but he swallowed it.

"Charcoal powder mixed with others. Tastes nasty, don't it? Now lay back. It's all right, I killed the snake. Keep your arm up in the air. No, up! Damn, don't you listen? Up is this way. You're a dumb one, ain't you?"

He couldn't stop shaking. Something else was rubbed on his hand.

"Sleep now. Come mornin' you'll be feelin' dizzy some and that hand is like to swell, but not too much as I got to it right quick."

All he could make out was a shape bending over him. He licked his lips and croaked, "Get away from me."

"Now why'd you run this way for? The canal is the other way if you was lookin' for a boat. You got me all off course. I'm not sure where we're at."

He wanted to say *go away* again but couldn't because he'd been bit by a snake and she had given him something else in that potion besides charcoal.

THREE

When he opened his eyes he was blinded by the sun. The rain clouds of the night before had marched westward. He was lying in smashed ferns only inches from sluggish water that glinted metallic where the light broke through the trees. Above his head was a canopy of green. The springtime opened leaves of slender cedars, junipers, and swamp oak, fluttered like iridescent wings. Great cypress trees stood big trunked, their wild tangled roots home to otters and snakes. Birds told each other things, some sang. A shimmering damselfly flitted by the boy's face. He watched it alight on the sunny side of a pawpaw tree where it was swiftly picked off by a warbler. The bird flew with its prize into the treetops, a bright yellow dash. Close by, something splashed in the bark-colored water.

"Was a mushrat," said somebody.

His head was filled up with thick clouds, but he managed to pull himself upright and sat, leaning against a tree trunk. The woman was sitting on a fallen gum tree across from him. Her dress was blackened with soot, hem burnt irregularly so that one of her calves was bare. Miraculously, she appeared to be unburned herself. Her feet were shod with mud, her face streaked with dirt and ash. Her hair was long and the bluest black. It covered most of her face and exploded around it in wild brambles. It looked like it hadn't seen a comb since the day it had started growing out of her head. He caught a flash of her eyes through the tangle; first he thought they were green, then gray. She brushed back some hair and he saw then that she was young—only a girl. She held a piece of paper. "What's this?"

He reached weakly for it. "Give it back."

The girl pulled it out of reach and turned it upside down. "What's it say?"

Leaning against the tree, he studied her as she turned the paper around again. "It's a map."

"Oh, I see now," said the girl, sounding like she didn't at all.

"Can't you read?"

"I ain't never had no schoolin'. The witch kept me close."

She was clearly crazy, sucking on the burnt end of her mad hair and staring up at the sky. He pretended to ignore her, hoping she'd go away. He examined his hand bound in a muddy red calico scarf. He winced as he began to unwrap the cotton from the wound.

"See that? That's a bonepicker up there."

He glanced up and saw a turkey vulture circling in the distance. He looked back at his hand, doing his best to keep it from shaking. She was a murderer. He slowly peeled away the scarf and gently touched the two punctures in the soft place between his thumb and forefinger. They were surrounded by a dark purple bruise. He tentatively flexed his fingers. They still worked.

"Y'all be glad that weren't no rattler what bit you." She squinted at him through her hair. "You're a runaway. I seen others out here afore." She looked around the little clearing: briar bushes, tupelo trees, pawpaws, surrounded by torpid water. "I'm all turned about. Can't tell where we're at." She wiped her nose with the back of her hand. "What you gotta go gettin' me lost for?" She dropped the map on the ground.

He snatched it up. Stone-cold killer. He shrank back against the trunk of the tree.

"Oh, she were already dead if'n you was wonderin'. Heart quit."

Had she read his mind? He stood and grabbed at air, feeling he was going to fall, catching a tree branch at the last moment.

"I tole you you'd be dizzy."

He steadied himself, then folded the map along the creases and put it back in his pocket. He took a step toward the edge of the marshy clearing.

"I could turn you in. Get me a reward."

He turned to her. His mouth was dry. He licked his lips. "You say that woman was already dead. Even so, you can't just burn down houses with dead folks in them. I'll tell I saw you do it."

"I s'pose you could," she mused, pulling up some leafy thing and sucking on the white root. "But you're a nigger. They ain't gonna believe you." She scratched her ankle and squinted at the sky, then looked at him with alarm. "Bones don't burn up, do they? Lordy. What if they find her bones?" She chewed the root, apparently full of this thought, and slapped her cheek where gnats were swarming.

He started toward the undergrowth again.

"Wait up now!" she called out.

For a reason he couldn't explain, he turned around.

"Jist hold on a minute." She leaned toward him and tapped the side of her temple. "Listen. How they know I didn't burn up in the fire too? Huh? How's 'bout that?" She clapped her hands triumphantly. "Then I'm gone! Ha-ha. I'm not but a ghost. Burned up. Dead as a boiled rabbit. That's what they'll figure, why it's jist perfect!"

He looked at her, the big gleeful grin on her face, and said, "Maybe they'll count the bones and see there ain't enough for two."

Her mouth turned down. "Damn me now. You think? Count them bones?"

He had no idea if it was true or not but nodded anyway. "Um-hum," he said. "That's what they do, I hear." It was oddly satisfying to see her dirty face fill up with worry. She got all worked up, began walking in a little circle and pulling on her mad hair.

While she was acting crazy, he tried to determine his next step. It was already hot. He was sweating fierce. Flying things whined by his ear, others bit him. Pomp had warned him of the Dismal's dangers. Not just snakes but bears and giant cats Pomp called panters. They'd eat your beating heart while you were still screaming. That's if the sucking mud didn't get you first. He bent beside the tree and scooped a handful of water and swallowed what didn't escape through his fingers. It left a gelatinous smear in his mouth. The girl was crazy but she was white crazy. She could turn him in and it wouldn't matter what he said.

He was worth one thousand two hundred and fifty dollars. He knew because he'd seen the account book when he was supposed to be polishing the dinner silver. The old man had left it lying on the table in the dining room, never dreaming the boy could not only read, he could count far more than his fingers. In the account book he was listed as *Prime House Boy: $1,250.*

The dizziness had faded a bit. The slant of the sun through the trees was east. West led back to the world he'd come from. Which was north? He wasn't good with outside things like Pomp who could read the moon, read birds. Knew from the way ants went when a storm was coming.

Pomp had run off last year. The old man put up a reward but the field hand hadn't been found. Still the master wouldn't give up, though Pomp was so bent with rheumatism he was next to worthless. Reecie told him the old man would hunt down a run-off head of cabbage, so hell-bent to keep what was his.

He was much more valuable than a head of cabbage. And not just because he knew which fork for fish and which for meat. He'd been trained to lay a table just right with all the china and silver. He knew some French too. The second wife was from New Orleans. When he was eight years old she'd bought him blue velvet livery, buckle shoes, and white gloves to wear when he fanned the guests at table. When he was thirteen she had a black frock coat of the finest fabric and knee breeches to match made for him. This suit of clothes had cost twenty-five dollars, once you added in the shoes and two shirts.

But it was more than the money with the old man and he well knew it. It was the reason he would never be taken back alive. He'd die first. He pictured himself, hands folded on his chest, eyes forever closed—yet even the Reaper unable to erase the courage etched on his tragically young dead face. The only frustrating part of that fantasy was he'd never see the old man crying his eyes out if he were already dead.

He picked up a long stick and poked at the marshy ground ahead. It didn't sink. He took a tentative step toward the trees edging the little clearing.

"Oh my day," moaned the girl behind him. "I'm lost. We both is lost."

This time he didn't turn around. He plunged into the tangled growth and swamp shadows. In but a moment one of those shadows knocked him to earth and threw a corn meal sack over his head.

FOUR

"You got the other?" hollered a man. Blinded by the sack, he felt his hands twisted brutally behind and bound before he could react.

"You git up now. You try anything and I'll knock you back down but good. You hear?" Inside a near airless darkness he heard perfectly well. The man shoved him through the trees back to the clearing where he heard the girl screaming high-pitched and ragged.

"This one's slippery as a snake," said another voice.

"I'm gonna take this sack off your head, darky, and don't you try nothin'."

For the second time that new morning, the sun glared at him. When his eyes focused he saw a fat man struggling to hold on to the girl. Though much smaller she fought with the fury of a cornered rat. "Lemme go! I ain't a nigger! I ain't no runaway," she screeched. She lashed and spit and tried to bite.

"Damn you!" the fat man cried, shoving her arms behind her with such force it seemed they must be broken. If so, it didn't stop her from kicking and screaming bloody murder.

"Shut her up, can't you? Shut her damn mouth closed afore she wakes the dead. Use this here," said the one who'd captured him.

The girl gagged as a rag was roughly shoved in her mouth and another tied around her head to hold it in. She grunted with pain as she was hog-tied, hands to ankles, and left facedown on the spongy ground.

"Whooeee," said the other one. "Easiest damn day we ever had. I tole you it'd be worth it to go deeper in."

Sweat ran down the fat man's face. The girl had been a lot of work. "Shit. This boy ain't no five feet ten inches. This one's near six feet if he's a day." He poked him in the chest. "Ain't half old enough. Look at him. Just a bony kid. And the hair, that's pure wool." He dropped a paper to the ground where it landed faceup:

FIFTY DOLLARS REWARD

Ran away from our sawmill in Washington County on the 4th instant, a Negro man named Ned. About 34 years old, copper color, nearly straight black hair, about 5 feet 10 inches high, and downcast expression when spoken to. We will give the above reward of $50 if he is returned or put in jail for us. He is supposed to be at Lee's Mill.

"Sit," commanded the man who'd thrown the sack over his head. The man was no more than about five feet five but muscled like a pygmy bull. "Sit your ass down. Don't you look at me."

The boy awkwardly sank down on a rotted log.

"What's your name?" asked the short man.

He wasn't about to tell them his real name or he'd end up where he started and no matter what, he wasn't going back. Looking at his shoes he said, "Hawk."

"Hawk? That your name? Hawk what?"

He shrugged his thin shoulders. "Hawk's all they call me."

"Who calls you? Where you run from?"

"Kentucky," he lied.

"Kentucky! Damn, boy, you did some runnin', that's for sure."

"What about Ned? That's what we was sent for," said the fat one.

"What difference it make?" said the other. "They's runaways. Who cares if it's Lee's Ned or not?" He grabbed the boy's bound hands. "Baby fine," said the short man. "Soft as a momma's tit. This one's more likely than Ned anyhow. Worth more'n fifty." He lifted the girl's face out of the spongy earth by her hair. "His gal ain't much, though."

"She ain't mine," said the boy from the rotted log.

The man dropped the girl's head and swung around. "What did you say?"

"She's white."

The short man stared at him incredulously, then down at the girl, who at that moment was wriggling sideways toward the surrounding brush. He put a boot on her back and shoved her flat. "Why, this gal's black as your Africany ass, don't you be foolin' around with me. You got somethin' else to say to me?"

He dropped his eyes. "No, suh." In his head a flurry of red thoughts whirled, but his hands were tied and the thoughts were useless.

The short one turned to the fat one. "Bind 'em with the irons. They're runners, we know that. What's this?" He picked up the little tattered suitcase as the girl grunted beneath the gag beside it. "What's in this here grip, I wonder? Something stolen? Y'all run off with the silver?" The short man yanked it open and fished around, pulling out a patched calico dress, colored potion bottles, and dried herbs. "Ain't but shit." He kicked the portmanteau into the sullen water. It sat on the surface openmouthed a moment, and then with a gurgle it sank.

"What's this one got?" The short man dug roughly in the boy's pants pocket (stolen from the old man's laundry so the dogs would have the wrong scent) and pulled out the map. He unfolded it, peered close, and laughed. He leaned to the boy and shook the map in his face.

"This here didn't do you a lick a good, you dumb nigger. You was goin' the wrong way."

The short man dropped the map in the water. He watched it sail away. All those states had looked as traversable as stepping-stones on paper. Now he realized he'd doubled back, hadn't even gotten out of North Carolina.

The girl was hauled to her feet and the rope around her ankles was cut, but not the one that held her hands. She twisted and coiled until the fat man cracked her across the thighs with a wooden cudgel. She stopped winding this way and that and sank to her knees. He held it threateningly above her head, and she bent toward the ground.

The fat man stuck the club back in his belt and yanked open a collar like prying apart a great metal jaw, then snapped it shut around the girl's neck. Another was locked on the boy's. It weighed down his shoulders and forced his back to bend with the weight. He was connected to the girl by a chain.

Hands bound, they were marched double time in front of the two men. The girl's dress was torn by sticker bushes, her ankles whipped by briars. The air was thick, steam rose. Unseen little birds twitted and chirped above their heads. A brilliant blue-and-orange butterfly swooped lazily, then rose in a spinning spiral. He followed it with his eyes as they stumbled forward, watched it disappear. They were herded to an inlet of green water flanked by leaning cypress and spindly cottonwoods. There sat another man in a twelve-foot flat-bottomed boat. A rifle sat across his knees.

FIVE

"Well, well, well. What you got there, Sim?" she heard the man holler from the boat.

"Two, Mr. Aubrey," shouted the bull-muscled man. "Two good as hard money, I'll be damned." The short one grabbed hold of the chain hauling the boy, which likewise hauled her. So this way they were pulled, splashing one after the other, into the knee-deep water. They were shoved over the side of the shallow boat where they landed helter-skelter. The slave catchers climbed aboard after them, setting the boat to rocking. The other man set his rifle down as the two men seated themselves across from him on a plank bench with the two captives piled between. The boat listed to port so severely that one side was about submerged.

"Mr. Sim, shove that lard-assed brother of yours over," said the man who had waited on the boat. He studied the two at his feet. She had landed faceup and couldn't avoid looking up at him as he looked down at her. He had a neatly trimmed blond mustache and big long-lashed eyes of china blue. Bits of curling gold hair peeked from under a broad-brimmed hat of soft felt. He wore a burgundy silk cravat tied at the neck of a finely woven Irish linen shirt. Her cheek lay up against the toe of a polished boot. He smiled down at her. "Well, bless my soul."

She was so scared she had to concentrate to hold her water. But she knew about fear. Knew how it could be smelled, how it drove some people to want to hurt a body more. It had done so with the old woman, who liked to see her shake and tremble until she learned to never cry out. Beneath her gag she bit her lip hard to feel the quick shot of pain and sucked the blood to keep from showing her terror.

"We found 'em in a clearing up yonder, Mr. Aubrey. The pair of 'em. She's a mulatta, though hard to speculate how light with all that dirt. And look at this likely darky here." He yanked the chain. "Soft as a kitten, this boy. He's somebody's pet, I 'spect. Look at the hands on him, not a blister on 'em. I'll be swarn if he ain't worth something rich. His gal is 'nother matter. Looks half-wild. Might not be right in the head. She screamed and hollered somethin' fierce. Fight me like a spurred cock."

"Your metaphor is lacking in proper gender, Mr. Sim," said the blue-eyed man in the soft felt hat. "I believe you mean a hen. Get up, you two, and set them down across from me where I can see what's what." The man called Mr. Aubrey stared thoughtfully at the girl as Mr. Sim shoved her and the boy down on the rough wooden bench.

"Though I do believe," he mused, "that we may have more of a downy chick before us." The girl stared at him, sucking blood from her cut lip to keep from shaking. Mr. Aubrey went, "Hmm, let's see," and pulled a lace-edged white handkerchief from his back pocket. He reached over the side of the boat and dipped it down into the murky water. "If I take that off your mouth, do you promise not to say a word unless I tell you to?"

She wanted the dirty rag pulled out of her mouth; she felt about to choke. So she nodded her head. Aubrey untied the rag. She spat the wadded ball of cloth from her mouth and, wheezing, leaned her head back and sucked down a big mouthful of air. Before she saw what he was about, Aubrey leaned over and rubbed the mud and soot off her face with the handkerchief. She pulled her head back, swinging her black hair over the left side of her face. He whistled soft at what he saw and said, "How old are you, girl? Speak up now."

How old? The only birthday she remembered had been long ago across the sea. After that she'd just grown bigger. A face floated up in her mind—tired eyes magnified behind spectacles. He sat at a scratched desk in the old brick building where everything sagged from the roof to his shoulders. *She's five years old, she says. Her mother died aboard the* Star of the East, *one of several Irish immigrants. Now, my dear, you are fortunate, for Mrs. Guthrie here will care for you now.* The old woman sitting across from the desk had smiled at her with teeth worn to gray stumps.

No.

The Orphan Man had peered at her then with eyes that made her think of abandoned bird eggs. *Now now now, don't cry.* He'd handed her a handkerchief. *Dry your eyes. You're a lucky little girl*, he'd said, glancing at the old woman. He'd cleared his throat and held up a paper. *You are hereby bound out to Una Guthrie, midwife, resident of Gates County, North Carolina, until you reach your majority. Be a good and obedient girl*, said the Orphan Man. *Never forget Christ our Lord and Savior loves you.*

"Cat got your tongue?" asked Aubrey, leaning toward her and setting the boat in motion. "Or don't you know how old you are?"

How many years had it been since then? The witch hadn't cared how old, only if she had arms and legs. Arms to carry, legs to fetch. "Don't know," she muttered. "Sixteen, I think."

"Lovely," said Aubrey, reaching over and smoothing the hair away from her face. "Good Lord!" He stared at her. She swung her hair back in her face. He grabbed her by the neck and roughly pushed her hair aside.

"Oooooh eeee, that's ugly," said the fat one.

"That'll cut the price down," said the other.

The left side of the girl's face was scarred in a jagged deep line from the tip of her ear to right below her chin. It looked as if someone had cut the flesh nearly to the bone, which in fact was true. It had been badly sewn back together. The stitches had left tracks like railroad ties laid by a drunk.

"Well, least she's young," said the shorter Sim. "Mebbe someone want her for the kitchen where no one'd see her."

Aubrey grabbed her chin and turned her face so the scar was exposed to the sunlight. "Might be some covet something like this if properly advertised. One side angel. Other side: surprise!"

"You mean put her up as a fancy? Her?" said short Sim doubtfully.

"You don't understand certain nuances of attraction, Mr. Sim," replied Aubrey, smiling.

She yanked her head away from his hand. "You can't sell me. I ain't no runaway! I ain't no nigger," she cried.

Short Sim jumped up and began to shove the rag back in her mouth.

"Noooo!"

"That's enough, Mr. Sim. Sit down." The boat dipped in the rear as Sim sat down. "Shhhh now." Aubrey put a finger to his lips. "Are you going to mind me?"

The girl wanted to claw his pretty face but she did not want that rag choking her again. She nodded slowly.

"What's your name?"

An emerald hummingbird buzzed over the boat and hung suspended over Aubrey's hat for an instant. "Birdy."

"Birdy what?"

"Birdy Moon," lied Alice Brown.

"What you think of that, boys? Birdy, she says. Birdy Moon."

"We gonna sit here all mornin'?" Short Sim slapped the back of his neck where a cloud of mosquitoes hovered.

"Birdy," repeated Aubrey, smiling at her. "Well then, Birdy, who is your master?"

"Master? What you mean? What I have a master for?"

"If you say you're not a runaway, what are you doing out here in the swamp with this run-off nigger? Why were you together?"

"I found him snakebit is all."

Aubrey looked into Alice's eyes with his pools of blue. "What happened?"

She turned her face away. Dark water slapped the boat as it rocked.

Aubrey turned to the boy. "What happened to her face?"

"I ain't seen none of her until last night. I got snakebit like she said."

Aubrey squinted at him. "You don't know her? You're not lying?"

"Why would I?"

"I don't know," said Aubrey, looking at him closely, noting that he met his eyes directly before lowering them. "I don't know," he repeated softly. After a moment when the only sound was the caw-caw of a crow, Aubrey said with a smile, "I thought you were a pair but since you were never together, there will be no pain on separation. Easier for everybody not having to split folks up." Aubrey stroked the scarred side of the girl's face. "How'd this happen to you, Birdy?"

"Got cut," she mumbled.

"Still think you'd git a fair price if you feature her as a cook. She looks like a strong gal. Remember that cook you sold for fifteen hundred up to Richmond last fall?" said the short man.

"Mr. Sim, you are more agitating than a pair of horsehair drawers. I have excellent powers of recall. Please stop flapping your gums and go sit down beside your idiot brother." He turned back to Alice. "Now, if you say you ain't a negro, who are your people? Why, they must be looking for you, child."

Her mind was racing from place to place, trying to see a way out. She figured the short Sim would hurt her and enjoy doing it. The fat one was stupid but did whatever his brother told him to. Combined they possessed the brain of something like an inbred dog, a mean biter that would shake you till you dropped. A rusty croak rose up on the bank. For a moment the sun was blocked as a great blue heron lifted itself over the boat, enormous wings spread wide.

Aubrey said, "Tell me and I'll take you home right now."

She looked at him sadly. "Well, I ain't from round here," she said softly.

"Mmm-hum. That so?" Aubrey squinted at her. "Just where you from then, girl?"

She let her eyes fill up. "My folks is dead, see? I ain't got no one. They up and died on me. So's I set out walking and got myself lost and I run into this boy and he'd been snakebit so I fixed him up 'cause I wouldn't let even a cat die like that, and then, and then, why those two"—she tried to turn her head but the collar prevented her—"they snatched me!"

The Sims began spitting and cursing: She sure as hell was a runaway; why look at her, listen to her! And what the hell would a white girl be doing out in the swamp with a runaway nigger? "Let me at her," said short Sim. "I'll hold her feet to the fire."

Aubrey held up his hand. "Leave the interrogatories to me, Mr. Sim." He bent his face to Alice. "Where exactly was this home you walked away from?"

Alice swallowed. Everyone by the swamp knew old Granny Guthrie had raised her—Alice Brown, orphan. Now she'd burned down the witch's house and left her bones behind for them to find. Where's Alice? they'd all ask. Where's that ugly orphan ol' Granny in her goodness raised up? The tip of her tongue found the torn place on her lip. She looked up at Aubrey with wide mossy eyes. "Let me go, won't you?"

The boat rocked. The wind picked up, whipping Alice's hair across her face. Aubrey reached over and gently moved the hair aside. He lifted her face by the chin. "Poor gal. She's got nobody, she says. Nobody in the whole wide world to look for her." He shook his head sorrowfully, gently stroking Alice's good cheek. "Boys, we need to help this poor lost lamb."

"Oh, thank you," said Alice, letting tears fall, drip-drop, onto her lap. "I knowed you were a good Christian."

Beside her the boy leaned away, pulling the chain tighter as he let out a derisive snort.

Aubrey didn't move his head but his eyes rotated like a salamander's. "You got something to say, boy?"

"No, suh." He dropped his eyes and studied the warping wood of the boat.

Aubrey had called her a lamb. He'd surely let her go. She looked sorrowfully at her bare feet. "I come from New York," she whispered.

"What's that?" asked Aubrey, his blue eyes even bigger. "New York City?"

"What the hell!" sputtered a Sim.

Aubrey patted her knee and grinned. "Well now, boys, before that sun fries the contents of my skull, let's get a move on."

With that, both brothers stood and picked up long poles. "'Bout time," grumbled fat Sim. They began moving the flat-bottomed boat through the winding water. Alice leaned toward Aubrey; the links connecting her with the boy ching-chinged. "You believe me, don't you?"

Aubrey leaned back against the side of the boat. "Course I do, Birdy dear."

"Then take these chains off'n me, won't you?"

"Oh, now you just rest up a bit. You must be awful worn out after walking from New York to North Carolina." He pulled his hat down low and folded his hands over his bright silk vest.

The boat skimmed through the swamp. All around were green and new budding things. Trees leaned over their heads, mirrored in the still water until the boat broke the reflections and sent them in tiny waves to the bank. "Move over some," she whispered. "No, the other way, you damn nigger. You're like to choke me." When he didn't budge, she moved a bit closer to ease the chain between them a bit.

"You're a awful liar," he muttered. "You know how far New York is? It's way past Washington, past Delaware, past New Jersey."

"You shut it," she hissed. "He's gonna let me go when he wakes up and you're gonna git sold downriver and pick cotton till you die."

"That man ain't *never* gonna let you go," he hissed back. He turned his dark eyes to hers. "Not since you told him nobody's looking for you. We're just alike now, you and me."

"Shut your mouth, the both of you," barked short Sim behind them.

The boy gazed out at the swampy wilderness, watching his freedom ripple away. If it hadn't been for her he'd have been long gone. He gave a furious little tug to the connecting chain by leaning sideways, resulting in a surprised yip. That gave him only the smallest satisfaction, but he'd take any right now. He stared glumly at spring flowers as they floated by: violets, buttercup, pink lady's slipper. *Ha,* he thought bitterly, *never dreamed the whole place was filled up with poison.* He sunk down, his back bowed, trying to find some relief and not succeeding in the least. His mind was half-full of red and half-full of hopeless, one dancing around the other, feinting like equally matched boxers. The man Aubrey lit a cheroot. The odor reminded him of the old man at Our Joy. Never see him again. Never see anything he'd hoped to see now. He dropped his gaze, staring at the green-tinged mud caking his worn shoes, and thought about where they'd landed him. He glanced at the rifle resting against Aubrey's thigh and imagined snatching it, watching the man's head explode to red chunks like a dropped watermelon. Behind him one of the Sims whistled something, but it wasn't a song, just air sucked in and out. Tuneless.

At noon the sun lifted itself to full glory. There was not a cloud to be seen in any direction. Hatless, the captives suffered its white blaze while Mr. Aubrey napped beneath his soft fedora. The Sims poled through the swamp; at times the only sound was the slap of water against the sides of the boat. Every once in a while it seemed they'd lost the main waterway, for they were in a portion of the swamp known as Deep Dismal. They were hedged in by thick reeds on either side while overhanging trees blocked the sky. In this green twilight, vines, some thick as thighs, descended like serpents. The water smelled of sulfur. Sometimes a towering cypress rose directly in their path, exposed tangled roots so enormous they had to navigate between them, floating on slime full of pus-like bubbles, reminding them that things somehow lived below.

Alice shifted herself on the bench so that the boy couldn't tug the chain tighter without throwing himself overboard. She was glaring at Aubrey—at his hat anyway, since he'd covered his face with it.

SIX

They changed the flatbottom for a large rowboat in Elizabeth City. No one had paid any attention to the shackled boy and girl seated in the back. In the dying light they tied the rowboat up in a little channel on the outskirts of Norfolk, Virginia. As the boat rocked, gulls circled overhead, crying in the fading light. The air was salted and wind played with the water, tossing up white-headed waves. Aubrey jumped in one graceful motion onto the bank without getting his shiny boots wet. "Keep them quiet. I'll be back in an hour or two."

"Thought we was headin' on toward Richmond tonight." Short Sim stood up but quickly sat back down as a sequence of waves almost rocked him overboard.

"Depends on what I find out." Aubrey set his felt hat securely on his head and straightened his tie. Despite the seemingly endless day on the canal, he looked well rested. As Aubrey vanished through the shrubs lining the bank, the sky was violet on the horizon but inky above. There was enough to see a bit but not enough to make out details. Lights winked not far off. The wind carried singing and laughing from the taverns on the waterfront.

The Sims murmured together at the front of the boat, the fat one spitting tobacco juice with clocklike regularity into the river. The boy kept his mind from going as numb as his bound hands by estimating the time between each ejaculation. He reckoned it to be around three minutes by counting in his head to sixty. By the time he reached twenty sets of three, he figured an hour had passed, and the moon had risen in a sky gradually speckling with stars. His shoulders ached from the unnatural position of his arms; his hands were numb. But that pain didn't matter. The real anguish was being caught.

He stared now at the backs of the slave catchers, the fat one leaning down to hear what his trollish brother was saying. Spit, splash. Two hours. He could rush up behind and maybe knock them overboard. He glanced at the girl. He'd have to convince her to move with him. He leaned to her. "Get off'n me," she said loudly.

The Sims swung around. "Shut up," said one. They turned back around and the fat one continued: "Goddammit, I tell you it's true, the damn horse sat on him, sat on him like a dog sits, crushed him flat . . ."

The girl said, "I gotta go."

In the starlight the short one shrugged. The fat one giggled.

"Unchain me so's I can go up in them bushes yonder," she said.

Short Sim pulled a tin pail from under the bench and banged it down in front of her.

"I ain't gonna do that in front of you!"

Short Sim looked down at her with the slink of a smile. The boy somehow sensed that her face had reddened. She scooted off the bench and hitched up her skirt. He bent forward to give some slack to the chain but looked away as she squatted over the pail. She finished, then sat down on the bench. With a swift kick, she sent the bucket over, sending its contents flooding over the brothers' boots.

"Why, you bitch," hollered short Sim, raising a leather strap. He whacked her across the shoulders with it, the crack cutting through the saw of katydids on the bank. He lifted it again, but a voice called out, "Don't."

"The worthless bitch kicked piss all over me, Mr. Aubrey. She done it deliberate."

Aubrey stood on the bank holding the reins of a sag-backed mare harnessed to a little dogcart. "Don't assign a value to what isn't yours. Put that strap down now and bring them up here."

He instructed short Sim to retie the girl's hands in front but release her from the collar. The fat one lifted her up and set her down on the back of the cart facing backward.

"Tie the boy behind. He can trot."

He was roped to the rail at the back of the cart. He tugged at the tether, knowing it was hopeless but having to try. When it did no good at all, he stood there stiff as a statue. Standing took all his effort.

Aubrey pulled some bills out of a leather wallet. "Twenty for you, Mr. Sim. Ten for your brother."

The old horse stamped and blew. Even though the air was warm, the boy shivered. He looked up at the stars. The wind was blowing clouds to cover them. Free of the collar, he swiveled his head owlishly, trying to get a bearing on where they'd landed.

Short Sim was saying, "He'll fetch more. This ain't half enough. That's valuable stock and you know it. You cuttin' us loose, Aubrey? We worked for you nigh on two years and now you figure on cheatin' us? You'll get a big bounty on them two and you know it. You think you can just toss us the hind end?"

"What bounty?" cried the girl. "I ain't no slave."

Aubrey walked around to the back of the cart where she sat. "Your lack of trust saddens me, Mr. Sim." Aubrey pinched the girl's thigh. She screeched. Aubrey pulled a knife out of his boot and held it up. "Want me to cut your nose off?"

The girl squeaked and shook her head.

"I'd hate to cut a nose to spite my profit, but I'll do it."

She clamped her mouth shut.

"Now, Mr. Sim, as I was saying, this here is merely a partial payment. I'm taking them to the Norfolk jail until I am able to ascertain what, if any, reward for this boy has been posted. The gal might have someone looking for her too, despite her tall tale. Mr. Sim, if there is money owed beyond what I've generously advanced, there will be proper remuneration."

"What you mean?" asked the fat brother. "We don't speak no French."

"Means he'll give us more," said the short one. He shoved the money in his trouser pocket. "But if you is tryin' to cheat us," he began.

Aubrey wagged a finger at him. "Cheat you? When you'll know exactly where they are? Why, friends, they'll be in jail! As you know, the runaway notices are posted in the paper. I checked today's already; there was nothing about these two, but I'll check tomorrow's first thing. You can as well. That is, if you can read?"

"You know damn well I kin read," retorted short Sim. "I ain't no dummy."

"Then how could I possibly cheat you when you will know everything that I know myself? Meet me at the jail tomorrow morning. Nine o'clock."

"Why ain't you takin' us with you now?"

Aubrey climbed up on the cart. "Because there is no room. Of course, you and your brother are welcome to travel the same way as the boy back there, though I had a notion you might prefer one of the fine establishments down on the wharf. However, if I'm mistaken . . ."

"He's puttin' 'em in jail, Oslow," said fat Sim. "They ain't goin' nowhere. I'm starved. Let's get us some supper."

"I'm gettin' mighty fed up with your la-de-dahin', you always actin' like we're idjits, Aubrey. Mark me good," said short Sim, "if I get wind you're foolin' with us . . ."

Aubrey shook the reins. "Until the morrow, Mr. Sim and Mr. Sim, I bid you both a good night." He clucked the horse forward and turned the cart toward the port city's lights. "Git up," he hollered. The old horse bolted with unexpected vigor, nearly toppling the girl while behind her, the boy was forced to run or be dragged.

"We'll see you at the jail in the mornin'!" shouted short Sim, but his voice seemed already in the past.

SEVEN

Aubrey flicked the whip over the horse's ears, and it clipped into a trot. Soon they were clattering on a narrow cobblestone street overhung with leaning buildings, a damp mist blowing in their faces. People appeared like forlorn spirits, then receded as the cart moved on. A light rain had begun to fall, the type that at first seems inconsequential but gradually chills to the bone. "Well, Birdy," said Aubrey cheerily, "what's your opinion? Are they idiots?"

"I don't care if you cut me, I ain't goin' to no jail!" shrieked Alice from the back of the cart as they rattled through a warren of dingy, ill-lit streets.

"No, you aren't, my dear," replied Aubrey, weaving around a pile of old clothes humped in the street. But now Alice noticed that the pile of clothes had a human head and something was leaking from it. A man dashed past a hissing gas lamp and into the shadows. "I doubt you'd like me to drop you off here, though." Aubrey turned to her, his face a milky moon. "It's a rather unsavory neighborhood."

The boy was running behind, his arms nearly pulled from the sockets as the dogcart careened around a corner. After several more labyrinthine turns, the cart halted before a redbrick building. Yellow lamplight pooled from a window. There was a sign above the doorway, but it was too dark to make out. Two women in wide skirts and feather-bedecked bonnets stood on either side of the closed front door.

Aubrey climbed down from the cart. "Now, Birdy, promise me you will be good and I won't put the rag over your mouth again. Will you stay hushed?"

Alice looked wide-eyed at the building, the tallest she'd ever seen in her life. Her heart pumped ragged. "This the jail?"

"The sign there says it's called Henley's Heavenly Hotel, though from the look of it, I believe Henley got his directions confused. I'm afraid I'm unable to offer you finer accommodations at the moment, though if things go well, tomorrow may see all our fortunes changed." He smiled at Alice, revealing a row of yellow corn-kernel teeth. He turned toward the rear of the cart. "Now you. Listen here. I'll make you a bargain."

I could scream, Alice thought, eyeing the women dressed in satin and feathers in the doorway, bent in conversation with a man. But before she could open her mouth, both followed the man inside. There was no one else on the ill-lit street and the soft drizzle had snuck through her dress, turning it cold and heavy. She couldn't make out what Aubrey was saying behind her because of a strange loud clicking. It took her a moment to realize it was her own teeth. She clamped her jaw tight.

"You have two choices," Aubrey was saying to the captive tied to the back of the cart. Aubrey's felt hat had gathered a reservoir of rainwater. Now each motion of his head resulted in a miniature waterfall that flowed over the tip of his nose. "You can come with me willingly or"—he pulled a newspaper from inside his coat and waved it with a theatrical flourish—"I can contact Mr. Micah Bourn of Bertie County."

When he reacted by recoiling from the paper being waved in his face, Aubrey grinned. He held the newspaper up to the light in the window of the hotel. "Let's see what it says here. Oh, look at this!

Ran away from the subscriber's plantation, Our Joy." He looked thoughtful a moment, then said, "Sounds nice. Is it nice? No comment? All right, let's continue . . . *in Bertie County, North Carolina, on the fifteenth instant, Bledsoe* . . . Bledsoe? What kind of name is that? . . . *a likely boy of seventeen years. Chestnut brown color, six feet tall, thin build, good countenance, quick spoken. He is wearing stolen clothes of his master, viz; dun wool pants and white linen shirt of good quality.*"

Aubrey fingered the filthy torn trousers. "Pity," he murmured. "These *were* good quality." He bent back to the notice. *"Have learned he can read, may write as well and will no doubt use every cunning and wile and head for northern parts. Bears recent marks of correction on his back. One hundred dollars if returned out of this state, two hundred if returned to this property.*"

Aubrey leaned to him. "It seems this Bourn fellow values you highly, young Bledsoe, as he's placed a two-hundred-dollar reward. That's rich." He walked around and lifted the back of the sweat-stained shirt. "Ow. Now, consider this. Bourn must want you back badly—of course, only you know what awaits your return. So. Let's review: number one, take your chances with me, or two, you are returned to lovely Our Joy and Mr. Bourn. Decide," said Aubrey. "You have ten seconds. Climb down, Birdy."

She stared at him, mouth agape. "I can't, I can't," she stuttered, "I can't 'cause my hands is tied. I can't climb down." He'd spoken to the boy named Bledsoe in a near purr, but it didn't hide the underlying menace and she'd heard that very clearly. She leaned away, but Aubrey grabbed her around the waist and swung her down. He held on to the rope tied around her hands as he turned to the back of the cart. "One or two?"

"One," Bledsoe mumbled.

"Good. Now then I'm going to untie your hands. Both of you. When we go inside, you will act as my personal servants, is that understood? If either one of you makes a move or opens your mouth, you will immediately really and truly be thrown in the Norfolk nigger jail."

"You're going to sell me to someone for more than the reward," said Bledsoe, looking straight at Aubrey. Aubrey untied Alice's wrists, ignoring him. Then he pointed toward the stairs. "Go on up to the door there, Birdy, and wait for me."

Quick as a whipsnake she took off down the wet cobblestoned street. "Dammit!" she heard Aubrey shout. There was an odd popping sound just as she reached the corner. She couldn't understand why her legs wouldn't work anymore. She didn't feel Aubrey lift her up a few moments later because she'd fainted clean away.

EIGHT

When she opened her eyes she was looking at a bug-specked, paint-peeling ceiling. It was day, but the light was dirty wool. Water flowed down the window as if it were being poured from a bottomless bucket. A coal fire burned in a small grate but did little to dry out the damp in the room. Her foot throbbed. She lifted her head from the pillow and saw it was bandaged in white cotton at the ankle.

"Drink this." A cup was thrust under her nose. Aubrey was sitting on the edge of the bed beside her. Alice dimly noted that there was only one bed in the room, but he looked as if he hadn't slept a wink. Without the hat, his white-blond hair hung in soft curls any woman would envy, but his face was porcupined with stubble, pale as flour.

"Shooting her robbed you some profit."

In a corner of the room Alice saw the boy called Bledsoe sitting on the floor, a thin blanket wrapped around his shoulders. He stared defiantly at Aubrey.

"No profit at all if I shoot you both," replied Aubrey, smooth as silk, despite looking worn out. "But if you don't shut up I may decide I don't much care. Drink your tea, Birdy."

"Go on and shoot then," said Bledsoe. "What difference it make?"

"None to me," said Aubrey. "But then I'm not the one who'd be dead on the floor of a Norfolk flophouse. Here, my dear." He turned to Alice and held the cup under her lips. "There, there," he said. He tucked a hunk of hair behind her ear. "Face of a baby," he murmured, smiling at her, "a wounded child." Aubrey stroked her bare arm. She was too dazed to move away but inwardly recoiled. She groggily sipped the tea and sloshed some. Her eyes didn't seem to want to stay open.

"That's the laudanum. Fortunately I found a doctor, though I had to pry him loose from one of the fair but frail. Lucky, Birdy, I'm an excellent shot or I might have maimed you for life. It's a mere flesh wound, just a graze, though since it nicked the anklebone, it's no doubt painful. This has altered my plans for you, I'm afraid. You rest up. We'll wait until later. I have someone who would like to meet you."

He stood up and rolled down his sleeves, buttoned his embroidered vest. "I've brought you food. Eat and clean yourselves up. There's water in the bowl, clothes in that parcel on the chair. Dress for you, Birdy." He set the empty cup down on the floor beside the bed and turned to Bledsoe, still sitting on the floor with the blanket around his shoulders.

"There's a good suit of clothes for you, boy. However, if your attitude does not improve in the next few hours, I'll show you in the filthy rags you're standing in, instead of presenting you as quality house stock." He held up his hand as if Bledsoe were about to interrupt him. "Yes, I know. It will bring the price down, but you're young, seventeen! Prime for a hand down south since they wear out after ten years or so."

Aubrey put on his hat. It was a different hat. A new gray stovepipe with a trim brim and a satin hatband. "I'll be back this evening." He opened his frock coat to reveal the revolver at his waistband. "Do not disappoint me. Either of you." The lock clicked in place after him.

Alice tried to force her eyes to stay open, but it was no use. She was sunk into a place with sparkling edges, swallowed in a swamp of sticky sleep from which there was no escape.

After several quiet minutes Bledsoe rubbed his wrists. There were deep lines in them where the bonds had been. His legs ached but he walked over to the bed. Her lashes curled like young tendrils; she was pale as the bandage around her ankle. The damage to her face was clear now. The scar was a deep trough of pink where the stitches had failed to close it completely. It was long and jagged. Looking at it hurt. Her breath lifted the cheap cloth of her dress up and down, up and down. Her hair fanned out on the greasy gray pillow. He still smelled smoke in it.

He turned away and walked to the window. He shoved it open and stuck his head out in the rain. They were on the top floor. He could throw himself out but he'd be lucky to only break his legs. He closed the window and swiped his face with the once-fine shirt. Outside in the hallway he heard a woman giggle and a man's hoarse whisper. Even if he raised a ruckus, all that would happen was he'd be sent back to the old man.

Why do you try my soul, boy? Why?

He kicked the chair, shoved the paper-wrapped parcel off it, and studied the small room. A washstand with a mirror just large enough to see half a face, a scarred chest of drawers with one drawer missing, the chair he sat on, and a small table were the only furniture except for the sagging bed.

He'd maybe slept four or five hours since he'd run from the North Carolina plantation. Day and night were all jumbled in his memory. He had to think, get his head straight so he could plan what to do. There had to be something. You didn't just give up.

He unwrapped the greasy package on the table with shaking hands. He had to control himself. He wouldn't be a savage. A roast chicken and two apples. He was salivating and wiped his mouth with the back of his hand. *Stop,* he said to himself. *Don't be like that. Calm down.* He pulled a leg off the chicken, noticing it had been poorly plucked, but he bit into it anyway. He tried to eat slow, but it was hopeless. The leg was cleaned in less than thirty seconds. He ripped into the breast with his fingernails. When he finally took a breath, he slowed down, chewing slower. He looked at the girl. She was lying on her back; he could only see the right side of her face. He had to admit it wasn't too terrible, which was what made the other side worse. Why'd she burn that place down with the old woman still in it? Who'd do something like that? *Crazy people, that's who.* He crunched the other leg bone in half and sucked the marrow. The girl turned on her side and let out a little snort. He could put that stained pillow over her face. In her drugged dream she probably wouldn't notice. He'd hide behind the door and crack the white man on the head with the washbasin. Then what? *Hang.*

He wiped the grease from his lips with the bottom of the shirt. The girl muttered; her arms flailed as if dreaming of swimming. "Bones!" she hollered.

He waved his hand at her dismissively. He ate an apple. A little later his head tipped back toward the wall. He fell asleep in the chair, chicken bone in one hand and apple core in the other.

NINE

"Oh, look here!"

He opened his eyes. The girl was hopping on one foot and holding a bright red and black striped dress against herself. He shook the silt from his brain as she struggled to pull the dress over her head. She wriggled it down over her dirty calico, the skirt falling in a gaudy tumble over her hips. "I tole you. I tole you. Mr. Aubrey figured out I ain't no slave like you. Look at it, prettiest dress I ever seen. Pretty as them women had on last night."

The dress was runched up in back, caught on her old dress beneath. He watched as she preened, having to catch hold of the bedpost to keep from setting her bad foot down and calling out, "Ow, ow, ow," whenever she forgot.

"That man just shot you and he'll shoot you again, no nevermind about it. He's dressing you up to sell, you fool."

The girl turned to him. "He can't. I'm white as him."

Bledsoe got up and splashed his face with water in the washbasin. Dripping, he turned to her. "The old man had twin girls out of Jeanine and they were pale as lard. He sold them, and Jeanine too, to a planter in Georgia when the new mistress wouldn't stop going on about them. You can bet that man Aubrey will sell you to whoever pays the highest. Though," he added, looking at her critically, "you ain't even as white as those twins, might even say you're more yellow, though don't worry none. Some eighty-year-old with no teeth who likes bright gals ain't gonna be that particular." It was satisfying seeing her eyes widen with terror.

"I ain't yellow. I'm white 'neath my clothes," she replied, hopping to the little shard of mirror. "I'm this color 'cause of the sun in the swamp."

"Yep," replied Bledsoe, holding up the back of his hand. "Sun do that to you. Sometimes it takes a thousand years before it sticks."

She hopped to the door and twisted the doorknob, then began to bang on it. "Help!" she cried. "Help!" If anyone heard, no one came. She whirled to Bledsoe on one foot. "My momma was from Ireland."

Bledsoe half laughed. "No wonder," he said scornfully. He knew about Irish. The poor ones anyway. How they'd come over in droves on boats because they ran out of potatoes and signed their lives away. He'd heard the talk at Our Joy's table. In places like New Orleans no one used their slaves for the hardest soul-sucking, killer work. Irish weren't worth a penny to a pound, whereas slaves were money in the bank. Irish. No wonder.

"What I'm gonna do?" She pulled the bottom of the gown up over her face and rocked back and forth on the bed.

"Stop crying, for one. It ain't gonna do you no good. Best is clean yourself up. If you get yourself pulled together you might get lucky and get yourself fixed up as somebody's fancy gal, though I figure it'd have to be someone blind on account of your face."

The girl howled, "He can't sell me! I ain't no nigger."

Ignoring her, he dug around in the paper parcel and pulled out the clothes Aubrey had bought for him. Black pants, not too poor quality, white shirt, simple but neat. A black coat, not near as well cut as the one he'd been given once the blue velvet had worn out. But not bad. There were shoes too. Not clothes to outfit a field hand.

He grabbed the blanket off the bed and hung it from the scarred chest of drawers to one of the bedposts. He quickly changed his pants. When he pulled off the linen shirt he winced. Wet, then dried by the sun, then wet again from rain, the material had partially stuck itself to the wounds on his back. He sucked in his breath as he ripped the shirt loose over his head.

"Oh, lord a mercy. You been whipped somethin' awful."

He spun around. The blanket had slipped off the bedpost. He quickly pulled the new shirt over his head.

"You should rub a potion in that. Cottonwood's best, but you can make a rub with chamomile. Stingin' nettles bring down swellin'."

He sat down on the chair and covered his face with his hands. "Just shut up, would you?"

"I was jist suggestin' a treatment is all." She sniffled and wiped her nose. She looked at him with brimming eyes. "Oh Lord have mercy, what we gonna do?"

He dropped his hands and looked at her furiously. "We? You is you and I am me and I ain't got nothing to do with *you*."

"But I ain't a slave!"

"Look," he said through gritted teeth. "Listen to me. That man smells money off you. He doesn't care what color you are. He can sell you because he knows you got nobody and nothing."

She sank onto the bed. "I never did have nothin' 'cept my momma, and the sea ate her."

"What you mean, the sea ate her?"

"They threw her off the ship we come in from Ireland." Her chin was lowered to her chest and tangled black hair covered her face. He felt a twinge of something but dismissed it, turning his back to her.

Bledsoe pulled on the new jacket. The girl hopped over to him, a hand on the table for balance. He stood half a foot higher and she craned her neck to look him in the face. "Y'all listen. I'm real sorry 'bout you tryin' to git free, but you need to be sorry 'bout me too. It's only Christian. I done saved your life. If it weren't for you, I'd be long gone and them men never woulda caught me."

Her hair had fallen back and the scar seemed to pulse angrily on the side of her face. He suppressed a wince. "If you hadn't set that house on fire, I wouldn't have saved *you* and *I'd* be free!"

His eyes burned into hers with such ferocity it seemed they'd set her aflame all over again. She limped back to the bed and dropped on it with hiccupping sobs.

He sat down on the chair and pulled on the shoes, leaned back, and closed his eyes. Maybe she'd get sold down south. *Ha.* That would be rich. He pictured her stooped low under the Louisiana sun, her white skin peeling in hideous strips. He'd noticed how she always held her head a bit tilted to the left, always trying to present the good side of her face. How'd she get that? Like someone was trying to cut the meat from the bone. *I don't care.* He heard her hopping to the dresser to look in the mirror again, heard the rustle of the cheap fabric of her gown. He wouldn't look at her.

A key turned the lock. The bolt slid back and his heart slid with it.

TEN

It had stopped raining but the street was flooded for lack of drains. Wagons sprayed waves of muddy water as they passed. The girl winced after a few hobbled steps. "I can't go no faster. My foot is hurtin'."

"Pick her up and carry her," Aubrey commanded. Bledsoe noted that the man's eyes didn't look blue in the dying light, more silver, hard as coins. "Go ahead of me through that alley there. I've arranged for a coach to meet us on the other side. Hurry up now."

"You ain't goin' to sell me? You can't," she protested as Bledsoe reluctantly swung her up in his arms, the red and black striped dress trailing to the ground. "Put me down!" She hit him on the chest with a clenched fist. "You put—"

Aubrey bent his head to hers, nearly nose to nose. "No more out of you. Not a word," he growled. "I had enough trouble explaining your face. If he asks about your ankle, tell him you were kicked by a horse, and if you don't shut up, I'll have to also explain why I've cut your throat."

The girl whimpered and shrunk in Bledsoe's arms, no doubt wondering who the *he* was. Aubrey pointed them toward the alley. After the spring rain the air off the bay was chill; it whipped through the narrow alley, sending her vivid skirt sailing behind Bledsoe. Aubrey's heels clicked on the slick paving stones behind them. The air was fishy; a mist was creeping toward the city. Bledsoe looked up between the buildings on the alley at the sky spread with inky clouds. His new shoes were thin soled and already his feet were damp. The girl was heavy in his arms and he paused a moment to shift her weight. Her eyes caught his, wide and frightened.

"Why're you stopping?" Aubrey's breath was on his neck.

"She's heavy."

"Get moving."

He knew the thing that prodded his back was not Aubrey's finger.

They were in the middle of the alley when two men in naval uniforms burst into view, running right toward them. Bledsoe saw terror on their faces. They fanned around the three of them and raced past just as a crowd swept in after.

"There they go!" yelled a man leading the pack. He was waving a hefty piece of lumber. "Git them Yanks." The pursuers didn't part for the three in the alley. They plowed right through, knocking Aubrey to the pavement and shoving Bledsoe, the girl still in his arms, against a wooden fence. Whooping and hollering, they were gone as suddenly as they'd appeared. Bledsoe shifted the girl in his arms, looked at Aubrey lying facedown in a puddle of sewage. He hadn't moved. He gave Aubrey's shoe a tentative kick.

Someone in the distance yelled, "Where'd they go?"

"Let me down," said the girl.

"This way," hollered someone else, closer this time.

Bledsoe swung her over the wooden fence behind them and scrambled over behind her.

"What's—"

"Shhhh," he whispered, putting an eye to a crack between the boards. There was a clatter of feet on the wet pavement. Two men paused beside the still-unmoving Aubrey.

"Lord, wh—" she whispered.

Without taking his eye from the scene in the alley, he slapped his hand over her mouth.

"Well, lookee here." Short Sim rolled the unconscious man over. "They wasn't at the jail. But here's ol' Mr. Aubrey goin' somewhere without 'em."

"Where you s'pose he put 'em, then?" asked his fat brother, picking up Aubrey's new silk hat.

"He sold 'em, that's what. Sold 'em to someone private. Sold 'em so's nobody'd know. And he wasn't gonna say a word, was you?" Short Sim spat in Aubrey's face. "Check his pockets there."

Fat Sim rummaged through Aubrey's pockets. "Not more'n a couple of dollars."

"Check his boots."

The fat man pulled off Aubrey's boots with a grunt and shook them. There was a clatter. "Nothin' but this knife here."

"Fuckin' bastard. Musta got it put somewheres. You think you can cheat us?" shouted short Sim.

"Damn you," hollered the fat one. He hammered a brick into Aubrey's face. The blow smashed the aquiline nose, flattened the high forehead, and sent corn-kernel teeth spraying.

Short Sim let out a shriek of fury and swung at his brother, sending the fat man staggering. He slipped and crashed to the pavement and began to howl like a stick-beat dog.

"Shut your mouth, you dummy! Now we'll never git the money. You killed the fucker!"

ELEVEN

Bledsoe led the way past a house that backed the alley. He stopped in the shadow of a tree. The street ahead was filled with men, some dancing drunkenly, some shooting off guns at the sky.

"What's goin' on?" asked the girl in a shaky voice as she peered around the tree. "Is that man really dead?"

Bledsoe buttoned his jacket and brushed it with his hands. "Can you walk?"

"What we gonna do? Why them folks actin' crazy?"

"I don't know."

A man in the crowd started singing:

I'm right from old Virginny wid my pocket full of news,
I'm worth twenty shillings right square in my shoes.
It doesn't make a bit of difference to neither you nor I
Big pig or little pig, root, hog, or die.

A lamp was lit in the window of the house beside the tree. Light spilled out around them. Bledsoe ducked back into the tree's shadow. "We can't stay here. Here. Birdy, is it? Lean on my arm."

"What for? Where we goin'?"

"We got to get out of here and we got to go out in that street to do it. Lean on my arm then, and let folks think I'm your servant escorting you."

"Whatcha mean escortin'?"

"Helping you along. You understand?"

"That ain't my name."

"What?"

"Birdy," replied Alice.

"Well, what is it, then?"

"It's . . ." She paused and gave him a dark look. "How I know I can trust you?"

"You want to get out of here alive?"

Alice looked up at him, truly frightened. "You think they might kill us?"

"I know for sure they ain't gonna roll out a carpet for us to walk on. I don't care what your real name is; just do as I tell you or we're both gonna end up right back where we started."

As she leaned on his arm, they stepped out of the dark and into the celebration in the street. Faces were lit up in torchlight. "We, we got 'em runnin'! They're licked right off at the start," bellowed a redheaded man next to Alice. He patted Bledsoe on the back. "You best git your mistress on home, boy. No lady ought to be out here. Folks are riled up."

"What for they so riled up, Marse?" asked Bledsoe as another man jostled him from behind.

"Why, Sumter!" hollered the man. "The Yanks are already runnin'! Tails atween their legs! Damn cowards." With a whoop he was swallowed by the crowd.

Bledsoe bent to Alice and said, "Keep going. Don't stop for nothing." Alice leaned on his arm and they wove their way to the sidewalk.

"Oh Lord, look," said Alice. The crowd cheered as a noose was put around a man's neck. "They gonna hang him!" she gasped. "They gonna hang that man!"

"Keep going," muttered Bledsoe. The crowd roared as the man was hoisted up to the arm of a street lamp. He shoved her in the small of the back ahead of him, glancing over his shoulder. "That ain't a man, it's a big rag doll. They dressed it to look like Lincoln."

Behind them the crowd was shouting, *Sumter, Sumter, Sumter!* Then suddenly a mighty cheer went up. A hundred voices roaring. It turned Alice's legs to jelly because it didn't sound human. She stopped and turned. Someone had set the Lincoln doll on fire and men were dancing around the gaslight firing guns into the air. Red sparks lit the sky.

"I told you not to stop." Bledsoe yanked Alice away so abruptly she squealed.

"Oh, stop it! You're hurtin' me."

"Shut up. Move faster. Faster!"

After a couple of blocks they found themselves in a neighborhood of warehouses and empty brick buildings. The roar of the crowd and the gunfire grew faint. Their shoes echoed on the cobbles. It was very dark. Once a carriage passed, its windows curtained. The liveried negro driver had looked at them curiously, a black man with a white woman leaning on his arm, but the carriage clattered past.

Bledsoe stopped in front of a livery stable. He pulled at the doors but they were locked. Crouched low, he signaled Alice to follow him around the side of the building. He found a missing board and pulled its neighbor. The board came free with a groan of nails. He threw it aside and squeezed through the opening. "Come on," he whispered. "Duck down."

Alice wriggled through after him, taking care not to rip her skirt. It was pitch-dark inside. They held their hands out before them to feel their way. She bumped into Bledsoe's back and gave out a little shriek. He whirled around and clapped his hand over her mouth. She pried his fingers loose. "Git off me," she hissed. "You 'bout broke my foot out there."

"Shut your mouth, goddammit," he hissed back.

They both stood silent a moment then, listening. The air was warm with animal heat and the green smell of manure. Horses nickered softly. Bledsoe collapsed on a hay bale and wiped sweat from his face with his sleeve. His eyes had adjusted, but he could only make out shapes.

Behind him, Alice dropped down in a pile of straw in an empty stall. "What was it they was yellin' back there? Who's Sumter?"

"Quiet."

"What we gonna do?"

"Can you not shut up? You want someone to hear?"

"Ain't no one here, jist horses. They ain't gonna tell nobody. Listen. You figure that Aubrey's really dead?"

He leaned his head against the wood of the neighboring stall. *Sumter.* That's what they were shouting. *We got 'em at Sumter.* Had the war already started?

"What we gonna do now? Where are we?"

Running back north. Had Lincoln's army already lost? Why else would those Virginians be so jubilant? The doll dressed like Lincoln. The animal joy when it was set ablaze. Bledsoe shivered. If the war was already lost at this place called Sumter, then the South had won. He had to get north immediately. Get to Canada. It was another country. Slave hunters couldn't snatch him from there. He'd be safe.

"I said, what we gonna do?" asked Alice in the dark. "What town's this?"

He blew out an exasperated sigh. If only he could get a hold of a newspaper. Find out what was going on.

"Don't answer me then," muttered Alice. "See if'n I care." She rustled angrily in the hay behind him.

"It's Norfolk."

"Don't know it," replied Alice. "It near Mocksville? Had a preacher come to Geegomie from Mocksville. They had a fella name of Dan'l Boone from there, he said. Wore a squirrel on his head. Can you imagine? Didn't say if it was live or not."

Bledsoe ignored her, ruminating on various strategies, but none made sense. He couldn't walk around without free papers. He couldn't forge them, he'd never seen any. He couldn't work and make money without free papers.

"That preacher got caught with Rule Chizwan's wife. They dunked him headfirst in a mudhole in the swamp and held him down. He jist 'bout died. Then they run him off."

Runaway. That runaway notice Aubrey had read was in the Norfolk paper. Likely the old man had put it in papers in every major city from here to New York. Two hundred dollars was a lot of money. Enough to make folks look at him twice if they'd seen the notice.

You try me, you try me. You were a good boy once.

He sighed and pulled off his wet shoes and set them on a bale of hay to dry. His eyes were burning. He brushed them with his sleeve. *I'm not crying.*

A soft snore whistled from the stall behind him. He looked over his shoulder. He could make out the shape of her curled up, careless as a puppy. The horse in the next stall shifted restlessly. Bledsoe reached over and stroked its velvet nose. "Ho there," he whispered, stroking it. "It's gonna be all right." His heart gradually slowed as he felt the horse relax beneath his hand.

He sank down and leaned back against the wall of the stall, inhaling the scent of green straw. He'd rest his eyes a few minutes. The girl muttered in her sleep. *Hell with her,* thought Bledsoe. He'd be gone before sunrise.

TWELVE

"I'm starvin'." Alice stood beside Bledsoe outside the livery stable. "I thought you'd never wake up. Ain't you hungry? I could eat one of them horses I'm so hungry. What we gonna do now? Which way you figure we oughta head?"

Bledsoe looked at her. Her hair flew madly one way and lay flat on the side she'd slept on. She was oblivious to the black and red striped dress that looked even tawdrier now that the sun was rising.

"Well, how we gonna git somethin' to eat?"

"I got other things on my mind."

Alice carefully rested her weight on her injured ankle. "Mind don't hardly work without food . . . aw, look! It's better. Hurts some, but I can near about walk." She peered down the still-sleeping street. "Where we gonna go?"

Bledsoe brushed a piece of straw from his trousers. "How many times have I told you that *you* are you and I am *me*?" He stepped away from the stable and looked toward the river. All was quiet, no one about yet except a driver dozing in his milk cart as the mule plodded down the street.

Alice grabbed his arm. "You ain't runnin' off and leavin' me here."

He shook his arm free. "I don't need you."

Alice looked up at him, eyes narrowed. "You need me 'cause you ain't got no free papers. I know you got to have papers or they'll snatch you. So where you goin'?"

He glared at her because she had a very good point. "There's ships. I saw them from the hotel window. Must go north."

"I reckon them ships don't haul folks around for free. How you gonna git on it with no money?"

The milk cart disappeared at the end of the road. His stomach growled. Alice jabbed him in the arm with a finger. "I got an idea. Don't look like that! Jist hear me is all. Why you gotta look like you're about to git sick? I ain't as dumb as you think maybe."

She limped around him in a circle, holding the skirt of her dress out like two red and black striped wings. "Now y'all listen close and don't say nothin' till I'm finished tellin' you. I could be a lady, you know, like last night? I got this here fancy dress, so's you kin pretend to be my slave. Now stop for a minute. Hold on. Come back here! *Pretend*, I said. Listen, Bedso, no one'd ask you for papers 'cause they'd all think you's my boy. We can git to them boats and go north thataway." She grinned up at him and dipped down awkwardly in what he supposed was her idea of a curtsy.

"Bledsoe."

"What?"

"My name is *Bled*soe."

"I don't care if your name is Sweet Potato Pie. I jist care we git outta here and git somethin' to eat. Now I'll be a lady and you . . ." He was eyeing her so coldly the rest dried up in her mouth.

"Won't work."

"What you mean?"

"Ain't no lady looks like you."

"What?" asked Alice, truly baffled.

"That dress."

She grabbed hold of the skirt and waved it at him. "Why, it's beautiful! Whatcha mean? Nary a hole neither. Brand-new."

"Whore wear something like that."

"What? You're crazy. What you know about dresses? You're jist a dumb boy."

"Ain't ladylike. Cheap."

"No it ain't!"

"My mistress would have used that thing to dress a scarecrow."

Alice looked down at the red and black gown. She ran a hand across the fabric sadly, as if it were a dying pet, as Bledsoe said, "I'm going to take my chances at getting on a boat. You go your way and I'll go mine."

She whirled to him and lifted the skirt up to her knees.

He gaped a moment, then turned away in shock. "Lord's sake! You outta your head? Put your clothes down right!"

Alice ignored him, wrestling with something under her skirt. "I got this. Here, look."

He cautiously turned his head, terrified he might find her standing naked as a jaybird in the middle of the street. God only knew what would happen if anyone saw that. Saw him standing there next to her white naked body. They'd likely hang him right then and there.

"My momma said it's old. Look. Look, I said!"

Thankfully, her dress was where it should be and she was holding something out to him. He bent to it. An ivory cameo set in gold and ringed with red stones.

"I pinned it under my dress 'fore I left the Dismal. I kept it buried under a willow tree in the swamp so the witch wouldn't find it. It's good as money, ain't it?"

Bledsoe took the pretty brooch and turned it over. Surprised. It was quality. The sun pecked free of the clouds and he held it up to the light and the stones caught fire.

Alice grabbed it. "It's mine," she growled.

"Act like it's the foot bone of Jesus or something."

She held it tight in her fist. Then she slowly opened her hand, displayed it on her open palm. The cameo featured a girl and boy in a bas-relief of elephant ivory on a background of jet. "My momma said they's lovers, these two." The cameo was framed in red stones rimmed with ornate gold filigree. "Rubies she said these are. Rubies stand for blood beatin' in the heart. Stand for love." She touched it with one finger very delicately. "She give it to me on the boat. 'Twas my great-gran's. My momma pinned it inside my dress. I kept it hid, see?"

Bledsoe looked at Alice, looked at the sky, bright and clear. People would be about soon and he didn't want to be here. "So what you saying?" he asked as she sniffled.

"I was *askin'*, if I was to sell it could I git money?"

"I reckon."

"I git money, then I kin git me a lady's dress, you'll be my slave, and we git a boat to New York," she said. "There it is."

"You don't even know where New York is."

A man across the street unlocked the door to a shop. He looked at them curiously before going inside. A cart clattered past. Somewhere a bell rang.

"Well, I know it ain't here." She turned on her heel. Whirled in a flounce of red and black and began walking down the street. Behind her he said just barely loud enough, "Well. Maybe it ain't the worst idea."

She didn't turn around. "Come on then."

THIRTEEN

An hour or so later they were again near the docks. This time in front of a dusty window displaying watches, clocks, and a model of a three-masted schooner propped against a sea of faded blue satin and an oil painting of a miserable-looking dog with a dead duck in its mouth.

"Do it like I told you," said Bledsoe.

"I git some money, it's mine."

"I don't give a damn. Turn around, that man's staring at us. Just make sure you say what I told you to say."

Inside, Alice watched the crane-thin man stoop over the cameo when she laid it in his palm, saw his pale eyes brighten. It took all her willpower not to snatch it back. He looked up at her sharp and it was as if she could read his mind. He didn't care one way or the other if it was stolen; all he wanted to know was if somebody might show up looking for it. Bledsoe had gone over this with her.

"It was my granmomma's. It was left to me. I was hopin' you could help me out to git back home. I ain't from around here. I come up from Charlotte and my things got stolen from the hotel."

He poked at the face of the cameo. "This might be ivory, but these are just red glass," he said. "I'll give you half a dollar."

"They ain't!" she replied hotly. "Them's real rubies. That's from Ireland, that is! It's real old. If'n you don't want it, I'll take it somewheres else." She reached for it, but the man pulled his hand away.

"All right, all right, simmer down there, missy. We'll see what's what." He laid the cameo down on his counter and peered at it through a glass he stuck in his right eye. Alice fidgeted and looked out the window where Bledsoe waited, dropping his eyes to the sidewalk if anyone passed.

"Well," the thin man said after poking and peering at the brooch, "they don't look like glass, but that's all I'm saying. Still, the filigree is good. Though I may be a fool, I'll give you five dollars."

"Fifteen." That was what Bledsoe had told her to go for.

"Fifteen! Are you right in the head, young lady? Even if they are real, they're hardly the crown jewels of England. Seven."

"Twelve."

"Ten and I'm done. You can take it somewhere else."

Alice took it. It was more money than she'd ever seen. She tucked the bills in the sleeve of the cheap striped dress and walked out of the shop.

"Well?" asked Bledsoe, following as she walked away.

"It was all I had of my momma. All I had of Momma and me and Ireland. I hid it from the witch all these years. It was mine. Only thing was *mine* in all the livewide world." She stopped and flopped down in a puddle of black and red on the wooden sidewalk's edge.

Bledsoe turned away from her tear-streaked face, hoping no one would become curious about a sobbing white girl and a nervous-looking young black man shifting uncomfortably behind her. "Sorry," he mumbled.

"I don't need your damn sorrys," replied Alice, drying her face with the hem of her gown. She struggled to her feet, getting one foot caught on the hem, and staggered. Bledsoe grabbed her before she crashed to the street.

A woman dragged a little girl past them so fast the child's feet were off the ground. "Hurry up, Lorna," said the woman with a look of disgust at Alice and Bledsoe. "This part of town is not for decent folk."

"Well?" said Alice, oblivious to the other looks they were getting now. "Whatcha standin' there starin' at me like a damn hoot owl for? Let's git me a lady dress and somethin' to eat." She set off down the street.

Bledsoe followed, telling himself that breaking her neck would not be the wisest course of action. Once he got headed in the right direction he'd get shed of her. But if eyes could shoot silver daggers, the girl stomping ahead of him with all the grace of a North Carolina field hand would surely fall down dead.

A few blocks away they found another shop, this one down a set of stairs. It was musty and close with a floor spotted with mice droppings. Light filtered dimly through one round window, illuminating piles of mildewed velvet and disintegrating crêpe de Chine. Ladies' shoes, some missing a mate, were piled on a table.

However, it was there Alice found a gray moiré silk blouse boasting a modest neckline and long sleeves ending in a most decorous trim of fine lace and a matching skirt. Both were in perfect condition. She peeled off the calico and black and red dress, pulled on a pair of lace-trimmed drawers behind a curtain made of an old stained quilt. The skirt belled around her due to the four only slightly yellowed petticoats beneath it. The proprietress had told her to fasten up the half corset herself as she had arthritis.

Alice had never worn a corset, half or whole. She'd never known anyone who did. She couldn't breathe right. But she wasn't going to let that woman know it. The way she'd looked at the two of them when they walked in the door—like they were too low for words. *Damn her,* thought Alice. *Ol' drunk sow.*

Her tune had changed when Alice flashed a couple of banknotes. Then she'd shown teeth; the front two made Alice think of a shifty rabbit. The dove gray skirt and blouse were dull to Alice's eyes, but even she could tell the fabric was nearly fine enough for a lady. She'd known a *real lady* once. That had been in Ireland. It seemed a thousand years ago. More than a memory of the actual gown the lady had worn, Alice remembered the shimmering sound of it—rustling and whispering as the lady moved. And the fan! The snap of it as the lady opened it on that hot July day. She'd even allowed little Alice to flutter it like an enormous moth inside the great coach that had taken her and her mother to the Belfast docks.

Now Alice picked a fan out of a pile on the littered counter—black lace with an ebony frame. And, because Bledsoe had told her to before they'd gone inside, she grabbed a small suitcase of alligator hide and a hat with a black grosgrain ribbon. It was plain, but suitable, Bledsoe said, for a young lady neither rich nor poor.

All of these secondhand goods were purchased from the woman with a nose mapped with broken veins, the cause of which was obvious from her breath. "Finest quality, that dress," said the woman, her rabbit teeth showing in what Alice assumed was a smile. "Came from London, England. Belonged to Miss Lemmon. She lived upstairs. Took strychnine. They were going to bury her in it, but put her in the blue instead."

FOURTEEN

"Damn me, I kin scarce breathe," said Alice a half hour later as she finished a paper bag of salted pecans. She wriggled; the corset was digging into her flesh. "How them ladies stand these things?"

"They don't chaw nuts like squirrels," replied Bledsoe. "Look up there. I'll tell you what to do."

The Baltimore Steam Packet Company ticket offices were up a long ramp. Alice stared with awe at the steamer *Adelaide* and her enormous paddle wheel. Bledsoe carried the alligator suitcase—empty, but nobody needed to know that. He leaned down behind her and said softly in her ear, "Now listen up. You're gonna be dumb as a stick."

"What you mean?" asked Alice indignantly, the gray skirt belling from side to side as she whipped around to him. "I ain't dumb and you best stop actin' so smart or I'll smack you."

"You won't or I'll choke you when you're sleeping. Now pipe down," he said softly through clenched teeth. "You want folks staring at us? What I mean is, you don't talk like a proper lady talks. What comes out of your mouth don't match what you got on, so I'm going to say you lost your ability to speak after a great tragedy. You can't talk except in some kind of hand language, which you taught me."

"Hand what?"

"Shut. Up," he whispered out of the side of his mouth. A well-dressed man passed and Bledsoe fell silent until he was out of earshot. "Now listen. My first mistress knew a lady couldn't make a peep after seeing her husband run over by a wagonload of tobaccy. Happened right in front of her face. Head squashed flat as pie dough. Shocked the speech right out of her. She only talked with her hands to her maid after. So you're gonna be like that. Fix your hair up."

Alice reached up under her hat and moved her hair to cover her scar. They stood aside as a man in a frock coat and a lady in pale green muslin passed by. The man tipped his hat to Alice and the lady nodded. "Nod back," whispered Bledsoe behind her. Alice felt her head tip up and down. "Smile." She did.

Bledsoe signaled to Alice to let others pass, leaving them at the end of the line. "Now you got to act like you can read, so here's what you do. You look up at that board over the man up there like you're reading the times, and then you make some kind of wiggle-waggle with your hands and I'll say you said you want two tickets for the eleven-fifteen to Baltimore."

Alice covered her mouth with her hand and pretended to cough. "New York, dammit."

"This boat don't go that far north, but at least it's more north," whispered Bledsoe back. "And we'll be out of here. Pay attention. You give the man the money. It says tickets are fifty cents each for the parlor and that's what you want. That's where the quality go."

The man in the ticket window and those waiting behind them murmured or shook their heads in sympathy as the poor dumb girl spoke in a complex sign language to her servant. She smiled at the ticket man when he passed her the tickets, but her heart was hammering under the gray silk blouse.

"We don't allow no coloreds in the parlor, miss, 'less it's a nursemaid for a baby," the ticket man hollered as Bledsoe and Alice started toward the boat's gangplank. Alice turned back to the ticket man, a look of genuine terror on her face. Without Bledsoe she'd be lost.

"Sorry, young lady, but rules are rules."

The woman in the green muslin stepped up beside Alice and turned to the ticket man. "Well, you need to change that this time, sir. This poor child needs her servant if she's to have anyone understand her."

Her companion stepped up to Alice's other side. "Indeed. Rules, as they say, are made to be broken from time to time. You must make an exception here. Why, she's traveling all alone."

Two hours later Bledsoe was seated across from Alice on a grass-green velvet sofa. The parlor was furnished with polished tables of inlaid wood displaying bowls of fruit and vases of flowers. Deep Turkey carpets covered the deck, so thick it was like walking on clouds. Chinoiserie urns filled with dozens of blush-colored roses perfumed the air. The man and woman who had spoken up for her were seated nearby. Other passengers politely averted their eyes when the young girl performed odd acrobatics with her hands and the colored boy responded with even stranger ones.

At first Alice was terrified of being discovered as a fire-setting Dismal Swamp charlatan and tossed overboard by enraged *real ladies*. But that had mostly subsided. The paddle wheel swept the water up and let it tumble in mesmerizing arcs of foam. Occasionally a great belching bellow erupted from one of the two giant black smokestacks. The sun flirted with the river, turning it from brown to green. The blue sky was dotted with puffy clouds and the air smelled of summer coming. She snuggled deeper into the velvet cushions and let out a sigh. She'd never been more than four miles in any direction since Una Guthrie had dragged her off to the Dismal. She'd been planning to get someplace else when she'd burned down the shack, though she had only the haziest notion of what other places might be like. She certainly hadn't imagined it would be anywhere so fine.

The lady in green had brought her a glass of iced lemonade. She crunched chips of ice with her strong molars as she stared dreamily at the wake left behind the churning paddle wheel. A gentleman passing by politely offered her his newspaper. Alice took it with a smile since she figured she should, but let it lie unopened on her lap.

As Alice stared out the window, Bledsoe read the headline upside down. It was easy as it took up nearly half the front page.

> WAR! WAR! WAR! SUMTER A REBEL ROUT!
> LINCOLN CALLS FOR 75,000 VOLUNTEERS.
> DAVIS CALLS ON ALL VOLUNTEERS.
> RICHMOND NAMED CAPITAL OF SOUTH!

The war wasn't over, it was just starting! It was all he could do to keep himself from jumping up and shouting hallelujah. He'd join Lincoln's army. Nobody could send him back to the old man then. And it was the right thing to do. The exact right thing. Just as soon as they got off the boat he'd find a way to get to wherever it was he could join up.

"Fan me with this here paper, wouldja?" said Alice, holding the newspaper so no one could see her whispering. "This dress is like to strangle me."

"If only," muttered Bledsoe.

"What?"

He snatched the proffered paper and waved it with such ferocity that it nearly blew her hat off her head.

FIFTEEN

He followed when she was invited to join her new friends in the dining room. He stood behind her chair as she enjoyed fried oysters and boiled fish in caper sauce. She kept her head low and tilted a bit right. She'd swept her hair across her cheek, but a bit of puckered scar showed near her chin. Bledsoe knew these people would be too polite to stare.

"To Jeff Davis in Richmond and all our gallant Confederates," said the gentleman, holding his wineglass aloft. The man and woman beamed at Alice. She smiled back, wondering who Jeff Davis was.

Bledsoe kicked her chair leg when she began to pick up a broiled quail with her hands. Just as she grasped the little bird, Bledsoe shoved a silver knife and fork into her hand.

"Yes, Marse, yes, Mistress," drawled Bledsoe when the couple asked if he could tell them about her. "Her name is Miss—" His eye fell on a crystal dish. "Miss Birdy Pickle."

He ignored her odd snort. "What's that, Marse? How come the poor chile can't talk none? Huntin' accident. That's right. Her daddy, that is Marse Pickle, uh-huh, Mistress, that her name, Miss Birdy

Pickle . . ." Bledsoe paused to pound Alice's back; it sounded as if she were choking. "Yessir. Marse Pickle got him haid shot off right in front this poor incent lamb when she was itty-bitty. Blew his brains to Heaben, hep him Jesus. She ain't talked none since. Nah, suh, her momma daid too. Had them whatchacallit? Them pappitations of de heart. Where she from? Near Charleston, Mistress, outside dere. Her daddy was a planter, but loss it all, that 'fore his haid got shot off, a course, and had to sell all dem slaves de had. I'se all dat's left for the po' chile."

He pulled the knife and fork from Alice's hands. "Now slow down dere, Mistress. See, I gots to keep her from stuffin' herself sick. She not quite right in de haid. Hmm? Where we goin'? Well, she goin' to her aunt Pickle up to Balimore."

"You poor dear," said the pretty lady. "Now I'm trying to place your South Carolina Pickles." She turned to her husband. "Don't we know some Pickles in Baton Rouge?" She leaned to Alice. "I've got a brother in Charleston, maybe you know him? Judge Billingsly? No? Well, of course you're too young for that old crowd. No matter." She raised her glass for another toast. "Here here for brave South Carolina!" she exclaimed, patting one of Alice's hands. "Y'all had the gumption to go out first."

Alice was relieved she couldn't speak because she had no idea what the woman was going on about. Instead she smiled wide, then dug into a syllabub whipped from air and spun sugar, followed by a slice of fruity cake drenched in a sticky sauce.

"You poor thing, you must have been starvin'," said the lady, watching Alice eat with some alarm.

Bledsoe soothed himself with the knowledge he'd soon be shed of her.

By the time they made Baltimore all he wanted to do was slap the silly smile off her face. When they'd docked, Alice made an intricate flourish with her hands at the lady in green and her gentleman companion.

"Oh, I can read that, you sweet thing," cooed the lady, and she kissed Alice softly on the good cheek. "I do wish we could escort you to your aunt's, but I fear we must go on to Boston to my sister. Foolish girl married a Yankee and he up and died on her. We're bringing her home to Virginia before this war starts. I'm sure it will only last a minute, but you still must take care."

"You look after her, boy," commanded the man with a stern look at Bledsoe.

"Oh, I will, Marse," replied Bledsoe through clenched teeth.

"Take this of mine, darlin'," said the lady to Alice. "I didn't see you had one with you. Y'all keep that and think of Harold and me sometimes."

Alice's face was flushed with excitement, her eyes shining as the lady pressed a lace-edged handkerchief into her hand. She used the lilac-scented handkerchief a few minutes later to wave goodbye to Harold and the lady in green, whose name she had already forgotten.

"Hope you're full up," growled Bledsoe, as he followed her down the pier with the empty alligator suitcase, past seamen loading tobacco, bales of cotton, and barrels of whiskey.

Beside a cartload of fish covered in a blanket of ice and sawdust, Alice pivoted to him, her skirt continuing to rock to and fro even though she'd stopped. She held out a white cloth napkin. "Here."

Bledsoe unfolded the napkin. Inside was a perfect little browned quail.

"Ha," said Alice. "I sneaked it while they was watchin' me make them silly hand moves. I wiggled my hand around like so." She made a complicated loop and flourish. "Their eyes were lookin' at *this* hand, not the other one. Well? Don't just stand there like a dumb rock. Come on then. Let's git ourselves someplace to stay tonight 'fore we head on to New York."

He'd go along. Just for now. Maryland was still a slave state and he had no papers. But soon. Soon. She struck out down the pier, her skirt swaying to and fro, toward the great city of Baltimore. A trail of delicate bird bones followed.

SIXTEEN

She ate strawberries sitting on the brass bed. She'd been up half the night. The moon sat above the rooftops, full and fat. From her window it looked as if the city never ended, just went on and on, roof to roof. She'd finally fallen asleep after midnight, the quilt pulled tight under her chin, and dreamed of swimming in a strange milky lake that she gradually realized was moonlight. She was surprised to find in that murky half-caring way of dreams that she wasn't swimming at all; rather she was drowning. The moment she realized this, she began to rapidly stroke upward but instead of bursting through water, she broke into daylight with its cry of "Crabbie crabbie! Buy my blue crabbie!" and the sound of horses clip-clopping, carriage bells ting-linging. A steamer horn brayed in the harbor. Somewhere near a man kept yelling, "Move your damn wagon."

Alice threw back the quilt and leaned out the upstairs window of the redbrick boardinghouse on Baltimore's Pratt Street. The wide avenue was filled with drays and carts piled with goods. Elegant carriages with liveried drivers scattered pedestrians in the street below. Directly across, a bakery window displayed petits fours, strawberry savarin, and cardamom palmiers. She didn't know what they were called, but she could smell the butter and sugar in the air. A dress shop exhibited the latest summer muslins from Paris on jointed dolls, and a milliner boasted ladies' hats elaborate as wedding cakes. She saw all these things and thought she would burst.

The only shop she had ever set foot in was the dry goods in Geegomie, a bump of a place too small to even qualify as a true village. Its inhabitants were mostly impermanent, coming and going with work on the canal or fur trapping. The dry goods sat on stilts like many places built on the butt of the Dismal, to keep out critters and other things that bite. Its weathered wood and knobby legs made Alice think of a great gray water bug. It stocked things like flour, molasses, gunpowder, and whiskey; the walls were done up with the hides of skinned creatures. As for fashion, there were bolts of twenty-year-old dusty gingham and several yards of denim so stiff you might as well coat your legs with dried mud. There were no baked goods, though occasionally some dried thing fished out of the swamp might be on offer for those with enough teeth to chew it.

Alice leaned over the sill and looked down where, in the light drizzle, the tops of fancy umbrellas protected the tops of fancy hats. A man in a bowler smoked a cigar, sending aloft the peaty scent of bright leaf tobacco. Amazed, she noted that some of the well-dressed people passing below the boardinghouse were colored. If Baltimore was this grand, what must New York be like?

She pulled the gray skirt up over her bloomers and buttoned the shell buttons of the blouse over the thin chemise. She ignored the pile of petticoats on the floor and the half corset flung on a chest of drawers. She ate another strawberry from the bowl a colored girl had brought up to her room with a pot of tea on a tray.

The arrival of the breakfast tray was her first experience of being personally waited on, and Alice had stood by nervously while the girl had set it down and dipped a little curtsy at the door. Alice didn't understand why the maid looked hit over the head when Alice, dressed only in her unmentionables, dipped an awkward curtsy in return. She didn't understand why the girl had stifled a giggle behind her hand as she left the room.

"Hell with you," said Alice once the door was closed. She'd discovered many of these city people were stuck-up types. But even if folks were all high and mighty here, at least she could breathe free. Nobody in Baltimore knew a thing about her except what she chose to tell them. And, since Bledsoe had told her to continue pretending she'd lost her ability to speak, she didn't have to tell them anything at all. Alice fluttered her juice-stained fingers in front of her. "Now *that* means you, a smelly ol' cow." She snorted a laugh, then covered her mouth, for fear someone might hear.

The woman who owned the ladies-only boardinghouse was a fat German with thin stretched lips. She had grudgingly permitted Bledsoe to sleep on a pallet outside Alice's door. Ordinarily she would have sent him to the back shed, she'd said. No men allowed. "If any of my boarders complain, I will not have it. It will not do."

Alice had wiggled her fingers worriedly and Bledsoe had wriggled his back. Alice answered with a wild pantomime of what appeared to be the tragic death of something winged and hid her face in her hands.

"She mighty worked up, Mistress," Bledsoe had said, keeping his eyes downcast on an especially ugly hooked rug. "She ain't never been away from home afore."

A woman with a face like an aged monkey was sitting in the parlor. She said, "You won't hear me complain, Mrs. Claussen. This poor little girl needs her servant. Why, what would she do without him? Poor child. Look how modestly she hides her face. Not like some of these brazen Jezebels you see on the streets today. No hat! Hair down! Why, this innocent is far from home. That Lincoln wants to take them away, Mrs. Claussen. What's a God-fearing woman to do? Who will protect us? Why, my daddy had thirty-eight slaves and you never saw such happy smiling faces. It's plain the child depends on this boy of hers. Can you imagine how cruel it would be if he takes our niggers away? No, Mrs. Claussen, you won't hear me complain."

Alice ate another strawberry and frowned. The people around the Dismal were generally too poor to own slaves. Except Warren Shaw. He owned a lumber boat and had five. One of them died. It was said she'd drowned herself. He was an ugly man, Warren Shaw. She shuddered with the memory of the witch pulling his abscessed tooth. Pasty faced and loose fleshed, he reminded her of something that lives under a stump.

She'd glimpsed runaways out in the swamp, flickers of dark skin darting into a thicket. One time there'd been a woman with a little girl. She'd come on them sudden and they were both surprised. The child had begun to holler and the mother put a hand over her mouth. Alice had backed away behind a tree to let them know she meant no harm. Later, she took a sack with a ham bone and oatcake she'd managed to steal. When she checked the next day the sack was gone and she hoped they'd got safe to wherever they'd been going. She had nothing against them.

But how could anyone think she was one herself? Alice stood in front of the oval mirror hanging over the dresser. With her hair swooshed around her face like half-pulled draperies, the rest elaborately wound into a nest at the back of her neck, and her high-necked gray dress, she looked nearly as much a lady as the ones out the window. It would be nicer if her dress weren't drab as a wood pigeon. It ought to be a happy shade. She unclasped her lace fan and held it spread wide against her face so that only her eyes showed above.

"Hullo," she breathed to her reflection. "My name? Why, Birdy—" She paused, her brow furrowed. "It ain't Pickle, damn you. It's Moon. Miss Birdy Moon."

Moon was the name of the lady who had paid their passage to America. That was why she'd picked it for herself. A real lady with a real lord for a husband. Lord and Lady Moon of the great house—too many windows to count—and deer in the park. Oh, she remembered the deer running through greenness. And Lady Moon with her golden hair and ginger cake eyes. A smile for Alice. Sometimes a candy. Young as she'd been, Alice knew Lady Moon was not like her mother. Lady Moon's fingers sparkled with rings and there were no deep creases in her pale forehead. She took them to the ship in Belfast in a carriage nearly as big as their cottage. Lady Moon.

Now Alice fluttered the black fan as she had years ago in the grand carriage in Ireland. "Why, how'd ya do? Birdy Moon. *Miss* Moon. Oh, this here?" she said aloud, fingering the gray skirt. "This ol' thing? My granny bought it for me. My grandma*ma*. Oh Lord, she's rich as King David. Lives in New York. Gimme some of that cake there." She shook her head at her reflection. "I'll have the cake if you please. What? No, siree! Damn me if I ain't already got all the books I kin bear. I'll bust out with all them words, I'm so full of 'em!"

She dropped the fan. What if they asked her the names of the books she was supposed to have read? Well, she could say the Bible. She nodded to herself. That was the biggest book of them all, wasn't it? She knew some Bible stories. There was the lion eating Daniel, the whale swallowing Jonah. When you got to thinking about it, there sure were a lot of people getting eaten up in the Bible. She finished the last strawberry and jumped when someone knocked loudly on the door.

SEVENTEEN

"Open up."

Alice looked guiltily at the empty basket on the bed. Maybe she should've saved him a couple of strawberries. Well, she wasn't going to feel bad about it. He could fend for himself. Eat in the kitchen with the rest of the servants. Matter of fact, he could just blow away with the wind, always telling her what to do.

"Open the door."

Except he seemed to know his way around. He could read too, though he needn't act so smart about it. Alice flung open the door. "What you poundin' like that for?"

"Why didn't you open when I knocked?"

"You say *Mistress, please* and I might."

Bledsoe looked right and left down the hallway. There was no one in sight. He leaned into the doorway, leaned right in her face. "You ain't my mistress."

"You best say it or else. Wait a minute, where you think you're goin'?" Alice ran after him. "All right then," she said when he didn't stop. She jumped in front, blocking his way. "It don't matter."

He kept heading toward the staircase.

"I was just funnin', that's all. Hey! Where you goin'?"

Bledsoe was at the top of the staircase when Alice grabbed his arm. "Don't leave me. I can't talk good. I can't talk with the hands without you. I'll be nice. Here." She reached into the sleeve of her gray gown. "Here's the rest of the money. It's all I got that's mine. I'll give it to you. Don't leave me. They'll know I'm false and put me in jail."

"Let go." He shook his arm free.

"Who's up there?" yelled the landlady from below. "I won't have men in my house."

Alice looked up at Bledsoe, eyes full of green. "Where you gonna go? You ain't got no papers."

His eyes met hers. They were cold as dead stars. "You ain't worth it."

"I'll help you git up north."

"Who is up there?"

Alice said softly, "I'll be worth it. I promise."

"No men in my house."

Alice looked up at him. Her unbound hair fell back from her face and the scar seemed to pulse. "I was wrong."

"I ain't yours nor nobody's."

She lowered her face, and her hair dropped around it like a black curtain. "Sorry. I'm sorry, Bledsoe."

He closed his eyes and inhaled deep. "It jist me," he hollered and shook Alice's hand off. "There were a mouse in my mistress's room and she got all skeered. I was jist chasin' the critter out."

"Mice!" huffed the fat woman coming up the staircase. "I have no mice in my house." As her frizzled gray head came into view, Alice quickly pantomimed something running across her skirt.

"Now, now, it all right now. I done chased it clean out." Bledsoe ran his fingers on the stair railing, then clapped his hands loudly.

"No mice in my house." The landlady peered tentatively from the top riser of the staircase down the hallway. "Where is it?"

Another woman, this one twenty-five or so, began climbing the stairs behind the landlady. She was hatless but wore a long, heavy black wool coat over her dress though the spring morning was mild. She climbed slowly behind the landlady, gripping the banister for support.

The fat woman turned her head. "Oh, there you are, Mrs. Nelson. You have forgotten yet again? It is by now the nineteenth."

Mrs. Nelson's face was pink from exertion. She paused on the staircase a few steps short of the landlady, breathing deeply. "I did not forget, Mrs. Claussen. Pray give me a moment to get to my room and I will give you what I have."

The landlady lifted a sausage finger to the perspiring woman. "What you have? You mean you do not have it all?"

Mrs. Nelson stumbled on the staircase. "I mean, oh, God," she began, rocking dangerously backward. Bledsoe quickly rushed past the landlady and grabbed hold of the woman's arm to keep her from falling down the stairs. He helped her slowly climb past the landlady to the landing. "Thank you. I'm afraid I must lie down," whispered the woman. "I must . . ."

"What is this?" The landlady hefted her weight up the last stair as the woman sank onto the carpet. "Are you ill, Mrs. Nelson?" The woman's eyes had closed and her breathing became more rapid. She opened her mouth and let out a long howling scream.

Alice dropped to her knees and unbuttoned Mrs. Nelson's heavy coat. When it fell aside it was clear why she screamed again.

"Hush!" yelled the landlady. "Stop that. Oh, I should have known. Always wearing that coat hot or cold. Shameful, shameful. Not in my house you don't."

A bloody fluid ran from beneath Mrs. Nelson's skirt in a thick dark stream. "Git some hot water," Alice said to the landlady.

"She's dirtying up my carpet," screeched the landlady, as the woman groaned. She peered close-sightedly at Alice, who was unbuttoning the woman's high-necked blouse. "Wait. What is this? You can talk?"

"Git some water. You want her to die? Take off her shoes," she commanded Bledsoe, rolling up the sleeves of her blouse.

He stared at her openmouthed. "I can't," he began, but the pregnant woman's eyes were open so wide they seemed ready to pop from her head. She screamed again and he quickly bent and unbuttoned her shoes.

Alice, kneeling, bunched the woman's skirt up over her knees. *"Mein Gott!"* shrieked the landlady.

Alice reached up under the skirt and felt the woman's abdomen. "It's a bad 'un," she said softly. "Turned wrong."

Bledsoe was an odd shade of gray. "What's that mean?"

"Hold her legs apart," Alice said to the landlady without looking up from Mrs. Nelson.

"I will not! I forbid this in my house." The landlady, her chins jiggling in horror, shrieked as Bledsoe kneeled beside Alice. "That nigger is, *Gott im Himmel*, the nigger is touching her!"

"The baby's backward," said Alice to Bledsoe, ignoring the landlady.

"What you mean?" Bledsoe stared horrified at the flesh that now protruded between the woman's thighs. Neither noticed when the landlady rapidly thumped down the stairs.

"It's comin' ass first. It got to be quick now or it'll die, can't get no breath with the head coming out last. I got to feel where the legs is. Bring me water and some butter," she yelled at the top of her lungs. "Hurry!"

"God!" screamed Mrs. Nelson.

"Shush now," said Alice soothingly. "It gonna be all right."

Bledsoe backed away and stood against the hallway wall. The servant girl ran up the stairs sloshing a pot of hot water and a dish of butter. "Oh no," exclaimed the girl. "That nice Mrs. Nelson done got herself knocked up."

"Gimme that water over here." Alice plunged her hands in the hot water, then inserted her fingers around the flesh emerging from the woman's body. "I got to feel which way the legs is goin'," she whispered. "Please let the legs be right. Now, honey," she said to the laboring woman, "I need you to be like a dog after a hunt. Pantin' like. I know you wanna push it out, but we gotta take this slow. So go like this, hah, hah, hah."

The woman panted like she'd hunted for miles. Alice felt deeper and the woman fell silent. She had fainted. "Oh Jesus God, wake up now, help me. I can't do this without you," whispered Alice. But she continued coaxing the baby out slowly.

It soon became apparent it was a boy. Alice's fingers gripped one tiny arm, then the other. "We got to get the head out quick but careful or it'll git mashed. Pass me that butter."

Bledsoe leaped forward and handed the dish of butter to Alice. She quickly greased her hands. "Oh Lord. Oh Jesus and all Stump Toe's devils, help me now, I pray."

With a sucking sound the baby's head emerged. The face was covered in a white chalky film. "Mermaid child. Born in the water sack," announced Alice, smiling. "Some say good luck, some bad. It gonna be able to tell the future, I reckon." She bent to the little face, gently snipping the membrane. It fell to the rug like a transparent handkerchief. "Sailor man buy that for luck."

But the baby wasn't moving. Alice bent and blew into the tiny mouth. "Come on now, come on now, come on now, my pretty li'l baby," she sang between breaths. Bledsoe looked down at the discolored thing. Then it opened its lips and screeched. "Thank you, Lord Jesus," whispered Alice on her knees beside Mrs. Nelson. She clasped her hands. "And thank ol' Devil too." She smiled at Bledsoe, lifting the baby up in her arms. "Best to spread the thanks all around, just in case."

EIGHTEEN

Bledsoe carried the still-insensible Mrs. Nelson to her small, neat room, and Alice carried her pinking son. "Motherwort and bayberry bark for the bleedin'. Chamomile and lavender flowers for the pain. Red raspberry to tonify the womb. Can you get me any of these?" she asked the servant girl.

"Doubt we got none of that," said the girl skeptically. "Mistress got some cherry brandy hid in her clothespress, though. I'll fetch that, though she like to skin me for it. She mad as a hornet," she added. "You best be 'ware of that. I think she mean to do somethin' about it too, jist so you know." She left the room, closing the door behind her.

"Forgit about that ol' smelly cow for now," said Alice, cleaning the baby with a pillow sham she'd found in Mrs. Nelson's bureau. Alice's dress was sopped under the arms with sweat, the skirt dotted with blood. She would have liked the new mother to eat the afterbirth to get her strength up but knew it was unlikely the fat woman would let her cook it up proper. She sank down on a hard chair on one side of the bed and wiped the woman's forehead with a damp rag. Mrs. Nelson groaned weakly and opened her eyes.

Alice threw her head to the side and let a cascade of hair fall on the left side of her face.

"Look here," she said, putting the baby in his mother's arms. The baby mewled, punching tiny fists in the air. "He's a fine 'un."

The woman's eyes misted. "Bless you. Bless you."

"You got yourself a fine boy. You rest now, hear? I'll sit by you till you feel stronger."

"Why," said Mrs. Nelson, smiling up at Alice. "You're just a girl! However did you know how to do that? What is your name?"

"Oh! My name? Ain't no nevermind. But it's Birdy," replied Alice. Her hands were trembling and she squeezed them between her knees. It was just beginning to hit her that she'd delivered a baby.

"How pretty. What is your last name?"

"Moon."

"Lovely," murmured the woman, her eyelids drooping. "What pretty hair you have. I've never seen anything like it. Well, no wonder. You are an angel, Miss Moon. I shall give him Robert for the first, and Moon will be for the middle. We will never forget you and . . ." Mrs. Nelson's eyelids fluttered. She kissed her baby's little head. "Robert Moon Nelson."

"Oh now, don't you worry about names and such right now. You got to git your strength up." But secretly she was pleased Mrs. Nelson wanted to name her baby after her, even though it wasn't her name at all.

Mrs. Nelson closed her eyes, the baby resting in the crook of her arm. Alice wiped the woman's forehead again and looked at little Robert Moon Nelson, his newborn eyes the lilac of wild clover. "Ain't he beautiful?"

"How *did* you know how to do that?" asked Bledsoe when Mrs. Nelson had fallen asleep.

Alice straightened the bedclothes and pulled a clean nightgown from the woman's chest of drawers. "When she wakes, I got to clean her up. How you ask? I helped the witch when she brought babies." She took a deep breath and smiled at Bledsoe. "Lord Almighty, I never done it by myself afore. I guess I learned more than I thought. The witch had me hoppin' since the first week she brought me to the Dismal. I was barely old enough to fetch the pot of water, but she didn't care none."

Bledsoe sat down on the only other chair on the far side of the bed. "That old woman back in the swamp? Why you always call her a witch?"

Alice sat down on the other chair and nodded. "Granny Guthrie went to church when the circuit preacher come once a month, but she really prayed to the Devil."

"She was your granny?"

"Kin a mine? No!" snarled Alice furiously. She tugged at her hair and pulled it halfway across her face.

Bledsoe eyed her. He thought for a moment she was going to spit at him. She was the most awful, ignorant excuse for a female he'd ever run across. "Forget I asked then."

A little clock on the dresser tick-tick-ticked. Finally when the baby yawned, she said, "Look at that, so tiny, all them fingers and toes. Well then. How 'bout you? Your folks?"

"You think I hunkered around the fire playing games and singing songs? Then I got tucked in with a fairy story?" His lips were drawn tight.

"Well, no. I guess not." She was quiet a moment. Then, "Now, Bledsoe. Isn't that a funny name?"

"All I got."

"What's your other?"

"Other what?"

"Name. Last name."

"I don't have any other. Just Bledsoe, then House Boy. Writ like that on the ledger between Soosie Kichen Girl and Hert Barrel Maker, and that came after two cast-iron kettles." He turned to the window, arms crossed over his chest, mouth set in an angry line.

She looked away and down at the baby. It had a sprout of hair on its head like the plumes of a carrot. She glanced at Bledsoe. He was the grimmest boy she'd ever met. Lord. Of course she didn't think he'd had some nice kind of life; he was a negro, he was a slave, but he didn't need to snap her head off about it. It wasn't her fault, was it? She snuck a look at him. He'd picked up a flimsy pamphlet on the table next to the bed.

Bledsoe opened it, read a bit, and looked at the sleeping woman with surprise.

"What's that book 'bout?" asked Alice.

"It ain't a book like that."

"Give it here. Lemme see."

"What for? You can't read." But Alice reached out over the woman on the bed and Bledsoe reluctantly handed her the pamphlet.

She flipped the pages but saw nothing but inky squiggles. "There was a teacher man come to Geegomie for a spell. He come from Elizabeth City and schooled Dolantha Shaw and her brother and a couple of others, but not me; Granny Guthrie wouldn't let me, said no need and I was too dumb anyway, though I ain't. She couldn't read none either, but she'd pretend to read the Bible if anybody came around doubting she was a good Christian. She'd stick her nose in it and say parts of it that she remembered from the preacher. He didn't last long, though."

"The preacher?"

"That teacher man. Scarce anyone cared about readin' and scribblin' in the Dismal. Can't eat words. How come you can?"

"How come I can what?"

"Read."

"I learned."

"But you're a nigger, why'd anyone learn a nigger to read?"

He turned his face away and crossed his arms over his chest.

She bent to the pamphlet, flipping the pages again so she didn't have to look at his face. He was awful thin-skinned, she thought, sitting over there, growl faced. Seemed a smile would kill him, no matter how nice she tried to be. Somewhere a church bell chimed. A pigeon paced the sill outside the closed window. Bledsoe cracked his knuckles. She tried to catch his eye, but he wouldn't look at her.

"We best git out of here afore nightfall," she said finally. "That fat cow looked fit to be tied; I don't like it. She puts me in mind of Jemimah Crandall."

"Who's Jemimah Crandall?"

"One of them women acts all Christiany, but really's mean's a wild turkey. You ever run across a wild turkey? So best we git on to New York tonight."

"Just like that?" Bledsoe snapped his fingers. "It's a hundred miles at least. Maybe you can fly."

Alice rolled her eyes. "I ain't stupid. Stop callin' me stupid."

Bledsoe cracked his knuckles again. He looked at the wallpaper. Finally he said, "Well, maybe we could get a train. Trains go to New York."

Alice leaned across the bed toward him, her face alight. She had never seen a train, though she'd heard of them. "Where we find one?"

Bledsoe had never seen a train either. Not a real one, though he'd seen pictures. But then he'd never seen a great number of things he'd read about. "Trains are at train stations," he replied confidently. "We'll ask where . . ."

The door of the small room swung open so hard it bounced against the inner wall. The landlady filled up the narrow doorway. "There they are." She pointed. "That slut in the bed has not paid me for four months. And that girl over there? She is a liar. The nigger said she could not speak, but she can, she can, and oh, *mein Gott,* he had his hands all over Mrs. Nelson. Disgusting, touching her where no nigger ought. There's laws against that. And *she* there insisted on keeping him right outside her door! Who knows what went on? Look at her, not even dressed proper. Unholy. Who knows what they've been up to? This is a godly house. Arrest them."

The landlady moved out of the doorway to make room for a uniformed Baltimore policeman. "I'll ask the girl and the negro some questions, ma'am, but I don't think there's anything you can do about that woman there."

Alice and Bledsoe turned to Mrs. Nelson. Beside her the baby began to wail. Alice quickly put her ear to the woman's chest. "She was jist a little weak is all. I don't know what happened. Oh Lord have mercy, this poor li'l baby. That poor woman, must have been a weak heart." The baby was crying louder. Alice gathered it up and held it against her, but the landlady tugged at it.

"Why? What you gonna do with it?" cried Alice, only letting go when it seemed the landlady would just as soon rip the infant in two as surrender it. Once the landlady had the baby, she looked at it with disgust and thrust it at the servant girl with less regard than a dinner ham. "Make it stop crying," she commanded the servant. The landlady pointed at Bledsoe and Alice. "Now, Mr. Policeman, you will do your job, *ja*? I will not have this in my house. No dead women, no dirty bastards, no lying niggers. I am a Christian woman. Not in my house!"

NINETEEN

Bledsoe and Alice were prodded ahead of the policeman down the stairs to a small parlor that looked very elegant at first glance, but Bledsoe knew better. The oriental scarf on the table didn't hide the scratches, and the vase with dried flowers was polished tin meant to look like silver. The dull wood floor was only partially covered by a moth-eaten red Turkey rug that wasn't really dark, just dirty. The only other furniture was a settee Alice was sitting on, upholstered in mud-colored velveteen.

Bledsoe stood behind the settee and focused his attention on the faded curlicues in the carpet.

The policeman kept Mrs. Claussen out of the parlor by shutting the door in her face with a curt "Best if I question them alone." But Bledsoe could still see the landlady's bulky shadow pacing back and forth under the door.

Alice didn't realize she still had the little pamphlet. She was twisting it in her hands. Her hair fell in black wildness nearly to her waist, her dress hung limp without her petticoats, her skirt was splattered with blood, and her bare feet were pale against the dark rug. "What about the baby?" asked Alice. "You ain't gonna let that mean old woman keep it, are you?"

"That's not your concern." The policeman wore a billed cap and a uniform with a shiny badge over his heart. He pulled a notebook and pencil from his brass-buttoned uniform pocket. "Your name, miss?"

Alice clutched the pamphlet nervously in her lap. "My name?"

"Your name."

"Birdy."

"Birdy what?"

"Birdy what?" parroted Alice with frightened eyes.

"Your last name. What is it?"

"Oh. It's Br—Moon," replied Alice, dabbing her eyes with the limp lace of her cuff.

"Broom?"

"Moon."

"Birdy Moon?"

She stopped drying her eyes and looked at him, startled. "Why? Somethin' wrong with it?"

The policeman shifted his gaze to Bledsoe, but Bledsoe continued to pretend to be enraptured by the rug. He looked back at Alice. He pointed with his little pencil. "Well then, Miss Moon, what happened to your shoes?"

"Happened? Why nothin', they're jist fine."

"Are you in the habit of going about in, um, your current state, Miss Moon?"

Without looking up from the rug, Bledsoe said, "It account of dat mouse."

"What? What mouse?"

"Dat mouse up in her room dere, then that lady fell to birthin' the baby and Mistress ain't had time to git dressed proper."

"I wasn't talking to you."

Bledsoe shrugged. "I jist tellin' it like it is, Marse."

"This negro yours, Miss Moon?"

Alice glanced at Bledsoe. "Uh-huh. He's mine. And what he said's right. About my shoes, I mean. I didn't have time to put 'em on nor git dressed right on account of all hell breakin' loose around here this mornin'."

The officer stared at her a moment. Alice stared back.

Bledsoe tried as hard as he could to melt into the wall behind him.

"Your last place of residence?"

"Resi-what?"

Bledsoe inwardly closed his eyes, though outwardly he'd shifted them from the rug to an oil painting of a long-haired white cat playing with a ball of yarn on the far wall.

"Where is it you lived before Baltimore?"

"We come up from Norfolk. On the paddle wheeler."

"Traveling all alone, are you? Just the two of you?"

"Well, ain't got nobody else," said Alice. "So's I suppose that would mean jist us."

The look the policeman gave her made Alice lower her eyes. She fiddled with the pamphlet and wiped her sweating palms on her skirt.

"How old are you?" he asked, looking at her closer.

She pulled her hair closer across her face. "Nineteen," she mumbled.

The policeman wrote something in his notebook. "Now the landlady said you pretended to be a mute and insisted on this negro sleeping right outside your bedroom."

"I loss my voice on account of I had a bad throat. What's wrong with that?" said Alice, looking at the policeman. She stood up, hands on her hips; the forgotten pamphlet tumbled to the carpet. "You never heard of a body losin' their voice? And *he*"—Alice tossed her head toward Bledsoe—"I needed him to talk for me till it come back. It come back now. See?" Alice crossed her arms.

The policeman picked up the pamphlet. *"A Former Slave's Flight to Freedom."* He tossed it to the table, where it knocked over the tin vase of dried flowers with a clatter. "One of those abolitionists, are you? I see now."

"What you see? I don't know nothin' 'bout that." Alice looked wide-eyed at Bledsoe. "What's he mean?"

The policeman put away his notebook and pointed at Bledsoe. "You got papers on him?"

"Papers? Why, I—"

Outside voices rose and fell. It sounded like chanting but was muffled by the closed window. The officer shoved Bledsoe toward the parlor door. "He'll be at the jail at Pratt and Howard. If he's your property, prove it."

"He didn't do nothin'. Let him go!" exclaimed Alice, grabbing Bledsoe's hand.

The officer pushed her away. "Good God, you nigger lovers disgust me." He opened the parlor door, shoving Bledsoe in front of him just as the landlady came rushing toward them, her voluminous skirt raising a small tornado of dust.

From outside, the sound of angry voices swelled.

"Arrest her! She's a thief!" The fat woman yanked open Alice's crocodile bag, reached inside, and triumphantly displayed a small gilded bust of a balding man with enormous muttonchop whiskers. "She stole my Emperor Franz Joseph!"

The policeman turned to Alice. "That true?"

"It musta fell in there somehow," muttered Alice.

Outside the sound of chanting had risen to a roar. The policeman opened the front door, pushing Bledsoe and Alice ahead of him. "What the . . ." began the policeman. "Hey!" he shouted as a man in the surging crowd jostled him. As the policeman shouted angrily at the man, Bledsoe stepped back and was immediately engulfed in a sea of hats and bonnets.

TWENTY

Alice found herself wedged between a tall man in a bowler hat and a woman in a gingham gown. The policeman had been swallowed in the crush that lined both sides of the street. Alice stood on tiptoes, trying to spot Bledsoe, but it was useless. She tried to push her way to the back of the crowd toward the buildings but was jostled and shoved in the sea of people. All pretense of manners had been dropped in the melee. Alice watched as the woman beside her craned her neck around another man, trying to get a view of whatever was coming down the street. Was it a parade of some sort? The shopkeeper's wife in Geegomie had once seen a circus parade in Raleigh. There had even been a big humped thing called a camel. It had been amazing, she'd told Alice. But there were no smiles on the faces surrounding her. Instead a man had a pile of cobblestones at his feet and another had a pistol pulled and was waving it over his head. She tried once more to shove her way toward the rear of the pack, but she was only crammed in more tightly.

"Look there! Here they come!" someone shouted, and the multitude roared, "They will not pass! They will not pass!"

The crowd carried Alice forward, trying to reach whatever had appeared in the street. On her right was a woman in a wide-hooped skirt, holding on to a little boy with one hand and a good-sized rock with the other.

"Here come them Yanks!" yelled a young man with bright ginger hair. "Come on now, don't let 'em through!" He hoisted a flag with a single star above a coiled snake and the motto *Don't Tread on Me* stitched below. "Don't let 'em reach Camden Station, boys!" he yelled, waving the flag above the crowd. "Don't let 'em get through!"

Alice was thrust toward the street, very nearly knocked down by the eager throng.

"Hooray for Jeff Davis," screamed a woman behind her. "Hooray for the South!" The cheer was taken up, drowning out the sound of soldiers in dark blue marching four abreast down the center of the street. They looked neither left nor right, ignoring the shouts and insults.

"Remember 1776!" hollered the ginger-haired man with the flag. "King Lincoln can't take our freedom. Damn the Federals!" The crowd was pressing in ever closer to the company of blue-clad soldiers marching down the middle of the street, forcing Alice along with the swell. A man a few feet away threw a rock, knocking the cap from a soldier's head, but the soldier barely flinched and kept marching.

"Damn you Yanks," screamed someone. "This is our land!"

"Give it to 'em!" shouted another. "They won't shoot! They're too afraid of their cowardly necks." A man broke from the crowd and ran right into the street. He hit a Federal soldier over the head with a paving stone. The man reeled a moment, then collapsed to a deafening *hurrah!* from the mob. With howls people began pelting soldiers with rocks and bricks. Alice was terrified of being trampled but couldn't extricate herself. She either moved with the melee or risked being crushed beneath it. Somewhere an unseen woman wailed, "Help me, they hurt my baby!"

Then someone in the crowd fired a gun. The soldiers now quickly formed a defensive circle in the middle of the street, the barrels of their rifles facing outward. It was suddenly so quiet Alice could hear a chink-chink when their rifles were cocked in unison. Then, from the crowd another gunshot rang out, blasting away the silence. A soldier faltered a moment, then collapsed onto the street.

"Kill 'em," shrieked a girl.

Suddenly everything was noise. Horses, women screaming, men shouting. Alice put her hands over her ears, shoving herself backward, elbowing and kicking herself away from the street. She heard the report of the rifles as the soldiers fired. Clouds of white smoke rose, accompanied by the acrid odor of gunpowder. The young man with ginger hair pushed past Alice, his flag abandoned as the soldiers continued firing. Pop-pop-pop went the guns. A horse, its rider lost, pounded through the crowd and galloped past Alice into an alley. The window of a bakery shattered, spraying glass into the crowd. A man beside Alice screamed, a hand held to his bloody face. She felt someone grab her by the shoulder. She whirled, her fists raised.

"Come on," yelled Bledsoe. "This way." He began to weave along the back of the crowd toward the next corner. When Bledsoe disappeared, Alice shoved a woman out of the way and jabbed a man so hard with her elbow he bent double. At last, with the shrieking mob behind her, she picked up her soiled skirt and ran.

TWENTY-ONE

When she caught sight of Bledsoe, he was far ahead running down the eerily empty street. "Wait!"

He didn't turn around, but he slowed some, allowing her to catch up. She followed him as he zigzagged from street to street, until at last the sounds of gunfire and shouting gradually receded. Somewhere something was on fire; she could smell ash. Turning, she saw a pillar of gray smoke rising near the harbor basin where they'd docked in the paddle wheeler.

After several twists and turns, Bledsoe paused beside a shop. She stopped next to him panting, trying to catch her breath.

"Get down," he snapped suddenly, ducking quick behind a wagon.

"What?" she puffed. "Why?"

Bledsoe dragged her down beside him. "Here." He scurried under the wagon; she followed. They lay on their stomachs staring out at the street. Bledsoe put a finger to his lips. Two white men were approaching, zigzagging down the middle of the street. "Drunk," he whispered. One man, his hat askew, waved a bottle. The other swung a sword wildly above his head. They paused as the one with the bottle pitched it through the window of a shop across the street. A colored woman ran out cursing, only to be pulled back inside by someone unseen.

"Burn them niggers out," yelled the man, and he lit a torch drenched in kerosene. He threw it, and it crashed through a window.

They stayed under the wagon until the men, whooping and hollering, passed out of sight, the sound of breaking glass following. "Is this the war?" said Alice, trembling, as flames started tonguing the window across the street.

"Come on, get up. Keep close to the buildings."

"What are they fightin' about? Where we goin'? What we goin' to do? What—" A gunshot close enough to send a flock of pigeons flapping skyward cut her off.

"Run," yelled Bledsoe.

An hour later smoke hovered over the streets behind them like a malignant cloud. A colored man passing on the sidewalk stared at Alice. She stared back with frightened eyes. Bledsoe glanced at her. Her hair had exploded in wild black frizz, her dress hung baggy without the petticoats and was filthy, and her bare feet were grimy.

"Why'd you steal that thing anyhow?" Bledsoe asked.

"The head? 'Cause it was gold! I found it in the clothespress in my room. I figured we could sell it like we did my rubies and git that train to New York," said Alice.

"Who'd leave a real gold head in a clothespress? It was just painted wood," said Bledsoe scornfully, and he walked faster, hoping no one would think she was with him.

Behind him, Alice sighed loudly. "Well, *maybe* I was thinkin' 'bout more than jist myself. Maybe I was thinkin' it might help you too." Which wasn't true. What she'd really thought when she'd found the gold head was that it surely was worth more than her little brooch. And with the money she'd buy fancy dresses and a pink parasol like a woman had twirled hypnotically beneath the boardinghouse window. Alice lifted the hem of her skirt to step over a pile of horse manure. "But guess thinkin' 'bout you as well as me makes me jist a big ol' fool."

For a second Bledsoe's eyes met hers. Alice looked away and pretended to brush away a tear.

"Well," he said brusquely. "No time for blubberin'. Come on. Hurry it up." Inwardly, he cursed himself. Why hadn't he just left her back there? Something had seemed to compel him to grab hold of her when all he really wanted was to get rid of her.

"What was that thing the policeman said? Abowlinist? How can I be a thing I don't even know?"

"Abolitionist. A person against slavery. That's what the war's about."

"No, it ain't. It's 'cause Lincoln wants to free the niggers so they'll runny muck among our southern flowers."

He stopped and wheeled to her. "What?"

Alice bent her head. "*He* said. He said that. The preacher. The preacher in the Baptist church in Geegomie, and everybody got all riled up, and the witch made me wear those damn shoes that cuts off my circulating 'cause they's too small. What you lookin' at me like that for? He preaches in Wilmington too; you ever been to Wilmington? So he knows what the war's about, I reckon."

"You're the dumbest . . ." He left off disgustedly.

"I ain't neither. I jist said *he* was the one said that. Wait!"

"Get away from me." Bledsoe turned a corner and nearly bumped into a well-dressed colored man. "Beg pardon," he said as the man hurried past. Everyone in this neighborhood was colored. Bledsoe tried to smooth down his coat a bit. He straightened his shoulders. These people were free. He could tell by the way they held themselves. How could they live here, he wondered, and still hold their heads high when drunken white folks could burn down their houses?

Alice had paused a moment in front of a shop window with strange cages, then realized they were hoops for ladies' gowns. Inside she saw a colored woman sewing. "Maybe we kin git me a new dress here." Alice reached for the door handle. But just as she did, the woman inside locked the door. "How do you like that?" exclaimed Alice. "She locked me out."

When she turned around Bledsoe was looking down at a little sandy-haired colored boy. He was no more than seven or eight and had a red india rubber ball. "You saw the soldiers?"

Bledsoe nodded. "I did."

"They tried to stop them, didn't they? Those were Lincoln's soldiers going to Washington to fight the war. My daddy said so," stated the little boy. "But they can't stop 'em. I'm gonna join the army. Are you?"

"I am," said Bledsoe solemnly. "Just as soon as I can get there."

"Jeffrey!" shouted someone from a row house across the street.

"You'll get there before me most likely. *She*"—he nodded behind him—"makes me go to bed soon's it's dark. But I got this." The boy pulled a pearl-handled pocketknife from his waistband.

"Jeffrey, come here this instant!" A colored woman rushed down the steps of the row house.

"Here." The boy thrust the pocketknife at Bledsoe. "She's gonna take it from me anyhow." The woman, reaching the sidewalk, yanked the boy up the steps of the house and slammed the door behind them.

"What you tell that boy you joinin' the army for? We're goin' to New York. Hey now! Slow up some."

TWENTY-TWO

It was growing cold and getting dark. A tidal scent filled the air. The neat row houses of the free black neighborhood were behind them. The cobbled streets near the boat basin were narrow and layered with filth. Buildings tilted toward each other, sharing thin walls with their neighbors. Alice stepped on a piece of broken glass but her feet were tough; she'd rarely worn the shabby shoes on even the coldest days in the swamp. When she pulled out the shard of glass, her foot didn't even bleed.

They passed a drunk vomiting in the street. Someone in an alley yelled, "Ellen Lee, Ellen Lee, you gonna git it." They could still smell the remains of a fire a few blocks away. Alice's ankle was throbbing and she was so hungry she felt faint. The last thing she'd had to eat had been the morning's strawberries.

In the distance the sound of riders approaching made them recede into the shadows of a warehouse. After they passed, Bledsoe dug in his pocket. "Here. Take it."

Alice started to snatch it, then pulled her hand back and looked up at him, confused. "What you givin' me that money for?"

"It's yours, ain't it? See that place?" He pointed to a clapboard sign above a door advertising rooms to rent. "You can stay there tonight and get you a boat in the morning wherever you want."

Alice didn't even try to hide her panic. "What you mean? What you talkin' about?"

"I have to get north."

"But I'm goin' with you."

"I'm joining the army. But until I can find where to, I'm a runaway and now you're wanted for thievin'. You're white and I'm not. We stick out, the two of us."

"You said I was more yellow," pleaded Alice. Her ragged dress flapped against her legs. The April wind remembered winter and she shivered, teeth chattering. Over her head a wooden sign creaked and a light in a lonely window blinked out. He walked away, his coat billowing behind him like a black sail.

"Wait," she shouted. "Don't go." But he disappeared. *Oh my day,* she thought wearily, her shoulders slumping. *He's gonna leave me here.* Was it only this morning the whole world seemed ready to open for her like a new-bloomed flower? Just hours ago she'd felt finally free? She didn't notice the sailor with the blue scarf draped around his neck. He had sidled up next to her. The sailor reached to touch her black hair blowing wild in the wind.

"Evenin'."

Alice screamed. Surprised, the sailor took a step back but grabbed her wrist. "Whatcha hollerin' for? I'll pay. Shut up." He pulled her toward him.

"Let me be!" she hollered. "Don't you touch me, git off me!"

Alice's mouth opened again, but with silent surprise. Bledsoe was behind the sailor and in one motion yanked the blue scarf off and jammed the blade of the pocketknife against his naked throat. "Let go of her."

"Sure," stammered the sailor. "Sure. I was just foolin'." The sailor let go of Alice so suddenly she staggered. Behind the sailor, knife still to the man's throat, Bledsoe was taller, but the sailor was wide and clearly strong. "Hey now," said the sailor. "I don't want no trouble." But he grabbed Bledsoe's hand at his throat and squeezed it so hard that Bledsoe howled and dropped the pocketknife.

The sailor spun around cat quick. "Ha! You ain't nothin' but a skinny boy."

"Get going, go on," yelled Bledsoe, grabbing up the pocketknife and jumping backward. He danced in front of the sailor, stabbing the air.

The sailor grinned. "She yourn?" He pulled a long-bladed bowie knife from his belt. "I like 'em bright," he said, giving the knife a fancy twirl. "I like 'em young and I like 'em bright."

Bledsoe stepped backward again, nearly tripping, still stabbing air. He should have kept going. Now it was too late and he was going to die. Not gloriously in a war of righteousness, but pitifully on a street in a city still south.

Out of the corner of his eye, Bledsoe saw that Alice had the sailor's blue scarf. It was whipping in the wind. He took another step back. The sailor was playing with him now. The sailor twirled the bone handle of the bowie knife and, still grinning, took another step toward Bledsoe.

Behind the sailor, Alice threw the scarf over the sailor's head and around his neck. She pulled it tight so quickly he had no time to react. Bledsoe watched, stunned, as she pulled the scarf's ends with both hands with all her might. The sailor fell to his knees; his bowie knife clattered to the pavement. "Ugh," she grunted, but she didn't stop. She pulled the scarf tighter and the sailor reached up, clawing and gasping. His mouth gaped. She shook the hair back from her face and the sailor's eyes widened in horror, seeing the scar. She stood over him then, the scarf knotted around her wrists. "There you go," she shrieked. "Damn you, there you go, there you go."

Even in the dim light Bledsoe could see that the sailor's face was turning dark and his eyes were bulging. "Go on now," she snarled. "Touch me agin, damn you."

"Stop!" Bledsoe shouted.

She twisted the scarf another turn. Bledsoe shoved her hard and she fell backward to the street. "You want to kill him?"

"Why not?" she said dully, still on the ground. "He'd'a killed you." They stared at one another a moment as behind Alice the sailor gasped and began to crawl away across the paving stones. Someone yelled out a window. "What the devil's going on?"

"Don't you see?" called Alice, rising from the pavement as the sailor staggered into the shadows. But all Bledsoe could see was the blazing shack, the fire she'd set in the Dismal, with the old woman still inside. He turned and ran. Through an alley, over a back fence. A dog barked wild as he dashed through a new-planted garden. He barely made it over the next fence, the dog so close he could feel its breath behind him. He kept going and didn't dare pause. Not until he was certain he'd lost her.

TWENTY-THREE

He was afraid of what would happen if he was still in Baltimore by morning. Several times he'd seen policemen before they'd seen him and had managed to hide in the shadows. He heard a man as he passed say something about a curfew—police were sweeping the streets for anyone still about "after the riot." A fragment from the encyclopedia popped into his head.

> *BASTILLE, a medieval fortress used as a prison destroyed on July 14, 1789, by a mob . . . Women and children were trampled underfoot in the rush to the drawbridge. The Marquis de Launay was violently beheaded and his head was put on a stake and paraded victoriously all through Paris after the riot had ended.*

Heads on stakes. Rioting was another word for madness. He wanted away from this city. But one street led to another, around and around. He looked up. Stars glittered. Before Pomp had run off from Our Joy, he'd told Bledsoe about the drinking gourd. You were supposed to follow it. How could you follow something that just hung over your head? Wasn't like bread crumbs in that fairy tale. Every time he heard footsteps he pressed himself into a corner or ducked behind a fence. He found himself on the same street again. He felt like screaming. He turned around. *No!* But there she was.

"Bledsoe?"

He ran again, slipping on the pavement. But it did no good. He could hear her heavy panting breath heaving right behind him.

"Wait, Bledsoe, please wait."

She was so close behind him that if he turned around she'd run right smack into him. Hearing someone coming, he ducked into the shadows. He felt Alice's heat as she pressed herself into the wall beside him. A man raced by. A policeman followed a moment later without a glance in their direction.

He felt a nudge at his side and reluctantly looked down at her outstretched hand. He could smell the partially crushed ripe berries.

"Go on. Got 'em out of a garden back yonder. They're real sweet."

He was starving. So he let her dump them into his hand. He ate them in seconds and licked his palm, keeping a wary eye on the street.

The big city was oddly quiet. There were few lights in windows. In the distance a steamer horn blew, but it sounded very far away, almost distant as the stars. A cat skitted from behind a fence, making him jump. A bird twoo-hooed.

"Dove callin' at night's a bad sign," she whispered. "Where you goin'?"

"I don't damn know." He started off again.

"Well, you best slow down some 'cause 'don't damn know' is where I'm headin' too."

He wouldn't cry. He sniffled and wiped his nose on his sleeve. Where was the *out* of this city?

"I kin help you, I kin." She'd snuck up right beside him.

"Get away from me."

"What's that?"

He whirled to her. "Go away!"

"You cryin'?"

He stopped. A delivery wagon and a team of horses sat outside a building. He'd been down this street and it hadn't been there before. A lamp burned in the window of the building. The street was lifeless except for the double team hitched to the wagon. Bledsoe could just make out the gold lettering painted on the box. *Millibrand & Sons* it said. Below that all that was visible from where he was hiding was a gold *W*.

"Whatcha lookin' at?"

He motioned for her to be quiet. A man in preacher black came out of the building. He was haloed by the light in the window. Bledsoe quickly ducked behind a wrought iron fence wreathed with spring honeysuckle; Alice crouched behind him. Two more men emerged from the building, struggling to carry a big wooden box. They set the box on the ground while one unlatched the double doors at the back of the wagon.

"How long to Winchester?" asked the man in the black suit.

One of the others replied, but he couldn't hear what was said. The men hefted the odd box through the back doors of the wagon. "Better hoof it," said the man who looked like a preacher. "Did my best but couldn't get ice today with the station blocked."

"Dang 'em," said one of the men. He had a long shaggy beard that nearly obscured his face.

"Bastards," agreed the other, and he spat on the street.

Bledsoe was certain they were talking about the riot, but what side they sympathized with he had no idea. Baltimore seemed half one way, half the other. The people rioting in the street obviously considered themselves southern, but then you had free negroes and abolitionists like that poor Mrs. Nelson. The black-suited man said they were to deliver the box to Winchester. "*A Former Slave's Flight to Freedom*: Colvin Publishing Company, Winchester, Ohio." It was right there on the front page of the abolitionist pamphlet. It was surely a sign. Ohio was a free state.

If the poor woman in the boardinghouse wasn't an abolitionist, she was at least a sympathizer. Most of what he knew about the movement was gleaned from disparaging table talk at Our Joy and purloined copies of the *Carolina Watchman* or the *Richmond Daily Dispatch*. Anyone who made the white folks at Our Joy so damn mad had to be doing something good.

Alice tugged his sleeve but he shook her off. This was his ticket. If only he could figure out how to get aboard. Then the man in preacher black said, "Come in and have one for the road; it's going to be a long night."

Apparently they weren't worried about anyone stealing the box. They left the back doors of the delivery wagon wide open. He scrunched low and started crabwalking toward it. Alice crouched down and imitated him. He waved a hand at her angrily. But it didn't do a bit of good.

TWENTY-FOUR

The Baltimore night was perfumed with honeysuckle and April lilacs. But once they were inside the wagon, the only air came from a few small cracks between the floorboards. After the back door banged shut, it hit him that there was no way out unless someone swung the latch from outside. What if no one opened it for days? It was so dark he couldn't see Alice. There was also a strange smell. It had been growing steadily stronger. After a while it became nearly unbearably hot. His shirt was as wet as if he'd jumped in a lake.

The wagon rocked from side to side. He felt every jolt. Nearly all the interior was taken up by the big box. They were pinned behind it with their backs against the wall separating them from the driver.

After what seemed a week, the wagon had gradually tilted upward, climbing steeply. The box had slipped backward as they ascended, banging so hard against the doors that they'd both held their breath for fear it would smash right through. But not long after, the wagon tilted downward and the box had skidded in the opposite direction, nearly slamming into them. They kept it at bay by bracing their feet against it. His legs ached from the strain but he didn't dare move.

Since it was so dark he lost all sense of time. Whether it was morning or dead of night, he hadn't a notion. By now it felt they'd been traveling forever. He didn't dare say a word. The bearded driver and the other man were right outside. They could hear every squeak of the bench seat springs and the snores of one of the men.

He was exhausted but terrified of falling asleep. He set himself to trying to imagine what would happen once he finally got to freedom. Alice's head had fallen on his shoulder. He didn't dare move for fear she'd make noise. He could smell her breath. It was strangely minty. He was shaken alert by a jolt. The road beneath the wagon had changed from dirt to paving stones.

"Smells like butter gone bad in here," whispered Alice.

"Ho," shouted a man outside. The wagon stopped.

They peered blindly at the rear of the wagon, their feet still propped against the box. But the doors remained closed. They heard the crunch of boots on gravel, the sound of horses thirstily drinking. Then a woman screeched high and loud, "My God, my God. Daddy, it can't be true!" An awful sobbing commenced and another woman said, "Oh darlin', hold strong now. They said it was a vein busted in his head." The sobbing rose in pitch and fervor.

"Reckon we're in Ohio now?" breathed Alice in his ear.

"Shhhh," said Bledsoe. "Listen."

"It can't be true!" howled the woman outside once more.

The back doors swung open. Behind the box Bledsoe and Alice blinked like sun-trapped moles. A tiny woman in a plum-colored gown and matching bonnet squinted at the box. "What's this? Why ain't he in a proper one?"

"It was all the undertaker had on hand, ma'am. He had a delivery of new coffins down at the train station but couldn't get 'em on account of they'd set the depot on fire to try to stop the soldiers gettin' through."

"Damn that Lincoln. Keepin' Daddy from a proper box." The woman put a handkerchief to her nose and burst into a wail of high-pitched sorrow. The other man from Baltimore pointed at the back of the wagon. "Who's them two?"

The bearded driver stuck his head in the back of the wagon. "Couldn't say, Luther," he replied.

"This Winchester, Ohio?" asked Alice in a small voice, feet still propped against the box.

The tiny plum-gowned woman poked her head inside now too. Holding her scented handkerchief to her nose, she shrieked, "What them niggers doin' in there with Daddy?"

"I reckon they's runaways," replied the bearded man. "Help me with Miss Camdale's father here, Luther." He shook his head at Bledsoe and Alice. "Y'all in Winchester all right. Winchester, Virginia, that is. Well, ma'am, Luther. I reckon after we get Mr. Camdale here unloaded I best take 'em right on over to the sheriff so's he kin put 'em in jail and put out a runaway notice."

Miss Camdale commenced more earsplitting sounds of sorrow as the box with her father was set on the ground with a loud thud. The double doors of the wagon were slammed shut again and the wooden latch clacked into place.

"Oh Lord have mercy," cried Alice. "Oh woe! We're done for now."

Again they were pitched and rolled in the dark. Bledsoe decided that when the doors opened he'd run for it. No doubt he'd be knocked senseless or shot in the back, but at least he'd go down knowing he'd tried his best. He wished he had a gun. Or even a knife. *Wait,* he thought, his hand in his pocket. He unfolded the pocketknife. If he stabbed him in the eye . . .

"Where's this jail?" moaned Alice. "Why's it takin' so long? Oh Lord, I jist about want to die!"

"Then do it and be quiet," he said. "I'm thinkin'."

"What good's that gonna do?"

On the other hand, it might be better to beg for mercy. One thing was certain. He'd never be free if he was dead first.

At last the wagon creaked to a stop. The back doors were flung open. Once more they were blinded. The man with the beard had the light behind him so they couldn't make out his features clearly. "Get out."

Bledsoe climbed out slowly. Alice jumped off the back of the wagon beside him. They looked wonderingly at their surroundings. The narrow dirt road was edged by thick woods behind them, and looking eastward, hills rose higher and higher until the green of them turned blue.

Alice felt her knees go weak. He'd brought them to the wilderness to kill them. She reached for Bledsoe's arm and clutched it. "Oh please, mister," she began.

The man handed Bledsoe a wooden canteen and an old horse blanket. "Down there's the Shenandoah Valley," said the man. "That's where we come from. You want to stay out of it. East are the Blue Ridge. Don't go that way. Get yourselves west over the Alleghenies if you can do it. West is Ohio."

He climbed back up on the delivery wagon and turned the team around without another word, leaving them at the bottom of a trail in the foothills of the Appalachians.

TWENTY-FIVE

They walked as far as they could before the light gave out, skirting the dusty ribbon of road, backing into the woods at the sound of anyone approaching. They hiked up above dips and hollows, some with cabins tucked in them. Dogs barked sometimes, but they only saw one other human before dark—a woman beating wash in a rocky creek. She was humming to herself and didn't see them.

Toward dusk the air grew chill again. Shivering and hungry, they followed a cow, bell ringing as it went, to a little homestead. The cow walked itself through an opened gate and into a pen and set to working on a salt lick, taking no notice of Alice as she climbed into the henhouse. She wrestled five brown eggs from the reluctant hens.

They ate two apiece, huddled behind the henhouse. Alice dropped the fifth in her rush to eat it. The bright yolk splattered red veined on the grass. "Oh, damn me," she mourned.

She started back for more but the rooster gave notice and someone let out a dog. It ran them deep into the surrounding woods. They splashed across a creek and lost the dog but also lost the trail the man with the beard had pointed out to them that climbed up a long ridge. By then it was dark. The eggs just made them hungrier.

They slept in the woods, the horse blanket wrapped around them. Even dogs that fight will sleep close to keep warm.

*

They went opposite the sun in the morning. Alice dug up roots and they ate them, spitting out dirt. But they were small, new growth; it was only April. They saw smoke rising from a hollow and made for it. They were desperate now. A small house was set below, painted white with green trim, and a front porch with a pair of gay yellow chairs. They smelled bacon frying. It was too much.

"Hold up," said Bledsoe when they got nearer. "Might be dogs."

"I don't care. I'll wring their damn necks." Alice scooted down the slope to the right of the house, but it was steep and she began slipping and sliding. She would have tumbled right down in front of the place if Bledsoe hadn't grabbed hold of her wrist.

Wash snapped in the breeze on a line tied between two walnut trees. A blue gingham dress filled up with air and danced. Seedlings sprouted green headed in a fenced-off supper garden. No dogs barked when they snuck up to a window in the rear of the house. Alice peeked through the window. A woman in checked calico, her blond hair neatly coiled on the back of her head like a lovely golden serpent, was frying bacon with her back to the window. A man, golden haired like the woman, sat at a table. A baby cooed and wriggled on his lap as the man spoon-fed it milksop. The woman said something and the man laughed, and then she shoveled bacon and fried eggs on a plate and set it down on the table.

Alice huddled down beside Bledsoe. "I'll tell 'em we're lost and ask 'em for some food. They look like good folk. They got a little baby." She began to stand up, but he pulled her back down roughly.

"No," he whispered through clenched teeth. "You got your stupid head on? Don't matter how they *look*. Can't trust any of them. This ain't a free state."

Reluctantly, Alice backed away from the window just as the woman opened a side door, with a large bowl. They watched as she dumped the contents into a tin pail in the small barnyard, then went back inside the house. A moment later a great pink and gray hog emerged from a shed and waddled quick toward the pail. Alice ran faster and started over the fence.

"You crazy?" asked Bledsoe, racing to grab her, one eye on the huge beast, the other on the house. But Alice was already over. She kicked the hog in the snout. It squealed with shock and she grabbed the pail.

They could hear the hog snorting miserably as they squatted behind the barn. They dined on bacon rinds, nearly a whole buttered biscuit still lathered with peach preserves, and a stew of potatoes and some sort of meat. The stew was likely from the bottom of last week's pot, but they didn't care. The gray muck was gone quick.

Alice ran a finger around the edge of the tin. Bledsoe watched and remembered that first night he'd seen her. He couldn't remember if it had been days or weeks since then but he did remember his first instinct had been to get away.

She looked at him with a grin. "Let's check the barn."

There was a brown mare and a two-seat buggy, a mule, a small plow—not many more farm tools. There wasn't much land in this hollow. Still, it looked as if these people managed all right. The horse nickered when they came in. The sun shone through the hayloft above, spinning the straw into gold. "We could sleep here," said Alice. "I'm so tired."

"Someone's coming," whispered Bledsoe. They hid in the hayloft and watched as the man saddled the mare and led her out of the barn. The woman held up the baby's little hand and waved it as the man rode away.

"She's alone now," said Alice, chewing on a piece of straw and watching the woman walk back into the house.

"So?"

"What's she gonna do? She'll have to give us what we want. What?" she asked. "What you lookin' at me like that for?"

"She tells her man when he gets back, they're gonna come looking for us."

"Oh, I ain't scared. I'll tell her I'm lost. You wait."

Alice snuck up on the porch, the better to consider her approach before knocking on the door. She paused, caught by her reflection in the window glass. Her black hair was greasy and beginning to mat. Her eyes stared back in a sunburned face smeared with grime. Glimpsing the bottom of her scar, she pulled her hair over the side of her face. Her once-gray gown was nearly black and ripped under one arm. Alice shuddered. She wouldn't open a door to the thing reflected in the window, not even in the swamp.

The sound of a piano startled her and she peered past her reflection. Inside the little house, the woman sat with her back to Alice, her fingers confident on the piano keys. Alice had never heard anything like it. The woman's golden hair had lost a pin and a tendril dripped down her neck. On a rush-bottom chair beside her the baby kicked its feet in a basket. For a moment Alice forgot why she was looking in the window. It was so beautiful—the golden-haired woman, the pretty baby, the music. The baby began to cry and the woman stopped and rocked the basket.

Alice ducked down out of sight.

"Come on," whispered Bledsoe, as the piano started up again. "Let's go."

"Oh Rose of Allendale, sweet Rose of Allendale."

"I ain't leavin' without somethin' to eat."

My life had been a wilderness
Unblessed by fortune's gale
Had fate not linked my love to hers
The Rose of Allendale.

TWENTY-SIX

Bledsoe turned his head while Alice stripped off the filthy gray skirt and blouse and dropped the blue gingham over her head. The dress was warm from the sun and smelled of soap. "Look now! Look, ain't it nice?"

"All right, I guess," he said, turning his face away as she twirled, revealing calves and knees.

"Lookee here." She'd also grabbed a faded patchwork quilt off the clothesline. From the kitchen she'd grabbed a basket and loaded it with a jar of pickled beans, several biscuits, a generous hunk of bacon, onions, and a bag of spring peas.

They heard a scream from the hollow below. "Well, how you like that? 'Pears she found us out," whispered Alice, looking at Bledsoe with a mouth full of biscuit.

"Guess so," agreed Bledsoe grimly.

"Oh well," said Alice. She didn't notice he was doing his best not to grin. She opened the jar of pickled beans.

He said, "Slow down. We got to find a place to sleep and save as much food as we can."

She made a face but closed the jar, then dug down in the basket. "And I got these." She held up two packs of lucifers. "Now we kin have us a fire. And here's this." She pulled out a newspaper. He grabbed it.

"What's it say?" Alice was eating another biscuit.

"It's from the *Richmond Daily Dispatch*."

> THE FIRST ENGAGEMENT! Northern volunteers Repulsed at Baltimore. Massachusetts soldiers killed! Murder of Marylanders! The Railroads Decline to pass any more Northern troops.

"We was there," exclaimed Alice. "It say anything about us?"

"Don't be dumb. Why'd they write about us?"

"On account of us gittin' arrested and all!"

Bledsoe quickly thumbed through the paper. "No. Nothing. Of course they got more to worry about. Just listen."

> On Friday morning, the excitement which had been gradually rising in Baltimore for some days, with reference to the passage of Northern volunteer troops southward, reached its climax upon the arrival of the Massachusetts and other volunteers, some from Philadelphia, at President street depot, in that city, at 10 ½ o'clock. A large crowd had assembled, evidently to give them an unwelcome reception.

"Unwelcome, ha! That ain't even half of it!"

Bledsoe nodded, frowning. He turned a page and read to himself about a gentleman who was offering ten of his hardiest slaves to help build up Richmond's fortifications and admonishing all other slave owners to volunteer their own. . . . *there are not less than a thousand Negroes in this city who could be well engaged at this time.* Well engaged? There was only one way for a negro to be well engaged now and that was by joining Lincoln's army. He rattled the paper furiously.

Alice was licking biscuit crumbs off her fingers. She'd reopened the jar of pickled beans and had just about finished them off. "What else it say there?"

"Accidental Death of a soldier," began Bledsoe.

> We learn with regret that Private Boswell, of company A, 13th Virginia regiment. (Col. August) stationed on the Peninsula, lost his life a few days ago by an accident. He was cutting down a tree for the purpose of catching a squirrel which had taken refuge in the branches, and when it fell Mr. Boswell was unfortunately in its way and was crushed to death.

"He cut down a tree to git a squirrel?" They both laughed and laughed. "Go on," said Alice. "More."

> Amelia Co., Va., April 21, 1861,
>
> On Saturday, April the 20th, the students of the Amelia Academy, after a spirited address from the Principal, Wm. H. Harrison, with great joy flung proudly to the breeze, from

> the top of a staff 60 feet high, the flag of the Confederate States, organized themselves as a Home Guard, and made arrangements to elect officers and procure arms, Amelia is fully aroused. The ladies, God bless them! show the spirit of 76. One of the first in the county, in fortune, family, and every grace and quality that can adorn her sex, said to me yesterday, with great feeling, that if she had ten sons she would gladly send them to the war. With such a spirit animating men, women and boys, and God and truth on our side, we may surely defy Lincoln and his myrmidons.

"That's real good, Bledsoe."

"What? What the hell's good about it? They're joining up to fight against the North."

"No, I mean you *read* real good. Better than the preacher in Geegomie."

He could feel his cheeks grow hot. He shook the paper as if annoyed but knew it was true. Words seemed to run to him, as if they knew how much he craved them. He treasured the round sounds they made in his mouth, the careful drawing out of them. He practiced speaking them correctly, like he heard whites do at Our Joy. It pained him when words were treated like trash from folks who ought to know better. Words were everything. Words were power.

"Bledsoe!"

"What?"

"I asked you what it means."

"Means?"

"All that you jist read, what's it mean?"

He looked over the paper at her and breathed an exasperated sigh. "It means the damn war's starting and I'm not there. That's what it means, goddammit."

"What's a murmeydon?"

"I don't know."

"I thought you was so smart."

"Quiet, damn you." Bledsoe bent to the paper.

"Thank you. That's what I'd say if'n a body was to git me somethin' I wanted, like a biscuit or a newspaper," said Alice. "But that's just me."

Bledsoe ignored her, reading to himself:

> Missouri's response to Lincoln's Proclamation.
>
> Gov. Jackson, of Missouri, has replied as follows to the requisition from Lincoln's Secretary of War:
>
> Executive Department of Missouri,
> Jefferson City, April 17.
> Sir,
>
> Your dispatch of the 15th inst., making a call on Missouri for four regiments of men, for immediate service, has been received.
>
> There can be, I apprehend, no doubt but that these men are intended to form a part of the President's army to make war upon the people of the seceded States. Your requisition, in my judgment, is illegal, unconstitutional and revolutionary, and in its object inhuman and diabolical, and cannot be complied with.
>
> Not one man will the State of Missouri

furnish to carry on such an unholy crusade.

(Signed,) C. F. Jackson

"'An unholy crusade'! That's what he called it."

"What who called it?" asked Alice.

"To hell with Missouri," said Bledsoe furiously.

"I ain't never been there, but Loraleen Maguire's daddy went to Missouri and never come back. So's either he got murdered or he liked it so much he jist stayed. Oh, look at them clouds, Bledsoe. I think it's gonna rain."

But he had his face in the paper.

$25 reward.

Ranaway, on the 29th of March, a woman named Nancy, whom I purchased of H. Stern, of this city. She is of medium size, rather spare made, of a ginger-bread color, has a diffident look when spoken to, is twenty-three years old, has a blister scar on her neck. She was sold last Christmas at the sale of Wm. Andrews, dec'd, nine miles above the city. She may now be in that neighborhood, or near Slash Cottage, as she has a mother living at

> Mr. Wm. Winn's, near that place, in Hanover county. She was hired to Mr. Samuel Allen, of this city, last year, and has a husband hired to Mr. Ballard at the Exchange Hotel, by the name of Dolphius. I will pay the above reward if delivered to me in Richmond.
>
> R. B. Woodward

"We ought to see if we can find a place for the night. There was that old fallin' cabin we passed up yonder. Not sure it had a roof, though," said Alice.

Bledsoe didn't answer. He was beginning to feel sick to his stomach.

> Committed to jail as a Runaway.
>
> Was committed to the jail of the corporation of the city of Norfolk, on the 2d day of January, 1861, Negro Man Wm. Johnson. The said Negro man is five feet three inches high, and weighs about 135 pounds; has one scar on right arm above his elbow; light complexion; about thirty years old. Had on when committed to jail, black cloth coat, black pants, glazed cap, and says he was born free, in Baltimore, Maryland.
>
> J. Corprew, Sergeant City of Norfolk

"Don't answer me then. I don't care none. I jist ain't gonna talk to you no more."

He stared at the newspaper:

Stolen Property $300 Reward.

"That's the last time I bring you a paper. Sky might fall on your head for all the care you got."

He didn't hear her.

> BLEDSOE, a house boy aged seventeen years, stole himself from his owner on the 15th instant. Chestnut brown color, approx. 6' tall, thin build, likely featured. Can read, may write, though doubt that would pass intelligent muster. Will attempt all cunning and artifice in order to deceive as illustrated by recent marks of correction on back. THREE hundred dollars if returned to undersigned direct. Two hundred fifty if remanded to jail in any state so that I may retrieve him myself.
>
> Micah Bourn
>
> Our Joy, Bertie County, North Carolina

Bledsoe was still looking at the newspaper but no longer saw it. Instead he was six years old looking up at the old man who was smiling down at him.

Happy birthday. You like it?

Yes, sir, I surely do.

Don't let Teeny or none of them other pickaninnies take it from you, hear? You love me, don't you, boy? Say I love you. Say it now.

Yes, sir, I surely do.

"Hey!" shouted Alice. "What you doin' that for? You're tearin' the paper all to pieces."

TWENTY-SEVEN

A week snuck by and then another. They'd gone farther up and for the past few days had not seen anyone. The western hills rolled on and on, endlessly it seemed, like an undulating sea of green. Getting across to Ohio seemed about as likely as crossing the ocean by jumping. Every time they got to the top of a ridge, another was revealed in the distance.

They camped out in the woods, moving every day to avoid detection. One evening, looking for a place where they felt safe from being seen if they built a fire, they came on a cave in a dell where water flowed down a granite face, clean and clear. It was ringed by woods that rose thick as fur around it.

When they came upon the pool below the cave, a buck deer, new velvet sprouting, was head down, lapping water. When it scented them it raised its head curiously for a moment, then casually walked away into the bushes.

"I don't think it ever seen a person afore," whispered Alice. "This place is like Edenland."

"Edenland? Where's that?" asked Bledsoe in a hushed voice beside her.

"Oh it's a wonderful place, better'n Heaven but near as hard to find. I heard tell of it once, can't remember where. All was beautiful in Edenland till people noticed each were different. Then they got to quarrelin' and fightin' one another, started wars and such. They was thrown out by the angels and the gates were locked and nobody knew where it was no more. But lookee here," she said, turning to him with a wondrous smile. "This must be mighty near it."

Bledsoe nodded. It did seem as if they were the first human beings to lay eyes on this serene place. A bird trilled and the trees rustled softly, almost as if they were whispering *welcome*.

"Nobody'll find us here," said Alice. "We got it all to ourselves."

They would have been unlikely to see the cave in deep summer when it was hidden by overhanging growth, but things were just sprouting and Alice caught sight of an opening on the ledge overhanging the pool. She climbed up first and Bledsoe followed.

Inside it was about ten feet wide and fifteen or so deep. Alice could stand up in the center; Bledsoe bumped his head. But it was dry, the rock floor nearly smooth. Green tendrils of honeysuckle were already fringing the opening and perfumed the interior. In the dying light they'd looked at one another. Bledsoe nodded and climbed back down to gather wood for a fire.

He didn't intend to stay long. Spring was pushing into summer. One afternoon—had it been a whole month? Tuesday and Sunday were the same by now—they were down a ridge collecting greens and herbs. All around were new blooms. Alice called out their names as if saying hello to old friends: "Why, there's Jack-in-the-pulpit! Bishop's cap, pussytoes, and look yonder! Yarrow comin' in and there's, oh, there's spring beauty."

Bledsoe bent to examine flowers that looked almost like feathers.

"Don't touch that," she said suddenly, sharp as a bite.

"What is it?"

"Called doll's eye. Let it alone."

"Don't see anything looks like eyes." Bledsoe curiously peered closer.

"Berries come in fall," she replied flatly. "Leave off it." She stomped on the plant and ground it into the earth with her naked heel.

"What you do that for?"

She didn't answer, just took off running across a meadow. He caught up with her a few minutes later. She was squatted down on her haunches, black hair raining down her back, sweeping tiny flowers in the meadow grass. She moved under a tree and cleared away twigs and old leaves. She batted at a swarm of gnats and picked a stem from a plant. "Oh, lookee here, Bledsoe. This here is called self heal. It's rare by the swamp, but look how much is here! It's good for jist about everything," she said, gathering a sizeable amount. "If you git a sore, it'll heal it clean and is good for all manner of hurts. I kin dry it out and take it with us."

She smiled bright at the rusty green plant as she dug down into its roots. He watched her gather it in her skirt, wondering what had just happened. It was as if she had walked through a dark cloud, then back into the sunshine. She began to sing: "*Peaches in the summertime, apples in the fall, if I can't have the girl I love, I don't want none at all.* Sing with me, Bledsoe."

"No."

"Oh you're sour milk, you are. You're 'bout as fun as a one-legged dog!" She ran on ahead under flowering dogwoods, singing, *"Grasshopper sitting on a sweet potato vine, along comes a chicken and says you're mine."*

He shaded his eyes and looked up at a ridge where he thought he'd seen something glint in the sun like metal. He squinted but it was gone.

"When you find 'em we gonna join 'em, right?"

He jumped; he hadn't heard her come up behind him. She could do that. Move quiet as an animal. He dropped his hand from his eyes. "I told you a hundred times, they don't take women. Ain't no army takes women." He started up a rise, walking zigzag to keep from slipping on steeper parts.

She poked him in the back with a stick. "I kin fight good as you."

"Maybe they'll let you clean their slops." He grinned, but she didn't see it.

"You shut it," puffed Alice behind him, struggling through a rough patch of briars. "Bet they don't want your skinny black ass neither."

TWENTY-EIGHT

It was raining. Just poking a head out was like drowning so they dashed out quick to do their business and ran back in, shivering and teeth chattering. Alice knew how to make a snare, so she'd trapped a rabbit and made a stew. They huddled round the fire eating. It wasn't much past noon. The firelight danced on the walls. The rain drew a misty curtain on the outer world. The cave was a warm womb.

Bledsoe whittled. He'd gotten good at it, had a natural feel for finding the hidden shapes in wood, their burls and gnarls that looked like eyes or arms. He'd been working closely on something. Alice bent close over his shoulder.

"Whatcha makin'?"

Bledsoe studied it. He shrugged. "Tell me about Ireland," he said.

"What?"

"All I read is that it's part of the British Empire. It's also called Erin and the Emerald Isle," said Bledsoe, reciting from the encyclopedia.

"No, it ain't." Actually, she had no idea if it was or it wasn't but didn't like being told. "What you ask me about it for if'n you already know all about it, huh?"

"Well, I read that, but you oughta know best."

Alice pulled a hunk of hair over her shoulder and began to plait it. "Things grow wild there. It's real green," she said softly.

"Why they call it the Emerald Isle," muttered Bledsoe, but she didn't seem to hear him.

"And it smells like wet flowers," continued Alice. "This place—" She looked out the opening of the cave at the trees, their green leaves shiny and slick with rain. "This place puts me in mind of it."

"How'd you get here?"

"Here?"

"America."

"Oh. On the boat we come. My momma and me. The lady bought us tickets to come. Lady Moon. My momma worked in her house. It was grand, it was. So many rooms you couldn't count. I never went in none but the kitchen, but you could see how many rooms by the winders outside."

"Isn't your name Moon too?"

Startled, Alice opened her mouth, but Bledsoe held up a hand. "I don't care," he said, poking the fire. "What was it like? Crossing the ocean?"

"The *Star of the East*. It wasn't like no star, though. It was dark," whispered Alice. "They put us in the bottom. One end was horses, cows, and pigs and other end was us. So many. On shelves the animals was, all of 'em, stacked like goods in a shop, one, two, three, up the sides of the boat, you see. And more in the middle. So close they all was that you had to crawl across 'em if you wanted to git to the other side. They hung blankets up so's it would be separate, but it wasn't at all.

"The shipmen come down a ladder and brung us food, and it were awful." She looked across the fire at Bledsoe, but her eyes were on something else. "Bread all gray, meat full of white worms. And the people got sick and babies too and they die. The shipmen come down and throw 'em to the sea then. You couldn't see it. The ocean. Not from the bottom of the boat. But you'd feel it, feel it roll like a great humped snake, big ol' serpent waitin' for a meal.

"It was so dark. There was only a little light from candles and they made dark shapes on the walls like devils with tails and it scared me bad and I cried, 'Momma, make it stop,' but she didn't answer me no more.

"Then they come down. The shipmen come down, and they took her from me. Pulled her away from me. They took her up top and threw her in the sea, and inside? I laid up there on the shelf and I heard it. Splash, it went. They fed her to it. The sea ate her."

She wiped her face with the hem of the blue gingham skirt. "And that was that."

Alice poked the fire and held her hand over the flames.

"You're gonna burn yourself."

She smiled at him. "No, I ain't. I don't even feel it."

After a while Bledsoe said, "What about your daddy? He on that boat too?"

"He died in prison."

"Oh," said Bledsoe. "Oh," he repeated, because he couldn't think of anything else.

"I was playin' in the kitchen one time. This was afore we left Ireland. My momma was the cook for them all, his *lordship*, my momma called him, and a girl who worked with my momma said my daddy was a gyppoe and got what was comin' to him. I didn't know what she meant, I was jist little, but I knew the girl said somethin' wrong 'cause my momma dropped the pie she was makin' right on the floor and she pushed that girl up 'ginst the wall. 'Don't you ever talk about my man again or I'll kill you,' she said. That maid went white as rich man's flour.

"Later I asked my momma what she'd meant and she tole me he got blamed for stealin' somethin' but it wasn't him, it was another done it, but they put the blame on him. No one liked him, see, on account of he was a Traveler."

"Traveler?"

"They call 'em tinkers or travelers, gypsies. Lotsa people hate them back there; no one never said why. Anyway they put him in jail. He died 'fore I was borned."

The fire was almost out. Bledsoe piled on some more kindling. Damp, it hissed and smoked. They both coughed and fanned the smoke toward the cave opening. At last the wood caught. Both watched the flames awhile.

"How'd you end up in the swamp?" Bledsoe leaned back against the wall of the cave.

"I got bound out. It's what they do to orphans. Bind 'em to someone who'll use 'em. They's supposed to teach you a trade so's when you're growed you can do somethin'.

"The Orphan Man gave Una Guthrie a piece of paper, you know, sayin' I be hers till I git my majority, but she never tole me when that was gonna come. She tole the Orphan Man she'd teach me midwifin'. I s'pose she did, if you mean fetch and carry. She didn't tell him she'd teach me witchery too. I sneaked to watch her. Her evil deeds. When she ketched me she'd whip me with a hickory switch. Said if'n I ever tole what she done, she'd roll me in a barrel filled with pitch and light it afire. Roll it with me screamin' inside, deep into the swamp. She would have too and I knew it. Look at Keenan Wheeler."

"Who's that?"

"Who *was*, you mean. Handsomest man round the Dismal. He'd smile and women would jist trip all over themselves. But the one he wanted he couldn't have, for George McDermott had already married her. So Keenan Wheeler had Granny Guthrie curse George McDermott 'cause he wanted his wife. Now sometimes I'd hide when the witch did her work. I'd watch through a hole in a board outside. But this time when she cut the chicken's throat she said, 'Come ye Lord of all unholy, ye most rude and vile, Prince of Flies, come forth an' aid me, O Lord

Beelzebub.'" Alice spat over her shoulder three times. "When I heard that, I ran out into the swamp, 'cause he's Satan's greatest demon."

Bledsoe's mouth was half opened but he closed it shut. "No such thing."

"No such thing as Satan?"

"I suppose there might be a Devil, but ain't no demons."

"You shut it, fool!" Alice whispered and spit three more times over her shoulder. "You do it too."

"No, I won't," said Bledsoe. "Foolishness."

Alice leaned toward him; the fire had died down again and the cave was filled with shadows. "Foolishness? Well, how 'bout this? Next thing George McDermott come down violent with scrofula, awful weepin' sores big as onions all over his neck. Within a day or two he was coughin' up blood. By the end of the week he was dead as a runned-down dog and Keenan Wheeler married his widow. But"—Alice held up a warning finger—"he never paid Granny Guthrie. Not one penny. He laughed in her face.

"He had two great dogs, near big as ponies. He used 'em to hunt bears in the swamp. Granny Guthrie lured them to her and whispered in their ears. I seen her do it. They stood there and listened and then they trotted off.

"Next mornin' Keenan Wheeler was found by his new bride. All that was left was blood and bones. She only knew him by a scrap of his weddin' shirt. Them dogs were sittin' right beside him, sweet as Sunday, blood drippin' from their snouts."

He wanted to shout hogwash except suddenly he felt a bit afraid to.

"She was pure evil. Oh, she'd git up on the mule and ride it over to the meetin' house when the preacher come once a month, for she didn't want nobody sayin' she weren't a churchgoin' woman. But all round the Deep Dismal everybody knowed Una Guthrie was a witch. They knowed she didn't worship the Lord God, no matter how loud she sang in that shed they used for church. She worshipped Master Shiny

Hoof. But they was too scared to say a word. She'd stir up a potion for lovers gone astray or for sickin' a milk cow. She'd boil up nasties to kill a babe in the womb, and even more horrible brews for women what wants one but can't have."

Alice shuddered and rocked herself. "She were good at it, if there's any way to call evil good. When I first come to the Dismal she used to tie me up to the leg of her ol' iron stove. She'd tell me awful stories of what happened to people who wandered into the swamp, how they got torn to pieces by slobberin' bears, snakebit and left to the bonepickers, sucked down slow and swallowed by mud. She broke me down, see? Scared me so that I never reckoned I could get away.

"She made this nasty berry mash and she'd drink it all day long sometimes. Maybe I was eight? Nine? She'd been at it all day long. I kept out of her way but it was wintertime and it was cold. If I'd stayed outside I'd'a froze to death. After dark I sneaked in. I heard her snorin' and I hid myself under the bed and fell asleep. All a sudden I feel claws on me; her nails were long and sharp. She had me by the arm and dragged me out from under the bed and she got on top of me, legs on each side so's I couldn't git away. Her breath smelled like rotten meat and she lowered down into my face with her great gob of a mouth wide and screamed right in my face. Screamed! I was so scared I wet myself.

"'Goddammit,' she hollered then, 'li'l pig, look at you, pissin' like a dog.' And she pulled out a knife. 'I seen you lookin' at yourself in the water. You think you gonna turn out purty?'

"If I hadn't turned my head right then she woulda stabbed me in the eye. All she got was my face. Right after, she rolled off me and passed clean out."

She turned her face so that Bledsoe could clearly see the dark rose-colored river that wound down to her chin between ridges of puckered skin. It was crisscrossed with a haphazard trail of long-ago stitches. "Yes, sir," she said. "Git you a good look."

Bledsoe swallowed and turned away.

"Oh, don't I know? Too damn ugly for words." She parted her hair with her fingers and smoothed one side over the scar as she usually did. "I bled out so bad you could have swum in it. The witch commenced snorin'. If I wasn't 'bout to die I woulda had sense to drop a rock on her head, but I was too busy holdin' my face together. I got me a big needle and some thread."

Bledsoe looked at her with horror.

She spit into the fire. When she looked at him her eyes were blank.

"Well," he finally mumbled, "well, at least she's gone now."

"Oh yes," said Alice. "She went hard too." She looked out of the cave at the falling rain. "See them berries look just like eyes popped out of a china head." She looked at him. "That's how come they's called doll's eyes. They got little black dots in the center"—she pointed—"jist like the black circles in your own eyes there. The stems are blood red like veins in the human heart. I mixed them berries up in her beans."

"What do they do?" he whispered.

"Oh, poison. They stop the heart. Boom boom bang!" She laughed. "But not before a lotta pain." She stopped laughing. "You kick a dog enough, one day it's gonna turn and bite." She leaned back against the wall of the cave. "So I was gonna bury her. But I'm sworn if she didn't weigh more dead than alive. So I set to diggin' right at the bottom of the porch."

Bledsoe remembered a shallow ditch he'd almost fallen into when he'd first crept up to the listing cabin in the Dismal. He shivered.

"I was hopin' I could drag her fat ol' carcass and roll it right down them steps into the hole, 'cept I got so tired diggin' and diggin'. That's when I got the idea to jist burn the whole damn place down. I got so glad at the thought, it made me wanna dance."

He saw her through the window again, whirling around with the wooden bowl in the lantern light, her black hair swinging across her face. And the old woman behind her on the bed.

She put another stick on the fire and sang softly,

Who killed Cock Robin?
I, said the sparrow, with my bow and arrow,
I killed Cock Robin.

"What song's that?" asked Bledsoe. Maybe it was just the echo in the cave, but it was giving him chills.

Who'll dig his grave?
I, said the owl, with my little trowel,
I'll dig his grave.

"Momma used to sing it to me." She stopped and sat stirring the fire, watching the sparks fly and snap. She hummed the tune, breaking into a new verse now and then. He kept his head down and whittled. A part of him was afraid to look at her. But when he did at last, she was curled up by the fire. He watched her, breathing in and out, her mouth slightly ajar. Her lips were curled up sweetly. *You'd never guess.* He found himself in a sort of awe.

TWENTY-NINE

When she woke at dawn she found something on her chest. She held it up but couldn't make out what it was. She scooted to the opening and in the pale pink light she saw it was a tiny little woman whittled from a willow branch. It was no bigger than her thumb. She held it close and studied it. The features on the face were remarkable, considering he only had a pocketknife to work with. "That's somethin'," she said out loud. But there was no one to hear. Bledsoe was nowhere to be seen. It didn't worry her at first, but by afternoon she started getting scared. She hunted for him but was afraid to call out in case someone heard. Finally, she went back hoping he'd already be there. He wasn't. It wasn't until nightfall he came back. He said he'd been scouting.

"Is it mine?" She held up the little carved woman.

He smiled.

He smiled. She hugged the little thing, a tiny carved woman, to her breast.

They gathered ramps, pokeweed, and spring fiddleheads. Sarvisberries were just now ripe. One morning they hiked over several ridges to the east. Late that afternoon they scouted a cabin that appeared empty—its owner perhaps off hunting. No dog barked when they skidded down into the yard, and Alice knocked a hen in the head with a perfectly aimed rock.

They laughed like fools as they raced away, panting as they crossed one high ridge and then another, near exhausted by the time they made the cave. Later, full up of chicken and boiled greens, they lolled in the afternoon sun, lying on their backs beside the pool under the trees.

"Tell me more 'bout that book, that Injun one you like so much."

"All right. Remember what I said. Even though his name is Natty Bumppo they call him Hawkeye. You know, because he's like a hawk, brave, can see a rabbit from way up there. He's crafty but he's honorable. He's more like an Indian than a white. Oh, he's also called La Longue Carabine. Means *the long rifle.*"

Bledsoe held an imaginary musket to his shoulder. "Boom! He moves like the Indians in the forest, wears skins like them, knows how to track like them—most whites think he *is* an Indian. It says in the book, *Whoever comes into the woods to deal with the natives, must use Indian fashions, if he would wish to prosper in his undertakings.* You see? If you go into their world, you best be like them, so that's Hawkeye. He and Uncas and his father save these English folks from Magua and—"

"Magua?"

"He's also called Le Renard Subtil, the fox. But he's more like *le rat.*"

"What's that mean?"

"*The rat* in French."

"How you know French?"

"Second wife was from New Orleans. A lot of them speak French."

"Did she talk French all the time?"

"No."

"Did you like her?"

"No. Do you want to hear this or not?"

Alice nodded reluctantly. She was more interested in hearing about him.

"He's a scout for the French."

"Who?"

"Magua *Le Renard Subtil*! Now listen. The French and the English are at war. See, Magua is from a different tribe from Uncas and Chingachgook—that's Uncas's father. Magua is a Huron and he's on the French side. The whites use Indians as scouts because—"

Alice yawned. "Your story's confusin' and it's makin' me tired."

"Shut up and listen. All right. Hawkeye and Uncas and his father save two girls; they're sisters. Cora is one, her mother was from the West Indies. Her mother was colored, but they were married—I didn't understand how that can be, but must be on account of them being English. She had another sister—half sister, Alice, her mother was white. So Hawkeye is trying to get those sisters to Fort William Henry, 'cause that's where their father is. So Cora and Alice are traveling through Indian terri—"

"Alice?"

"Huh?"

"Her name is Alice? There's a girl named Alice? In a book?"

Bledsoe held up his hands. "That's it. I ain't wasting more of my time."

"That's my name."

"What?"

"Alice." She scrunched up her face. "Alice Brown." She tossed a stick. It landed in the pool with a splash.

He threw a rock in after it. They both watched the circle of ever-widening ripples. "Alice Brown. That's a good name."

Alice shrugged. "Plain as dirt."

"A rose by any other name would smell as sweet," said Bledsoe, and he tossed another rock in the pool.

"A rose? What you talkin' about roses for?"

"It's from a play. It's about these—"

"Hey! Who learned you to read anyhow?" asked Alice, lying back in the long warm grass.

Bledsoe pulled his knees to his chest. "Dorathea."

"Who's that?"

"She was my sister."

Alice leaned up on her elbows now, interested. "Sister?"

"Half. She was white."

Alice studied his face and he smiled, but it was a twisted thing. "Hold up a minute. Oh, that means your daddy . . . ?"

Bledsoe nodded.

"Your momma?"

"Dead when I was born."

Bledsoe stabbed the earth with the sharp point of a stick he'd whittled. He watched it quiver for a moment. "I told you he got twins out of his wife's maid, Jeanine. They were blond headed like him and green eyed and bright as the moon. Mistress stamped around until he finally sold them and Jeanine too. But no matter how she carried on, he wouldn't sell me, though Reecie says I got his nose and forehead, which Jesus God I hope ain't true, but at least I am surely colored," he said with sour pride. "Ain't no doubt about it."

He looked at Alice and she looked away. Bledsoe laughed quick and sharp. "See? Long as you don't look too much like them, they can bear it, but the minute you get to looking like their own brats, the wives cry and carry on. Well, I'd slept by the old man's bed on my little pallet since I was weaned. He'd lie up there and tell me stories and if it was cold he'd have me come and tuck in with him. He'd give me candy when he came back from town and sometimes a toy. He'd say, 'You're my special boy.' He told me to keep it secret that he loved me best of all. All I had to do was shine up his boots and empty his slops, then just play with the others too small to do any work yet.

"But Mistress said I was spoiled and it was wrong. She kept on him as I got bigger. So I was taught to stand at table and fan guests to keep the flies off. That wasn't enough for her. She said the old man acted unnatural in front of everyone, petting on me.

"One day at dinner when it was just them at home, I was fanning the back of her head and the old man said, 'I think I'll take the boy here to town this afternoon. His shoes are too small.'

"Well, guess what?"

"What?" breathed Alice.

"She threw her plate full of ham and gravy. It went all over. '*Cela me dégoûte*,' she yelled. 'I cannot bear it, you doting on that *abhorrent* little nigger.'

"Abhorrent. Now there was a word I hadn't ever heard. And I never forgot it. I looked it up in Johnson's dictionary when I could read. Know what it means? It means—evil, foul, obscene, and odious." He smiled grimly. "Anyway, her face had gone pink as the ham I was now on my hands and knees cleaning up under the table. A little bit of gravy had splashed on her shoe and when I dabbed it with a napkin, she kicked me so hard I let out a howl. But that didn't stop her. I couldn't see the old man's face from under the table, but I imagined it. When the mistress went at him, he would shrink till you couldn't scarcely see him. I think he actually tried to disappear.

"'Get up!' she screamed at me. She grabbed me by my velvet collar and shook me till I thought my head would snap off. 'It is clear to *everyone* this is your *sale petit bâtard*,' she screamed. '*Vous m'avez humilié*.'"

"What was she sayin'?" asked Alice.

"He'd humiliated her, I was his bastard. '*Vous êtes un ver* not a man!' She pounded on the table so hard the biscuits jumped clean off the plate. 'How do you think it makes *Wilson* feel?'

The old man looked sucked dry. He sighed loud enough to be heard in the next county. I knew it signaled his defeat to her once again. 'What do you want, Eulalie?' he asked.

"'He is a slave,' she said. 'Give him to Wilson!'"

Alice leaned toward him. "What you mean? Give who? You mean you? Who's Wilson?"

"My half brother." Bledsoe got up and bent to the pool, cupped some water and drank. "Wilson was a year younger than me. Had one eye went this way"—Bledsoe put a finger on the left side of his face—"other stared right at you. Even though he was younger he was bigger than me. He and Dorathea were halves too 'cause she was born from the first wife. But unlike me, they were pure white halves."

"You were your own brother's slave?"

He looked at her. "What do you think happens to us born like that?"

"Where you going?"

Alice watched him until she couldn't see him anymore. He'd disappeared in the woods and didn't come back until long after dark had fallen. He said nothing about where he'd been and she didn't ask.

THIRTY

It was almost summer. Sometimes the sky was so blue it hurt. Everything was green and growing. The air smelled grassy. Bledsoe had lost track of days. *It must be the end of May. Moon's come and gone. Is it June? Tomorrow I'll leave.* But he didn't because he didn't know how to get anywhere better than where he already was.

Sometimes Alice would tell him about the Dismal. She knew its plants and creatures and assorted odd inhabitants and spoke of them fondly. "I knew a old woman had a pet snappin' turtle. She trained it to bite them she didn't take to. Her name was Miz Whesher. She was a hundred and three and still fished in the swamp."

"Jonah Flint died of an explodin' stomach. Just blew up big and boom! All over."

"I had me a cat once. Fancella Tansey give me one of them kittens, black as the Devil. Had to hide him from the witch or she woulda wrung his neck. I named him Wish, I treated him good, but he run off one day. He never come back."

Sometimes she'd look at him and laugh and wouldn't tell him why. Or she'd sing. She did silly little dances, waving her arms like a lunatic, kicking her feet, as if she were drunk. "Just to see that mean ol' pucker of yours break down," she'd say. "You always like this." She pulled a long solemn face. "You worse than a damn preacher most times, I swear."

He'd roll his eyes.

Though she still held her head a bit tilted, a habit so ingrained by now it was like breathing, sometimes her hair fell aside and he saw the scar clearly. The thought of her stitching her own skin. He couldn't hold on to the thought. Didn't want to.

She made a hair wash from white clematis boiled with witch's broom and mint and combed her hair with willow sticks bound to a piece of bark. Her hair shone nearly blue in the sun; the thick tight curls hung to the middle of her back but reached to her hips if pulled down straight. She wore the stolen gingham, faded to nearly turquoise. It was too big and hung awkwardly. It buttoned to the neck, but she didn't button it that far and kept the too-long sleeves rolled up to her elbows. It was sturdily hand sewn, most likely by the blond woman herself. Sometimes she tied the skirt into a big hank at her knees, to keep it from hampering her as she climbed in the hilly forest. He'd find himself watching her ahead of him, sunbrown calves muscular as a colt. Coils of black hair escaped from the turban she made from the old gray dress. He'd get a sickly feeling in his gut and look away.

He whittled sticks to sharp points and set off by himself, saying he was going to hunt. He tried to move through the woods like an Indian, or at least, as he imagined an Indian would. The wildlife was not impressed. He didn't get within twenty feet of a flock of wild turkeys before they flapped away, and the red squirrel didn't even budge from the tree limb after his spear clattered to the ground. Instead it glared at him and chattered furiously. One day there was a brown rabbit, back to him, fat from spring greens. All he had to do was plunge the spear in its neck. It was nibbling a flower, ears twitching back and forth, content. Rabbit happy. He just couldn't do it. *But,* he thought, watching it hop away into the underbrush, *she could.* She'd wring the neck of anything left alive in her snares. Quick and efficient. He turned away when she did it.

❧

She picked purple clover and began weaving a flower chain. "Why they say it against the law for a nig—a colored to read?"

"Because it scares white people. When I was little, there was a man from the Coombs place, slave name of Oliphant Griffin. He was a carpenter and got loaned to the old man to build him a new barn. It got around amongst the slaves he knew how to read, so he started teaching some in secret. Some fool, don't know who, said something and the old man found out.

"Coombs gave the old man leave to have Oliphant whipped before all the slaves at Our Joy. The old man rang the big cowbell out back and called every slave from the fields and all the house slaves too. 'Why you want to hurt me?' he said to all of us.

"The slaves looked at each other. They didn't know what he meant. I sure didn't. I was just a child.

"'Ain't I good to you?' he asked.

"And all the slaves hollered, 'Yes, Marse.'

"'I give you plenty to eat and new clothes when it ain't even Christmas. Ain't I kind to you?'

"'Yes, Marse, yes,' they hollered. 'You good as gold.'

"'Little Bill. Stand up there. Ain't you got a new glass eye?'

"'Yes, sir, Marse,' hollered Bill. 'You wants me to take it out for you like I does sometimes?'

"'Nah,' said the old man. 'You keep it plugged in. Ain't y'all happy here at Our Joy?'

"'Oh yes! We so happy we about to bust,' they hollered.

"'Then why you want to hurt me? Y'all know readin' ain't for you. See that donkey over there? Can that donkey read? No, sir, it can't. How 'bout that Mulefoot hog? It read? No. These creatures ain't got the sense and neither do y'all. But each has its place and each has its work to do on God's green earth. So that why y'all 'bout broken my heart and God's too with this readin'.'

"'Oh no, Marse, we never wants you to feel bad,' said one. The slaves cried out they were sorry. 'We won't never read nothin' agin,' said another.

"'Too late!' cried the old man. 'That cat already drowned. Bring that nigger and tie him down.'

"So Oliphant was pegged down and whipped near to death by the driver and salt rubbed in. I stood beside my master the whole time and cried out with each cruel stroke.

"When all the slaves were sent back to work, he caught me by the arm. He looked around before he bent down to me. 'Wipe your eyes now. Don't cry. You're my special boy,' he said. 'But don't you ever go hurtin' me like that, you hear?'

"I mumbled something and he hugged me quick, then pushed me away before Mistress saw him."

Alice was looking at him, perplexed. "But how it hurt him that you or any of them could read?"

"They don't want us to *think*, don't you see? We're to smile and dance when they want to watch us and work ourselves to death and get sold and die like mules and Mulefoot hogs and not complain. They don't want to know we can *think* same as them."

He sat on the edge of the pool, back to her. Alice watched him for a minute, sitting there ramrod straight. "But didn't Dorathea know you wasn't s'posed to read?"

"Course." His shoulders slumped and he turned around. "Mistress hated her. She was born from the first wife who died. I guess nobody would call Dot a beauty, but compared to Wilson, she was a stunner. And she was smart too. Wilson was dumb as a sack of rocks."

Bledsoe picked a blade of grass. He sliced a slit in it with his thumbnail. "He was mean just for the fun of it. Always whupping on me or tormenting Dorathea. Mistress knew Wilson smacked and pinched her and worse, but she didn't lift a finger. Course Wilson was allowed to do whatever he wanted to me," he added bitterly.

"There was an old cabin down by the crick. Everybody said it was haunted on account a slave murdered his wife and children in it." He paused and held the blade of grass between his thumbs, raised it to his lips, and blew. A high whistle pierced the air. He blew one more time, then rolled the grass into a ball and flicked it away.

"Dot read to me there: Peter Parley, 'The Three Golden Apples,' you know, that sort. I'd lean back and listen. Drink the words. Get drunk on them. Everything would go away—Wilson, Master, Mistress. Me. Me that was a slave, I mean. I got inside those stories. Lived in them. While I was in those stories I wasn't on a list with silverware and hogs. I was free.

"Dot saw how I gobbled it up, so she decided to teach me. She said, 'I hate Wilson. You're my better brother even though you are a negro. I guess you'll have to be a slave forever unless someday I marry someone rich and they let me buy you. But don't count on it. Ol' Pissy Face says Papa's gonna send me to a convent where I'll likely turn into a nun, and they don't get married except to Jesus.' She patted my head. 'Least you'll be able to read the Bible. That ought to give you some comfort. But you must keep it secret or I'll get in terrible trouble.'"

"I went from baby books to grown-up fast. She stole me magazines, books, newspapers, whatever she figured nobody would notice. Like Shakespeare's plays. Nobody read those except me and her. We acted them to each other." He stood up and threw one arm in the air:

"How now! What means death in this rude assault?

"Villain, thy own hand yields thy death's instrument."

He grabbed a stick and brandished it, then ran at an invisible enemy and plunged it into air.

"Go thou, and fill another room in hell."

He was apparently surrounded by invisible enemies; he parried, feinted, but then gasped loudly.

"Oh no!" shrieked Alice. "Watch out!"

"That hand shall burn in never-quenching fire

"That staggers thus my person. Exton, thy fierce hand

"Hath with the king's blood stain'd the king's own land."

He stumbled, reeled, and clutched his chest. He threw back his head and roared to the sky:

"Mount, mount, my soul! Thy seat is up on high;

"Whilst my gross flesh sinks downward, here to die."

Bledsoe fell with a bang to his knees and then boom! Face-first into the grass.

Alice didn't say anything for a moment. Bledsoe remained still. She slowly crawled over and poked him in the arm. "Hey. King. You dead?"

"Arrrrbhhhh!!!!"

He opened his eyes. She jumped away with a little yelp and threw a handful of pulled clover at him. "I knew you wasn't."

Bledsoe sat up and rubbed his knees. "One day," he said, continuing as if he'd never stopped. "Dot brought me *The Last of the Mohicans.* It was like she gave me a star in the sky of my very own. All summer I snuck away to read it. One afternoon when the mistress and Wilson was away in Charleston, it rained. The book got ruined; all the pages were stuck together. I was still crying when I got back to the house. Reecie saw my tears and said, 'Oh Lawd, how you know already?'"

"Know what?" asked Alice, picking more clover for her chain.

"That Dot was dead."

"Dead! What! How?"

"She fell down the stairs. Broke her neck." He threw his pocketknife at a tree. He missed and it clattered to the ground. Tears dripped off his chin into the grass.

"Oh Lord," whispered Alice. "Oh no."

Bledsoe lay down on his stomach, his chin on his hands. "They had a fancy funeral. People came up from Charlotte and all. But soon as it was over, it was like she'd never existed. To them, I mean."

"Even to your daddy?"

"He just drank more."

Two squirrels chased each other around and around a tree. A chickadee sang. Bledsoe took a deep breath and wiped his eyes. "One day not too long back, I heard him come in the study behind me. I was reading the encyclopedia. Sometimes I've wondered if God just likes making fun of me because I was at the letter *G* and I was reading about Johann Gutenberg." He looked at Alice, and as she said, "Who's . . ." Bledsoe recited, *"John Gutenberg was born about 1410 at Mainz of noble parents, his father being Frielo zum Gansfleisch, and his mother, whose name he adopted, Else zu Gudenberg—"* Seeing Alice's blank face, he shrugged. "Never mind, it's not important. What mattered was I didn't slam the book shut, or pretend I didn't know what I was doing. I didn't care anymore. I *wanted* him to know I was smart. Smarter and better than Wilson. He didn't say a word to me. Just turned and left the study. And I thought, *Yes! He understands!*

"Next thing I knew his driver, Samuel, dragged me out of the study. Mistress was standing there in the hallway. 'He's ruined for the house now,' she hollered to my master. 'I won't have him spying on me. Beat him, then sell him or put him in the field. I never want to see him again.'

"I was dragged out of the house to the drying shed. He sent Samuel away. We were all alone. At first I thought maybe he'd just pretend he was going to whip me to please Mistress. Maybe he'd just keep me in the shed awhile and then let me out. But I was wrong. He tied me down. I was scared but sure I could take it. Be brave like an Indian. And he *was* my father. He wouldn't really hurt me.

"It wasn't bad at first. But it got that way quick.

"'I tried to keep you safe,' he yelled as he laid into me. 'But you had to bite the apple, didn't you? You were clean, you were perfect. You were mine!' he said, as he lashed me. I could hear that he was crying. 'My sweet good boy! I loved you! Who ruined you? Tell me!' But even though he was sobbing it didn't keep him from lashing me again and again. It didn't stay his hand one bit and at last I couldn't help it, I started begging.

"'*Who was it?*' he screamed at me. '*Who was it taught you?*'"

"Lord," said Alice, grabbing Bledsoe's hand fiercely, "there ain't a shame in the world if'n you tole. And, anyway, your sweet sister was already in Heaven."

Bledsoe slowly smiled.

"What's funny about that?"

"I said to him, 'Please, please, Marse. Have mercy and I'll tell.'

"He stopped then. I could hear him panting behind me like a spent hound.

"'Who was it, boy? I'm gonna rip the hide off 'em.'"

Bledsoe turned to Alice. "So I said loud and clear, so loud I reckon you could hear it all the way up to the house, 'Wilson.'"

Bledsoe laughed then, but Alice heard the bitter in it. She set the ring of clover atop his head. "King wears a crown."

THIRTY-ONE

They came on a stag mounting a doe. Alice put a finger to her lips, peering through the bushes, watching with fascination. Bledsoe felt a rush of blood to his face. He rustled the bush, and the buck bellowed furious when the doe bounded away in fright.

"What you do that for?" asked Alice, bewildered.

Bledsoe stalked away. He picked up a stick and knocked it against the trees as he passed.

"You're crazy!" she shouted, racing past him, darting ahead through the trees. "Crazy crazy crazy!"

"Stop hollering," he yelled, then shut his mouth. He was louder than she was if anyone was around to hear. He caught sight of her ahead, a blue will-o'-the-wisp, jumping over a fallen tree. He stubbed his toe on a root. "Damn," he hissed, biting his lip to keep from crying out. He'd given up his shoes weeks ago. They were meant for show, not purpose, and the soles had been nearly thin as cardboard. He hadn't gone barefoot since he'd been a little boy, and at first his feet had been tender as a baby's. Gradually they'd grown a horny toughness, but he didn't like it. He didn't want to be barefoot.

He lost sight of her. He couldn't hear her moving through the brush ahead either. But then, he rarely could. She moved nearly silently when she wanted to. Like an Indian, he had to admit grudgingly. Lost in thought, he tripped. "Ow!" he exclaimed, pulling his hand away from the bony tree he'd grabbed hold of to keep from falling. It was called devil's walking stick and for good reason. It was covered with spiky thorns and one had pierced his thumb. He pulled it out. His thumb was bleeding. He stuck it in his mouth and sucked it.

From somewhere up ahead he heard, "Come see here!"

He stepped cautiously over a fallen log, pressing a leaf into his still-bleeding thumb. Indians wore moccasins. He should make some moccasins. But they were made from deer hide, weren't they? Those deer they'd seen earlier—the blood rose to his face again, his ears burned.

"Come on!" she called again. "Over here."

When he found her she was gathering mushrooms under a ring of oaks. There were hundreds of them in the dark shaded soil. She said one was called hen in the woods. "These we got back in the swamp. Good for medicine mostly. I don't know what these others here is called. Look here, Bledsoe, they look like they got on little pointed hats. I'm gonna taste one. If it don't kill me, then we kin eat more." She pulled a tiny bit from the cap, avoiding the mushroom's gills.

Bledsoe grabbed it. "Don't be a fool."

Alice shook her head at him. "How we gonna know if it's good to eat? Why, if I look like I'm gonna die, then you stick your finger down my throat and I'll spit it up." She took a tiny bite. A minute passed. She sat there without moving, staring straight ahead.

"Well?"

She didn't move. It looked to him like her eyes had gone glassy.

"You all right?"

She toppled over and lay still on the ground.

"Alice?"

Bledsoe lifted her by the shoulders. She fell back limp and rubbery, her hair across her face. She still hadn't moved or opened her eyes. "Alice? Come on now." He pried open her lips and stuck in a finger. She moaned. "Alice? You all right? Talk to me."

She sat up as if pulled by strings. Looked at him and laughed. She was laughing so hard she was holding her stomach. She gasped, "Oh, ha! Look at your face!"

He grabbed her by the shoulders and shook her hard, so hard her teeth rattled in her head. She was startled by the fury on his face. She reached up a hand and he knocked it away.

THIRTY-TWO

In the middle of the night Bledsoe opened his eyes. He sat up, alert, listening. He thought he'd heard something but wasn't sure if the noise had been in a dream. It was quiet now. He peered out of the mouth of the cave, but the moon had slipped behind heavy clouds. Wind sighed and branches swayed. His skin prickled and the hair stood up on the back of his neck. He thought he saw something moving between the trees. Something pale enough to stand out against the dark. There it was. Then it wasn't. A chill crawled up his spine. *Goose trod over my grave.* This lonesome place shut off from the world hid not only them but perhaps others. Other people, other *things.* He strained, listening to the night. There was the cry of something far off, a breathy whoosh of wings overhead. "Ain't nothin'," he murmured. But his skin was still cold with goose bumps. A rumble of thunder was followed by a huge burst of lightning over the farthest ridge.

Slowly, he backed farther into the cave as the moon lifted free of the passing storm clouds.

The moon poured creamy light through the cave opening. Alice was asleep. Bledsoe kneeled beside her and leaned down. He could see the little depression right above the swell of her upper lip. She mumbled.

He leaned closer and turned his ear to her lips. He felt the heat from each breath, rhythmic as a heart. "Bones," she said.

He jerked his head away. He sat at the entrance to the cave for the rest of the night, watching.

❧

She was skinning a rabbit beside the pool. The sky overhead was gray. It was humid. Flies gathered on the hide she dropped beside her as she worked. He was gathering firewood before it rained. He didn't like to watch her gut the thing, yet somehow he couldn't keep himself from looking as she pulled the gray intestines from the rabbit. It didn't even look like a rabbit anymore, he told himself. Yet that wasn't true. Her hands covered with blood, she looked up and smiled at him. When she was done she laid it on the ground and squatted at the pool to wash the blood from her hands. She leaned forward, splashing water on her face. Her back was to him. Through the thin cloth of the gingham he saw the ridge of her backbone.

She turned to him and said something. About the rabbit. He didn't know what it was she said. He kneeled beside her and ran his finger up the line of her spine. She turned to him, water dripping from her lips. She reached out, touched his cheek feather soft. He pulled her to him.

Afterward she'd turned to him from the pillow she'd made of his chest. "I'm yours now and you're mine. Don't you reckon we're as good as married now?" Light shone from her face. She lay all that night in the circle of his arms. She fit perfect. A thing in her brain hissed, *Can't last, won't last, can't last.*

Hush. We are one now. He's mine, she answered and lifted up to kiss him fierce. *I'm his. He's mine.*

Bledsoe gently lifted her head and pulled his arm away. It had fallen asleep and he shook it, feeling the itch as his blood flowed free. *June, it's got to be June, near July.*

THIRTY-THREE

The morning had come up in smoke mist and she'd woken to trees dressed in billowy film, the sun a ghostly silver dollar through the fog. She peered out of the cave. "Bled?" she called softly. She slid down the damp rocks to the creek below, the cold water making her jump onto the bank. "Bledsoe? Where are you?" She called louder. "Bledsoe! Damn you, answer me! *Bledsoe!*" she screamed.

She felt a hand over her mouth and was pulled roughly behind an oak tree. She struggled and kicked. "It's me, goddammit, shut your mouth." Bledsoe dropped his hand and let her go.

"What's the matter with you? What you do that for?" she sputtered, glaring at him. "Where were you?"

"We can't stay here anymore. I went north a ways and down in the valley is a camp. Might be even a thousand tents."

"What army?" asked Alice, her stomach dropping away.

He shook his head. "I couldn't tell, they were too far away."

"Then we best stay put." She took his hand. "Till we find out. Can't do nothin' till we know, and ain't none of them gonna come up here this mornin'. Come on. I'll put a fish on the fire. Come on, honey." She smiled at him and took his hand. He pulled it away.

"I ain't spending the war in a damn cave." He picked up his spear and started for the woods.

"What war?" she yelled after him. "I don't see no damn war."

When he returned hours later he couldn't help but notice that Alice had been crying. She didn't speak to him. She continued stuffing things into makeshift sacks, sniffling and wiping her nose on the hem of her skirt. He finally grabbed her.

"I couldn't get close enough to tell. So might as well stay another night or so."

She glared at him. "I was gonna curse you. I thought you'd run off."

"I didn't, so don't. Let's go check your snares."

She smiled then. He smiled back, though all he could think about was the army camped below. He prayed it was the North but was pretty sure it wasn't. He'd seen a lone soldier across a deep gorge, but there was no way to tell which side he was on. The soldier had mounted a horse after obviously surveying the area, and Bledsoe watched him wend his way down the ridge until he disappeared in the tree line. His heart pounded double time all the way back to the cave. But Alice was happy as a puppy again and he didn't want to ruin it. Not yet. Not yet.

The morning mist had dissolved by the time they set out. It was just right warm. Alice laughed, drunk with sunlight. They crossed a large meadow. Everything was blooming: ox-eye daisies, live-forever, bright orange poppies. Queen Anne's lace swayed in the breeze, filled with the buzz of bees. Trees waved their leaves, birds burst forth with frantic love songs.

As they passed, a bear cub watched them curiously with little black eyes from the crook of a tree. Bledsoe pointed to it and Alice grabbed his hand, pulling him back the opposite way. "Baby bear means momma bear," she whispered.

She gathered greens, tying them up in her skirt. They checked the snares and found nothing but a strangled opossum. "Poor blind thing," sighed Alice, picking it up by its hind legs and dropping it into a feed sack she'd grabbed on one of their marauding expeditions.

"Oh, Bledsoe, look." They hushed when they came upon a mossy clearing ringed by pale birch trees. She ran her finger up the ghost-white bark, then bent and felt the lushness of the moss with the tips of her fingers. "Soft as a kitten," she said.

Light dripped between the leaves, leaving puddles of gold. She sat down in the center of the ring of trees. "This is just the type of place they like," she said.

"Who?" Bledsoe sat down beside her and ran his hand across the living carpet of green.

"The ones my momma tole me about. She called them the *sidhe*. Beautiful, like nothin' on earth," she said in an awed voice. "Sometimes they snatch humans clean away and make 'em live with them in the fairy world. They feed 'em all manner of grand food and give them magic wine to drink and it all seems like Heaven." She turned to Bledsoe and tapped his nose with the stem of a fern she'd pulled. "But it's a trick."

He lay down on the moss, arms under his head. "What kind of trick?" he asked, batting the fern away.

"They keep 'em there always." She tickled him with the fern again. "They never let them go."

She laughed. Her eyes smiled into his. He reached up and gathered a hank of her thick black hair and pulled her to him. Their noses touched and she giggled like a child.

Her mouth was sweet as rock candy. Her skin was near brown as an acorn now but her breast was more butter. There he traced a blue-green vein, delicate as spider silk. "I ain't never had nothin' my own, no one since my momma," said Alice, soft.

A memory flashed through his head, his father holding out his hands to him in the quiet of the bedroom: *Give me a hug, boy, you love me, don't you?*

Bledsoe stroked the velvet of her belly. His once baby-fine hands were now callused; the rough of them made her let out a breathy sigh. She interlaced their fingers. He pushed back her hair and traced the scar. She pulled her head back. He pulled her to him and kissed it, each crisscrossed track. "Alice," he said. "Alice, Alice."

They lay side by side on the carpet of moss without speaking for a while. What was there to say? His hand rested on her thigh. They looked up together at the sky and watched the clouds marry, then break apart, then catch again.

"Do you think we'll be together when we die?"

Bledsoe turned his face to hers. "We're here right now. Don't talk like that."

"But we got to be together even then, we have to be together always. I won't never let you go." She put her head on his chest and timed her breath so that it came and went with the thumping of his heart. "My love," she said. "My honey." He said nothing but closed his eyes and held her close. They slept.

He sat up. The sky was pink. "Bat." He pointed at the little brown thing flitting above the beech trees. He stood up. "We got to go." Alice reached her hand up to him. He pulled her to her feet. He turned away and reached for his worn shirt he'd tossed to the ground.

"Oh, your back, your back. I'll kill him if'n I ever see that man." Alice laid her cheek against the closed welts.

"Sun's going down. I'm not sure which way we came."

"I know," replied Alice. "I kin find it."

He was already halfway into the woods. "Come on then."

"Bledsoe?"

He turned back. "What?"

She stood in the center of the ring. A last ray of rose-colored light sluiced through the leaves, bathing her in an unearthly glow. "You ain't never gonna leave me, are you?" She looked like something from another world and he felt almost afraid. She came toward him.

"Don't act a fool," he said, turning away.

She threw her arms around him. "You're mine," she said. "Ain't it true?" He held her to him a moment, felt her heart beat. She clung tighter. Her skin smelled sharp and salty. "It's you and me," she said. "We got each other."

A twig snapped. They turned in unison. A few feet away a soldier had them in his rifle's sights.

THIRTY-FOUR

A bearded man wearing a double-breasted frock coat flush with gleaming buttons sat at a makeshift desk of two wood planks set atop a barrel. A book lay open on his lap. His forehead was high, his dark brown hair slightly receding. He had a long elegant nose and eyes of such a startling blue it made Alice think of the way ice burns when held against skin. "These are the captives? I took you to mean you'd captured something useful."

The soldier snapped to attention and saluted. "Yes, General. Yes, sir, these two were caught up yonder. They were up on a ridge where they could spy on everything down here clear. When I seen the female in the light, I almost thought she was white."

Alice's eyes darted to the sentry who'd captured them and back to the man he called General. It was right on the tip of her tongue—*I ain't a runaway; I ain't a nigger.* But if she said these things they'd take him away from her. "I ain't no spy," she said instead. "Him neither."

The general placed a cloth marker in his book and closed it. Alice saw it was a Bible by its black cover and gilt-edged leaves. He stood.

He was taller than Bledsoe. He studied Alice silently for a moment. She pulled her hair across her cheek.

"Shot or hanged?" Alice's eyes widened. "What you mean?"

"We hang spies, but since you're a woman I'm offering you a quicker way."

"You gonna shoot me?" Alice felt her knees go weak. "Oh no, don't, please." She looked at Bledsoe full of panic.

"What's your name?"

"Birdy," she stammered.

"Are you a spy for the Union army, Birdy?"

"No, sir. We didn't even know if y'all were North or South till that boy there caught us up yonder." She looked at the general imploringly. "We don't even know where that other army is at, so please don't, don't shoot us." She took a deep breath. "Nor hang us neither."

"Untie them, Private."

"But, sir, how do you know they ain't . . ."

"Now, Birdy, can you cook?"

She nodded.

"Sew?"

"Not so good."

"Honesty is a virtue. We need more cooks than seamstresses anyway." He indicated that the private was to untie Bledsoe as well. Alice massaged her wrists as the general turned to Bledsoe. "And you? Would you leave us now when all hands are needed?"

The man's eyes seemed to cut to the core. Bledsoe looked at the ground.

"The only true freedom for any of us, white or black, is in relinquishing ourselves to His divine will." The general stepped away and pulled the tent flap back. "Look out there. Look past this camp."

Bledsoe, Alice, and the sentry peered out. In the distance the Blue Ridge Mountains were buttered with moonlight. The sky was swept clean of clouds and thousands of stars blazed.

"In this beautiful valley I sometimes get a faint glimpse of what Adam lost." He indicated to the sentry to pull the tent flap closed again. "Now we find ourselves on the brink of war, fighting for what God in His mercy has left us poor sinners after our banishment." He looked at Bledsoe and Alice. "God has ordained our stations in this life for His own divine reasons. We must remember that our reward is not in this world but in the next."

He sat down at the makeshift desk. "Take the boy up front with those others. Give the private here the name of your master. He will notify him that you are now in service to the Army of the Confederacy. Have Second Lieutenant Harper come to me for tomorrow's orders."

"Yes, sir," said the sentry.

"Dismissed."

"Sorry, sir, but what about her?" He pointed to Alice just as a colored man, somewhere past forty, stepped into the tent carrying a silver tray with a china teapot, a teacup, and a bowl of blackberries. He stepped past Bledsoe, Alice, and the soldier as if they weren't there at all. "I brung your tea, General."

"Thank you kindly, Jim. Just set it on the table."

The servant pulled out an old bandana and flicked imaginary dust off the table, then placed the tray gently upon it. Slowly and with great elaborateness, he poured a steaming cup of tea. "I gots you the English but I think mint's better when you gots your stomach all worked up, but you will do as you will do. Now these here berries come from up yonder. They's sweet. You wants anything else, General? You stayin' up all night agin? You ain't had no supper. I betcha them Yankee generals et jist fine tonight. I bets Gen'ral Booregard and Gen'ral Johnston et too."

"Bring me just a bit of milk and bread, Jim. That will do fine. And I've written a letter to Anna in Charlotte. Will you see it on its way?" The general folded the paper on his desk and sealed it.

"You know I will, General," he said, taking the envelope from the general's hand. "I'm a-gonna bring you that bread and milk and I'm gonna bring you a chop with it. No use starvin' youself." The servant glanced at Bledsoe and Alice with disdain as he passed out of the tent.

The private said, "Beg pardon, General, but . . ."

The general rubbed the bridge of his nose between his thumb and forefinger. "Take her to the cook tent." He bent back to his work.

THIRTY-FIVE

When Bledsoe was taken away, Alice tried to run after him but the sentry held her by the upper arm. She couldn't shake free. "Where they takin' him?"

Up close the soldier had the face of a fat-cheeked baby. In the dark behind the tents he pulled her close. "You're the army's now. Come on then, let's go." He shoved her ahead of him.

"Where you takin' me?"

She felt his breath on her neck. "Where you wanna go?" He grabbed her breasts from behind.

"No!" she hollered.

He snapped her head backward. "Shut your fuckin' mouth." His other hand raked up the side of her dress. "Goddamn you, hole still," he hissed in her ear. "Ow! Goddamn!"

"Soldier?" A man, hair lit even redder by the light from his tent, stepped out of the back flap. He was in pants and boots; one half of his face was soaped. His shirt was untucked and flapped in the warm breeze. "Well?"

The private stood at attention and saluted. "I'm taking this slave to the cook tent, Captain. General's order. Caught her up on the mountain with another nigra. Runaways, sir."

"Was she attempting to run right now?"

"Yes, sir."

The captain looked at Alice, with her arms crossed protectively across her chest, and back to the soldier.

"Odd way to prevent someone from running away."

"Sir?"

Alice looked down at the young soldier's cheap homespun pants, his awkward boots thick and worn.

"Grabbing hold of her anatomy like that."

"What you mean, sir?"

"Her bosom, Private. Grabbing a hold of her bosom is what I mean."

"She bit me, sir!"

Alice gathered a gob in her mouth and spat on the boy's boots.

"Why, what you damn . . ." The private raised his hand but the captain caught it. The soldier swung a furious face to him. "You gonna let this nigger get away with that?"

"You gonna let this nigger get away with that, *sir*."

The private lowered his eyes. The captain dropped his hand. "Now get out of my sight and back to your post. And if I catch you messing around with any of the female servants again, I'll tan your hide in front of the entire company. Do I make myself clear?"

"Yes, sir." Even in dim light it was apparent his face was flushed and heated. But he whirled about smart and marched the opposite direction.

The captain wiped the lather from his face with his shirttail. "What do they call you?"

"Birdy," Alice mumbled to the dirt path. *What will they do with him? With me?*

The captain pulled up his suspenders. "Come along then." He walked beside her, not behind. "Most of these men have no former training. They're volunteers. Just boys really. Never been away from home and have the manners of a mule. You have nothing to fear about something like this happening again. Or, if it does, you come straight to me. My name is Captain Brennan."

He stopped at a large dark tent. A guard stood aside as the captain lifted the flap for Alice. "But if I ever hear of you showing disrespect for a soldier again, I will also tan *your* hide."

The flap dropped behind her.

It was so dark inside the tent she stumbled and nearly fell. On the far side someone was snoring loudly. A hand grabbed hold of her ankle. "Who're you?"

Alice bent to the whisper. As her eyes adjusted she was just barely able to make out the woman she'd nearly tripped over. "Let go."

"You best not wake Lettie, she'll skin you. You new? Got you a pallet?"

Alice squinted and made out two other shapes on the other side of the tent.

"You ain't got one yet. I s'pose you kin share." The woman flicked a blanket aside. "You best git you some sleep; it be light afore you know it."

The tent flap glowed an odd orange in the light of the campfire outside. The guard coughed.

"You gonna sleep standin' up?"

I'm gonna tell. I gotta tell. "I ain't a—" she began.

"What you say?" whispered the woman.

"Nothin'." Slowly Alice sank to the pallet. The woman rolled on her side away from her. She smelled like bacon grease. Alice lay down back-to-back with the stranger.

"I'm Jubilee."

Alice shut her eyes tight. A tear escaped anyway. She felt it slide down her cheek.

"What you called?"

The tears were rolling freely now. "Nobody."

"Night, Nobody," giggled Jubilee.

I'll tell in the morning, thought Alice miserably. *They'll let me go then. They're the army, not no slave catchers.* But what could she answer when they asked why she was with him? The preacher in Geegomie had said, "Thou shalt not let thy cattle gender with a diverse kind; thou shalt not sow thy field with mingled seed, neither shall a garment mingled of linen and woollen come upon thee." His face had puffed red with righteousness. He pointed a finger at his motley congregation: wood haulers, fur trappers, tree cutters, boatmen. "Amalgamation is an abomination!"

Alice remembered shrinking on the hard wood bench of the hut that served as a church once a month. The forty or so men and women in their drab grays and browns hallelujaed when this new preacher paused for air, though he didn't seem to appreciate it. He was Lutheran and the former one had been Baptist. Granny Guthrie held a wad of tobacco in her cheek and spat delicately into a stained hanky. "Sit up," she hissed to Alice. "He's talkin' about sin, girl."

Stone Burham stood in his homespun trousers held up with a snake-skin belt. "Whatcha mean, Preacher? Plain so's we kin understand."

The circuit rider turned his accusing finger to Burham. "The fat will always rise! It must be skimmed off, for it will never mix! Never. White with white. Negro with negro, for not even all the seas of the earth have enough water to extinguish the fires of Hell! Amalgamation of the races is an abomination to the Lord, an obscenity, like as to the worship of false gods. Did not the Lord God force the Israelites to drink the water of their iniquity? No white with black, no white with brown, no white with red, no—"

Stone Burham grabbed the woman next to him and pushed her toward the door. The preacher got more red and righteous after the trapper and his Yawpim Indian woman left.

I'll go to Hell then. Alice licked tears from her lips. From across the tent came a whistling snore. It was hot and airless. Besides the bacon smell of the woman beside her, there was an aroma of onions and cooked cabbage. Outside crickets whirred and metal clanked. There was a tide of voices, in and out, hushed and muted. She knew she wouldn't sleep but she closed her eyes to stem the tears. The next thing she knew she was on an enormous plain. Not a tree, not a flower, not a blade of grass grew. There was only red earth. She heard thunder but when she turned her head she realized it was the pounding of thousands of feet. People behind her, all running. She was running too. Ahead was the sea. It reared up green, teethed with froth. She felt herself sucked under and she waited to drown like the others. They bobbed and floated around her, empty eyes open, limbs spread like starfish. She continued to sink as though weighted by stone.

Below, the water hissed and bubbled from a great chasm. The witch was trying to grab hold of her legs. Then something grabbed her and began to pull her up through the green sea. She didn't have to look. She knew it was him pulling her toward the light.

"Come on now. Wake up."

She swam into his arms.

"Wake up." Alice opened her eyes. Jubilee let go of her arm. A bugle was blowing outside the tent. "Git up now."

THIRTY-SIX

There was singing outside and it was getting louder. Alice rubbed her face with her hands and sat up, baffled. A girl not much older than herself was tying a bright yellow rag around her head. Her black skin gleamed in the muted morning light of the tent. The eyes that looked at her with obvious amusement were almond shaped above high cheekbones. She smiled. "Mornin', Nobody."

A fat colored woman, this one older, brushed by toward the tent flap. "You won't sleep like Queen Sheba come tomorrow," she huffed, exiting the tent.

Another, hair the color of smoke, sat on an opposite pallet staring at her. Though her hair was gray, her honey-colored face looked no older than twenty or so. "You mighty bright. Don't be thinkin' that gonna git you anywhere round here."

"Leave her be, Janine," said Jubilee. "She gots to git her bearings straight."

The singing outside the tent grew louder. Alice went to the tent flap and pulled it aside. In the center of the campground on a great open field, hundreds of soldiers stood singing.

Am I a soldier of the cross,
A follower of the Lamb,
And shall I fear to own his cause
Or blush to speak his name?

"General's called all to gather," announced almond-eyed Jubilee. "Ain't no drills this mornin', they says. He's gonna preach. Come on now, Miss Nobody, he preach to us colored folks too."

Shall I be carried to the skies
On flowery beds of ease,
While other fought to win the prize
And sail through bloody seas?

"But fix yourself up some first. Lord, look at you. Like the cat dragged in." Jubilee squinted at her critically. "But you be all right, I 'spect, if you weren't dirty as a mud-rolled hog. Too bad 'bout this hair, though."

Alice smacked Jubilee's hand away and found that her hair contained several twigs and a dried leaf, which she combed out of the tangle with her fingers. She dug in the little bag made from the gray gown she kept tied at her waist. It was filled with scraps of this and that, bits of cloth, dried herbs, and the little willow woman Bledsoe had carved. She pulled a rag from the bag and wound it around her hair, leaving a portion hanging to cover the scar.

"You missed some your hair." Jubilee reached to tuck Alice's hair into her turban, but Alice quickly turned her head away.

"Let me be," she said.

"Ain't you got no shoes?"

Alice shook her still-fuzzy head. The night before was just beginning to filter into her consciousness.

"Well, come on then, we gonna be late." She grabbed Alice's hand and pulled her out of the tent behind row after row of still, hymn-singing soldiers. To the rear, colored men and women sat on the grass singing along.

"What's wrong?" asked Jubilee as Alice frantically scanned the colored faces.

"I'm lookin' for somebody."

"Nobody lookin' for somebody," laughed Jubilee.

Ignoring her, Alice walked over to a tall black man standing apart from the rest of the slaves. "You know a man what was brought here last night?"

He looked at her and squinted. The sun was full in his face. He shaded his eyes with his hand. "Who's askin'?"

"They caught me and him last night up in the mountains where we was hid. Said we with the army now. His name's—" She paused. *He'd never tell them his real name.* "Hawk."

"Tall? On the lanky side?"

Alice nodded eagerly. "That's him. Where's he at?"

Jubilee had followed Alice. "He your man?"

"I saw where they was takin' him with some others early this mornin'," said the slave.

"Where? Where'd they take him?" asked Alice, ignoring the panic in her voice. She didn't notice the singing had stopped. "Tell me. Where'd they take him?"

The general's distinctive voice rang out across the field. "The angel of the Lord came."

Alice tugged at the slave's sleeve when the man turned toward the orator. "Please."

"Hush now," whispered Jubilee, trying to pull Alice away. "The general's preachin'."

". . . and sat down under the oak in Ophrah that belonged to Joash the Abiezrite, where his son Gideon was threshing wheat in a winepress to keep it from the Midianites. When the angel of the Lord appeared to Gideon, he said, 'The Lord is with you, mighty warrior.'"

"Amen!" shouted one of the slaves on the grass near Alice.

"You got to help me," Alice implored the man.

The general's voice rang out across the field. "The Lord turned to him and said, 'Go in the strength you have and save Israel out of Midian's hand. Am I not sending you?'"

"Yes, sir, he sendin' us!" sang out the slaves.

"Your man be all right." Jubilee continued pulling Alice away. "Stop pesterin' Homer now." Alice tried to yank her hand away, throwing her head back in fury. Her hair fell back, revealing the scar. "Lord have mercy," said Jubilee, staring. "What happened to your face?"

"Leggo a me, you dumb nigger!" shouted Alice, pulling her hand free. "Lemme alone!" she screamed. Jubilee's almond eyes went wide. Dimly, Alice realized the sermonizing had stopped. A crow caw-cawed as she slowly took in the faces staring at her.

"Sit down and shut your mouth or I'll damn well shut it for you." Alice recognized the general's servant from the night before. The old man eyed her coldly and Alice sank to the ground like a ship going down. The faded blue dress ballooned around her. Quickly with shaking fingers she rearranged her hair to cover her scar. Everyone moved away. She sat there alone.

"For God is on the side of the just," shouted the general. All faces turned toward him in the center of the field. "Let us pray." More than a thousand heads bowed. "Oh Heavenly Father, lend us a sword like as to Gideon that it shall free us from the invader. Grant us fortitude in our most righteous cause. Men of the First Virginia," continued the general. "Strike your tents and leave them where they fall. Leave all but your guns and your stout hearts. We have been called to battle by the Almighty. We march on the hour."

THIRTY-SEVEN

A bugle blew and across the field drums began to beat. Soldiers and slaves ran to and fro.

"Where we goin' to sleep without our tents, Marse?" asked a colored man.

"The ground was good enough for Adam and Eve, wasn't it?" replied a lieutenant supervising the slaves as they readied the wagons.

"But that was in the Bible, weren't it?" the slave grumbled. "That ground was a whole lot softer." He bent and began pulling up tent stakes. He stood up and pointed at Alice. "Sky fall on your head or you got too much white?"

The soldier pointed at her. "Help him with that tent there."

Alice felt herself flush. She looked around. Slaves eyed her hostilely. She bent to the next stake and wrestled it loose. Two privates stood guard as they rolled and tied their pallets. Though where these slaves might possibly run off to with thousands of Confederate soldiers surrounding them was a mystery, thought Alice as another tent came down.

Before the cook tent was dismantled, Alice ducked inside where she had left her little bag of belongings. She'd forgotten to tie it to her waist before leaving the tent.

"Move outta mah way."

Alice didn't look up at the smoke-haired woman. "I ain't in it."

The woman squatted down and grabbed Alice by the chin. Her sharp nails dug into Alice's skin as she said, "You up so high, when you fall, you gonna break your neck."

Alice knocked her hand away. "Don't you touch me. You touch me agin, you'll be sorry."

"Ha. You'll git yours." The woman ducked out of the tent. Across the tent Jubilee and the other women glowered at her. She felt their hate. With shaking hands she began to tie her cloth bag to her waist but fumbled. Everything spilled out, strips of cloth, dried herbs, bits of bark, and the tiny woman Bledsoe had carved from the willow branch. Jubilee grabbed it and held it up to the light.

"What's this?"

Alice reached for it. "Give it to me."

Jubilee clenched it tighter. "It a charm?"

"It's mine," Alice growled. "You give it or I'll . . ."

Jubilee laughed and dashed outside. Alice ran after her screaming, "Give it back, goddamn you!" She jumped on Jubilee and they both slammed to the ground. The willow woman flew into the air.

"What's going on here?" boomed a voice.

"No!" Alice shrieked, scrambling on hands and knees to grab her treasure before the horse's hooves smashed it. "Move your horse!" she hollered.

"What did you say?"

Alice looked up at Captain Brennan. He was seated on a tall bay, dressed grand in a high-collared coat of gray with two rows of gold buttons. "What are you doing down there?"

"Your horse! Your horse 'bout to step on it," she said. "Move it so's I kin git it."

The captain frowned down at Alice. "Get up from there this instant."

But Alice didn't move from in front of the horse. "Haw, Romeo!" said the captain finally. The bay stepped neatly left.

"Damn me," muttered Alice, snatching up the little thing and examining it carefully. "It's all right, it's all right," she whispered.

"What is it that's so precious?" asked the captain, bending from his saddle to see what Alice was cradling in her palm.

"It's mine." She snatched it to her breast and glared at Jubilee. Jubilee, brushing dirt off the back of her skirt, glared back.

"Then keep it close." The captain wheeled his horse and shouted, "Move out to the wagons. Anything you cannot carry will be left behind."

The cook wagon followed the artillery, which in turn followed the infantry. Up ahead, company drummer boys beat a marching cadence. The drums were so loud it seemed the ground vibrated. Alice sat on a hay bale, straw poking through the gingham of her skirt. She felt made of pudding, shook and jarred with every jolt. Sweat formed half-moons under her breasts. She felt the sun burning another layer of her skin a deeper brown. Jubilee and the other women rode in the back as far away from her as they could get. "Bitch," she heard one of them say, but she ignored it. Her mind was awhirl with plans and plots, none of which ended up passing muster. No matter whom she asked as they rode or filed by, she could find out nothing about him. She was tempted to jump out and run ahead, but the wagon was surrounded and she knew she would get nowhere fast.

The Virginia Brigade wound for miles through the Shenandoah Valley; thousands of men marched for hours without stop. Finally a halt was called. An officer rode down the line. Each company he passed let out a great cheer. When he got toward the rear he read from a paper that he called The Order:

"Our gallant army is now attacked by overwhelming numbers. The commanding general hopes that his troops will step out like men and make a forced march to save the country."

Alice figured the commanding general he was talking about was the Bible thumper with the high forehead and the light blue eyes. He was the one who'd sent Bledsoe somewhere unknown. She stood up in the wagon and yelled to the officer who'd read the order. "Where's that general at? I wanna ask him somethin'."

The officer was clearly shocked speechless at this boldness from a slave. She didn't care. She started to ask him where the general was again when all around them the troops began to whoop-de-doo and holler at the top of their lungs. The officer rode off. All around the cook wagon the men could barely contain themselves. It had seemed their marching prior to hearing this order had been fairly plodding and mostly cheerless. Alice leaned out to a soldier on a mule. "How come they's all so glad?"

"Gonna whip the Yanks!"

"That mean a battle gonna happen?"

"Hell yeah, gal!"

"There gonna be as many of them as there are of you?" Alice asked, but someone started singing. All up and down the line the men joined in:

Get out the way, old Dan Tucker.
You're too late to git your supper.
Supper's gone and dinner cookin';
Old Dan Tucker's just a-standin' there lookin'.

Some broke ranks to link arms and do-si-do. As far as Alice knew, battles meant people got killed. Yet they all looked thrilled to death. The drummers beat time and the valley rang.

Get out the way, old Dan Tucker.
You're too late to git your supper.
Supper's gone and dinner cookin';
Old Dan Tucker's just a-standin' there lookin'.

Back in the Dismal she'd known a fiddle man who'd taught her "Gathering Home," "Poor Robin," "Weevily Wheat," and more. But singing was the last thing she wanted to do now. She bowed her head. *Oh dear Lord Jesus, don't let him git killed. Help me find him and I'll be good as gold.* Head bent to her knees, she opened her eyes to the faded blue of her dress. "Oh Great Devil," she whispered to her knees, "whichever one helps me, I'm yours."

She glanced at the back of the wagon. Jubilee had made a cross of her forefingers. Alice knew it was the sign against the evil eye. She laughed.

"Oh you gonna fall, gal," said the smoke-haired woman. "You wait and see."

THIRTY-EIGHT

A halt was called sometime in the middle of the night. The soldiers, exhausted after marching for miles, dropped where they'd stopped and fell asleep in the road; the slaves slept alongside the road or in the wagons. At daybreak they learned they were to travel the rest of the way to the battlefield by train.

They arrived at Piedmont Station at around six in the morning. In the little town flags were flying to welcome the army; a band consisting of a coronet, flute, and deep-throated saxhorn played an earnest if out-of-tune "Camptown Races" and "Lilly Bell Quickstep." A troop of small boys paraded in imitation of the soldiers as they marched to the train, dogs barking at their heels. Ladies in bonnets handed up plates of fresh-baked cookies and baskets filled with picnic luncheons to eager soldiers hanging out the windows. The train was so crowded that many of the men had to ride atop the cars, but they didn't mind. There were smiles all around.

Alice was hurried into a boxcar along with slaves and crates of worried chickens. There were no windows, so she saw nothing of the countryside they passed. She felt the vibration of the rails all the way to the top of her skull. Where were they going? How would she find him? Click-clack click-clack. The sound was maddening after two hours. The other women were asleep. Two men played dice. The chickens squawked with alarm whenever the train whistle blew. A wasp droned. She watched it fling its armored body fruitlessly against the walls of the car. Sunlight fell in blinding stripes through the wooden slats. Her neck ached from holding her head up. She was so tired.

She was jarred awake by the whining screech of the brakes. They had been traveling nearly eight hours. The door to the boxcar was rolled open. A hot cinder hit her cheek and she quickly brushed it away. She heard someone say they were at Manassas Junction. She had to jump from the car; no one helped. They were herded together and a soldier with a rifle signaled them to walk from the depot and out on the road that passed by woods and fields. Though the sun had gone down, the heat hadn't. It was in the nineties and the humidity was awful. Alice looked at this alien landscape that surrounded her. Campfires bloomed red all along the banks of a creek for miles. Between the fires and the almost full moon the Rebel camp was lit nearly bright as day.

Orders were yelled and orders were ignored. She was almost run over by a wagon hauling barrels of something, the driver pulling up the team just in time. A man in his shirtsleeves shouted, "Somebody help me with my supplies. I'm a doctor!" but was ignored. She was pushed and shoved. Confused, she tried to get some sense of where she was, but all she saw were uniforms. To her right a company was marched off to the rattle-tat of drums. A few feet away a woman dressed in tartan plaid silk was scolding two colored men struggling to unload a piano from a wagon. "You drop it and you'll get it," she warned.

She kept her head down, but no one paid her any attention. Cavalry wheeled to one side, and infantry marched this way and that. The tents of the army they'd come to meet lined a creek someone told her was called Bull Run as far as she could see. Slaves scurried, rousing songs were sung. The moon rose higher.

"You. Yes, you," barked an officer, as she frantically searched for Bledsoe in what was now something more like a circus than an army campground. "We got men to feed. Why aren't you cooking with the others?"

Perspiration created a mustache on Alice's upper lip. A woman had handed her a strip of cloth for a bandana. She wrapped it around her head to keep her long hair safe from the campfire. The woman looked at her scar a moment, then handed her a tub of batter. All she could think about was when this fight started, he might get shot.

She kneaded dough for biscuits until her arms ached. After midnight she was allowed to sit down and eat a couple. She chewed mechanically. *What now?* She was surrounded by Rebel soldiers. The only colored men she managed to speak to so far were servants who had accompanied their masters to war and didn't know anything about some impressed slave.

Exhausted, she wiped sweat with her ragged sleeve. Mosquitoes were at work on every naked bit of skin. She slapped her neck and scratched one bare foot with the other. She stood and stretched her back. She felt like she might drop. But if she did she'd never find him. The company she'd been cooking for had at last been fed and the other woman had gone to the cook tent. She pulled the sweat-soaked rag off her head and her hair fell around her face.

She started walking without a real destination, hoping by some miracle she might spot him among the soldiers. She passed a man playing a squeezebox, another dancing a jig. A young long-haired soldier had a board across his knees, penning a letter while a little colored boy sat at his feet, stifling a yawn. A couple of soldiers called out to her, but she ignored them and they made no move to follow her.

In the distance she saw a woods and the light of a campfire among the trees. She started toward it but a voice called loudly, "Halt."

"What?"

"Advance and give the countersign," said a voice in the darkness.

"I ain't got no sign. I was jist takin' a walk."

The sentry stepped into the light, rifle aimed at her. "Take a walk the other way 'fore I shoot you just for practice."

"You go to hell," mumbled Alice, but she turned back. Miserably, she sat down cross-legged beside a lone campfire on the fringe of camp. A soldier pissed against a tree not less than ten feet from where she sat but either didn't see her or didn't care. He disappeared back into the thousands of tents. There was no one else near except the lone sentry, and he was way up on the edge of the field. She fumbled in her bag and pulled out the willow woman. In the firelight the eyes, each with a tiny pupil cut in its iris, stared at her accusingly. The lips seemed to frown.

"What are you doing here?"

Alice started to scramble to her feet. "I was jist . . ." she began, clenching the little figure in her fist.

Captain Brennan nodded at her hand. "Will you show me?"

Reluctantly, Alice handed him the little figure. She watched him sharply as he turned it this way and that in the firelight. "What a wonderful little doll. Amazingly lifelike. Look at the face, almost looks like it could speak. Wherever did you get it?"

Alice reached up for it. "It was give to me. It's mine."

"Fine whittling." Captain Brennan handed it to her and smiled.

Alice grabbed the little woman and dropped it in the pouch tied at her waist.

"You have an awful lot of hair, gal. But I did get a glimpse of your face yesterday. How old are you?"

"Why?" Her calves tensed, ready to spring.

"You look so young is all. I figure my Katie was about your age." He lowered himself on his haunches next to her and stirred the fire so that the flames caught bright. "Would have been sixteen this month."

She tilted her head so only the right side of her face showed in the firelight. "Somethin' happen to her?"

"Fell into the river last April playing with her cousins. Couldn't swim." He smiled sadly. "Not something young ladies learn, though I think she would have liked to. When she was small my wife was always trying to get her to sit quiet, but Katie would sneak out the window and climb a tree soon as her back was turned." His eyes glistened in the firelight. "Do you know how to swim?"

She nodded. She'd taught herself to stay afloat in still ponds in the swamp—one of the only escapes. She'd float ears submerged, eyes skyward. Deaf, she'd watch tree leaves flirt with sunlight.

"That's good. Good." The captain reached inside his coat and pulled out something. He unwrapped it. "Black Jack. My wife knows I have a sweet tooth. She sent it to me in Winchester. Have one."

Shyly, Alice took a stick of the molasses candy. No one had treated her kindly since the man and woman on the paddleboat. Of course, she knew they wouldn't have if she'd looked the way she did now. But this captain didn't seem to mind. What if she told him the truth? Would he believe her? He handed her another candy stick and smiled.

Doesn't matter how they look, you fool.

The captain looked up at the sky. "We're going to be moving out before daybreak. But don't worry, you'll be safe here with the other servants." He stood up.

"Why you call them servants when they're slaves?"

The smile on his face dissolved. "Good night, Birdy." She heard the chink-chink of his brass spurs as he walked away.

Alice called out softly, "Captain?" She could no longer see his face when he turned back to her.

"What is it?"

"I was with a boy when they brought me to camp. Soldiers took him. That general said to send him ahead. You know 'bout that?"

In the distance someone laughed and a dog barked. "Well," said the captain, "some boys were sent ahead to the Alabamians."

"Sent to Alabama? Lord no!"

"An Alabama company. The Fourth, I believe. Sent them to the woods. To build breastworks for the artillery."

THIRTY-NINE

Up in the woods Bledsoe stopped and scratched his bug-bit leg. They weren't building breastworks. They were digging trenches. They were not allowed to talk and dug in the dark, flinging dirt over their shoulders. At last, pale light bleeding through the trees and the stars had gone filmy. They had dug through the night with only a brief break for cold meat and corn bread, made soggy by the sweat on their filthy hands.

One soldier had gone to sleep under a tree. There were only the two to watch them and now one wasn't. Still, the one that was had a rifle with a fixed bayonet that looked even meaner than the gun. Gradually the sky turned from violet to a rosy blush. The birds woke up and in the trees a tremolo rose, clear and bright as running water. The one guard slept on but the other motioned with his rifle for them to keep at it.

Bledsoe bent, flinging earth along with worms, homeless now. He didn't want to think about her but his brain was against him. She kept edging into his mind as if peeking around a corner. She would have told someone by now she wasn't a slave. She was free and white.

Don't you reckon we're good as married now? But that was impossible.

Still. That bright bird voice, her eyes. He could see through those eyes clear to her beating heart. Her fierce heart. Fierce as any Indian. But she wasn't an Indian. She was white and it would never work. *Forget her.*

"Hey there!" The private threw a half-gnawed apple at him. "Git busy."

A white woman in Beaufort had taken up with a free negro named Eli Mundy when he was a boy. He remembered Mundy. He was a skilled glazier and had come to Our Joy to replace the glass in several of the big house windows. Bledsoe had followed him around while he worked. He was a quiet man, didn't say much, but he shared the contents of his lunch bucket with the boy. He also had a pocket watch with a see-through back so you could watch the gears turn. He let Bledsoe examine it whenever he asked. Years later he heard that the white woman had her throat cut and Mundy was shot dead one winter night.

But maybe north it wouldn't matter.

An enormous boom sent birds flapping from their roosts. The slaves dropped their shovels as another blast ripped the morning awake. The soldier who'd been sleeping jumped to his feet. Bugles blew in the distance; drums began to call. "Get up outta there, boys. War's started!"

FORTY

"Git up." Alice cracked open her eyes, swallowed the taste of glue in her mouth, and looked at the girl standing over her. It was barely light. Alice had fallen asleep beside the now-dead campfire. "What?" she mumbled. "Go 'way."

"You come with me." She jabbed Alice in the chest. "Right now."

Alice scrambled to her feet and shoved Jubilee aside. "Git off me." Somewhere a piano played. She heard women singing *"I know not, oh, I know not, what joys await us there."*

"You better come. They said you s'posed to help me," said Jubilee.

The sun was rising a red ball, the air already sticky. *"Oh sweet and blessed country,"* sang the women. Bugles blew clear and crisp. Horses trotted by, their riders bellowing orders or following them. *"The home of God's elect!"* Drums beat marching tattoos. Men squatted by fires fixing fry bread and coffee. Artillery rolled by. Confused and disoriented, Alice turned her back to Jubilee and scooped a cup of water from an open barrel. *Alabama.* He was somewhere building something.

"You best come." Jubilee stood behind Alice scowling, arms crossed.

Alice splashed some water on her face. There was clang and clatter as a troop of Virginia volunteers lined up behind a mounted officer on the edge of the field. A little boy, no more than twelve or so, hefted a drum over his shoulder and rat-tatted it a couple of times. Soldiers scrambled as officers shouted to form ranks. A group of soldiers in homespun and baggy sack jackets stood by the nearest campfire, laughing and joking.

"We gots to take water to the sick tent." Jubilee poked Alice again.

Alice took a swallow from the cup of stale water. She was wide-awake now.

"It's an order!"

Alice rinsed her mouth and spat the water out on the ground. Her heart was tripping and she felt it miss a beat. Overhead the sky turned a fleshy pink. Over the whine of a fiddle came a popping, like corn jumping in a hot skillet. The soldiers swung their heads toward the sound.

"What's that?" asked Jubilee, turning to them.

"Yankee guns!" shouted one of the soldiers joyously. They grabbed their rifles and raced off to join their troop beginning to move out toward the road. Drummers thum-tummed the call to battle and fifers gaily played "Frog in the Well." A smile was on nearly every soldier's face as they fell in with their company.

In the distance Alice saw Captain Brennan on his handsome bay. As his company moved out, alongside marched the company band. A color guard snapped the Stars and Bars on the Confederacy's new flag to the right and left as he stepped smart to approving applause from those left behind. Then Captain Brennan's cavalry company trotted down the macadam road and disappeared.

The camp was hardly empty though. Slaves, wives, dogs still worked or sang or barked. Livestock needed feeding, sick soldiers needed tending, bandages needed rolling, and prayers needed praying. To this last end, a preacher had gathered a troop of wives come to witness this battle that they were certain would be over in time for a lovely picnic luncheon. They sat on parlor chairs brought from home, their colored servants standing attentively behind.

Alice headed toward a blacksmith pounding out a new shoe as a horse waited patiently. "Look here," said Alice, pushing Jubilee away again. "I'm tryin' to find a boy they took to some kinda works with Alabama soldiers. Might you know 'bout that?"

The blacksmith clanged his hammer on the red-hot shoe. He dropped the shoe in a bucket of water where it hissed angrily. "Nope."

Over the noise in camp came the pop-pop-popping of guns, but it was difficult to tell exactly where it originated. "Well then, where's the war at 'xactly?"

The slave looked her up and down. "Well, lessee, gal." He pointed with his hammer. "It's over there by the crick, up by the turnpike yonder, down by the bridge, up in the woods. Fact is, I do believe them Yankees is tryin' to surround us right this very minute. Least that's what I'd do if I was them." He pulled the cooled horseshoe out of the bucket with a pair of tongs, then whacked it with his hammer. It rang. He stuck some nails between his lips and lifted the horse's rear hoof between his knees.

Jubilee nudged Alice from behind. "Who you think you are?"

"Git off me."

"They caught them some Yankee spies sneakin' round 'bout yesterday. They gonna hang 'em later. Maybe I say you a spy too," said Jubilee. "They hang you wid 'em." A boom as a shell exploded. The ground shook. They all looked toward the woods. Alice felt her heart pitter-pat. *That's where they sent him. To the woods.*

"Artillery," said the blacksmith calmly, soothing the horse. "Them's the big Yankee guns."

"The general'll stop 'em," said Jubilee, forgetting Alice. "He got the Lord."

"They got Father Abraham. They get over Bull Run, they'll be in Richmond tomorrow."

"They ain't gonna, though, are they? What happen if they do?" Jubilee looked part worried and part excited.

Alice watched black smoke cloud up the distant skyline.

"We be free," said the blacksmith, spitting a nail into his hand.

"Oh," said Jubilee. "It's true? My mistress say they lyin', jist say we be free to whip us up."

Another enormous boom. Smoke rose high as hills. A strange whistle made all three suck in their breath. The explosion seemed to rip the sky open. Smoke rose from the woods. The blacksmith gentled the horse and, smiling, pounded the last nail into the hoof. Bang went the answering artillery. Jubilee grabbed hold of the blacksmith's arm.

Artillery. That was what it meant. Those big guns. The captain had said they'd been sent to the woods to build breastworks for artillery. Alice started running and no one stopped her. She was running toward the woods from where right then came a blast so ferocious the entire sky seemed aflame.

FORTY-ONE

The stream, wide at this spot, glistened in the muted light of overhanging trees. The coolness was enthusiastically welcomed by the soldiers, pouring sweat in their mismatched uniforms, pale blue jacket from here, gray trousers from there. Two wore kepis. One had on a red shirt. His hat had fallen off a while back. It was sometime on the distant side of noon. The July sun had turned from red to white and it was mean. The air was thick as paste. Gnats swarmed in black clouds; they'd fly right into a mouth if it was left open.

Earlier by the ford, the 4th Alabama had exchanged fire with the Yankees. Bledsoe, however, hadn't exchanged anything with anybody, except his shovel for a heavy haversack of extra ammunition. He was lugging this on his back as he followed the three infantrymen. Two were the ones who'd overseen the night's trench digging.

These three had somehow managed to get separated from their company when a retreat was called from the hill they'd been on. There were two hills on this battlefield that Bledsoe was aware of. Both were apparently prizes to be won for some reason since generals ordered their opposing forces to form lines and march up them despite getting shot dead or blown up by cannon fire. It was clear these Alabama boys with their hot blistered feet now dangling in Bull Run creek weren't expecting the type of war they'd found. Neither was Bledsoe. He'd hunkered down behind a big boulder. He hadn't been prepared for the screaming or seeing a body shot apart.

It wasn't only Yankees they had to worry about, said one of the Alabamians as they made their way farther from the fighting. He'd heard down the line that the 4th Carolina had fired at the 1st Louisiana by mistake and shot a number of them in the back. The Louisianans no longer gave a hang about shooting Yankees. They'd turned and fired in retaliation at their fellow Rebels. "Can you believe it?" asked one.

Seemed everything in this battle was a mess, observed Bledsoe. Some of the raw volunteers, both North and South, plain disobeyed orders either deliberately or from a lack of understanding the maneuvers their generals commanded them to execute. Who would *want* to march straight at enemy guns? Did they think they were stupid? And it was hard to make out which side was which in all the smoke and confusion. Both sides had similar uniforms, or lack of them; though some Confederates wore gray, a great many of them wore blue. From a distance the Union flag and the southern Stars and Bars looked alike. So it wasn't just confused Rebels shooting Rebels; it was Yankees shooting Yankees as well.

When told to fall in with another general's regiment after a scrambled retreat down one of the hills, the three soldiers, Bledsoe following, had just kept going, making their way farther and farther until they were downstream from the Yankee fire and the deafening blast of Rebel artillery.

Now none of them appeared much interested in Bledsoe, so he splashed water on his face and sat down behind them, leaning against a big hickory. One of the men tried to rally the other two back toward the hill where the Virginia's general had stationed himself. "If we don't go back we're deserters."

Bledsoe watched them through half-closed eyes. He was hoping for a fight between them, a distraction, a chance to fade back into the trees and make his way far enough downstream to cross over to the Yankee lines.

"We ain't desertin'," replied one, pulling an apple out of his pack. "We're just restin'."

The other boy looked younger than Bledsoe. He said nothing, scratched his arm, and threw a rock in the stream.

"They'll line y'all up and shoot your danged asses. The shoot deserters, don't you know? Follow me back."

"Ain't got to follow you nowhere, John Henrick. You ain't no general."

"Goddamn you, Griggs, you want everybody back home to know you run off?"

"Like I said, we're just restin' a bit is all. We'll go back soon enough."

Above Bledsoe's head something scurried at the sound of new artillery fire. "Well, I'm going back," said the one called John Henrick. "Y'all can hang and you will."

"We're right behind you, Johnny," said Griggs, lying down beside the stream and fanning himself with his sweat-stained kepi. The boy next to him turned and grinned.

"Hell with y'all then," Henrick said. "Come on, boy." He motioned to Bledsoe to follow.

Griggs sat up. "Wait. You can't take him."

"Come on," repeated Henrick. Bledsoe, head lowered, got slowly to his feet and hefted the pack.

"You got no right to that nigger. He's got the extra ammunition." Griggs picked up his rifle. Two seconds later he was down again. Another minié ball spun John Henrick around in a full circle before he crashed down dead on the bank of Bull Run—the top half of his head gone.

The third and youngest boy tried to pick up his rifle, but by the time his hand reached it he'd been shot through the heart. Behind the tree Bledsoe heard him whimper once or twice, then nothing. He was shaking. *Don't be afraid, they're Yankees.* Still they might think he was one of those fools like the general's. So foolish they'd fight to keep themselves enslaved. He had to let them know he was on their side. He'd read about the white flag. He pulled off what was left of his shirt. It was more yellow now than white, but he stepped around the tree, waved it madly. There was no one there. Across Bull Run creek, the hot July breeze rustled the bushes. Just then Bledsoe realized there *was* no breeze. Not even a sigh of air. The world smelled of sweat and blood. The last thing he heard was the rifle cocking.

FORTY-TWO

The sky had turned sullen but the clouds were obscured by the smoke of the pounding artillery. Her eyes wept constantly from the residual smoke from the gunpowder. A boom like the end of the world made her cover her ears and set her quivering. She passed a cartload of wounded men coming back toward the junction but merely gave them a quick glance. They were white. Soldiers ran past, one banging into her before shoving her roughly aside. Were they running to the battle or from it? A horse with only one polished boot stuck in the stirrup grazed beside the road. A team of mules pulled a cannon, a soldier on horseback hollering to the driver to "Get that howitzer up to the Fifth by the bridge." No one stopped her as she stepped off the turnpike.

Once she entered the woods she still heard the guns firing, but they sounded distant. She soon noticed no insects chirped. No birds twittered. The air was stagnant and her mouth tasted of metal. The sounds of a snapped twig, a crushed leaf, as she hesitantly made her way were too loud. She found herself stepping cautiously, quietly. The sunlight filtering through the trees cast squeamish shadows.

It was too quiet. She heard herself breathing too fast, nearly panting. Her blood seemed to pulse in her ears as loud as the guns in the distance. Sweat snaked between her breasts and dripped from her forehead into her red-rimmed eyes. She stopped and looked at the way she'd woven through the woods. She had a strange feeling that the trees had closed ranks to prevent her finding her way out again. *"Oh,"* she exclaimed, surprised and horrified, when she came upon a buck deer, its body a mass of mangled bone and blood. Looking away, she tripped and put out her hands to catch herself. She landed on a man's gray-shirted chest. Lifting herself away, with a gasp she saw there was nothing above his collar. His head lay beside him, eyes opened wide. She scrambled to her feet, hands flailing, then clapped her hands to her mouth to hold in the scream. That was when she saw they were all around her. Dead men, faceup, down, or faceless.

Ahead, where a line of trees once stood, all that remained were a few jagged splinters. Artillery shells had decimated a quarter mile of woods. Beyond she could see a field and more bodies. She stepped backward, a little mewling sound escaping. "Oh Lord Jesus," she whispered.

"Are you mad, girl? Why didn't you come with a guard? What possessed you to come through the woods?"

She looked up and saw an old man a few feet away. He wasn't wearing a uniform. He looked anywhere between sixty-five and seventy but was heartily made. His black suit was dotted with blood. He was hatless and bald but had a thick gray beard. "Don't just stand there. Help me." She backed away farther.

The old man bent to one of the dead men. "Thank you," she heard what she'd assumed was a dead man say when the old man struggled to lift him.

"In the name of Heaven, did they send me another ninny? Give me a hand," said the old man.

The wounded soldier began to slip out of his hands, and he groaned in pain. The soldier was bleeding from a head wound, blood dripping like thick red oil. The soldier turned his face to Alice. "Thank you," he said to her. "Thank you, ma'am." Alice bent down and took hold of the man's ankles.

"The wagon is right over there," the old man grunted as he struggled to hold on to the wounded soldier's top half. "Help me get him into it." Between them they managed to get the soldier onto a large flatbed cart. A team of mules stamped nervously. Alice stared in horror at the field. Men and horses lay crumpled as if dropped by a bored giant child.

"Let's get them to the house. I think it's about to rain. Must be the cannon fire that's done it."

Alice looked at the bald old man and the six half-dead men piled on the cart.

"You're not afraid of blood, are you?"

Alice found that her mouth would not open.

"They said they'd send me an experienced girl. Have you ever cared for the sick?"

Alice numbly nodded.

"Good. I already had a volunteer faint and another sick up my last clean sheet. Fine ladies aren't usually that fine about rearrangement of human anatomy. Tie up your hair. Don't want it getting in wounds. Here. You can use this." He handed her a bandana. "Climb up here in back. I think that young sergeant there could use your lap for a pillow. His head has had enough pounding. Climb up."

Numbly, she obeyed. She sat down and took the soldier's bloody head on her lap.

"They say they've taken that hill they're calling Henry House," said the old man, clucking the mules forward. He turned from the driver's seat toward her. "I heard General Bee fell." The man shook his head and turned back around. "Tragic, tragic. But Jackson's brigade stood firm. Like a stone wall, someone said. Already calling him a hero. The Yankees are retreating now. Running back toward Washington, they say."

That was the name of the Bible-thumping general who'd ordered them all here. Jackson. But she didn't care about hills or bees or generals. She closed her eyes so as not to see the faces around her. *But he wasn't fighting. The Yankees ain't gonna shoot slaves.*

"I am Dr. William Loveall," announced the old man. "I came up from Charlottesville yesterday."

Alice opened her eyes. One of the wounded men was attempting to smile at her, but his lips curled with pain. "Inside my coat there is a letter for Lenora. Will you see it gets there?" When the man spoke there was a strange whistling sound. She saw that he had a nearly perfectly round hole in his neck. A silk scarf, caked with blood, had been tied around but had slipped loose. Alice ripped a strip from the hem of her dress and bandaged his neck. "Tell Mother I shall see her in—" His eyes closed.

Alice gently put a hand on his heart. "I will," she said. "Don't worry none." But she knew he was already dead.

"Water," begged another. One of his legs was turned the wrong way.

Dr. Loveall held out a canteen and Alice took it, pouring water in the attached tin cup. She held it to the man's lips but he choked trying to swallow, so Alice dipped her fingers in the cup and gave them to the man to suck. The doctor gave her an approving nod. She tied her hair up with the bandana. Dr. Loveall eyed the scar but said nothing. He climbed down from the wagon to lift another wounded soldier aboard. Even though he told her that the Yankees were running, she still heard the pop of rifles and the boom of artillery. She gave the soldier some more water and hoped he wouldn't die in her lap.

FORTY-THREE

It was raining. There was mud on the floor of the two-story house. Mud and blood had ruined the carpets. Silk draperies had been torn down for extra bedding. The wounded, the sick, the dying, and the dead were crammed from the rafters to the basement. Most Confederate, but a number of Yankees too. The iron scent of blood and stench of bowel were overwhelming. Alice had tied a cloth across her lower face so as not to gag.

Dr. Loveall's bone saw had worked off a leg, and a foot and arm before it. He used a long silver hook with an ebony handle to quickly pull out the arteries from the stump end. He tied them off with thread as neatly as a crocheted doily.

Alice wrapped the stump with linen. It immediately spread with red.

"Unwrap it," he sighed. "I must have missed one." The old doctor wiped his face with his forearm, leaving a smear of crimson on his forehead. The other doctor, much younger, took a swig from a silver hip flask and passed it to the older man, who drank deeply and handed it back.

Two colored slaves hefted another soldier on the table who began to scream, "Don't cut it off, don't cut it off."

"Now, young lady," said the old doctor, ignoring the man being roped down to the table by the slaves. "Take the leeches off that boy there and put them in a jar. We'll need to starve them before we can use them again. They're of no use really," he muttered, "but at least it makes them think something's being done." He placed a cloth cone over the patient's nose and mouth. "Just breathe, son," he said to the still-struggling soldier. "It'll all be over soon."

The soldier on the table writhed a moment and then fell still. "Well, Hadley," said Dr. Loveall to the younger doctor, "that's the end of chloroform and we've got no ether. I warned them in Richmond about this, but apparently they think these boys just need to bite down on their sword and think of Jeff Davis. And this is only the beginning."

Dr. Hadley looked across the table at the older man with surprise. "The Yankees cut and run back to Washington. They're tripping over themselves to get away. It's over. They have to let us go now."

Dr. Loveall picked up his saw again, its metal glinting in the candlelight surrounding the operating table. He probed the unconscious man's mangled arm with a blood-covered finger.

"Not using the flap method any longer?" asked the younger doctor, peering curiously at the wound.

"Now hold that arm out straight, Hadley. No, straight so I can get a good cut. Young lady, apply the tourniquet above the elbow, please." By this time Alice knew what was expected and tied a scarf tightly above the soldier's elbow. "We haven't time. We'll just do clean cuts." Dr. Loveall began to cut in a circular pattern. "Plus the flap method raises chances of infection in my observation, which is, I confess, limited to a foot mangled by a wire cutter. Sadly that slave developed sepsis and died two days later. The other amputation was my bird dog, Sally. Used a clean cut like this and Sally lived to thirteen on three legs. Course she couldn't hunt worth a damn after that."

The old doctor worked fast. In less than a minute the saw made little scratching sounds as it bit into the bone. "Everyone thought this would be a picnic. Hot air overwhelming cooler heads. Speech making, politicking, ladies' auxiliaries knitting socks. Hurrah hurrah and parading. War. That's the way they see it. Glorifying death. Boys lining up cheerfully to be killed before they've even kissed a girl. Valor. Honor. Look at this one, he look full of honor? He's likely to die, no matter how careful I am. Sepsis is the true battlefield enemy."

"Are you saying these men are not dying for honor?"

"Dying like this? Look at him. Look at them out there. What do you think? You call it honor when the last thing on earth is loosening your bowels in the mud? Maybe I see it in all this blood like gypsies read tea leaves. But I'm telling you this is only the start of something much worse. And no, no. Lincoln won't let us go. We've humiliated them and the humiliated always want revenge. They'll be back, Hadley. And they'll be back in twice, three times the number. Yes, today they've been run out. But that will make them more determined. Mark my words, this is only the beginning." Dr. Loveall split the arm from its elbow. "But of course no one will. I'm just an old man they ran out of the legislature."

Alice breathed shallowly under her makeshift mask as the doctor severed the arm. She kept telling herself it was no worse than butchering a hog, something she'd had to do herself on the rare occasion one was traded for the witch's work. Yet it was. Far worse.

"Sir, I am not certain that you are not espousing treason."

"Treason? For having an opinion? And treason to whom? These boys? Jeff Davis? You? Take it away, young lady." Dr. Loveall indicated the arm lying disconnected on the table. "This poor devil has no use for it anymore. Tell those boys to bring the next one. I think that captain with the chest wound in the parlor. And, Hadley, I am not espousing anything but the fact that I find it utterly pathetic that mankind can think of no other way of settling their differences than bleeding each other to death. Henry, Jacob, come get this one," he called to the slaves who were acting as orderlies. "Young lady, hand me my surgery bag."

Dr. Loveall had never asked her name. Not her name or where she came from. When he needed her, which was always, he addressed her as *young lady*. It had been hours and hours. How many she couldn't guess. The doctor had shared some bread and fatback with her but had not ceased attending the wounded as he chewed. The fact that she hadn't stopped for a moment since they'd arrived at this house had kept the horror hidden in her mind. And so much eventually numbs the brain. At least for a while. Though exhausted, she was in a state of rare wakefulness. All her senses seemed vibrantly aware. Her eyes were sharper, her hearing accentuated. She moved quickly, but more like an automaton, movements precise and automatic. She knew if she stopped for even a minute she would fall to the ground.

But always in the back of her mind as she hushed some poor boy, or closed another's eyes, he was there. She saw him lying motionless on a field, left behind, forgotten. She saw him leaned against a fence post, dying and alone. She saw him crawling and collapsing in another field or on a hill. But what could she do? She'd only get killed herself.

The slaves carried in a man and laid him on the table. His eyes were closed, face bleached as raw cotton, the front of his gray frock coat rust red. Alice bent over the red-haired man. "Captain?" she called softly. His eyes remained closed.

"You know him?" asked Dr. Loveall.

"It's Captain Brennan." She looked up at the doctor. "He goin' to die?"

The doctor peeled back the remaining strips of fabric clinging to the wound. As he did a gold button popped off his coat and fell on the floor with a ping. The entry wound bubbled with pink froth like a volcanic spring. The doctor shook his head mournfully. "That is entirely likely, I'm afraid. Your captain has lost a lot of blood. And the bullet is lodged beneath the ribs. I have no way to get to it."

She bent and picked up the gold button from the floor and rubbed it between her thumb and forefinger as if it were a charm. It came to her that the captain could help her. He had been in charge. People listened to him.

The doctor was wrapping the captain's chest tightly with linen bandages. "Put him out in the hall," he told the waiting slaves. "That's all we can do."

"I'll care for him," said Alice.

Dr. Loveall watched her open the cloth bag at her waist and pull out a small packet. "What have you got there?"

"Self heal and other herbs. Give me some of that whiskey and I'll make up a potion for his chest."

"Potions? Superstitious nonsense," said the younger doctor.

"Give me that flask of yours, Hadley." The doctor hesitantly handed him the silver flask. Dr. Loveall poured a bit of alcohol in a tin cup. "Having faith in a God who is invisible might also be called superstitious nonsense, yet time and again, people say they were healed by the redeemer. And you know yourself that we use distillations of plants and herbs, have for centuries. Now this young lady has proven herself a more than capable nurse."

He handed the tin cup to Alice. "I would shake a rattle and call the Devil if I had faith it would save these boys. Make up your magic potion. Even if it does nothing more than let the poor man know that you care."

Alice took the cup. *But I don't care. I only care about him.*

FORTY-FOUR

He couldn't swim, but somehow now he could and the water was so warm and soft. Soft! Who would have thought water would be like a warm cloud? He was like a fish, finning down and down toward the light, shining like a silver moon. A beacon pulling him. A plant waved on the floor of this lake? Sea? Back and forth it waved. Beautiful. He reached out to touch it and discovered it wasn't a plant at all. It was hair. Blue-black hair and then she turned up her face to him. She was crying. How can you cry in the sea? But he realized he was crying too. Water in water. He reached up to rub his eyes. Then he opened them. Raindrops were splashing his face.

He was drenched through and through. He tried to sit up. He fell back, breathing in short startled gasps at the pain. He lay still for a moment, the rain falling harder through the leaves above. The pain radiated in hot waves. It was a pounding throb, a pulsing; when he turned his head it was as if his shoulder were being sliced open with a knife dipped in hot grease. He slowly turned his head again and then held his breath in shock for a moment.

He cautiously lifted his other arm and, finding it still worked, laid his hand on the burning place between his neck and shoulder. He took the hand away and held it before his eyes. The rain washed away blood in pink smears.

By slowly twisting himself upward like a reluctant screw he sat up. Only by saying to himself *I'm not dead* could he manage not to faint. There beside him was his once-white flag. He picked up the wet shirt and pressed it to the wound. John Henrick lay with what remained of his face turned up to the black clouds. The other Rebel had fallen facedown. He still clutched his rifle. The youngest boy's bottom half had slipped into the rushing water. Bull Run was rising and soon he'd be beneath it.

Groaning, he took the shirt from his shoulder and pressed it into the wet ground. She'd told him mud would draw out poison after the snake bit him. Maybe it would draw out a bullet's poison too. For a moment he thought he heard her voice. Quick and bright as gold. He winced from another sharp stab of pain. *Bledsoe,* he heard her call. "No," he muttered. No. He was losing his mind along with his blood. He'd never see her again. That girl Alice. *Alice. Alice Brown.*

His ragged trousers were rain-glued to his legs as he forced himself up, leaning against the trunk of the tree. He thought he still heard guns but realized it was only the sound of the rain ping-ping-pinging as it fell heavy into Bull Run creek. He'd thought of trying to get across it earlier but he could forget it now. It had swollen to three times its width and rushed fast enough to drag a man off his feet. He began to stumble back the direction he'd come with the boys of the 4th Alabama. Even if the Yankees were still on the other side, he couldn't get across. Anyway, they'd already shot him for trying.

FORTY-FIVE

Sometime toward morning another doctor arrived. He was with the army. This one was equipped with a soft-faced volunteer nurse of middle age. They stepped over the bodies that had been left in the front hall where it was easier to haul them out the door.

In the dining room Dr. Loveall had just bandaged a man's lower jaw with the unlikely hope of keeping it attached. Alice had handed him the last of the lint bandages for the task. The younger doctor was gone. He had disappeared over two hours previously, saying he was getting a drink of water, and hadn't returned.

For the first time in nearly eighteen hours Dr. Loveall sat down heavily in a stiff-backed chair. It had once been part of the set for the dining table that had served through the night as the operating theater.

Alice no longer wore her mask. She was used to the stink now. Her arms were lead. When she dropped them at last to her sides, she doubted she could ever lift them again. She was wiping her hands with a piece of a curtain when Dr. Loveall turned her face to him. He traced the scar tissue with a thick-knuckled finger. "Whoever did this ought to be skinned."

Alice looked at the floor.

He put his hat on his head and the army doctor helped the old man out of the house. Alice watched through the window as he climbed unsteadily into a buggy.

She was left alone in the once-pretty dining room. For a moment she thought she might faint and grabbed hold of the scarred dining table, splattered with congealing blood. Her eyes took in the blue-patterned wallpaper, the painting of a glossy chestnut horse, the English porcelain shepherd and his companion, her milkmaid face smiling on the mantel. A vase lay smashed on the floor; blood and gray matter stained the rug. *All this,* she thought. *All this dying. What for?*

In the hallway the army doctor began barking instructions. Alice heard him in the parlor telling the colored orderlies to begin moving the wounded. The soft-faced nurse came into the dining room. She took in Alice's dirty bare feet, kerchief-wrapped head, and scarred face.

"Who are you?"

Alice couldn't even lift her shoulders to shrug.

"What's your name?"

"Alice," she replied, too weary to remember to lie. Flies were feeding on the old doctor's saw he'd left behind on the table. It seemed they were buzzing inside her head. She leaned against the table to keep from sinking onto the stained rug.

The nurse cocked her head, clearly puzzled. "You the doctor's servant?"

"He tole me to help him. So I did."

Alice held on to the table's edge. She couldn't talk anymore. She tried to think what to do now but she couldn't seem to follow one thread long enough to get to an answer.

"Well, there's a wagon out front taking those that can be moved to the train station. Some are going to the hospital in Richmond, some are going home," said the nurse, kinder voiced. "You must want to get home yourself if you've been here all night."

Alice stared vacantly at the older woman in her prim brown dress. She watched as the nurse's lips moved, but the words seemed to float in syrup.

"Is your home close to here?"

"Bledsoe," murmured Alice, staring out the window. She put a hand to the windowpane, as if reaching out to the bodies piled in the yard. The sun was up, and raindrops on the glass cast little prisms across her hand.

"Is that nearby? Where are you going?"

Alice walked out of the dining room and down the hallway, neverminding the slaves hauling out the wounded and dying. Arms and legs dangled from the sides of a wagon as it rolled away toward the road. She felt a breeze brush her cheek, silky as a kiss. It flapped the gingham around her bare ankles. She smelled honeysuckle in it. Above her head a flock of birds chittered as they winged across the rain cleaned sky. Alice slowly sank down beside a wagon wheel into the churned mud. *And if he's dead?* She tried to cry. It did no good because she didn't believe it. *I'd feel it. I'd be empty.*

The nurse came out and said someone was calling for a girl named Birdy. Alice pulled herself to her feet.

"But I thought you said your name was Alice."

"Must be the captain. I clean forgot him."

The nurse looked relieved. "Oh yes, then you're the captain's girl."

In the parlor Captain Brennan turned his face to her. He was lying on a stained chaise longue. His chest was bandaged over the poultice she'd made hours earlier.

"I thought that was your voice I heard. I wasn't imagining it. You're the one who saved me. I knew it." He was breathing shallowly, obviously in pain.

"Don't talk," she said.

"Will you help me? Will you help me get home? The doctors said if I had a nurse or someone to look after me on the way, I'd have a better chance to get home."

Alice sat down across from him in a parlor chair, balancing the chair with her foot since one of its legs had been wrenched off for a splint. "Help you?" She looked at him intently. "If'n you help me."

He tried to smile. "I have to bargain?"

"Help me find somebody."

The captain tried to sit up, and Alice rushed over and gently laid him back down. "Who?"

"His name's, oh it don't matter. None of you care what his name is." She checked the bandage around his chest. "I tole you. He was with me when they brung us down to that camp of yours. You said he'd been sent to the woods. I been to the woods. Everybody there's dead. He weren't there."

Captain Brennan looked up at her. "I'm pretty certain I'm dying, Birdy, and I want to die at High Hope. I want to see my wife and I want to die in my own bed. Take me home and I promise I'll help you to find him." His lips clenched for a moment, then relaxed. "You have my word of honor."

Alice noted that the bandage was bright with new blood. "If'n you want to get home to your own bed you're gonna have to mind me right now." She pulled something from the bag at her waist. "Chaw on this." She put something in his mouth. He tried to spit it out. "It's willow bark. It'll help ease the pain some till I kin boil some up. And this here is a potion I made up from passionflower. This'll make you rest."

FORTY-SIX

He was moving across a field. He stumbled now and then, but he somehow managed to lift his feet high enough to step over the dead, to concentrate enough to not fall into the carcass of a dead horse. He tried not to look down, to keep his eyes on some sort of goal, getting out of this field for one. He didn't want to see them. It wasn't the torn-up bodies or the blood so much as the eyes. Sometimes he'd catch a glimpse. Many were still open with a look of surprise.

He kept moving forward. He thought he was still moving even after he'd fallen into a shallow ditch. In his mind he was still crossing the field. After a while he became conscious of something blocking the warm sun that he'd felt on his face. He wanted to open his eyes but he was too tired. He felt himself being lifted and wondered if there really was a Heaven and if that was where he was going.

He didn't hear the officer take the driver to task later for throwing a nigger in with the dead soldiers. By then the wagon had crossed the battlefield and arrived at the Manassas train station. There, soldiers were once again lined up except there was no marching. They were lying faceup to the blazing sun. No one thought to check if the colored boy brought back to the station in the wagon was still breathing. He was rolled off by a bush next to the railroad tracks until someone had time to cover him with dirt.

FORTY-SEVEN

Another soldier's head was in her lap as the wagon set out for the junction. This time it was the captain. He had been conscious when they'd taken him out of the house. Still, Alice kept her hand over his heart to make certain it continued to beat.

At the train station the dead had now been covered with blankets, hidden from view of the locals who came to cheer the heroes. There was word that Jefferson Davis himself was coming to make a speech. Shouting and hurrahing filled the air as the word of Confederate victory spread. The crowd fell silent as more than two hundred captured enemies came into view. Some staggered with wounds; others shuffled, heads bowed. Alice watched as the men were herded onto a waiting train. She asked Captain Brennan what would become of them.

"I imagine they'll be sent to Libby Prison in Richmond," he replied. His eyes were glassy from the passionflower.

She helped two colored men lift him gently off the cart to a litter. She told him to lie still lest he move the bullet around inside him. An officer stopped and spoke to him. She didn't listen, she was scanning faces. Though her body ached, her brain felt on fire. She felt she could almost see right through people, so intently did she search each face. But he wasn't there.

When she turned back around Captain Brennan was being carried toward the waiting train. She ran to the litter and grabbed one of the slaves, almost causing him to drop his end of the litter. "You can't git on the train, Captain. I got to find him afore you git on the train. I won't leave till he's found."

Captain Brennan, his hand protectively covering his chest, said, "But, Birdy. You see all of this. It's bedlam here. Once we are in more civilized circumstances I will make inquiries, I promise." The slaves started toward the train and again Alice grabbed the slave's arm.

"Leggo, girl. Marse needs to git on that train."

But she didn't let go. Instead she bent so close to the captain's face their noses were almost touching. "You make your 'quiries right here, right now. If'n you don't, well, I ain't your slave and I ain't goin' nowhere with you."

The men carrying the litter stared at her, mouths agape. "Put me down, boys," said Captain Brennan. He had to shout. Wild commotion had busted loose. Horses galloped by, men whooped, women sang, some cried. A band started playing "Lubly Fan." A little girl ran by singing at the top of her lungs, *"Won't you come out tonight and dance by the light of the moon!"*

Alice kneeled beside the litter. "You tell me who you want to do your 'quiring to. Tell me and I'll fetch 'em."

Captain Brennan blinked in the bright sunlight. Alice held her hand over his eyes to shield them. "My God." He looked at her with disbelief. Seeing she wasn't going to budge, he pleaded, "For pity's sake, Birdy. I'm a dying man!"

Alice remained unimpressed. "You tole me they sent him to them breastworks with Alabama."

"I did? I don't recall." He closed his eyes, took a breath, then opened them again. "Might have been with the Fourth. They were working up in the woods south of the creek. I know Lieutenant Law of the Fourth, heard he was with Bee's brigade up on the hill, suppose he might have some idea, but, Birdy, I don't know where he is right now or even if he's still alive. Birdy?"

She wasn't listening. She was watching a coffle of slaves going the opposite way toward the main road. One man in the back was being nearly dragged along by the slave in front. His feet kept giving out on him.

"So you understand that when I am home and able to write a few letters of inquiry . . . where're you going? Where's she going? Boys, don't let her run off. Stop her!"

The litter bearers ran after Alice, and Alice ran after the coffle. She screamed "Bledsoe!" so crazy that everyone within earshot turned to see what was going on. When she reached the last chained man, she stopped still. He turned his face to her. It wasn't him. The driver cantered to the back of the line, raising a small dust storm. "Git along, you!" he shouted at Alice, shaking his whip. "Git goin' or you'll git it."

The coffle started up again, the last man pulled along behind, head lowered to the road, and Alice turned away. The litter bearers grabbed her by either arm and marched her back to the captain. He asked, "You married to this boy?"

"No one said words, but I'm his and he's mine."

"I'll tell you again. We won't find him in this confusion. You see yourself, look. So please, you're a smart girl, Birdy. Though you belong to the army, I'm allowed to take you with me as a nurse to High Hope. It's a lovely place and certainly better than the army and we'll find your . . ."

She stood on tiptoes. Ladies with parasols, mounted soldiers, dogs barking. The train was belching smoke, heads were sticking out windows, people were shouting, mules were braying, the band members banged their bass drums, and the sousaphone blared, deafening all those in close proximity. Alice sighed and nodded to the captain. The colored men picked up the litter once more. The crowd parted to let the bearers through to the train, and that was when she saw him. "Wait!" she yelled. "Look there."

A man lay senseless on the far side of the track. A black man. She ran past the parted crowd, jumping the tracks in front of the belching locomotive. She fell to her knees beside a dusty bush and gathered him to her—pressed his cheek against her breast.

"Let go a me," he muttered without opening his eyes.

"Oh, thank you, Jesus!" shrieked Alice.

The crowd gathered to stare at the scar-faced slave with the nerve to yell for someone to come get the wounded black boy. They stared again when the Confederate captain ordered the bearers to place the colored man on another litter and carry it onto the train.

Tears pouring down her cheeks, Alice bent again to Bledsoe's face and kissed his forehead. Lost somewhere in fever land, he wondered if it was raining once again.

FORTY-EIGHT

High Hope sat back from the James River on top of a knoll. It wasn't a great big house. There were no columns or gewgaws. It was painted a muted blue that changed through the day's passing to a watery gray. When viewed from the river at dusk it seemed to float rather than sit on a foundation. It was flanked by towering hundred-year-old oaks that shaded it in summer. The roof was peaked and shingled with cedar that had aged a soft green. A long front porch faced the river.

Farther downriver were great plantations big enough to fit all of High Hope many times over. But to Alice's eyes the farmhouse was grand as a castle. Looking up at the place from the boat dock, she hoped the name was a good omen. She believed in signs. And they certainly needed hope. For here they were someplace else yet again. It certainly wasn't where they'd been aiming to get to. She had no idea which way was what. Only that they were in Virginia. But the captain had promised them good treatment. What choice was there? She moistened Bledsoe's lips with a wet kerchief. He mumbled something.

"What's that, honey?" But he said nothing further and his eyes stayed shut.

The captain was carried on the litter by two men who'd been hired to row the boat down the river from Richmond. They were slow and careful as they made their way up the sloping rise toward the house. From the front door someone ran down the steps to meet the litter. At first Alice thought it was a little girl all dressed in black, but then she saw it was a woman, fairy small. Her head was bare and her honey-hued hair flowed loose as she ran.

Behind her in the gently rocking boat, Bledsoe lay still as stone. He had opened his eyes but once since they had loaded him on the boat with the captain. He'd looked up into her face, then closed his eyes again. She couldn't tell if he knew her or not. There was an entry and an exit in the meat of the shoulder girdle, right through muscle and tendon but luckily not through bone. The ball had passed clean through. He had lost so much blood. On the train he'd fallen into a fever. She had licorice root in her bag and had treated him with some mixed with water but longed for yarrow. She had none. His forehead was dry and hot.

Alice gently checked the bandage running under his armpit and across his shoulder. He murmured something she couldn't make out. She looked up and saw the colored rowers carrying the litter onto the front porch of the house. The little woman fluttered around the captain as they carried him inside and the door was closed behind them.

Alice didn't know what to do then. Should she wait? Should she follow? She was about to climb onto the dock when an older colored woman came out of the house. She was also small and neatly dressed in gray with a white apron. She made her way down to the boat. She said her name was Jenny. The hired men from Richmond followed her. She told the biggest one to carry Bledsoe, and he picked him up in his arms. Bledsoe lay limp as a wet rag. "Come on thisaway," she said to Alice and the men.

They went around the side of the house, under the towering oaks, past a separate brick kitchen, until they were out of sight of the main house. Past a smokehouse, a milk house, a big green barn. Chickens scattered at their approach and a tethered goat brayed piteously. Behind thick hedges and other outbuildings was a line of one-room cabins. Jenny told the men to carry Bledsoe into one. "You go on and take care you man now. I'll call when Cap'n want you."

They laid Bledsoe on a cornhusk pallet. Alice sank down beside him. She was so tired. For a while she did her best to fan flies away from his face. She heard them buzzing long after she'd slumped against the wall, his head in her lap.

He'd been sunk in fever for two and a half days. It had finally broke. She moistened his lips with the rag and a few minutes later he drank from the gourd thirstily. He hadn't had a bite of food, only broth she'd drizzled between his lips, holding his head up so he wouldn't gag. Alice grabbed hold of him when he tried to stand. With her arm around his waist, he looked at his surroundings. There wasn't much light. The window was a missing board about chest high. Another board hanging from a rope made a shutter that could be dropped against cold and weather. It was currently propped open with a stick. There was a rush-bottom chair, not long for this world, and a three-legged stool. The table was an old door with the doorknob removed. A little soot-filled fireplace with a tin pail in it. A pallet was spread on the hard-packed dirt floor. He grunted with disgust.

"Why didn't you leave me?" Though he'd mumbled during his fever, she hadn't understood any of it. This was the first time he'd spoken to her since they'd arrived at High Hope.

"Ah, honey, you'd be dead if'n I did. I saved you. You don't remember. This is the captain's place. It's called High Hope and it's beautiful, Bledsoe. He brought you here. Captain's good to his people. And look here. He give us this cabin all to ourselves and they don't stint none on food here neither. We're lucky we got a place. You need to heal and git your strength up."

Bledsoe put his hand to his shoulder and winced. "*His* people?"

"He brung me here to nurse him. He got shot bad. It's on account of that we got to come here 'stead of stayin' with the army. We can stick here till we git a chance for somethin' better."

"Better?" He leaned on the chair so he wouldn't topple over, for he felt like he might. "This captain? I'm *his* now you brought me here. So are you. Where are we? I'll wager you I'm somewhere even further south than I was before you had to go and save me." He started toward the door and felt his knees buckle. He grabbed the edge of the table.

"Sit down before you fall down. It was them Yankees shot you! Captain saved your hide. They hauled your half-dead ass right up on that train 'cause he said so. Now sit down. You ain't goin' nowhere yet."

Leaning on the table, he knew she was right. He'd have trouble even making it to the door he was so weak. He stared angrily out the improvised window. A green barn. Hogs snuffling in the barnyard. A guinea hen pecking hopefully under a tree. A wasp whined near his face. He shut his eyes until it flew off. Alice reached for his bandage.

"I ought to change it."

He smacked her hand away. "Leave it."

"Oh, tell me you're still my honey, Bledsoe?" She reached up on tiptoe to kiss his lips.

He turned his face away. "I ain't nobody's."

Still on her tiptoes, she studied his face a moment, surprised at the vehemence in his voice. "I jist mean like we was is all." She reached for his hand and he pulled it away.

"Leave me alone."

"What's wrong with you?"

He glared at her. "Look around you, fool! See where we are? I ran away from this and you put me right back again."

"It ain't like that, Bledsoe. The captain's good and we'll leave . . ."

He fell onto the bed and covered his ears. "Go away. Go away, dammit!"

FORTY-NINE

"Danged fool," she hissed to a cat crouching under a lilac bush. She pinged a rock against the side of the green barn. *Damn you.* All she did was think of him, day and night. Worry, tend him, *save* him. Here she'd thought they were bonded so tight, two hearts, one beat. "I am a fool," she growled again as she entered the back door of High Hope.

As she crossed the threshold a tear snuck down her face. *Stop it.* It was true they were farther south and also that the captain thought she was a slave. But she wasn't really. She'd tell him in good time. At the right time. It wasn't the right time yet. *Maybe I'll jist leave him here . . . he calls me a fool, tells me to git away.* Angrily she blew her nose on a rag. But she knew she wouldn't. She never would. He was her love. Even if he was mean sometimes. But how would she explain Bledsoe to the captain? It was confusing. Every time she thought of something, some way to explain how she and Bledsoe ended up together, any explanation became a jumble in her head. *It'll be all right. Leave it for now.*

She rubbed her eyes with her apron and straightened herself up. She had on a new brown homespun dress and thick brogans, heavy but never worn, and a blue and white checked apron. The kerchief around her head was a pretty yellow, color of marigolds. She'd had a bath in a big wood tub out back behind the barn after the captain had sung her praises to his little honey-haired wife. Told her how she'd saved him from death, nursed him without cease.

She'd been given no chores and left to herself, except when she tended the captain. The wife's name was Tirzah but she was called Tizzy. Miss Tizzy. She wore deep mourning for her daughter drowned the past spring. But black brought out the gold shimmer of her hair and the high color in her cheeks. Still, whenever Alice was near enough, she noticed the gold-brown eyes burned too bright. Like someone with a never-ending fever.

Alice walked down the sunlit hallway to the staircase. The way was familiar to her by now, but she was certain its beauty never would be. Though the house wasn't overlarge, it was laid out in perfect symmetry. Each room flowed into the other and everywhere was light. The hallway smelled of beeswax. It smelled of roses too, opened big as plates in a porcelain vase on a side table. Delicate furniture and soft rugs. When she'd first peeked into the front parlor she'd seen a pretty little piano, looked like a gilded toy, and birds she couldn't put a name to. They were so lifelike she wondered if they'd fly off if released from their glass domes. Dainty china people danced beneath the branches of a silver candelabra. Everything was sunny. Everything shined bright.

She stepped up the first carpeted riser of the elegant staircase with its gleaming handrail and ornately carved balusters. She ran a finger over the French silk wallpaper. She forgot she wanted to throttle Bledsoe. Instead she pretended this was where they lived. She in a shimmering satin gown. He in an elegant suit with a waistcoat fancier than that man Aubrey had ever dreamed of. She smiled to herself as Bledsoe bowed over her silk-gloved hand.

"Hold up."

Alice stumbled on the stair and grabbed the handrail. She turned to see Jenny holding a tray at the bottom of the staircase. "Take this on up to Cap'n, won't you? I gots the wobble legs today."

Alice came down and took the tray from Jenny. On it sat a dish with a silver cover. The handle was shaped like a twig.

"My bone broth." Jenny was missing a front tooth, but it didn't stop her from smiling. Alice couldn't help smiling back. Jenny had been nice to her. She carried the tray to the upstairs landing. The smell of the rich broth filled the air. Alice was tempted to lift the lid by its silver twig and sneak a taste but decided not to risk it. The doctor was a nosy piece of work, popping up when she least expected him. The first time she'd seen him had been when she'd dared to step inside the wondrous parlor downstairs. There she'd spied a funny little creature, big round eyes and a long wrapping tail. She'd picked it up off the mantel to look closer at its comical face.

"Put that down!"

Startled, she'd almost dropped the figurine. "What is it?" she'd asked the elegantly dressed man in the doorway.

"If you break it I'm sure you'll be sorry."

"I wasn't gonna break it. I jist wondered what kinda critter it was."

"A monkey. Put it down."

Alice set the creature back on the mantel carefully, her face on fire. "I was jist lookin'," she'd murmured. The doctor had eyed her coldly and followed her out of the room. *Make sure I don't steal no monkeys, I guess, damn his sneakin' eyes.*

He came every afternoon to tend the captain. Or untend him, in Alice's opinion. Today, with the tray in her hands outside the bedroom, Alice heard him telling the captain the latest war news. The doctor had acted sorry that he couldn't have been there at Manassas to give them Yanks what for, like the captain had. That was what he said, and acted all sorrowful and all. Oh, but he was the sole provider for his poor sickly mother.

And the doctor's news, no matter how happy, always came with a spoonful of gloom. Right now she heard him saying, "Susanna Whealful has had a baby boy. It is fine and healthy. A pity her husband may never live to see it. But I envy Jonah Whealful, I do." The doctor sighed dramatically. "Would that I were free to die for my country."

But dyin' for your country might muss up your clothes.

The doctor combed his hair with so much Macassar oil it looked glued to his skull. He waxed his great mustache so stiff it could be carved from wood. As Alice walked in with the tray she noted he was again gussied up like he was going to a ball, although it was only eleven o'clock in the morning.

He was scowling at Alice's latest poultice. He hated her and she knew it. He didn't want her there, but Captain Brennan insisted. "I'd be in my grave if it weren't for her, Francis."

"It's a miracle you are not," replied the doctor crossly, peeling away the bandages. "What is this filthy stuff? My God. Is this mud?" he sputtered. "Weeds?"

"Coneflower and slippery elm mixed in. Cleans the hurt. Gits out the pus and shuts the wound."

"What? You would clean a wound with dirt? Are you mad? And the suppuration from the wound is a positive reaction; the corruptive discharge must be allowed to flow." The doctor turned his back to her and bent to his patient, suddenly sneezing right in the captain's face. "I beg your pardon, Tom. These pestilential weeds she's smeared you with make my nose itch."

He pulled a handkerchief from his pocket, blew into it, then folded it once and wiped away the rest of Alice's poultice.

"You ought not do that," said Alice. "Blowin' like that around the sick is bad luck."

The doctor ignored her and unwound the bandage. Something clattered to the floor. "And what in heaven's name is this?" asked the doctor, picking up a gleaming button.

"Keeps his heart safe," muttered Alice from the far end of the bed. "I spelled it."

"What? Slave nonsense now? For God's sake, girl, the metal will cause the wound to fester far worse. Tom, this is beyond the pale. Please keep her out of your room." The doctor tossed the button to the floor.

"It ain't dark work," replied Alice, striving to keep her voice even. "You close a wound with somethin' you love. Captain loves his Rebel army. You best put that back when you wrap him up."

From the bed the captain tried to suppress a laugh but failed. The doctor turned away from Alice. "For heaven's sake, Tom, it's barbaric."

Captain Brennan, pale as milkweed, smiled up at the doctor from his pillow. "Come now, Francis. Birdy is right. I'm fond of those buttons. Tizzy had them made special for me. And truth be told, I am feeling somewhat better this morning."

The doctor threw his hands up in the air. "I cannot be held responsible if you continue allowing this absurd hocus-pocus."

"What hocus-pocus?"

Alice and the doctor turned to Tirzah Brennan, who stood in the doorway dainty as a doll. Her gold-brown hair matching her gold-brown eyes was done up in the back and fell in ringlets in front of her ears, framing her pretty face. "What hocus-pocus?" she asked again, the silk of her black skirt rustling as she passed Alice at the end of the bed. She went to her husband's side and gently took his hand.

"Birdy put one of my cavalry buttons inside my bandage, my love." He smiled up at her. "Those buttons you had made for me."

"Why on earth did you do such a thing?" The captain's wife stared at Alice.

"Help his heart," mumbled Alice.

Tirzah Brennan bent to her husband. "Darling, you must listen to Dr. Lang. Is he feverish, Doctor? You"—she glared at Alice—"you get out of here."

Alice shrugged and started for the door.

"Sweetheart, I'm not feverish. Stay here, Birdy. What difference does it make? It's not a bad idea to have what you love near your heart." He grinned. "I wish I could wrap you up in this bandage."

"Tommy, stop it. It is not funny. You have to listen to Dr. Lang." She turned angrily to Alice. "Stay away from my husband."

"But, darling," said the captain. "Don't you understand? Birdy saved my life."

"She's going to turn his wound gangrenous," warned the doctor. "It will be her fault entirely should that happen."

Alice had her hand on the doorknob.

"Stay, Birdy."

Tirzah Brennan sucked in her breath. Alice could see her face twist, caught between humoring her wounded husband and hating her. The captain took his wife's hand and kissed it tenderly. "You wrote me we lost that house gal I got for you before I left. Give Birdy a chance, sweetheart. If only to make me happy."

"I don't want her. And we did not *lose* Bertina, Tommy. She ran off."

"Tizzy," said the captain, his voice firm. "It is my wish that you keep Birdy."

Alice opened her mouth to say, "Nobody gonna keep me," but just then Captain Brennan said, "I'm dying, aren't I, Francis? Don't honeycoat it."

Alice closed her mouth.

Dr. Lang sank down on a chair beside the bed. "It is in the tissue near your vital organs, Tom. An attempt to remove it would be disastrous, I'm afraid."

Tirzah turned to the doctor, eyes full of tears. "There must be something you can do. There must be."

"All we may hope for is that anomalous tissue might grow around the bullet and keep it from moving into an organ. I have read of it." The doctor began to repack his bag. "However," he added in a tone full of doom, "that was an exceptionally rare case."

"Remember that little nigger over on the Chaffin place?" said the captain. "He swallowed a fishhook and everybody said he'd be dead by morning. But isn't that boy still alive? Twelve years ago that was. Just think, Tizzy. I'll be that old man down the road that no amount of Yankee lead could kill."

The doctor nodded gloomily. "Well, that's the spirit, Tom. I will be back tomorrow with silver nitrate to paint the wound. In the meanwhile, here is a tonic he is to take every two hours. Also these blue pills for pain." He glared at Alice. "Administered by anyone but her."

Tirzah turned to Alice ready to send her away, but the captain tugged Tirzah's hand. "See Francis out, Tizzy honey. And what was that new book you wrote me about? The one you liked so much."

"Book, Tommy? Well, heavens, let me think." She smoothed the damp hair off his forehead. "I think you must mean *A Tale of Two Cities*."

"That's it. Two cities. Perhaps you'd read to me later?"

"Of course, my love, of course." She kissed his forehead.

"I'd like Birdy to stay for a moment. You and Francis go on now."

Tirzah glanced at Alice angrily but then appeared to compose herself for her husband's sake. "I'm not sure I understand, but very well. Do not tire yourself, Tommy." Alice ducked her head as if avoiding a blow when Tirzah rustled haughtily past her to the door. "I will be back soon." Alice heard the doctor's melancholy drone follow the captain's wife down the staircase.

"Close the door, will you, Birdy? I'd rather Tizzy doesn't hear what I need to tell you."

Alice hesitated a moment, then did as he asked. The bedroom seemed suddenly smothered in silence. In the great four-post bed the captain closed his eyes. She wondered if he'd fallen asleep. Alice stood motionless. She knew the captain's wife would be furious if she met a closed door. She strained to hear the sound of her small boots on the staircase, but there was nothing. Under the lemony eau de cologne that Tirzah sprayed each time she came in was the scent of a body gone wrong—blood circulating sluggishly, vessels constricting, cells colliding. Sunbeams floated soundlessly in a golden arc above the polished floorboards. She realized her right foot was asleep and tentatively tapped it on the floor. And then a small gold clock on the mantel chimed. The captain coughed, wheezed, and held a hand to his chest. Alice quickly went to his side and held a cloth to his lips.

He coughed dryly into it and waved the cloth away. "Argh. That's all right. I'm all right now. Listen to me. Be patient with Tizzy, Birdy. She lost her beloved child, her *only* child." He paused, tears pooled in his eyes. Alice held a hand out at that moment to him. He took it between his own. They were dry as winter leaves. He ignored the tears and let them fall. "Just this past year," he continued, "she lost, *we both*. Birdy, she needs someone with patience. To take care of her."

He closed his eyes. She thought once more he'd fallen asleep, but he opened them again. He shook his head and dropped Alice's hand. "Her family doesn't speak to her. Her father. Because of me, Birdy. She thwarted him and married me. She could have had her pick. Well, you can see why, of course. She's so beautiful. And talented too. I was a poor man compared to the others. High Hope." He laughed quick and sharp, plucked a down feather from the coverlet. Held it in his palm. "High Hope," he repeated.

He pursed his lips and blew on the feather. It drifted a couple of inches and fell to the floor. He looked at Alice intently. "Listen," he said, "you know how to do things. I know you do. I've watched you. You don't rattle easy. You're quick-witted. You're brave too. You're not afraid of much, are you? Remember when you told me that you could swim? My little girl couldn't swim and Tizzy can't either. I doubt she'd even know how to fry an egg, though she can certainly embroider a handkerchief like all get-out. Hell. Pardon me, Birdy, Tizzy doesn't know how to do *anything* practical except sew and you can't eat that.

"I worry . . . well, before I left to join the army, I had to make some arrangements. It may come out right if. Well. Never mind that." He paused and looked out the window. "But if not . . ." He looked back at Alice and smiled, sudden and wide. "Enough of this. Right? Just tell me you'll help her if I'm soon gone."

Even though she knew he was in a bad way, she still believed he'd pull through. He was such a big, handsome man. Except for being so pale the freckles on his skin had popped out bright, you'd hardly know he had a bullet in him. She pursed her lips disapprovingly. "Now that's just plain foolish. Talkin' like you're goin' somewheres when you're right here in this room talkin' to me. You act like you was marchin' to the cross like Jesus."

His face brightened. Or else it was the sun washing across it just then. The red hair gleamed with threads of gold, he smiled, his eyes danced. "You're right, gal. You're right, goddammit—pardon my French—I have surely fallen into a deep well of pity. Here I am boohooing like no tomorrow. Thank you, Birdy. You don't let things get you down, do you? If I were captain of myself, I'd have me shot. Indeed, maybe High Hope will just once, *once*, live up to its name and me with it."

He motioned Alice closer. She leaned down as he whispered, "Later I want you to put that button back in my dressing. Did you see ol' Francis's face?" The captain laughed.

"Don't worry 'bout buttons right now. You need to rest up." She tucked the quilt under his chin. "Jist rest. Close your eyes."

"Oh, now don't baby me. I'm not tired."

"Close them," commanded Alice. "Or I'll go git the doctor 'fore he leaves."

"All right," he grumbled. "Maybe for a minute or two." He turned to her. "But tell Tizzy to come read me that book when you go downstairs." With a sigh he closed his eyes.

She set the brass button softly on the bedside table. Alice was certain Tirzah Brennan would do everything in her power to keep her away from the captain from now on. She was sorry about it.

FIFTY

Alice sat on a low stool shelling peas with Jenny in the kitchen.

"Look out there now."

Alice looked out the doorway of the brick kitchen. The big room smelled of roasting ham and apples. There was a colored man currying the captain's big bay.

"That's my boy there. That's Hush. Cap'n put his name in the book as Robert, but I called him Hush, for he was such a quiet chile. Never cried. Never. He do all round High Hope, build things, drive the rig, butcher stock. He good at all. He's a good boy, he is, less he git round that Boaz and git to the mash."

Jenny was telling Alice about High Hope. There was Gracy, Arlund, and Lilly. They were mother, father, and daughter. They mostly worked in the fields. Boaz was the other hand, though he didn't do much besides eat and get drunk nowadays, according to Jenny. He was seventy or so. He mostly kept out of Miss Tizzy's sight as much as possible.

"We's all that's left. There was a gal that Cap'n give for Christmas to Miss Tizzy 'fore he join the army. She been trained to do hair down in Charleston. She run off at Easter time."

Jenny, Hush, and Boaz had belonged to the old master, she told Alice. His name was Hugh Brennan.

Alice shook the shucked peas from her skirt into the half-full pail. "And your husband? Hush's daddy? He belong to High Hope too?"

"He was sold 'fore Hush knowed him. He came in the spring, he was gone in the fall. Ol' Marster Hugh selled him to pay some kinda debt what he had. Hugh Brennan didn't have much 'cept what he lost. De specalator come and collected him." Jenny shook her head as she shelled peas. They sprayed into a tin bucket between her feet, pinging the sides like buckshot. "We ain't never had none of that kind round here afore dat. Got all dem poor niggers coffled up to sell like cattle. Afore we was kept away from such darkness by Ol' Missus. She took us to church, you know. But after she died? Oh, honey. It got bad.

"His name was Bill. Hush's daddy. He been gone, less see? Thirty years? He dead long time, I 'spect. Down south they die young."

"I'm sorry," said Alice softly.

Jenny wiped her hands on her apron. "I cried one time. Don't cry no more. Nothin' grow from salt. Cap'n ain't like his daddy. He a good 'un. What 'bout you? He bring you from the army, but where you from?"

Alice ducked her head to the peas. "North a ways," she mumbled. For a moment the only sound was the scratch of fingernails scraping the peas from the fleshy pods, the ding-ding as they bounced off the tin. "Baltimore."

"Balimore? Oh, that's how come you sound like you do." They were quiet for a while. It was peaceful in the kitchen. A yellow tabby wound itself around Jenny's ankles and she reached down to rub its head. "I know you gots your man out in the cabin there."

Alice looked up, eyes wild. That was right, Jenny knew. What if she told her mistress?

"You keep him outta Missy's way. She ain't seen him and I don't think she knows 'bout him yet, else she'd'a bin out there, look him up and down, figurin' his worth and all. Miss Tizzy? I'm'a warn you. You never know which way dat cat gonna jump."

"When the captain's better, he's gonna let us go," said Alice.

Jenny looked at her surprised. The yellow cat jumped up on the table behind her and began licking its paw. Alice looked down at the pile of peas in her lap. "Captain'll let us go. I know it."

"Free you? He say that?" replied Jenny skeptically. "He ain't never freed no one afore."

"We belong to the army," replied Alice. "Not him. That's how come."

"Well, mebbe that's so, but I'm'a gonna tell you right now that Miss Tizzy ain't gonna let no property walk off this place without bein' paid for. So you keep him outta her sight. You too, much as you can. Now here." Jenny got up and cut a big slice of bread, which she spread liberally with butter and sprinkled with sugar. "You take that to you man. Go on then."

As Alice walked into the slave quarters, the sun was hunkering low over the fields. The August corn was higher than a man. The tassels shimmered in the evening's last glow. Katydids had started their long-legged hum. The air smelled like sweet manure and Tirzah Brennan's big-headed roses that bloomed in late summer profusion.

Bledsoe was asleep on the pallet. She studied him, one arm outflung, the other cradled to his chest in the sling she'd made for him. Earlier she'd told herself she wouldn't care if she never saw him again. But even at that very moment she knew it was a lie. Why did he have this hold over her? What was it? She looked at his face asleep, all the anger and hurt erased. "Damn it, Bled," she whispered. "I don't know why because you treat me so cruel, but if'n they was to try to take you away like that they took Jenny's man, I'd fight 'em. I reckon they'd hafta kill me."

If he was aware of her, there was no sign. She pulled off the heavy shoes and curled up next to his back. She closed her eyes and inhaled him. She was dripping down into a warm dream when there came such a sound it froze her stiff. Bledsoe sat up. The keening didn't stop and Alice ran outside. The others were standing out front of their cabins looking toward what they called the Big House, though it wasn't very. The keen turned to a howl. It was a sound no human being should make. She knew then she'd never have a chance to put the button next to the captain's heart.

FIFTY-ONE

The funeral was three days later. The captain was buried in the small family graveyard surrounded by a stand of silver maples. There was an iron fence closing off the burial ground. On the ironwork above the gate was painted a red hand. That, Jenny told Alice, was a sign of the Brennan family. Jenny said the captain's family was Irish.

Like me.

Our Katie was young like you . . . fell into the river . . . can you swim, Birdy?

A preacher opened the gate and four men carried the polished wood coffin. The brass handles glinted in the sun. All the men were older. Too old to go to war. Tirzah followed the coffin through the gate. Draped in a black veil, she was a ground-bound cloud of darkness. Other mourners had come from neighboring plantations, ladies dressed in sorrow colors, men in black with high hats.

The slaves had followed the procession but stopped at the gate. Only the white people were allowed inside for the service. But Hush, Arlund, and old Boaz stood right up against the curlicued iron fence where they could hear the preacher. Jenny, Gracy, and Lilly stood behind them. Jenny wore a straw bonnet she'd woven through with black ribbon. She had dyed her homespun dress from gray to black with walnut hulls.

Alice stood off to one side where she had a clear view of the proceedings. Anyone who died in the Dismal just got a grave dug, maybe with other family members, maybe all alone. Many times the hole started to fill with water before you could even get the box with the body down in it. Sometimes the coffin floated right back up to the surface by the morning. Folks knew their loved ones would eventually be sucked into the swamp but they did their best to not dwell on it. Most did their best to remember a patch of Bible verse or just sang some church-type songs—and hoped for the best.

Now Alice watched the ladies behind the little cloud of black. Their gowns ranged in tones from the purple of a bloomed iris to charcoal. They had silk and satin bonnets to match. Three were older, one bent with arthritis. Another looked about the widow's age, still young, but with a face like a surprised fish, pucker mouthed and bug-eyed.

The preacher wore a long black robe and high white collar that held up his double chin. He had a big cross on a chain of gold and beads at his thick waist. Sweat glistened on his pink forehead but his voice was rich and mellifluous, though Alice understood scarcely a word. *"Judica me Deus, et discerne causam meam de gente non sancta: ab homine iniquo."*

"The captain was a Catholic man," said Jenny. "They do things different."

Bless me, Father, for I have sinned. Holding her mother's hand. Singing. Kneeling on a stone floor. *It hurts! Hush a stór and fold your hands.* The smell of something too sweet. The preacher in a long dress with the same high collar. *I remember.*

Through her tears Alice watched the new widow drop a handful of earth into the hole where they'd lowered the coffin. Then the rest did the same. Tirzah Brennan took a red rose from a rush basket. It was perfect, full bloomed; the fragrance floated even to Alice. She dropped it down into the grave and turned away. Everyone had long sad faces. The fish-faced lady helped Tirzah toward the graveyard gate.

As the white mourners filed past, Jenny began slowly, rhythmically clapping. Stomping her feet to the beat of her hands. Boaz joined in. Then the other slaves. Boaz lifted up his gray head: *"Hark from de toom a doleful sound, my ears tend the cry, great God, is this our doom?"*

His voice rang across the fields. Jenny's voice rose above his in a clear soprano. The other slaves kept time with hand claps and foot stomps as the white mourners proceeded slowly back to the house, the new widow leaning heavy on the long-dressed preacher's arm.

Alice didn't sing. She didn't know the song. But she bowed her head to the earth, so mournful was the dirge that she couldn't hold it upright.

Just a while ago there he was, Captain Thomas Brennan with his rich red hair, buttons shining, on that fine bay. Now, whoosh! Down in a hole six feet deep and she would never see him again. Never. No one would unless he returned in spirit. The red hair would fade, skin sag, and things would feed on it. All would be bones. Click-clack. She wiped her eyes with the heels of her hands, rubbing hard to make colors flare behind her eyelids. To see. To feel. *Woe. Why do we live only to die? He was Irish. Just like me.*

Slowly she made her way back toward High Hope, sorrowfully dragging her feet through the high, hot grass. She'd forgotten that the captain never knew she was Irish. She'd forgotten he'd died thinking she was his slave.

FIFTY-TWO

The fever was gone, but when Bledsoe took his arm out of the sling it hung limply at his side. He tried to clench his fist and could barely move his fingers. He sank down on the pallet. In the distance he heard the singing from the graveyard. Though he had only the slightest feverish memory of seeing him on the boat from Richmond, he hated the captain. Hated him just as much dead as alive. Now he hated the slaves out there dirging for him, the mournful singing, hand-clapping and stomping. Walking Egypt, it was called. He'd heard the pounding of the feet and rhythmic clapping sometimes at Our Joy when a slave had died. *That's how they git funeralized,* Reecie had told him when he was small. *Like de Israelites outta Egypt.* He glared scornfully in the direction of the sounds of mourning. *The Israelites didn't Walk Egypt for Pharaoh, but you do it for a man who died to keep you slaves.*

His wound throbbed. She'd left some sort of muddy paste to rub on it if it hurt. He dumped it in the slop pail. From the moment he set eyes on her all he'd done was run and all she'd done was ruin.

He stood in the doorway. The sun was high and hot. It was about noon, he figured. Sweat dripped off him no matter how still he stood.

But for the distant singing, the only sound was the cluck of chickens and the high-up shrill of a hawk. The sun hammered his bare head. He raised his good hand and shielded his eyes. The corn was high enough to hide in and beyond were woods. What lay beyond he had no idea. But whatever it was wasn't here.

He grunted, struggling to pull on the homespun shirt Alice had brought him the day before. The sling got in the way. He wrestled with it and gave up on fastening the shirt, just let it hang open. He had on clean homespun pants. No shoes, but he'd gotten used to it. Last night Alice had sponged him off every place he'd let her. He only let her because he smelled so bad he couldn't stand it himself.

She'd prattled to him as she gently rubbed him with a rag as if he were a helpless baby. He wanted to stop her mouth with the cake of stinging soap, but instead he sat still and sullen. The sound of her voice in his head, singsong, bird bright. He wouldn't listen, wouldn't care. *Get out of my head,* he said to himself.

There was some leftover corn bread she had brought him that morning, some fatty meat. He wrapped these in a kerchief with his good hand. She'd told him it would take time for his arm to heal. The bullet had cut through nerves, but treated right, it would mend. She'd said to bide the time, the little woman in black he'd seen in the distance didn't seem to know of his existence. Bide time? He stuffed the little bundle of food into the sling that held his arm. He knew it would be difficult running with only one arm. He couldn't climb a tree or easily forage for food. But somehow he'd manage. And if he didn't? It was better than being here. *Biding time.* They were all distracted now. It was the perfect opportunity and he'd be a fool to miss it.

"Come in de kitchen and hep me out, Birdy."

He darted inside and peeked out the slat in the wall they called a window. The cook and Alice were walking right past. Alice caught him before he could duck down.

"All right," she said, nodding to Bledsoe.

He let out an aggrieved sigh and slammed his good hand against the cabin wall. Which hurt. So he kicked the little chair over. Then pulled the bundle of food out of his sling and threw it on the floor.

"Ho there, boy. I come sit a spell while your woman gone."

Bledsoe gave the old man a look that would have stopped most in their tracks but didn't do a thing to the black man with hair like popcorn. He walked past Bledsoe, picked up the overturned chair, and sat himself down. He took in the crumbled corn bread, the greasy meat on the floor. "Guess you figured out youself now ain't a good time to be takin' a walk nowhere. Never mind patterollers whippin' you hide when ketch you.

"Now, one of them come to funerlize Cap'n up at the house is a friend of Miss Tizzy. That be Mr. Hale Talbot. Hale Talbot the meanest man on the south neck and he don't go nowhere widout Black Shuck. That his nigger dog. That boar hound kin track a man to the moon. He et a boy's leg half off when they ketch him runnin'. Tole him to hole still and cover his privates, but he try to git away and Black Shuck go to work. Hale Talbot love that dog most when he ketch a nigger."

The old man leaned back on the rickety chair. "Lemme tell you a little story. When Black Shuck's daddy die, Hale Talbot make his slaves dig a grave and gib his dog a funeral. He tell 'em they better moan and carry on or he'll whip 'em good. So they cried they eyes out over that dog what ketch and bite 'em, and *that* dog weren't half as bad as this here Black Shuck." Boaz held out a brown glass bottle. "Here you go. Hep youself."

Bledsoe sank down on the lumpy pallet. Boaz bent down and retrieved a piece of corn bread and popped it in his mouth. The next time he held out the bottle, Bledsoe took it.

FIFTY-THREE

Alice placed the fresh rhubarb pie and the cakes, one a sponge and the other a raisin cinnamon iced with sweet butter, on crystal platters. She carried porcelain plates rimmed with gold for Jenny to serve the widow's guests.

"You pour for the wimins," instructed Jenny, carrying pie and cakes as Alice followed her into the parlor. "They gits sherry off de sideboard in de tiny glasses. You hand it round on de tray to all de ladies. Watch Miz Tibbins, though, that the ol' skin and bones out dere. She li'ble to drink it all up and we ain't got no more sherry."

What sounded like a squirrel chattering in the parlor turned out to be the fish-faced woman apparently trying to console the widow. Jenny nodded toward a crystal decanter and the smallest glasses Alice had ever seen on a silver tray. A scrawny old woman about drowned in her hoop-skirted dress stared at Alice's scar a moment before she snatched one of the glasses off the tray. The woman had a chin so sharp you could slice a ham with it. She finished her sherry before Alice had served the rest of the ladies, the widow and the fish-faced woman demurring.

"Girl," hissed the old woman, holding out the doll-sized glass to be refilled. Alice noted her hand was shaking. She filled the little glass to the brim. The woman immediately put it to her lips and drank it down. Alice refilled it a third time, then moved away.

The men were gathered around the fireplace on the far side of the room where they had been murmuring quietly.

"I will have a drink now," said the widow. Alice started toward her with the tray, but the widow held up her hand. "Not that. Bring me a whiskey."

One of the men stood alone. "Come here, girl. Fetch your mistress a drink." He was a very tall man but so thin as to be nearly emaciated. His wrists protruding from the white shirt cuffs were big bony knobs and his Adam's apple bobbed up and down when he spoke like a ball on a string. From across the room he looked no more than forty, but when she got closer, Alice saw he was much older. Sixty, maybe seventy. His hair was still black as pitch, but his face was webbed with myriad wrinkles. The back of his hand as he handed her a glass filled with amber liquid was mottled with liver spots. His eyes were slightly uptilted at the ends, almost slanted, and were so black you couldn't find the pupils. "Look at that," he said, staring at her. He took her chin and tilted her face this way and that. "Melpomene and Thalia all in one. What happened to you, gal?"

"Leave her be, Hale," said the widow across the room. He smiled. His eyes didn't. He dropped his hand. The room had fallen silent. Alice felt all eyes trained on her, felt they were waiting for something. She stood frozen in front of the tall, thin man.

"She's new. Where'd she come from, Tirzah?" said Hale Talbot.

"Bring that drink over here, girl," commanded the widow.

The whiskey in the glass sloshed as Alice walked across the parlor.

"Tommy brought her home from the war."

Alice handed the glass to the little woman in black.

"Brought her back from the war, did he? Gal this young, this bright? How 'bout that, fellas?" He grinned at the men.

No one responded. "Ha," laughed Hale Talbot, and he poured himself another whiskey.

One of the men by the fireplace turned his back on Talbot. He said in a too-loud voice, "How's that new colt coming along for you, Lowell?" A second or two passed and then the others took it up, talking of horses, weather, and types of corn blight. Standing by himself, Hale Talbot let out another short barky laugh and finished his drink in one swallow.

The ladies leaned forward in their lyre-back parlor chairs toward the widow. An old woman in eggplant purple said, "The Lord must hold you precious, my dear, for he has heaped the trials of Job upon you. Ah, the sorrows of this world. My niece lost her precious oldest boy, Abel Thompson, at Hoke's Run in July. Only eighteen and the most tragic part is, it wasn't even in battle. Tripped and fell down a well. They didn't find him for two weeks! Can you imagine? My poor niece went half mad when they brought back what was left of him, and it wasn't much between the heat and the water in that well. Fact is, they said it was more like pouring jelly into that poor boy's casket, so, my dear, at least you know the Lord took Captain Brennan as a battlefield hero. You had him back whole and in one piece and can look forward to seeing him in Glory one day."

The widow's veil was thrown back from her face. Her skin was so pale you could see the blue veins pulsing beneath her eyes. She sat sunken in her chair like a pile of black laundry, one small hand wrapped around the glass of whiskey. "God is a bastard," she said, tipping back the glass and swallowing deep.

After ten seconds or so, a chair creaked and Hale Talbot began to laugh. As if pulled on strings by the same puppeteer, the ladies rose in unison from the delicate chairs. "Why, Loren, I do believe it's time we got on home," said the woman who knew so much about the trials of Job. "Mrs. Brennan needs to rest." The fish-faced lady bent and mumbled sorrowful things to the seated widow, who ignored her and finished the contents of the glass.

"Dear, dear," mumbled Miss Tibbins, snatching a last little glass of sherry off the tray on the sideboard while Jenny rushed about to gather the ladies' wraps. The men were meekly herded out the front door by their womenfolk. Within five minutes they were all gone, except Hale Talbot. "Now, let's you and me talk turkey, Tirzah. You two can get out."

Alice felt those strange eyes on her back as she followed Jenny out of the parlor.

"And close the door," ordered Talbot.

FIFTY-FOUR

In the hot kitchen, Jenny stirred up a breeze with a goose feather fan. They each had a slice of Jenny's stone fruit pie. "That Hale Talbot sniffin' round and Cap'n ain't cold yet. Wonder what he want? Miss Tizzy hate him. I know that for a fact. That ol' fool, Miz Keffington, goin' on 'bout Job. What she know 'bout trouble? Missy loss her only chile a year ago and now her man. But don't feel too sorry." She nodded to Alice. "From Georgia. I tell you what. She brung a chile to High Hope, scarce six years or so, to run and fetch for her. That poor boy had scars back of his legs where he been cut with a tree switch if he don't run fast enough to please her." Jenny pointed at a shelf. "Fetch me some my med'cine there."

Alice handed down a small stoneware jug. Jenny pulled the cork and took a long swallow, pulling a face. "Law, it burn, but help my rhumatiz. The boy tole how it was down in Georgia. Place called Brightland. Go for miles and miles. Had more'n two hundred slaves. Cotton and rice, just grand. They whip all the time down south, you know, not for nothin', jist to keep 'em in line, 'fraid they might rise up, and when Missy come here to High Hope, she thought it the same, like sumpin' you do same as eat your supper. But Cap'n broke that tree switch over his knee. He tell her his slaves mind him 'cause he treats 'em right. His people go to church every Sunday.

"Miss Tizzy yell at him niggers oughtn't go to church for they ain't got no souls and they need whippin' or they won't mind." She took a deep pull off the stoneware jug. "I heard it all, see, 'cause I was dustin' in the front parlor. Well, Missy stomped aound the house after that, hit me with the hairbrush, broom handle, whatever she lay her mean hands on whenever she could git away with it. But then Miss Katie was born. Sweet as sugar that dollbaby was. Hair color of strawberries like her daddy. Miss Tizzy got near human then. But then she drown. Oh, it break my heart when they brung Miss Katie upta house drowned like that, her red hair like a put-out fire. Miss Tizzy lay down with her on the bed and wouldn't git up till they come put her in the box to bury her in three days after." Jenny sat silent for a moment and Alice did the same, figuring Jenny was mourning for the poor drowned redheaded Miss Katie.

"What ever happened to that little boy?" Alice asked after what she thought was a respectful enough pause. "He still round here?"

"Hmm?" Jenny took another swallow from her jug.

"That child she brung with her from Georgia?" asked Alice. "He still here?"

"Daid," she replied. "Daid as dust. Poor chile fell off the roof tryin' to git Miss Tizzy's Samese cat down off it. Cat was fine but the boy slipped, you see. Haid busted open on the lawn. Did that devil shed a tear? No. No she did not. Miss Tizzy say to Hush when that chile layin' there daid, 'Git that mess outta my sight.'

"He buried behind the barn over yonder. Hush did it. And I planted the rose called Galilee on top. He free to the Lawd now, bless him heart." Jenny blew her nose. "Riles me to think on it, but what the use?"

Alice shook her head. "Funny, ain't it? She looks so pretty and angel like. Guess that's how the Devil like to dress 'em up sometimes."

Jenny leaned to her. "Don't I know?" Then she said in a low voice with a glance first over her shoulder toward the house, "Now one them mens in there was the law fella. He read the will to Miss Tizzy. Figure she find herself rich, her 'heritin' High Hope and all us." She tipped the jug back again and held it out. "Here. Have you a nip. Don't worry none. I take care if she want somethin'. I 'spect she cry herself to sleep after that Hale Talbot leave. She take laud'num since Miss Katie die and sleep like she daid too. Go on, take a pull."

Alice took the jug. The sun slanted through the window, laying a dappled rug of light on the smooth floor. Flies buzzed in lazy circles. Chickens clucked and a dove called soft. The yellow tabby had curled up on Jenny's lap. Alice could hear it purring. She tipped the jug, figuring the alcohol would be harsh like the witch's home brew. But it was smooth, tasted like summer sunlight. She looked at Jenny with surprise.

The older woman laughed. "Good, ain't it? I make it from the sweetest peaches. What that you got round you neck?"

Alice put her hand to her breast and instinctively started to tuck the willow woman back inside her dress, but stopped and held it out for Jenny to inspect. Jenny bent to the carving that Alice kept tied to a long piece of string. Jenny squinted up at Alice. "A conjure woman up at the Mills' place do spell work if you gives her money. You know 'bout that?"

Alice tucked it inside her dress. "It ain't for no conjure work." Jenny looked at her carefully for a moment and Alice felt herself coloring up. "It's good luck," she said.

"Well. Have youself another pull then," said Jenny. "That's good luck too."

Alice drank deep. The liquor filled her with heat and comfort. At last the golden sun rug on the floor was gone. It was hot and stuffy in the dim kitchen. Her head felt funny. Had she been saying something? She couldn't remember. A tear rolled down her cheek and she brushed it away. She sniffled and another tear ran down her cheek. She wiped it away and self-consciously pulled her hair over her scar.

Jenny patted Alice's knee. "Whoever done that to you face gonna pay one day. Mebbe not in this world. Look at the time. That man ought to be gone by now." She stood and looked out the window of the kitchen. "Don't see his buggy no more." She sat back down a bit unsteadily. "What any of us doin' in this world? Law. It ain't gonna come round right till we gits to the next one. Have another pull, I will too, then you go on. I'm gonna rest a spell. Miss Tizzy crazy now with grief, but once she come round I reckon I ain't gonna git no rest till Jesus lets me."

It was late afternoon when Alice got back to the cabin. Lilly, Gracy and Arlund's daughter, was sitting on a stump in front of their cabin eating a roasted sweet potato. She was a big girl of about nineteen or twenty, her round face scarred bad from childhood measles. She stared at Alice with dull eyes and said nothing when Alice said hello. Jenny had told Alice that Lilly wasn't right. Though her body grew, her mind didn't. But she was strong and could do the work of two men in the field. Now Gracy, nearly wide as the doorway that framed her behind her daughter, nodded, but said nothing either.

That was fine with Alice. Her own mind didn't feel right. It was as if someone had poured a bucket of water over her brain. Thoughts sloshed around inside her skull, but she couldn't seem to fish a complete one out. She tripped over a rake someone had left and nearly fell.

That brandy was stronger than she'd figured. She'd never had much to drink before. Only a taste or two of the witch's brew and that was so nasty she'd spit most of it out. Everything looked wavy, too bright. She leaned against a tree and closed her eyes to keep the world from whirling. She was crying but she didn't know why. It was all she could do to pull herself through the door.

Inside smelled like sweat and dirt. No air came in the little window, but it was thankfully dim as twilight. Bledsoe wasn't there. She made her way to the lumpy pallet and sank down. Closed her eyes and clung to the narrow edges. *Oh my day, the earth is spinnin' round and round.* Her mind darted here and there like a bee drunk in a carpet of clover. Her mother held her hand. Her eyes gray as an Irish sky, hand chapped and rough holding her small one. She tossed and turned trying to pull the pictures in her mind clear: peat fire, rain on the window, cat stretching on the rug. But they faded and she was alone. There was nothing but a vast, rolling silver sea and she was sinking.

FIFTY-FIVE

After finishing the one bottle they'd moved to Boaz's cabin. He had a table and four mismatched chairs. His bed was covered in a bright patterned quilt. His wife had made it. She was long dead. He also had a guitar made of spruce. He was allowed to hire himself out for weddings and parties and the captain let him keep what money he made. That was why he had a few things, like the brass clock that ticked on a shelf. And the captain had given him the blue coat with the shell buttons he wore now, the good cut of the coat clashing somewhat with the ragged hem of his hemp trousers.

"He in Heaven now," announced Boaz in his gravel voice. They raised their glasses for the umpteenth time. Jenny's son had joined them. Hush was built opposite of his mother. He was tall and broad. They'd drunk from the first brown bottle until it was gone. Boaz had pulled out another. Now he played the guitar and sang, *"Five can't ketch me and ten can't hold me. Ho! Round the corn Sal-lee!"*

Bledsoe clapped along. He'd heard these songs at Our Joy but had never sung them. He wasn't allowed out in the quarter. Couldn't join in cornshuckings, holiday dances, weddings. He was *Prime House Boy*, not a field hand. But sometimes he'd sit in the dark back pantry, hams curing over his head, door propped open with a foot, listening to the music until somebody hollered for him and he had to run or get what for.

Now when Boaz sang, *"the Devil was a liar and a conjurer too; you must be pure and holy, you must be pure and holy, you must be pure and holy, or dat Devil conjure you,"* Bledsoe sang loudest. When they were worn out from singing, they drank some more. Then Hush leaned in toward them. "Time's a comin'. That man in there and all like him gonna git it."

Boaz lit a clay pipe and pointed it at Hush, nearly jabbing him in the eye with the stem. "That what you think?"

"Time's come at last," bellowed Hush, slamming the table with his palm. "You know it's true. God gonna smite. War!"

Boaz tipped back the amber-colored bottle. "This war? White man's war," he said, "ain't 'bout you, me, or this boy, Hawk, here. It 'bout the dollah in his pocket, and *me*, *you*, and *you* are silver dollahs, one and all. Money. That's all you is."

Bledsoe opened his mouth to say something, but the words blurred on his tongue so he just took another swallow from the bottle instead.

"What?" said Hush. "You shut it, ol' man; you just an ol' man, you don't know nothin'."

"Lincoln," said Bledsoe, or thought he did. He wiped his mouth with his shirttail. "Lincoln gonna."

Boaz looked at them across the table and shook his head. "Y'all ain't never been nowhere, have you? Well, I'll tell you. I been north and I been south and all them whites the same though they say you free. I seen how they do the colored man up there. Oh yes. I had a master once take me up to Conecktuk. Big ol' house, rooms and rooms. Colored gals workin' in the house just the same as down here. Said they ain't been paid for two years. Can't leave 'cause they starve if they do. Oh, and they was free, mind you. My master had business with the Quaker man owned that big house. And guess what? That business was cotton!

Ha-ha." Boaz sucked on his pipe and nodded. "That man? He come down real sick one night. They was way out in the country. All there was for miles was this one doctor. He was a colored doctor. But the man was sick? Northern man, mind you, Quaker man, mind you, wouldn't let that colored doctor touch him. No suh! White northern Quaker man rather be daid than have the colored doctor fix him up. Oh, that's free, ain't it! That's free, they say. Yet they don't do nothin' to keep a free man from bein' snatched away from his home and sold down south. They just smile and say, oh they free here. They gonna free you down here too? Free you the same? Free you to what?"

"Blood's gonna run," hollered Hush. "You a damn ol' fool."

"Shut your trap, boy. You want that woman come down here see what all the ruckus is 'bout?"

"She ain't comin' down here," said Hush. "She ain't been down here since Cap'n come home." But he said this in a whisper, looking over his shoulder.

Bledsoe's head was fuzzy. It felt as if fog had seeped in through one ear and gotten stuck in the middle of his head. "Connecticut," he pronounced slowly and distinctly. Boaz and Hush looked at Bledsoe wonderingly as he stood shakily. "One," he announced, holding a finger aloft. "One of the six New England, and one of the thirteen original states of the American Union. It is bounded north by Massachusetts about eighty-eight miles; east by Rhode Island, forty-five miles; south by Long Island Sound, one hundred miles; west by New York about eight miles in a direct line. The southwest corner projects along the sound under New York for about thirteen miles."

"What you talkin' 'bout?" asked Hush. "You crazy or what?"

"Nothin'," mumbled Bledsoe, sitting down hard in the chair. "Just Connecticut's all."

He was surprised a while later to find his head was lying on the table. He had no memory of how it got there. Boaz was talking and he heard parts of what Boaz said; in and out it went until it came to: "All them runs away go now down to Fort Monroe. Hundreds, thousand, Dick over at the Henry place tole me," said Boaz. "He knowed 'cause he heard his mistress talkin' 'bout it. That's where Yankees is at. They get to Fort Monroe and them Yankees got to take them. You gotta say contraband! Contraband the word, Dick said. Like magic it is. You say the word, then you with the Yankees. Course how you gonna git there? Army or patterollers gonna git you first."

Bledsoe unstuck his head from the table's surface. "Where's it at?"

"Fort Monroe? Downriver. End of the south neck. But you'd git shot to pieces 'fore you halfway." Boaz polished off the second bottle. "Now I'm gonna lie down a spell," he said. "Y'all git out."

"I'm gonna go," slurred Bledsoe, stumbling to his feet. He weaved his way out of the cabin. It was so simple. Just get down the river and you were free! "Conterband," he announced to nobody. *What's she gonna do if you leave?* He batted a rosebush. *I don't care, gotta go damn you.*

His bad arm flopped in the sling, but he waved his good one ahead toward the river. "Come on, lez go!" He fell down but it didn't hurt. He patted his face to see if his head was broken and laughed. Why? He didn't know. He rolled himself over onto his back. A star shot across the dark above. *"Angel flyin' cross the sky, free me to Jesus when I die,"* mumbled Bledsoe. "But I ain't comin', Jesus! You hear? I'm goin' to Fort Monno."

"Whatcha out here hollerin' for?"

A big black cloud had blocked the stars. Bledsoe sat himself up and tried to shove the cloud out of his line of sight. "Ah need to see tha sky."

"Best shut your drunken mouf afore Mistress hear you."

He was slowly realizing the cloud wasn't a cloud. It was the broad bulk of the woman called Gracy. He'd seen her heading off to the fields in the morning. A woman you did not want to mess with—broad as a man and all muscle. But right now he didn't care. "Go 'way," he said, struggling to his feet. "Ow!" he bellowed. He'd forgotten about his arm and it had fallen from the sling. He bent his head to tuck it back in. "Git outta my way, woman. I'm gettin' free, goin' conterband."

He began weaving his way around the house toward the river. "Move!" he commanded an oak tree. When it didn't, he finally staggered around it. He could see the water in the half-moon light. It was dark as blackstrap molasses, a rushing midnight road. He could smell its heat and sense its deeper cold. He zigzagged down the rise where cattails swayed like furry cigars in the hot night wind. Mud squeezed between his bare toes. Where was the boat? Wasn't there supposed to be a boat? He took another step and water rushed around his calves. Just before he took another, he was yanked out of the river.

"Well, you be free all right," said Gracy, "when you drowned." She turned him back toward the quarter. "This ain't how to do it." Gracy yanked him by the good arm up the rise toward High Hope. He wanted to fight her off, tried, but she just hauled him behind her. Dimly he realized she could likely snap him clean in two like a wishbone, so he gave up and followed to the cabin.

Inside he swayed a moment, looking down at Alice. The shape that was her on the pallet anyway. It was very dark. He felt sick and stuck his head out the front door. He retched and, groaning, fell backward onto the dirt floor. *I'm dying.* He turned his head and managed to focus on a bucket beside the doorway. He wormed his way toward it and scooped water with his good hand and dripped it on his face. *Water. Yankees.* That was it. He'd almost done it. Something happened. *That woman caught me. Damn her. Sleep a little, then I'll go. I'll go. I'll find a boat somewhere. Fort Monroe.*

He turned away from the shape on the pallet, wrestling with his suspenders. He couldn't get one down on account of the sling. He stubbed his toe on the table leg and cursed loudly. He could smell her perspiration. Like some evil perfume. He wanted to choke her. Everything in his blurred mind added up to her. The way he hated himself for being half his father made him hate the all of her. He reached out with his good hand and grabbed for her neck. But he was drunk and got her shoulder instead.

"Wassa matter?" she mumbled, reaching up for him. He groaned like something badly hurt. She sat up, groggy but awake, forgetting everything, only hearing pain in his voice. "Bledsoe? What's wrong?"

In the dark he could barely see her face, but it seemed when she touched him it burned.

"Is it your arm?"

He was on her then, thrashing. He wanted to hurt her until she screamed. He wanted to rake her eyes out. She pushed him off her. He rolled onto his side, back to her, and began to sob.

"Shhhh," said Alice. "Here now. Come here." She put her arms around him. He winced when she accidentally bumped his arm. "I'm sorry," she whispered. "It's all right. Come here." She rolled him over onto his back and he didn't resist. His arm hurt, head hurt, the world hurt.

"What you cryin' 'bout?" She pulled him up so his head lay on her breast. "Never mind," said Alice. "That's all right now. You drunk is all. I was too but I slept it off." She smoothed his forehead and wiped away his tears with her thumb. Gentle and soft. He didn't resist. He couldn't. He was glued to her by drink and some other thing he couldn't name. He felt her heartbeat under her shift against his cheek.

When he woke the sun wasn't up yet, but the light had gone that blue before dawn. She was on top of him, moving slow. "I'm jist like you, Bled," she whispered, leaning to his ear, her thick hair a black curtain. "'Member you said that to me on the boat when we got snatched from the Dismal? You said we're just alike, you and me. It's true. We belong to each other."

He was still swimming in a liquory soup. He didn't comprehend what she was saying, just felt her breath, heard puffs of sound. Her voice was a tide pulling him out to sea. She whispered something else and he answered though he didn't know what he said. The feel of her skin. A tiny light flickered in his brain, remembered something, just a wisp, a fragment. A memory floated—in—out. He was looking up at blue sky, lying on moss. Soft as a kitten baby skin, she'd called it. Something else she'd said. What was it? *. . . snatch 'em clean away . . . not lettin' a person ever go.*

"I'm yours and you're mine," she whispered in between night and day. "Don't you reckon we're good as married now?"

When daylight broke he thought his head would fall off. She brought him coddled eggs and milk. She smiled at him in such a way he couldn't help but smile back, though even his teeth hurt. But in a little while he looked around and saw where he was. *Got to get away from here. Got to go.*

"I love you," she said, her smile raining down on him. She looked into his eyes. "You ain't ever said it. How come you never say it?"

Bledsoe turned his head away. The window board was lifted and in the opening a butterfly had lighted and was pulsing its wings. He could smell the tissue-thin pages as he quickly leafed through the encyclopedia one afternoon. Outside he heard the drill of a woodpecker. Inside he heard the creak of the board beneath the Turkey carpet under his feet. The pages of the book smelled of decay and creeping mold from too many humid summers.

> *. . . Amongst those which belong to the period in question is Psyche, with a butterfly, which is placed on the left hand, and held by the wings with the right. This figure, which is intended as a personification of man's immaterial part, is considered as in almost every respect the most faultless and classical of Canova's works.*

Alice gently smacked his chest to get his attention. "Why don't you say it?"

"Say what?"

"Them words. I'd like to hear 'em jist once."

Why was it so hard? There was an ache in his center. *I'm scared.* It seemed his blood was beating, pulsing, like the wings of the butterfly inches away on the window board. Her head was bowed. She had covered her eyes with her hands. Her hair parted at the nape, revealing her neck before him. How white it was. The sun never saw that part of her. He felt a tear splash on the back of his hand. He lifted her face to his. He leaned to her. Her lips were slick and salted and he kissed them softly. "I love you, Alice Brown. There. I said it. So stop crying now."

"Oh!" she said, and her face burst with such light it was as if a new sun had been born inside her.

He found himself smiling wide at her joy. *What is this thing? What's wrong? Not wrong. Happy I'm happy. There. It's done.*

FIFTY-SIX

Tirzah Brennan hadn't come out on the back porch to ring the bell and assign chores. Something she'd done every single morning when the captain was away. The only ones who'd seen her since the funeral were Hush and Jenny. Hush when he'd been given a letter to take to Hale Talbot and Jenny, who brought her meals to her room.

"She ain't eat a speck. I fear she loss her mind," Jenny said to Alice, setting another untouched tray down on the kitchen table. "She worse than when Miss Katie die. Least then she smack you with the hairbrush now and then. Now 'pears she don't got the strength. Thought she'd come round by now. What we s'pose to do if her mind's gone? What happen to us? What we gonna do?"

Alice shook her head as Jenny went on, but secretly she was inventorying foodstuffs that could be packed up quick. There was a half loaf of bread. That half round of cheese. Jar of preserves.

Jenny went on. "Hush tell me up at the Wattle place a boy said big boats shoot their guns anytime they git wind of Yankees tryin' to come upriver. He tole Hush he hear his marse say the South is winnin' the war. Got camps all up and down the river to keep Yankees from gettin' to Richmond. That's where President Davis is hid at. Them soldiers up on there road marchin' and whistlin' and bangin' on drums? Don't look like Yankees gonna free us anytime soon."

Alice went, "Um-hum, I know." *There's pickles over in that crock; will she notice that sausage gone?* He said his arm had been tingling for a week, and yesterday he was able to pick up a spoon. Tonight was a new moon, which meant they could get downriver in darkness, he said. *Look, there's a whole jar of calf's foot jelly. Got to get that too.* When she asked him how far this Fort Monroe was, he couldn't say. But he was leaving tonight, with or without her. *Without me? You crazy?* She'd pulled his face to hers and kissed his lips. He'd kissed her back. *You won't really go without me? No. I won't leave you. He said that. He won't leave me.*

A bell began to clang. Such a racket. The sound made Alice jump up from her stool, dropping the potatoes from her lap. Jenny smoothed her spotless apron. "Lawd. Listen. There it is. There she go. She come round. We in for it now, damn her." Jenny hurried out of the kitchen.

Barely five minutes passed before she walked back in. Alice looked up from the potato she was peeling. Jenny gently took the knife from her hand. "Lawd, gal, fix that rag on you head and put on this here clean apron. She say she want *you*."

Alice stood in the doorway. Sunlight snuck around the edges of heavy brocade draperies. A mantel clock ticked over an empty fireplace. The ornately carved mahogany bed was unmade, linens and pillows tossed every which way. The bedroom smelled of burnt candlewicks and the rotted stems of the drooping lilies on a marble table. It also smelled of sweat and sadness, as if tears and perspiration had soaked into the rugs. At first Alice thought the room was empty. It was so quiet. Then there was a papery sound like dead leaves underfoot. Her skin prickled.

"Close the door. Pearl, is it?"

Alice's tongue stuck to the roof of her mouth as Tirzah Brennan glided toward her like an orphaned shadow. She was still wearing the same lusterless black gown as well as the floor-length weeping veil. The veil covered her from head to toe and fluttered as she moved in her self-made breeze. She stopped midway across the room. Alice could barely make out her eyes through the gauzy fabric but knew they were studying her.

"Birdy." Inside her head it sounded like a squeak. Alice nervously licked her lips.

"Help me." The voice had the grate of a rusty saw. The little woman sat down, back to Alice, at a dressing table. The veil flowed from the crown of her head to the floor. "Light the candles, will you? I cannot bear daylight."

Alice closed the bedroom door softly and walked deeper into the gloom, her steps muffled by the thick rugs.

"There are matches on the mantel."

Alice lit a three-branched silver candelabra. The glow lit up a painting of a girl in a filmy dress running from something that looked half goat, half man above the fireplace.

"My head aches," murmured the widow, throwing the veil back over her shoulders. Her cheekbones jutted out too prominently. Alice swallowed nervously. Her palms were sweating.

The hollows under the widow's eyes looked smeared with black ash. "My head," she said. "You would think it would be my heart that hurts, yet it is my head."

She leaned both elbows on the dressing table and rubbed her paper-pale forehead with her little hands. "I will have a bath, Pearl, and then I will change into the bombazine and crêpe. It is in the press there." She closed her eyes and rubbed the swollen lids. "I have written to my father."

Alice stood where she had stopped in the middle of the room. Did the widow want her to ask about her father? What she had written to him about? But she said nothing further, so Alice went to the press and pulled it open. Black after black. Four, five. She could not tell one from the other. She turned to ask which one when the widow said, "I have been wondering if perhaps I am dead." Tirzah Brennan's waxy face atop the high-necked black gown seemed to float in the mirror. The gold-brown eyes that had burned too bright now stared blankly at her wavy reflection.

"You're jist worn out is all," said Alice softly. She didn't think she'd ever seen such a wasting away of a person. Sorrow seemed to be eating the poor woman from the inside out. She wanted to say something to comfort her, sitting there so small and fragile. She struggled to find something right. "Captain's with your little girl now. Jesus and the angels—"

"Take this veil off, please."

Alice closed her mouth and gently removed the combs that held the veil from the honey-brown hair, now unwashed and oily. The widow smelled. She was staring in the mirror but not at herself. Alice's face was reflected above her own. "Were you my husband's whore?"

It took a long moment to fully digest what the widow asked. "Oh Lord, no! The captain? He—"

The widow fluttered a pale hand, signaling Alice to stop. "Enough. I believe you. My husband was a saint, wasn't he? He was. Too good for this world. Too good for me." Her eyes that had been so dull suddenly flashed in the mirror. "That Hale Talbot is a bastard. He likes to poke at any weakness. Stick a finger in a sore. Rub salt. And he knows my pain all too well right now. All too . . . It is my head. I cannot stand it. Tommy said you were a good nurse. Have you anything for this ache?"

"I kin make you up somethin'," whispered Alice.

"I *was* dead, you know."

Alice glanced toward the closed door.

"My eyes were closed. But then I found I could open them and I was still here in this damned house. Look. Come here and look." Tirzah motioned Alice to stand behind her as she gazed in the mirror. "I am thirty-seven years old, thirty-eight come January. I only produced one child and that was a girl. A dead girl. I'm a childless widow. A *poor* widow." She let out a bitter laugh.

Alice backed away.

"I should have listened but I was in love, and now see?" Tirzah went on. "See? Oh, I see so well. I opened my eyes and see where I am. High Hope. Funny. I thought that was a sign. Foolish. What is love? Oh, how would you know? You people aren't capable and you know? You ought to be grateful. I'll tell you what it is. Shit. No." She shook her head. "No, not shit. *That's* something tangible. It's like faith, isn't it? You have to believe in it, like you have to believe there's someone up there in the clouds. *Believe.*"

She looked at herself in the mirror and was quiet a moment. She folded her hands and set them in her lap and looked at Alice calmly. "So here I am. My father has written back to me. I have made my bed, he says." She picked up the veil and ran it through her fingers. "Now, *you* will say I am not dead." She leaned over and covered the mirror with the veil. "But I ask you, Pearl. How can you be certain?"

Alice stood in the center of the room, afraid to breathe. "The Bible say, it say, don't it? All things pass, everything in its time."

The widow stood and pulled aside the heavy curtain. She sat down in a chair facing the window, looking out at the river. She began to brush her hair with a silver-backed hairbrush. "Go tell Jenny to heat my bathwater. Then bring it and fill my tub." She brushed her greasy brown hair harder and harder. "And I don't need your nigger platitudes. Get out."

FIFTY-SEVEN

Alice was emptying pails of dirty bathwater in the barnyard when the bell began to clang on the back porch again. The sound shattered the hot afternoon, made her want to climb out of her skin. Well, after tonight it wouldn't matter. They'd be gone. Over the cornfield two crows were harassing a young hawk, diving at it, wearing it down. The bell kept tolling as the hair on her arms prickled. *Something's happening, something wrong.*

She could see the back porch from where she stood in the barnyard. She looked toward the cabin where Bledsoe was impatiently waiting for darkness. There was no sign of him. The board was down over the window.

Alice watched as High Hope's few slaves gathered in a little knot below the back porch steps. She heard Arlund say, "We's all sorry, Miss Tizzy, for your loss." Gracy nodded her head. Lilly stood between Gracy and Arlund on her big bare feet, her muscular arms hanging at her sides.

"I called y'all here because I am going." She stopped.

"Where you goin', Mistress?" asked Jenny.

The little woman in black took a step backward on the porch. "I can no longer care for you."

"What you mean?" asked Jenny.

The slaves looked at one another and Hush asked, "Is you sick, Mistress? Can we help?"

All heads turned toward the sound on the gravel drive. From where she stood, Alice couldn't see why the slaves began to suddenly cry out or why Arlund pulled his wife and daughter behind him. A wagon, its big wheels creaking, appeared. The tall man in it was Hale Talbot. There was no mistaking that man even from where Alice stood. There was a powerfully built colored man beside him.

They both climbed down out of the wagon. Hale Talbot had a rifle. The colored man had a whip hooked to his wide belt. An enormous black dog jumped out of the wagon behind them and loped to Talbot's side. Alice had never seen a dog like that. Looked the size of a bear with a huge head. She heard Lilly cry out, "I'm scared, Daddy."

Alice pressed herself against the side of the barn, trying to blend into the shadow of the overhanging eaves. She looked in the direction of the cabin. *Don't come out, don't come out.* The widow's voice broke through the sultry heat of the late summer afternoon.

"Y'all belong to Mr. Talbot now," said the widow.

"What you mean, Mistress? Me and my boy were borned at High Hope. You can't mean it," said Jenny, falling to her knees. "You can't mean it! Cap'n wouldn't sell us for nothin'. You can't," she sobbed.

Beside his mother, Hush said, "Git up, Momma."

"Please, Mistress, we work twice as hard for you. Three times. We won't eat barely nothin'. What you do without us?"

"Git up, Momma."

Tirzah Brennan seemed to shrink even smaller in her widow's weeds. "I'm sorry."

Hale Talbot had hold of his big dog by the collar. "No use babytalking 'em, Tirzah, just riles 'em up. They'll keep on and on and only makes it harder to settle 'em down. You go on inside now and George and me'll handle it." He turned to the slaves. "Come on now and be good niggers, or I'll turn Shuck loose on y'all. Get in the wagon over here." He paused and looked around. "Wait up a moment. Where's that gal?"

The widow had just opened the back door. She turned to Talbot. "I decided to keep her."

"Oh no," said Hale Talbot. "Hell no, Tirzah. That won't do. I bought *all* your stock. You think I'd pay that much for this lot? Half so old they ain't even worth their own grease? I paid for prime and I'll have it."

"Look, Boss, yonder!" The big black man with the bullwhip pointed. "That gal! Over there by de barn, why, she's fixin' to run!"

When the bell rang for the second time that day he knew something was wrong. Whether announcing someone else was dead or the house was on fire, he couldn't tell, but he'd ducked down inside the cabin, heart racing. When he heard the slaves crying out he'd sidled cautiously toward the doorway, ready to bolt through the corn to the woods beyond. But at that moment he saw a huge black dog jump the barnyard fence, teeth bared. Then he saw her. She was pressed against the barn. "No!" he yelled.

He ran toward the barnyard just as Alice grabbed up a shovel and swung it at the dog's great head. It yelped and crashed to the dirt of the barnyard. She lifted the shovel high over her head. He heard the dog's skull crack.

By the time Hale Talbot climbed the fence, Alice was already over the other side and racing toward the river, her skirts hiked to her thighs. "Get her!" yelled Talbot, sighting Alice along the barrel of his rifle.

Bledsoe didn't hear himself, didn't even realize he'd opened his mouth. He screamed, *"Run, Alice!"*

Hale Talbot immediately swung the barrel to Bledsoe. "Bring me that bitch!" he shouted. "She killed my dog. You! Get down on your knees. Get down now!"

FIFTY-EIGHT

She jumped from the dock in front of High Hope and hit the green water with a loud smack. Her skirt immediately ballooned and tangled between her legs; the heavy shoes pulled her down. By the time Hale Talbot's slave driver got to the riverbank, Alice was already well past the dock. But not of her own volition. In the lazy Dismal she swam in pools warm as bathwater, the only ripple the one she made herself. And it wasn't so much swimming as keeping her head out of water the same way animals do. She knew how to float flat on her back, looking up at the fluttering cypress leaves and sugary clouds. But that was no use now, as she was frantically realizing. She struggled to kick off the thick-soled shoes, her cheeks holding on to her last gasp of air. The current was so swift it had already pulled her nearly a quarter mile downriver from High Hope.

Bledsoe didn't kneel, and the man cocked the rifle. By the time Hale Talbot was aware that Hush was right behind him it was too late. As

Talbot turned, the same shovel that had killed his dog was already on its downward swing. It sounded a dull thunk when it hit Talbot's head. The tall man stumbled a moment and raised the rifle. Blood flowed down the side of his long, thin face. Hush wrenched the rifle free from Talbot's hands.

"Give me that gun, nigger!" Talbot shouted, grabbing for the rifle, blinded with blood. "You're gonna hang!"

Hush raised the rifle to chin level and pulled the trigger. The blast reverberated through the barnyard, scattering chickens and setting the milk cow to lowing and the goats to bleating. Hale Talbot dropped down like a sack of grain right on top of his dead dog.

The slave driver was waist deep when Bledsoe splashed in behind him, smacking aside reeds and cattails in the shallower water. He turned his head, startled, when he heard Bledsoe splashing into the shallows behind him. He backed farther and deeper in the river, stunned by the fury on Bledsoe's face. Two more slippery steps backward, and the slave driver's arms began wheeling madly as he struggled to keep himself from being snatched by the current.

Bledsoe barely noticed when the driver disappeared. He splashed along the riverbank. Up to his waist, then his chest, calling, "Alice Alice Alice." He stumbled farther out, deeper, and went under. He shot up swallowing, then spitting water. He kept on calling. Forever it seemed. After a while it came out cracked and barely heard. He'd grown hoarse. His voice was shot. He sank down in the mud on his knees. The river lapped and licked his chest but he didn't feel it. Sunlight winked on its surface, and it gurgled merrily as it raced by. He didn't notice the slave driver as he was swept away, spread-eagled to the sky.

I can't swim, he cried to the rushing river. But the river didn't care. It kept on going.

FIFTY-NINE

"She's still so pale."

"There's a bit of pink to her lips now."

"Yes. But that bump on her head, we need to get the doctor."

Alice didn't understand this dream at all. She looked up from the bottom of the sea. There was a little point of light far above. She felt herself being lifted by that light, up and up toward the glittering surface. She moaned softly as she blinked and sunlight flooded her eyes. She could barely keep them open and peered through the mesh of her eyelashes at what seemed to be a puffy cloud hanging far too close to her face.

"She's awake!" said the cloud in a booming voice.

"Are you feeling better? You gave us such a fright, you know," said a different voice.

"Yes," said the cloud, "you were absolutely blue when he pulled you out. No doubt you'd have drowned had your hair not caught on that log."

"Who are you? Can you tell us?"

Alice blinked and peered up at two faces haloed in golden light. "Angels?" she whispered.

"What did she say?"

"This Heaven?"

"Only Virginia, I'm afraid."

"Shhhh, Uncle." This from a girl with a face framed by butter-yellow curls. There was also an old man with puffy white hair beside her. Alice struggled to wiggle away, but she was pinned down by a quilt and her head was filled with cotton.

"Calmly now, calmly, lie back there, dear. You're still muddled. Understandable, but at least you can speak. We were worried being so long underwater that you might have damaged your brain. That happens, you know. Lack of oxygen to the blood vessels, you see." The white-haired man smiled.

"How gruesome, Uncle," remonstrated the girl. She looked at Alice with concern. "You must have fallen in the river. You hit your head on something. You have a nasty bump on the back. Do you want anything? Water?"

"I doubt she wants more water, dear, she has only just dried out."

"Oh really, Uncle Harlan, that's enough. Hand me that glass." The girl gently lifted Alice's head and put a glass to her lips. "Sip a bit of this. Go on. That's good. Here, let me get that for you." The girl dabbed Alice's chin with a handkerchief. "Lie back now. Just rest, we'll talk more in a bit."

"I thought I could swim," said Alice, looking around the sunlit bedroom in confusion.

"Just lie back," said the blond girl soothingly. "It's all right now."

"The James has drowned any number who thought they could swim it. I've never heard of a girl attempting it before. Luckily you were rescued by Attis. He was after bass when you went drifting by. He was afraid of you at first. He thought you were a naiad."

She was struggling to keep her eyes open. The faces were clouding up again.

"Can you tell us who your people are?" asked the girl. "They must be worried sick."

But she was sinking back into the warm green water of the Dismal. She barely heard the girl say, "Oh, Uncle, look at the side of her face. What do you think happened to the poor thing?"

SIXTY

He blinked. The sun was setting. Without thinking he smacked his arm where twilight mosquitoes were at work. He pulled his feet from the mud and fell backward on the soggy bank with effort and lay there. He rubbed his swollen eyes. Doves called. The sky was purple now and the last light was being swallowed by night. When he looked up the rise there were no lights at High Hope. The house looked dead. Numbly, he made his way toward it. There was no real thought in his head, no complete sentence. Just a sickening bile-filled feeling of empty. She was gone. He was here. He paused halfway up the hill. There was a light. A candle burned somewhere in the house. Its solitary flame triggered something. A dim memory. He climbed toward it.

The window was open. A breeze ruffled the silk drapes. He didn't know why he needed to look in the window, didn't pause to think it was a stupid thing to do. Hush had shot a white man. Whoever was inside might be sitting there just waiting for Hush or any of the others with a gun across their knees. But he couldn't help himself. So he looked around the edge of the window frame.

In the light of a single candle on a mantelpiece, a porcelain monkey wearing a bright yellow turban crouched as if ready to spring. Light streaked the top of a gilded pianoforte and bounced off the glass domes of birds trapped beneath them. He felt a tremor run down his spine. When he became aware of a clink-clink he looked up. The crystals dangling from a great brass chandelier were gently tinkling and clinking together as the chandelier swayed from the weight of the little woman in black suspended from a veil tied around her neck. One small foot dangled shoeless, the other wore a satin pump with a rosette. Both feet swung slowly like the pendulum of a clock above a fallen lyre-back parlor chair.

He pushed himself away from the window and threw up in the grass. He retched until it seemed he'd throw up his insides. When he was done he felt light as air and dull as dirt. As he raced down the hill, the widow's tiny feet continued swaying in his mind. He stood on High Hope's dock. Before him the black James River sluiced between banks nearly a mile apart.

Throw yourself in and get done with it. But a rowboat bobbed right below the dock. He jumped in, setting it rocking wild.

Grasshopper sittin' on a sweet potato vine.

He untied the rowboat from its mooring.

Along comes a chicken and says you're mine.

And pushed the boat off the dock with one of the paddles. Five minutes later the single candle in the window of High Hope had disappeared. Bledsoe dipped the paddles in the James River mechanically while in his mind the Sim brothers poled through the Dismal. *Move over some. He's gonna let me go. That man ain't never gonna let you go. We're just alike now.*

He looked straight ahead as he paddled. He was afraid of the water. What if he saw her, pale face looking up at him, black hair waving? What could he do? *She's dead. Gone.*

Ahead, a strange constellation of flickering orange stars seemed to be moving rapidly toward the rowboat. They hung too low in the sky. Then a blast of a horn split the night air. *Steamboat.* Bledsoe quickly rotated the oars and tried to turn the rowboat shoreward toward the reeds where he could hide, but the current was against him. It was forcing the boat toward the great whoosh and splash of the fast-approaching side-wheeler. Red sparks flew into the sky from dual smokestacks and rained into the water with hisses.

There were soldiers high up on the rounded prow. They held lanterns extended over the water on long pikes, sweeping the river with the light. He pulled deeper with the oars, ignoring the shooting pain from his injured shoulder, but it was too late. Bledsoe threw up his good arm to shield his eyes from the brightness.

"Pull alongside," bellowed a voice. But blinded by the lights, he sent the rowboat circling the opposite way.

"Pull abeam. Pull abeam now or get shot." The huge wheel flung spray, stinging Bledsoe's face. The churn as it turned was deafening. He paddled madly to avoid getting sucked into it. The water around the rowboat boiled as bullets smacked into the river. Gunpowder burned his lungs. He was blinded by a cloud of white smoke, expecting any second to be hit, and squeezed his eyes shut, preparing himself to die.

A minute later he heard the whistle of the Confederate gunboat, but it was no longer near. He opened his eyes. The lanterns were distant. His rowboat had been carried swiftly downriver. With a bang that vibrated through his body, the boat snagged on the roots of a fallen tree near the shore.

From upriver came another angry blast from the gunboat. Then all was quiet except the slap of the water on the rowboat's hull. He sat there in the boat. The sky grew darker and the stars shifted. Did they move closer? Or farther away? A bullfrog croaked. Katydids scratched their legs. He heard these things but it was a dream. The boat rocked like a cradle. He didn't know what to do. He didn't want to be alive, but he didn't know how to die. He looked out at the river.

> *KOKYTOS, the river of lamentation, one of the five rivers of Hades in Greek mythology. The others were the Styx, the river of hatred; the Akheron, the river of woe; the Pyriphlegethon, the river of fire; and the Lethe, the river of forgetting.*

He gradually realized he was wet to the waist. The boat was sinking. He jumped off the rowboat and onto the trunk of the fallen tree. He felt it bob up and down beneath him. He crouched there, watching the boat sink. First slowly and then faster and faster. With a sucking sound like a final breath, it disappeared.

He slipped off the tree trunk and waded chest deep to shore. He stood on the bank, dripping. Then he turned his back to the river and began to run. He ran inland, tripping and falling, ripped by thorns, bruised by rocks. He only stopped when his body refused to continue. He clutched his stomach, bent in half, and retched in the grass, but nothing came up. He sucked in air and pushed himself off the ground. He ran again. If he ran hard enough, far enough, long enough, maybe his heart would explode and he could die. He thought it surely would happen. His heart hurt that bad.

SIXTY-ONE

Alice woke up in a panic. She sucked in air. Once, twice, three times, until she realized she could breathe just fine. She found herself sunk not in the Dismal but in an overstuffed feather mattress. She looked around the bedroom, swung her feet to the floor, and stood on shaky legs. She plopped back down on the edge of the bed, dizzily surveying the bluebirds and vines climbing the walls around her. Sunshine streamed through a window hung with fawn velvet drapes. She smoothed a hand over her lap and wondered at the fine lawn of the nightdress, stared at the lace at her wrists.

There were loud voices somewhere. A little grunt escaped as she limped toward the door. She pulled up the gown and saw that her right leg was bruised black and blue. Someone was talking loudly. She hesitated before touching the ornate brass doorknob. Then she twisted it and opened the door. She limped toward a staircase.

"Have they called in your regiment, Cadan?" someone asked. "Have they? My God! This is the very end. The very end."

"We'll cut off their monkey heads and put 'em on sticks. Then they'll think twice!" shouted a man. "They want free, we'll free 'em to hell, by God."

"That's right! Mount up, let's get 'em."

There was a bloodcurdling cheer that nearly stopped Alice's heart. Who were these people, hollering about cutting off heads? She limped quickly back to the bedroom and leaned against the closed door.

When she peeked around the velvet drapes she saw there were at least ten saddled horses in front of the house, reins held by slaves. Hounds milled. Men poured out of the front door. She saw the tops of their hats and their gesticulating arms as they shouted for their horses. A man, blond hair shining in the brassy light, mounted a horse and said something. Others answered but Alice couldn't hear through the glass what they said. He wore a light blue frock coat with a single row of shiny buttons and a golden bar on each shoulder.

The men had mounted now. Someone whooped, another let fly a shot from his revolver into the air; the dogs were barking wildly, dashing between the horses. The slaves had retreated to the other side of a wide lawn as far away as they could get. As if somehow signaled, the blond man looked up at the window and caught Alice looking down at him. His face looked familiar, though she didn't understand why. They stared at one another for what seemed a long time but was really only a few seconds. Then he put on a jaunty hat with a feather in the band and Alice jerked her head away, letting the drapery fall back over the window. She sank beneath it to the wide-planked floor, her knees pulled to her chest.

There was a knock on the door. She glanced at the bed, wondering if she'd have time to hide under it. She didn't. A blond woman, tall, wearing a gown of buttercup yellow, stood in the doorway. "What are you doing there? Did you fall?" She rushed to Alice and took her by the arm and helped her up.

Alice turned to the window. "Them," she stammered, "out there."

"Don't be alarmed. It's all right."

She backed against the bluebirds and vines on the wallpaper, still trying to assess the possibility of if not escape, then a place to hide. The blond woman smiled and her face was transformed. *She's only a girl,* Alice realized. Didn't look much older than herself. "That man out there." Alice pointed to the window. "The one on the red horse looks like you."

The girl gave a little laugh. "Oh. That's Cadan. I forget sometimes how it discombobulates folks. We're twins. He's with the army camped on Jamestown Island but got leave to visit. Come sit down, won't you? Can you tell me who you are?"

"That your brother then? Who're you?"

"I'm Tamsin. Tamsin Bell. You're at Bell's Bliss, my uncle Harlan's place. You had an accident, you nearly drowned! Thank God you didn't. Please come sit beside me." She sat on the edge of the bed and held out a hand. Alice slowly sank down beside her. "What's your name?"

"Alice."

"I have a cousin Alice in Alexandria. What's your last name?"

Alice slapped her hand over her mouth.

"My goodness, what's wrong?"

Alice shook her head. *Don't tell or they'll find out. What'll they find? I can't remember.* She tried to recall what had happened but it seemed just out of reach. *The water.* "Was it the sea?"

"The sea?"

"Did they throw me in?"

"Who?" asked the blond girl, clearly confused. "Did someone push you in the river?"

"The river," echoed Alice. "It was the river."

"I think you ought to have something to eat. That will make you feel better. I don't know what I was thinking. Of course you're starving." There was another knock on the door. The girl opened it.

"Good morning," beamed a voice. The old man with the fluffy white hair stuck his head in the room. "How is our river sprite?" He smiled at her. "Harlan Bell at your service, my dear."

"What you mean?" said Alice, pulling the quilt up to her chin.

"Oh, I do beg pardon," said the old man, pulling his head out of the doorway. *"Vous n'êtes pas encore habillé."*

"We're getting acquainted, Uncle," said the girl at the door. She lowered her voice. "Are they gone?"

"Yes," Alice heard him reply. "They're gone."

"I almost pity them, the poor devils. Treeing them like animals."

"Don't be a fool, they're black murderers, niece," replied the old man. The girl said she'd be down in a minute and closed the door.

Alice went to the window and peeked through the drapery. She cautiously peered out again. "Who were they, those men out there?"

The girl shook her head sadly. "It's just terrible. Some slaves revolted upriver near Richmond. They shot a white man and hanged a woman in her own home. A widow. And her husband just buried. They even killed the man's dog."

Alice suddenly felt sick to her stomach. She leaned on the back of a chair.

"A place up near Harrison's Landing. Oh, goodness, look at you. You don't need to hear this. Let me help you back to bed. Just lie down and rest." She put her arm around Alice's waist.

Alice pushed her away and turned back to the window. She didn't see the long drive or a formal garden or in the distance, the silver glint of the river. *The man's dog.* The girl's forehead wrinkled with concern but Alice didn't notice. "What the place called?"

"Where it happened? Oh, let's see. My Hope? Our Hope? Something like that. I never heard of it. It was a farm, they said."

Alice sat down in the chair. "Those men, they after 'em? After the slaves?"

The girl said quickly, "Oh, you poor thing. I'm sorry. Don't pay me any mind. What a fool I am to talk about such things after what you've been through. Now what we are going to do is find out where you belong and get you home. Good gracious. Someone is worried near sick to death about you."

The girl pulled the drapes open wide and the room lit up. The birds were blue and the vines were a soft and sheltering green. The chair Alice had leaned on was elegantly gilded.

"Just a moment and I'll bring you one of my dresses and I'll have Eva fetch you breakfast. We don't need to say another word until you want to."

Alice wasn't listening. "I jumped in," she said.

"What?"

"The river. I jumped in."

"Why ever did you do that?"

Alice opened her mouth—and closed it. She eyed the girl. Tamsin, she said her name was. Tamsin Bell. She lived here in this beautiful house with her uncle. Bell's Bliss, she called it. *That's where I am and that's who they are. I don't know them. Don't tell her nothin'.* "I don't remember," said Alice to the girl.

But she did. It came in a great wave. As soon as the girl was gone she sank onto the bed. She didn't cry. She didn't make a sound. She just stared at the golden light that flowed through the windowpanes and the lovely papered walls with horror.

SIXTY-TWO

He wasn't dead. His body had kept on going. It didn't care about head feelings, heart feelings. It was a machine. He crab-crawled from under the corncrib. It was set on stilts covered with hammered tin to keep rats out. He'd scrambled under just to catch his breath so he could run again. He knew he wouldn't sleep. Time didn't happen anymore. Sleep didn't happen anymore. Now, peering out at the dull dawn, he realized a night had gone by and it was morning. The world had kept on and him with it. She was gone and he was alone.

He crumpled on the grassy ground under the clouds, gray and thick as dirty wool. The air was still, like a bubble waiting to burst. He looked up for anything, a hurricane, a bolt of lightning. There was only an atmospheric pressure that seemed to press down on the back of his neck. Far off he heard a rumble of thunder. He shivered in his sweat-soaked homespun shirt and pants. Behind him, about a quarter mile away, sat a house and outbuildings. Closer to the corncrib was a split rail fence. A shambling line of cows was heading his way, going to pasture. In the distance a rooster was setting up a racket. He couldn't see the river anymore. There was a pine forest a ways off in the other direction.

Then over the crow of the rooster came another sound. At first it was faint and it barely registered. He kept on sitting in the jimsonweed and Queen Anne's lace like a stunned animal.

But this other sound, louder now, made him turn his head toward it. It was unmistakable. He whimpered without realizing it and stood up, stumbling backward, arms flailing, nearly falling over. The chilling bay was closer now. *Run,* commanded his brain. *Run.*

He zigzagged, leaping over fallen trees, tripping over brush. He was running as he'd never run before. He was flying, all other thought erased. All he heard in his head now was Pomp as he made toward the pine woods.

> *Don't git up in no tree, boy, no, don't wanna do that. Them dogs'll tree you like a possum. Don't try to hide from 'em neither. They find you sure. You see a herd of cows? You run through 'em, git the scent of sumpin' else to mix 'em up. See somethin' you gotta climb over wid your hands? Hard for dogs 'cause dey got no hands. Slow 'em down if you can. Rocks is good. Dey can't smell you good on rocks. See some mint? Some wild onion? Rub it on you. Water throw 'em off the smell, but runnin' in water make you slow down so 'member that. You gotta stay ahead. Most of all, you gotta run fast, boy. Run fast.*

But even though he was flying, the dogs were closer. He heard the excitement in their howls. The air he gulped seared his lungs. He tripped over a root and crashed to earth. Nearly every particle of him was convinced he could not get up again. A whisper in his head said, *After a while it won't hurt anymore,* but he pushed himself up. Ahead was a stream. He splashed into it. He ran, slipping on the wet stones, splashing and sliding. The stream broadened and became deeper; he couldn't run now. The water swirled around his waist, tugging him.

He made his way to the muddy bank and scrambled up it, pulling loose grass, slipping back into the water, then swatting his way through brush and thorn. Finally, he couldn't breathe. He bent over. His tongue was out. He began to pant. Hands on his knees, he took a painful breath of hot muggy air. Then he stood stock-still, cocked his head, and listened. Birds chirped. The sky flashed with heat lightning. His hair rose with the electricity in the air. Standing in a little clearing, sweat running down his face, he heard a strange whispery scratching to his right. He slowly turned his head.

A man was sitting on a stump. A straw hat was set on the grass beside him. His back was to Bledsoe but over the man's shoulder he saw the man was drawing in a big notebook. The scratching was the sound of a stick of charcoal on the paper.

Bledsoe took a cautious step backward, back toward the brush. When a twig cracked beneath his feet, he froze and the man turned around. They stayed like that for what seemed a full minute, more likely about five seconds. Then the man turned back to his drawing. "River's up ahead there."

Bledsoe didn't move.

The man closed his notebook. He put it inside a large brown leather satchel. Not far away a hound began to yip excitedly and another joined. The man looked Bledsoe up and down. He threw the satchel over his shoulder and began walking rapidly through the oaks and scrub pine. "Come on then if you're coming."

Below the fat black clouds seagulls wheeled and cried. They skimmed the sky above as the canoe skimmed the river. He smelled ocean in the wind, the same as when they'd put in at Norfolk. The scent memory brought it back, the clank of the chains. Joined together. *Just jump in.* Bledsoe leaned over the side of the canoe, watching the deep green ripples left behind. The canoe was faster than the rowboat, seemed nearly to fly.

Bledsoe stared into the watery greenness, willing himself to slither over the side and down past the green, down to the darkness. *Will I find her there?*

"Hey!" yelled the man. "Stop rocking back there. You'll capsize us."

Instead of going over the side, Bledsoe scooped a handful of water and splashed it on his face. His eyes burned and he rubbed them with a wet hand. He licked drops from his lips and studied the stranger's back as he paddled the hide-skinned canoe, dipping the oar to one side, then the other with seemingly little effort.

After he'd launched the canoe in the river, the man told him to climb in and sit in the narrow rear. Though his hair was silver, he wasn't old. Thirty? Thirty-five? He was tall and slender, but well built. His skin was a warm olive; his nose was large, slightly arched, cheekbones high. His eyes were dark brown and heavy lidded, giving him an appearance of being either slightly sleepy or slightly bored. Beneath them were shadows of blue that looked permanent. He was wearing a well-cut frock coat, a silk cravat, checkered trousers, and fine leather shoes. He didn't look like someone who would be paddling a canoe. And what about the little brass spyglass?

What was he looking for? Every few minutes he'd put it to his eye and survey the river ahead and the shoreline to the right. Bledsoe dropped his eyes. What difference did it make? *Doesn't matter. I don't care.*

But the man was looking through the glass again. "Damn my balls," he exclaimed. "Hell in a hatbox," he added, pulling in the paddle and resting it across his knee. "Well, no way around it. We'll just let them come to us."

Bledsoe leaned forward, peering over the man's shoulder. "Who?"

"See it?" said the man. "Here she comes. Sits there like a fat spider waiting for boats to pass up and down from the bay." A tugboat, its hull gleaming dully with a coat of iron plates, was putting out of an inlet about a hundred or so yards downriver. As it steamed closer, the man straightened his shoulders and raised a hand in greeting. "Keep your mouth shut."

"I can't hear you."

Without turning he said, "When we get abreast, keep quiet. I'll do the talking."

"Who are you?"

"Quiet."

"Why'd you help me?" asked Bledsoe. Despite himself he was curious, more curious at the moment than afraid of the approaching boat. He eyed the man's tall back. "You're a Yankee, ain't you?"

The man turned to him. The heavy-lidded eyes no longer looked either sleepy or bored. They blazed at Bledsoe. "Keep your fucking mouth shut or I'll shoot you."

Bledsoe shut his mouth. His heart was banging in his chest. He held on to both sides of the canoe as it was hit by wash from the tug. He found he had no true desire to die. At least not yet. At least not this way.

As the tug, *Telchine*, came alongside, a rope was lowered. The man grabbed for it, missed, grabbed again. The canoe was slammed against the side of the ironclad steamer. On deck above, several soldiers had rifles trained at their heads. An officer in a high-necked uniform and a slouchy gray hat said loudly, "What's your business?"

"Sightseeing," replied the man, as Bledsoe nervously clutched the sides of the frail canoe.

Two big guns were mounted on the ship. He could see their wide muzzles, big enough for large ordnance. The tug flew a Confederate flag. The officer pulled out a revolver and aimed it at the man. "What kind of sights?"

"Just a bit of sketching this afternoon, enjoying the river. That sort of thing."

"What?" asked the captain. "Sketching? Don't you know there's a war on?"

The artist swept a hand toward the shoreline. "I'm an artist. I'm drawn to beauty."

The officer looked skeptically at the little canoe. "What kind of artist?"

The man bobbed his head. "Of little merit, Captain, but I do my best."

Bledsoe didn't dare to look up at him directly, but out of the corner of his eye, he saw the captain wasn't convinced.

"Let's see then. Show me what you were drawing."

"My pleasure. Shall I come up to you, or would you prefer to come down to me?"

Bledsoe now raised his head and said loudly, "I show him, Marse, if you wants me to." The artist turned to Bledsoe with a look of surprise, which he quickly erased. Bledsoe looked back impassively. "You wants me to show dat soldier, Marse?"

"If that's all right with you, Captain? If you lower a ladder, my boy will bring up my portfolio."

"Just who the hell are you?"

The artist took off his hat and made a small bow from the waist. "My name is Evans, Captain. Spencer Evans of Baltimore, Maryland. Undoubtedly you are aware that we were the first to stand up against Lincoln's tyranny after Sumter." He handed the large leather satchel to Bledsoe. "If you'll allow my servant to come up to you, Captain, you can have a look at my humble attempts to capture some of the beauty along the York River."

Bledsoe took the satchel and reached for the rope.

"Just tie it on there, boy," said the captain. "What you doing here from Baltimore?"

"I'm visiting my cousins, the Marshalls, in Yorktown," said the man. "Perhaps you know the Marshalls, Captain?"

"Nope." The captain hauled the leather satchel to the deck.

He disappeared, but the soldiers kept their rifles trained on the canoe. The artist wiped his hands and the back of his neck with a kerchief. Bledsoe sat in the rocking stern. Either he was going to be shot or he wasn't. He realized he didn't want to see it coming. He looked out across the water toward the shoreline. The York, the artist had said. So this wasn't the James. It was a different river. That meant he'd crossed the entire peninsula. He was miles away from her. *Oh, Alice.* The heavy leather satchel dropped back into the little canoe and set it violently rocking.

The captain poked his head over the railing and said, "Trees don't look like that."

"Ah." The artist smiled up at him. "I was trying to capture the light rather than the actual tree itself, but I take your critique to heart."

"Get off the river before you get shot," replied the captain. With long poles two soldiers pushed the canoe away from the tug. A blast of steam shot from its stern as it puffed back to its hiding place downriver.

"What's that jackass know about trees? Damn quick thinking on your part," said the artist, paddling past the inlet. "What's your name?"

"You're a Yankee."

"I'm an artist," he replied.

"Bledsoe." He had to yell because the wind had come up.

"Say again?"

"My name. My name is Bledsoe."

"Bledsoe? Bledsoe what?"

"That's all."

"Tatsall?"

"No. Nothing. Bledsoe Nothing."

"Funny name." Bledsoe heard him laughing into the wind. "Unique!" he shouted over his shoulder.

Bledsoe didn't reply because they were rapidly approaching the Chesapeake Bay. The wind was funneled here and the river had kicked up rough. Whitecaps raced alongside. A moment later as the canoe was nearly swamped by a wave, he grabbed hold of the gunwale. Clung to it so tight his hands numbed when another washed over them, leaving them both drenched. "We have to head to shore now!" shouted the man. "Paddle, dammit! Paddle with your hands!"

He paddled frantically.

SIXTY-THREE

They left the canoe hidden in brush, then walked through an orchard. The man who'd told the Confederate captain that his name was Spencer Evans pulled a peach off a tree and threw another to Bledsoe. The man bit into it and then tossed it with a wry face. Bledsoe bit into his. He didn't care if it was past prime. He sucked it down to the pit and pulled another. Evans was disappearing ahead. Bledsoe followed. They passed a house, but it looked abandoned. Evans kept going. He stopped when he reached a macadamized road. He offered Bledsoe a wooden canteen. He drank long and deep.

Evans didn't seem to care if they were out in the open. When Bledsoe glanced nervously toward the brush along the road, Evans said, "They don't come down the peninsula this far. Not during the day, at any rate. Our camp is just past Hampton. Or what's left of it." He pointed ahead. "The Rebels burned the town to the ground."

At first Bledsoe couldn't quite wrap his mind around what lay ahead as they walked down the empty road. This had been a town? Dozens of brick chimneys jutted into the skyline like crooked teeth, but not a single house. He could tell there was a grid of streets; there were even some signs left, but they led to nothing. All that remained was tumbled and blackened with soot; even the trees were gone. All that remained was char and rubble as if the town itself had been an enormous fireplace. "Why'd they burn the town?"

"General Magruder burned Hampton rather than see Yankees use it. The fire was so bright you could read a book by it. They did it very methodically, quadrant by quadrant. Come on."

"What about the people?"

"What about them?"

Bledsoe followed Evans down streets, stepping over rubble. He looked through a window miraculously still intact, though it offered a view of nothing but emptiness. Once-elegant granite sidewalks now fronted piles of bricks and twisted metal. The only whole structure remaining was the walls of a large church, but it was open to wind and sky. Weeds had already replaced its floor. An emerald gleam here, a sapphire glow there winked. Evans bent and picked up a shard of colored glass.

"Stained glass windows must have exploded from the heat. This was St. John's Church. Quite pretty," said Evans. "Old too." They walked past a baptismal font that had been carted outside to use as a trough. A teamster was making use of it for his mules.

"You asked about the townspeople. Magruder warned them they were going to burn it. Most of the townspeople had already moved away, gone up to Richmond or scattered somewhere else. They were Virginians. Southern through and through. They didn't want to be that close to Yankees. Afraid, I suppose, we'd rape their daughters and murder them in their beds." He laughed and slapped Bledsoe on the back.

Bledsoe looked at him stunned. "What you mean? Yankees? They afraid of that from Yankees?"

Evans looked at Bledsoe quizzically a moment and then smiled. "Never mind. Anyway, we're camped at Old Point Comfort right here at the tip of the peninsula. Magruder was afraid we'd use Hampton for winter quarters. He must have studied how the Russians defeated Napoleon. Leave nothing for the enemy. Scorch the earth. Except we had no intention of using Hampton. We didn't need it. We already had a camp. So they burned down their own damn town for nothing. Tragic, really. A fine place. History gone in the blink of an eye."

"What about the others?"

"What others?"

"You said most left. Most means not all." Bledsoe looked away from the charred remains of what looked like a cat. The artist was poking something on the ground with a stick.

"Any left were runaways. Slaves who were trying to get to the fort. No one warned them. That was Magruder's point, wasn't it? Yankees weren't going to be able to keep either Union troops or runaway slaves in Hampton town. What's this?" He picked something up and examined it in the palm of his hand.

"What about them?"

"Hmm? Look at this." He held up a ring with a red stone. "Who? Oh, you mean the negroes? Died, I imagine. Shame." He licked the stone and rubbed it with his sleeve. "Somebody's wedding ring, no doubt." He dropped the ring in his coat pocket with a cheerful whistle. "If you look around you can generally find a little something. A soldier I know found a gold piece just yesterday."

Ahead of him, Evans continued whistling. It was all wrong, thought Bledsoe with a chill. Like whistling in a graveyard. Like laughing at the dead. *Alice.*

"Come on," shouted Evans.

On the blackened earth, already beginning to bristle with tall weeds, lay scattered books. Some with covers chewed by fire, some appearing nearly untouched. He picked one up. It disintegrated between his palms, bits fluttering away in the wind like charcoal feathers.

"Hurry up," said Evans at the end of a barren street. "I have to get back."

A row of rosebushes, their late summer blooms frozen by fire, crumbled to ash as Bledsoe brushed by. He was surprised to see makeshift tents here and there, mostly blankets strung on ropes. A colored woman stirred something in a pot. A little girl clung to her skirt on woozy baby legs. The smoke from their fire rose above the ruins. A skinny dog barked furiously while a boy restrained it by the scruff of its neck. An old woman sat on a wooden box smoking a clay pipe. She was petting a buff-colored chicken on her lap and it was clucking contentedly.

"We have a ride," called Evans up ahead. He was climbing onto a wagon loaded with barrels of flour. When he hesitated, Evans held out a hand. Bledsoe stared at it a moment. At the white hand offered.

"I got it," mumbled Bledsoe. He climbed up behind the driver and sat down beside Evans. He blinked rapidly and licked his lips. "Where we going?" he asked.

"You'll see," Evans replied. "Just relax a bit. You've had yourself a helluva day, if I'm any judge."

Soon they were beyond the ruins and following a road lined with more tents, but these were white and uniform. "Camp Hamilton," said Evans. "Butler wanted more troops here, but after Bull Run they needed them elsewhere. But we've enough inside to do the job."

Bledsoe looked at the water, which stretched away to the horizon to the right and left of the wagon as the road became an isthmus. They were approaching a massive wall of stone.

"What is it?" asked Bledsoe.

"Fort Monroe," said Evans.

"Fort Monroe," echoed Bledsoe, forgetting for a moment everything else in sheer wonder of its mammoth reality.

"As you can see, it's surrounded on three sides by the Chesapeake Bay. But what you can't tell from here is that it's built in the shape of an octagon. You have more vantage points that way for the guns," said Evans. "See there? That moat is a hundred feet across and fed by the actual tides in the bay. Virtual suicide if anyone were stupid enough to attempt to cross. If you didn't sink, you'd be riddled with shot from the walls before you even got a toe in.

"They call this stretch of the peninsula Old Point Comfort. Comfort from what, I couldn't tell you. Pirates, maybe, in the old days. Certainly not from the wind," he said, his frock coat blowing open, revealing a vest embroidered with silver butterflies. "The wind out here can be savage. Fort Monroe is the oldest and largest fortress in the United States. Well, not so united at present, is it? As you see, the walls are granite, over thirty feet high and ten feet thick, and with that moat, it's damn near impregnable."

"It's like *The Castle of Otranto*," said Bledsoe, remembering another book he'd never had time to finish.

"What was that you said?" asked Evans, eyeing Bledsoe curiously.

"Nothin'," he muttered, lowering his head. *Keep your mouth shut, you fool. You don't know what's what.*

The walls loomed even higher as they crossed a bridge over the enormous moat. "From here we guard the entrance to Hampton Roads."

"I don't see any roads," said Bledsoe. Silver water stretched away to the horizon.

"It's a euphemism. Hampton Roads are the rivers that lead from inland to the sea—they empty here into the bay; the James, the Elizabeth, the Nansemond. The York also, but they merge, you see, all converge into the Chesapeake. They're the roads the South has used to supply itself ever since the first settlements in America. We're cutting off the South's feet here. The rest of the body suffers all down the coast from the blockade. No one can get a ship in or out of the rivers without passing the thirty-two pounders up there on the walls. See them? They have a range of over a mile."

Lining the moat were more tents. Hundreds. Made of whatever was available, they were a riot of color. In the wild wind they bellowed like sails. Bledsoe smelled meat roasting; a string of silver fish dangled from a pole, laundry snapped. Children ran between tents. Someone was playing a guitar. On a tall beam, a Federal flag snapped in the wind. No one paid the wagon any attention.

"Contrabands," said Evans. "Already over a thousand. As you saw, some have moved over into the ruins of Hampton. Fifty, sometimes more, arrive every day. They press as close to the fort as they can, afraid of being snatched by Rebels, though no Rebel would dare come this close anymore. No one is sure what to do with them all. They have to be fed and some are sick. Many are put to work, but some are useless. Just too worn down, I guess. What's wrong?"

He felt Evans grab his arm. He'd almost fallen out of the wagon. He forced himself upright. "I'm all right," he said. He sat up straighter. Here he was. Fort Monroe. He wasn't going to fall over dead now. "Contraband," he said. "I'm contraband!"

"Contraband?" asked Evans, eyeing him.

"Means. Means I'm free." Suddenly the sun was too bright. When Evans replied, his voice sounded strange, the edges of words blurred. He tried to sit up straighter, tried to listen closer to what Evans was saying.

". . . property captured from the enemy when at war. For instance, a horse might be considered contraband," buzzed Evans beside him. "Or a wagon, or even a ham. Because of the Fugitive Slave Law, slaves like you were supposed to be returned to your owner even if you'd gotten to a free state. But once the war started, some slaves ran away from a Rebel camp right across the river there, see? Oh yes, they've got a big Rebel camp right across there. We watch each other across the river. I'll show you later through my glass. Are you interested in how this whole contraband thing began?"

Bledsoe felt his head go up, then down. Though putting it up again took all his might.

"Well, one day these slaves, there were three of them I think, ran off from the Confederate army. Got themselves into a boat and rowed from over there to over here and said they hoped the North would take them in. They were given shelter and some food while General Butler, who was in charge of the fort, decided what to do about them.

"When the slaves were missed, the Rebel general from across the river marched over here under a flag of truce and demanded his property be returned in accordance with the Fugitive Slave Act.

"'Well, apparently you Confederates have declared yourselves a separate country,' said General Butler. 'As far as I'm concerned, sir, that makes you a foreigner. United States laws no longer apply and I've declared your property contraband. They're mine now. So the answer is no,' Butler told him. 'Now get out of my country.'"

He laughed. "Good one, don't you think? 'Get out of my country!' That's the story anyway. Well, you people certainly have a way of spreading news. More efficient than the telegraph, apparently. Within days you began flocking here to the fort. However, you should understand that like a horse or a ham . . ."

Bledsoe wiped his forehead; things were spinning. *What do you mean a ham? I ain't a . . .*

". . . so you see, you're not actually free. Not *free* free. You're now property of the army—contraband of the Federal . . . ho there! Stop, driver! The boy fell out of the wagon."

SIXTY-FOUR

Alice looked out the window at the dark. "Did they find them?" She tried to make it sound as casual as she possibly could.

"Who?" asked Tamsin.

"Them slaves they said killed that man and woman."

"I don't believe so. No. We would have heard, but don't worry, they'd never come here. Besides, Cadan is staying with us two more days. And we have Attis to protect us as well. Now you get back in bed."

Alice climbed back onto the bed and Tamsin covered her up. "You need to take care. Look at you, Alice. You have the face of a baby, did you know that? Sweet baby face. No, don't hide in your hair. It's true. Now here. Isn't this a pretty bed jacket? Put it on and I'll read to you. It's so nice having a girl here. We used to live in Richmond all the time—we have a house there on Clay Street you know—we only came down here for summers. We used to have dances and go to parties, but Uncle loves Bell's Bliss and two years ago he said he was going to stay year-round. What could we do? He's our guardian until twenty-one. Still, before the war we did have visitors come down to see us. Two Christmases ago we gave the most splendid party. Fiddlers and an opera singer from Italy."

She sighed. "At least Cadan gets to go join the army. Since this war I've been alone except for Uncle. And half the time he thinks I'm Aunt Freddy. Oh, Bell's Bliss is the end of the world, isn't it?"

When Alice said nothing, Tamsin took it as agreement. "Yes, I know it is. Well, there are those girls in Williamsburg, but frankly I'd prefer being alone to their company. I'm not the type to turn up my nose at anyone, but they're just plain hayseeds. Tamara Stubbin starts every sentence with *I hate to have to tell you,* when it's clear as day she just *can't wait to tell you* her dirty ol' gossip. Oh, I'm chewing your ear off, aren't I? My, look! That jacket is so pretty on you. Are you too warm? No? All right. What would you like to hear? Are you in the mood for Hawthorne? Or would you prefer Miss Austen?"

"Whatever you want's fine," mumbled Alice. "Anythin'." She sank down into the bed and pretended to listen to Hester Prynne's debasement by the jeering townsfolk while she sifted through her memories. She ordered each memory of their time together chronologically until she heard him one last time: *"Run, Alice!"*

SIXTY-FIVE

When he regained consciousness, Bledsoe was lying on a cot in a room with bright whitewashed walls. Evans sat in a chair beside him drinking a cup of coffee and reading a newspaper.

Bledsoe weakly struggled to sit up. For a moment he panicked. *Where am I?* Then it streamed back into his memory, images racing by as if painted on paper, slowly unrolling.

Evans looked up at him. "I had you brought to my quarters. Would you like something to eat? There's soup on the table there. Probably cold by now, though."

Bledsoe weakly swung his legs off the bed. He tried to stand and had to sit back down.

"You slept for nearly seventeen hours," said Evans, turning a page of the newspaper.

Bledsoe staggered to the table. He dropped onto a chair. The soup had a skin of grease, but he could smell the meat. His hand was shaking and it took all his concentration to navigate the spoon to his mouth. He felt he would choke, but the soup slid down his throat. It was as if a lamp had been lit. He was terrifyingly hungry. He wolfed the rest of the soup, stuffing pieces of bread in his mouth as he went. He finished in a matter of moments, wiping the last speck with a rind of bread. He finally took a breath and, wiping his mouth on his sleeve, saw he was being closely studied. He turned away, blood coursing through his face. He looked at his lap. *Fool.* "Thank you, Marse," he mumbled.

"So you can read?"

Bledsoe stared at the wood grain of the table. He felt sick. He'd eaten too fast. Thoughts tumbled in his head, scattering this way and that. The man had brought him to his room and put him in his own bed. Why? What did he want?

"I don't suppose someone in your position would have a great deal of choice, but *The Castle of Otranto* is a rather awful novel. Silly. For girls, really. Most novels are."

Bledsoe looked at Evans. He was clearly appraising him. This time he didn't lower his eyes or look away. "I can read some."

"Where did you run from?"

Bledsoe pushed the chair back from the table. "You gonna give me back?"

Evans tapped the arm of his chair in a rat-a-tat-tat, looking keenly at Bledsoe. Then he smiled. "Of course not. You're contraband now."

Bledsoe let loose the breath he hadn't realized he'd been holding.

"You don't have to tell me where you're from. I was just curious."

A banging began in the back of his skull. *$300 Reward. Stole himself. You used to be my good boy. Love me. Say it.* Bledsoe mumbled, "Kentucky."

"Kentucky! Quite a hike you've been on, then. Well, all right. Shows you've got some stamina, that's for certain. And some smarts too to navigate all the way here without getting caught." He looked Bledsoe up and down. "I've been thinking while you were asleep over there. Oh, you need some feeding up, but otherwise you look healthy enough. Look here, Bledsoe, is it? Would you like to work for the Union army, Bledsoe?"

"What?" Everything that had happened fell away. Astounded, Bledsoe watched as Evans went to the mirror over the washstand. He began to trim his mustache with a small pair of gold-handled scissors. Then he slapped his cheeks with Florida Water. He turned this way and that to admire his reflection. "Well? What do you say? Do you want to work for the army or not?"

"You mean join Lincoln's army?" He stood up. "I've been trying to all along, but didn't know how."

"No, no. Sit down. You can't actually *join*. But I am certain I'm about to have a new assignment in which case I could use an assistant. Someone intelligent enough to keep their mouth shut when required."

"Wait. What you mean I can't join?"

"Negroes can't enlist."

"Negroes can't fight in Lincoln's army?"

"There's talk later down the line, perhaps, only if necessary. But listen, why would you want to anyway? Do you really fancy getting your head shot off? I certainly don't. And you'll still be working for Mr. Lincoln, just in a different capacity. You'll be working for the army more like myself. You can see I'm not in a uniform. That's because I'm not regular army. I'm a cartographer."

Bledsoe stood at attention beside the table. "Ptolemy, however, could be said to be the first cartographer. He created the map of the Hellenistic world in his Geographia using mathematical calculations. The geographer Jayme of Majorca superintended Prince Henry the Navigator's school of navigation. In 1839 a monument to his memory was erected at Sagres."

Something dropped to the wood floor. Bledsoe closed his mouth and stared at the wall. It had just spilled out of him.

Evans was looking at him, eyes wide. "What in hell was all that about?"

"Encyclopedia Britannica," muttered Bledsoe. "Cartographer. Mapmaker."

"You read the encyclopedia?"

"Only parts," whispered Bledsoe.

"Well." Evans was still staring at him as he bent to pick up his gold-handled scissors from the floor. "Well, well. Interesting." His face relaxed and he laughed. His teeth were large and white against his olive skin. "Yes, you're right. I'm a mapmaker. It's my job to survey the landscape, sometimes merely illustrate with topography, other times to prepare an actual map. Here." He opened the leather satchel and pulled out several sheets of thick paper. He pushed one to Bledsoe. It was a watercolor of a river. Birds swooped overhead. Clouds puffed in the sky.

"That's good," said Bledsoe, admiring it. "How you get the sky like that?"

Evans pulled a flask from an inside coat pocket. "It's not good, it's awful." He took a pull off the flask, capped it, and put it back inside his coat. "But most people don't know a damn thing about art. Here." He pushed another picture toward Bledsoe. It was the head and shoulders of a woman with apple cheeks and blue eyes peeking from below a bonnet. Bledsoe looked at the artist questioningly.

"A portrait of a Miss Cuthburt of Goochland County, Virginia. Think she's pretty?"

Bledsoe stared at the pink and cream face. He wasn't about to answer *that* question. Once, when he was only five or six, he'd stood in front of a painting at Our Joy of a pink and white woman with a little tan dog on her lap. He had never seen a dog tiny as that. Like a toy. Before he knew it the second wife had boxed his ears so hard he saw a galaxy of whirling stars. "How dare you stare at my *maman*, you dirty little ape."

Evans tapped the picture. "Miss Cuthburt was actually cross-eyed and weighed forty pounds more, but she was pleased as punch when she saw it. People see what they want to see, you know. Well, here. Rub this over it." He wetted a corner of a handkerchief and handed it to Bledsoe. "Just the right corner there will do."

Bledsoe rubbed a corner of the woman's flawless milk-white bosom with the handkerchief. He looked up astonished. "Another picture underneath!"

Evans grinned and swept it back into the satchel.

"Is it a map?"

"I'm a painter of portraits. An artist for hire and as such, I'm sometimes in a position to gather more than just topography for maps."

"You mean a spy?"

"No. I'm an artist." Evans sat down across from him at the table. He spoke softly. "If you want to work for Mr. Lincoln, Bledsoe, then it's important for you to tell me, what is it I do?"

Bledsoe said without a pause, "You're a painter of portraits, an artist for hire."

Evans grinned. "Something told me the minute I saw you . . . Good. Now I have some business to attend to. Why don't you clean yourself up? You look and smell atrocious. The tub in the back room is filled. I used it, but it shouldn't be bad. Day's hot, water should still be warm enough. There are clean clothes in the cupboard there. I think my old gray suit should almost fit you. Shoes, though," he said, looking at Bledsoe's feet. "Yours are significantly larger. We'll have to get you shoes down the road somewhere."

"You want me to wear *your* clothes?"

Evans was reading a letter, which he tucked in his inner coat pocket. "I didn't notice you had any baggage from Kentucky. Yes. Put on something of mine. You look like hell and it won't do. Hurry up. I believe we'll be leaving soon."

"But you just got here. Where to?"

"You mean where to, *Master*."

His heart sank then. *You stupid fool.* The silver-haired white man was staring at him across the table.

"I see by your face you misunderstand, young Bledsoe. Behind enemy lines, I can use an assistant who will only *pretend* to be my slave.

A Yankee wouldn't have one. Makes it all look more legitimate." He dabbed his mustache with a handkerchief, folded it, and put it in his pocket. He sat there, twisting a ring on his finger back and forth. It was the ring he'd found in the burned ruins of Hampton. Someone's wedding ring. "Well. Do you want to help Mr. Lincoln or do you want to live in a tent out there with the rabble?"

"But you say I ain't free?"

"Not technically. But you'll be a lot more free working with me than you would be out there."

"It'll help President Lincoln win the war?"

Evans stood up and rolled down his sleeves. "It'll help Lincoln." He put on a yellow silk vest and a brown frock coat and smoothed his silky goatee. "Whether he knows it or not."

"Then all right. I'll do it."

Evans smiled. "Good man. Now, listen carefully, Bledsoe. I am a portrait painter from Baltimore. You're my servant." He looked in the mirror and stuck a pearl-headed pin into his cravat. "And I think the name Bledsoe is too unusual. Different enough to maybe attract someone's attention. Especially if you're wanted. So let's just call you Joe."

The artist didn't ask him what he thought of his new name. He didn't much like it. Then he dismissed the thought. He was working for Lincoln. He was almost in the army. But once he'd sunk himself into the chill bathwater, he remembered everything. As he washed himself he tried not to remember the feel of her fingers on his skin. But it was impossible. Evans had gone out so there was no one to see when he started to cry.

SIXTY-SIX

"I keep trying to place your sweet little accent," Tamsin said a couple of days later. They were sitting in Uncle Harlan's library. The afternoon light was better for needlework. "My mother had a relation come to stay with us when I was a girl. Cousin Talmada Hemple. She was from Tennessee. Your accent reminds me somewhat. Tennessee? That sound familiar?"

Alice shook her head. Her hands, which were also shaking, were clasped in her lap to give the illusion of calmness. She fought down panic. What would happen should her true identity be revealed? The Bells had been kind to her, but what if they learned she was likely wanted in North Carolina for murder? In Baltimore as a thief? And how would sweet Tamsin's face curdle if she knew the man Alice loved not only was a runaway slave but had apparently murdered a white man? Her only hope was to continue her role as a tragic amnesiac.

"Tennessee. Of course not," mused Tamsin. "How would you get washed down the James River all the way from Tennessee? Unless"—Tamsin turned to her eagerly—"unless you were visiting someone upriver? Say near Richmond? And fell in somehow?" This time it was

Tamsin who shook her head. "But we put that notice in the Richmond papers the day after we found you. Someone would surely have seen it, wouldn't they?"

Alice sniffled, ducked her head, and wiped alligator tears away with one of Tamsin's loaned handkerchiefs.

"Maybe you're an orphan like Cadan and I and that's why we've heard nothing."

Alice looked up at her, startled.

"I'm sorry. That was selfish, hoping to keep you with me a little longer. No doubt your people are beside themselves. Well, they must not be in the Richmond area, but don't you worry. We will solve this mystery together."

Alice got up and nervously pulled a book off the shelf and opened it. She bent to it and pretended to be intently reading. A moment later she realized Tamsin was looking over her shoulder.

"You're interested in Highland cattle breeding?"

Alice looked up and smiled weakly. "I don't remember." And she hastily closed the book.

Tamsin shook her head. "You're an awful funny girl. Oh!" She clapped her hands together and smiled bright. "Do you want to see my secret place?" Whether Alice did or not seemed of little interest to the blond girl as she grabbed Alice by the hand and pulled her out of the house.

She led Alice past the garden's late-blooming foxgloves, yellow wax-bells, and black-eyed Susans. "Where we goin'?" asked Alice, following past a fountain, then farther than they'd ever walked before.

"Come on," said Tamsin, picking up her skirt and breaking into a run. "You'll see!" She led Alice into a stand of towering evergreens. Alice looked over her shoulder. She could no longer see the house. They were surrounded by the great trees. The air was full of their pungent oil. "There it is!"

Alice inhaled in wonder at the miniature house sitting in a small man-made clearing.

"My own little Bell's Bliss. Attis built it for me when I was a child." She grinned at Alice, a dimple deepening in her cheek. "You'll have to duck down; the doorway was made for me when I was small. I used to hide here for hours, even Cadan couldn't find me."

Alice ducked and followed Tamsin inside. There was only one tiny room, but she marveled at the silk draperies hanging at the little window and the small soft rug that covered the floor.

"Oh, it's all so dusty. I haven't been here in ages. See my dollies?" There was a shelf above a miniature settee where four beautiful china-headed dolls sat. "I used to read to them. Come! Sit here beside me."

Alice gingerly sat on the edge of the fragile settee, amazed at the papered walls, the table and Lilliputian chairs that could never bear the weight of an adult. "And no person lives here?" she asked. "Nobody ever?"

"Oh no," replied Tamsin. "It's only for play."

"Only for play," echoed Alice. "A house jist for playin'." The thought of such a thing filled her with astonishment.

"I used to dream of a knight finding me, you know, like in the stories, pretend that I was waiting here in my bower for my lover." Outside the window the pine trees softly sighed. A woodpecker was at work with a rap-tat-tat. "I read Lord Byron to my dolls: *She walks in beauty, like the night of cloudless climes and starry skies.*" Tamsin smiled and sighed. "Isn't that beautiful?"

Alice wasn't sure how someone could walk like a starry sky, but she nodded in agreement. The woodpecker's steady tapping was like a heartbeat. Surrounded by the whispering boughs of the fir trees, the light was a muted golden green. Alice felt as if she were in a dream, as if it might really be possible to walk across the night sky like a star.

"Here, I'll read to you. Better than a silly doll. Oh, I'm so glad to finally have a friend. It's so lonely out here. Are you happy? Yes? I'm so glad. Now. Look, here's a picture of Sir Galahad. Isn't he splendid? He was one of Arthur's Round Table, you know."

Alice peered at the colored plate of a handsome man encased in a metal suit. "What's he wearin'?"

"Oh, silly, you know, surely you do. No? Well, it's a suit of armor. Sir Galahad was very brave and gallant." She leaned to Alice and said with a wide-eyed whisper, "I bet he was a good kisser too! Now I'll read you some Byron." She opened a book.

There be none of Beauty's daughters
With a magic like Thee;
And like music on the waters
Is thy sweet voice to me . . .

Tamsin read with a melodious cadence and Alice drifted, day-dreaming of Bledsoe finding her in this perfect little house. How she'd throw her arms around him, after he took off the metal suit, of course. *My knight.* They'd live here forever. Hidden in the pines, where no one would ever find them.

SIXTY-SEVEN

Wearing Evans's gray trousers, a neat white shirt, and gray frock coat, Bledsoe looked like a new man. Or, at least that was what Evans said when he saw him. "The bare feet are unfortunate," he said, "but that's the best we can do for now. Let's go."

Inside the walls Bledsoe was surprised to see what looked like a small city. As Evans led Bledsoe down a sidewalk beside a well-groomed lawn, he continued telling him about Fort Monroe. "Over five hundred seventy acres. Livestock, gardens." There were even brick houses shaded by towering oaks, a hospital, church, stables, barracks, arsenals, batteries. "See that?" Evans pointed to an enormous cannon being hauled by a team of six oxen. "It can fire a missile four miles." In the distance the sound of bugles and the tum-tum of drums sounded as troops were drilled and redrilled. "Come on, Joe. No lollygagging. We're on army property now and these army types are nothing if not devoted to the idea of being on time. What are you staring at?"

Bledsoe had stopped several paces behind Evans, head craned skyward. There was a bright golden ball sailing above the fort. Evans looked up beside him. "Oh, look there. That's the aeronaut, Lowe, and his balloon. Haven't seen him down this way for a while. Guess he's been getting a gander at the defenses at Yorktown and decided to drift down our way." There was a dull boom-boom-boom in the distance.

"There's somebody up there?" breathed Bledsoe, full of wonder. Others had paused, pointing and staring at the balloon as it leisurely sailed over the fort. Two women ran out of a house in a decidedly unladylike fashion, practically screeching in excitement. Soldiers and servants dropped whatever they were doing to marvel at the balloon. Bledsoe could just barely make out a small basket tethered to the bottom. "How's he stay up?"

"Hot gas. Lowe has a generator on board and can adjust a valve to go higher or lower. God, wouldn't I love to get up there with him? Imagine what I could get down on paper. I'll have to talk to the general about that. On a clear day like this he can almost look right into their bedroom windows." The boom-boom from the other side of the river intensified. "It drives them crazy. Of course it's out of range of their guns, but they can't help themselves and they waste all kinds of ammunition trying to shoot it down. They got themselves some kind of circus balloon a month or so ago and tried to fly it, but it never got up more than a few hundred feet before it caught on fire. There he goes."

They watched as the balloon picked up speed and headed north. Soon it was nothing but a tiny golden wink in the sky.

Evans, his portfolio case under his arm, approached a big whitewashed building. Bledsoe followed. Two soldiers stood guard on either side of the door. "Name?" asked one.

"You know my name," replied Evans, scowling at the guard. "It's the same name it was a few hours ago."

"Name?" repeated the guard, staring straight ahead.

"Gallagher," snapped the artist. "James Gallagher, cartographer for the Union army, as you know, Private."

"Business?" inquired the guard, his face an emotionless blank.

Bledsoe, standing a few feet behind this man who had been Spencer Evans but now was someone named James Gallagher, noted that the other guard was barely attempting to disguise a smirk. Bledsoe watched the artist clearly trying to contain his anger. But why did he say his name was Gallagher, not Evans?

"To see Colonel Campbell, which you also damn well know as you're the one who brought me his order three hours ago. And be very clear, I'm sick and tired of your idea of fun and games."

The guard, still staring straight ahead, saluted and said, "Just doing my job. Pass on."

Scowling, the artist started through the door of the officers' quarters but when Bledsoe began to follow, the guard blocked his way with his musket. "He's with me," said the artist. "Let him through."

"I have no orders about a negro," replied the guard.

"Private Miller, isn't it?"

"Morris," replied the guard.

"You can count yourself demoted, Morris," said the artist. "I'm reporting your continual insolence."

"I don't think you can get much lower than a private," drawled the guard, "but you go on and try." The other guard sniggered.

The artist, clenching his fist, face blotched, turned to Bledsoe. "Just wait here." He glared at the guard, who stared straight ahead. The artist shouldered roughly past him into the officers' quarters.

"You the new one?" asked the guard named Morris when the door banged closed.

"New one?" Bledsoe backed a couple of feet away from the two men in blue uniforms with rifles over their shoulders.

"Other one ran off at Big Bethel."

Bledsoe looked from one guard to the other. The soldier named Morris eyed him. On the road behind Bledsoe a company began to drill. "To the right," shouted the drillmaster. A drummer beat time and somewhere a church bell tolled.

"What's Big Bethel?"

"A place where the damn Rebels shot us up. My cousin was there. That one," the soldier said with a derisive sneer, "that one just went in to the general to weasel something or other, just sat up on a hill drawing pictures at Big Bethel while down below them New York boys got shot to bits by Reb artillery."

"What you mean?" asked Bledsoe.

"I mean, boy, he *saw* they were about to be blown to pieces, but did he warn them? No. Just drew fucking pictures. Oh, and his nigger ran off from there and never came back."

Bledsoe was bewildered. "But he's not regular army. He doesn't shoot a gun. He's an artist. He makes maps for Lincoln. He's a cartographer."

"My ass," said Morris.

Turning to Morris, the other guard said, "Shut it, Bill. What you telling this boy all that for?"

"'Cause maybe he oughta know"—Morris spat between the toes of his boots—"what a shitty yellow belly that man is. I know shit when I smell it." He suddenly snapped to attention and saluted as behind him the door to the officers' quarters opened. Bledsoe stepped away as an officer, sashed and gold braided, exited and mounted a horse a colored groom held for him.

The guards now stood at stone-faced attention. It was as if Bledsoe had become invisible. He turned and watched as the troops drilled, suited in new sack coats of dark blue. They stepped smart, eyes to the front; the metal on their muskets gleamed. He watched them march. Men in blue, four abreast repeated over and over, row after row. One two three four, they stepped in perfect unison. How he longed to fall in beside them.

He looked over his shoulder at the guards. Clearly they didn't like the cartographer. Why? The one named Morris had called Evans a coward. But the artist wasn't supposed to fight. He was supposed to draw the battle. That was his job. Bledsoe shifted from one bare foot to the other, turning it over in his mind. But then, what did he know about war or artists? Not much.

Across the parade ground, a colored man tended a flower garden in front of an officer's house. Another four or five were building a brick wall. It was hot work. They were all stripped to the waist and closely watched over by an armed Yankee soldier.

He was at Fort Monroe, wasn't he? So he had a choice. He could stay with the other contrabands instead of going with this man, this *spy*, who first said his name was Evans and then Gallagher, a man whose real name he didn't even know. The last of the drilling company passed; the drums rat-tatted as they followed the troops back to their barracks. The door to the big white building opened again and the artist walked out between the two guards without giving them even a glance. He beckoned to Bledsoe. "Come along now, Joe." He pulled his hat brim jauntily over one eye as he led the way across a wide green lawn.

Behind him, Bledsoe said, "There was another one. That's what they said back there."

The artist turned and clapped him on the shoulder. "Look what we've got!" A fancy red-spoked landau was just pulling to a stop beside the artist. The driver climbed down and the artist climbed to the driver's bench and took up the reins of a glossy chestnut gelding. "Come on, Joe," said the artist. "*Tempus fugit.*"

"The soldier back there said you had another one."

"One what?" asked the artist, smiling as he ran a hand over the soft leather of the landau's upholstery.

"Another . . . well, I guess, contraband."

The artist straightened up and smoothed his jacket. He leaned from the fancy buggy. "You listened to that claptrap? Good Lord. Those men are idiots, Joe. They're jealous! Green as grass. Envious as hell. Jesus. Look at what we've got here and look at them. Standing in the sun all day like the dullards they are. Which is exactly what they deserve. Now climb aboard."

Across the field a soldier was yelling at one of the gardeners. The nearly naked men building the brick wall looked like what they still were—slaves.

"I should never have let them get my goat. Look, Joe, while they march around in the mud, I'll dine at the finest restaurants and sleep on a feather mattress and you're coming with me. It's as I suspected. I've been given a plum assignment. Why are you still standing there? We've got miles to cover before dark."

"They said the other one ran off at a place called Big Bethel."

"Oh. Well, that's true."

"Why?"

The artist shrugged. "Had somewhere else he'd rather be, I imagine. Didn't care for army life. Who's to say? I'm not a mind reader."

Behind them, a wagon pulled by a team of oxen was blocked by the landau. "Git out of the road," hollered the driver.

The artist waved a gloved hand at him, then turned back to Bledsoe. "Well?"

"What if I want to stay here?"

"Fine. They need fortifications built all day long. All night too. Day and night. Digging."

Sweat was rolling off the men's bare backs as they piled up bricks. The soldier was still yelling at the gardener.

Bledsoe climbed up beside the artist in the landau. "I'm only coming for Lincoln."

"Awfully kind of you," laughed the artist. "I'm sure he'll be glad to hear about it. Gee up now," he called to the flashy gelding. Moments later the light buggy with its high-stepping horse was rolling smoothly toward the great gate leading out of the fort. The artist pulled a cigar from his pocket. "You know, Joe, I've gotta say. Don't find someone like you too often. I like a man who can quote the *Encyclopedia Britannica*. Here, take the reins, why don't you."

Bledsoe took the reins while the artist, whose real name was anybody's guess, lit the cigar. "Where we going?" he asked, as the road wove past the burned remains of Hampton.

"We're on our way to the new capital of the South," the artist replied, exhaling a plume of white smoke as they left the ruins behind. "Richmond, my friend, Richmond."

SIXTY-EIGHT

She was a good mimic. If Tamsin picked up the wide-tined fork, she picked up the wide-tined fork. Tamsin used the spoon shaped like a scallop shell to eat turtle soup, so Alice did the same. Tamsin ate small dainty bites of food; so did Alice, even if there were times she'd rather just lift the plate and lick it clean.

Tamsin dressed every morning, complete with corset and at least four or five petticoats, despite the fact the only people who would see her all day long were her aged uncle and the servants. For the first few days, Alice had worn one of Tamsin's wrappers. It was green and pink taffeta, roomy, and buttoned easily up the front. She arranged her own hair, meaning she just let it fall in her face. But eventually Tamsin was certain that her guest would like to be properly dressed, dismissing Alice's demurs to the contrary. She was quite happy not having to get gussied up in uncomfortable garments just to parade around a nearly empty house in the middle of nowhere.

Tamsin had loaned Alice several pretty day gowns, as well as all the necessary underpinnings. She seemed to delight in dressing Alice up, almost as if she were a doll. "Oh, pretty, pretty!" she'd cry, as she turned

Alice this way and that to admire a bow or rearrange a bit of lace. "Do you like it? I hope so. Oh, it's so nice to have a girl, Alice. I get so lonely sometimes." So when she also offered Eva's assistance to help her dress in the morning, Alice pretended to be grateful. If Tamsin couldn't dress by herself, then Alice figured she better not be able to either.

Eva was part Tuscarora Indian. Tamsin said she was sixty or so. She had been Uncle Harlan's dead sister's maid and then became Uncle Harlan's housekeeper and cook. After the twins came to live at Bell's Bliss, she also took on the role of Tamsin's maid. She was a tall, stately woman. Despite her age, her hair was still jet black and nearly perfectly straight. She wore it in a braided roll on the back of her head. Her skin was brassy brown and looked poreless. Her profile could have been cut from marble. There was never a hair out of place and her apron was always spotless.

She didn't speak to Alice unless absolutely necessary. She held the petticoats wide for Alice to step into but did not look at her. When Alice was forced to steady herself by putting a hand on Eva's shoulder, she felt the woman flinch in distaste. When she combed her hair in the morning she dragged the teeth across Alice's scalp deep enough to make Alice wince. And, though she did artfully arrange it so that most of the scar was covered, Eva wound the chignon in back so tight Alice had a continual headache.

Alice avoided talking as much as possible, but when required, she spoke so soft it was nearly a whisper. *You don't talk like a lady talks.* Days passed like cold molasses. Sometimes she felt as stuck in them as a fly in glue. Her mind was constantly wondering where he was. *Is he alive? Oh, he must be, I'd know. Is he thinking of me?* It was torture having to mince about in an enormous skirt and pinching shoes, sew little silly things, take a turn with Tamsin in the garden, stare at the river, eat supper, go to bed. And most of all it was exhausting having to remember to *never* forget that she could never let on who she really was, for that would be the end of her and she knew it.

She was sewing in the parlor while Tamsin worked on an embroidery. Cadan was on leave again. He sat there now in his gray coat, with its row of gleaming buttons, a few feet away, one leg crossed atop the other, boots so shiny it hurt to look at them.

Doesn't he have to go somewhere and be a soldier? He reminded her of a lizard, all cold blood. Eva had arranged her hair in glossy black wings that swooped over her cheeks, yet she kept her bad side tilted away. She knew he studied her. When she'd catch him at it, he didn't even pretend to look away. She feigned fascination with her sewing while he went on and on about the war—how he'd fight it if it was up to him. *Well, it ain't and I guess the South is probably damn grateful.* Tamsin smiled at her. Alice pretended a sweet smile back. She was as good as a prisoner of war here.

Cadan rolled an unlit cigar between his fingers as he announced that three of the fugitives from High Hope farm where the white man had been murdered were captured trying to get north. Field hands: a mother, father, daughter. Apparently, said Cadan, there had been a mysterious negro staying in the quarter at the farm. A tall lanky boy, didn't even look twenty, the runaways said. And a girl was with him too. The master had brought them both back from Manassas. Girl's name was Birdy; they didn't know what the boy's was. He kept to himself and didn't mingle. Where either of them were now, they couldn't say. Really couldn't, he grinned, because except for the girl who'd been sold down south, the other two had been hanged.

Alice felt the blood pulsing in her temples. She bit her lip to keep from crying out.

"A militia patrol came on the bodies of two others, old woman and a middle-aged male. They washed up from the river a few days ago."

She kept her head down, concentrating with all her might on cross-stitching a pink briar rose on the pillowcase, but her hands were shaking.

"What about that poor widow?" asked Tamsin.

Cadan wiped the tip of his spotless boot with a handkerchief. "Oh. Well. Turns out she did it herself."

Tamsin stopped stitching. "What? Hanged herself? Suicide? Lord have mercy."

Alice looked up.

"Apparently she left a note. Looks like she found out she was flat broke after her husband died. Though doesn't make sense. Hale Talbot had bought her stock—well, then that nigger shot him in cold blood."

"How horrible! What a traged—oh, sugar," exclaimed Tamsin, examining her embroidery. "Look at this. I chain stitched when I ought to have herringboned. I'm going to have to take all this out and start over now."

"That nigger and his wench haven't been found. I can't figure it," said Cadan, crossly, slapping his handkerchief against the arm of the chair. "The dogs were on them. It's like they were plucked off the face of the earth."

He's alive! Though she hadn't made a sound, Cadan looked at her just then. She covered her joy with a coughing fit. He tucked his handkerchief into a pocket. "I've been meaning to ask. What the hell happened to your face?"

Alice opened her mouth and shut it again. She scrambled her fingers in her hair, pulling it across the face.

"Cadan Bell! I never! What on earth happened to *your* manners?" Tamsin dropped her embroidery, clearly shocked.

Cadan pushed back his chair with a screech. "Good Lord, just asked a simple question. She ain't made a glass." He stomped out of the parlor.

Tamsin leaned to her and put her hand over Alice's shaking ones. "I'm so sorry, honey. He's been cross as a bear since he was assigned to Captain Allen. He has yet to see a Yankee, let alone shoot one. Anyway he's going back to camp this afternoon."

Tamsin put her arm around her and laid her head on Alice's shoulder. "Don't pay him any mind." She lifted her head and gently stroked the glossy swoop around Alice's ear. "Your hair reminds me of a blackbird wing." Alice felt Tamsin's warm breath on her cheek. "And, if you don't mind my saying," she said softly, "I think it makes you more interesting, like a heroine in a novel. The mysterious Lady of the River." Alice sat stiffly, afraid to move as Tamsin continued to smooth her hair.

Eva appeared with two tall glasses and set the tray on a small table. Sitting on the sofa with Tamsin's head on her shoulder, Alice wondered why she hadn't heard her come in. *She's quiet as a cat.*

"Here, Miss Tam. Last of summer lemons. Had to put lotsa sugar to hide the sourness. If you was to taste the real thing you'd not like it."

Tamsin sat up and took the chilled glass. "If there's any sourness in this room, it's the look on your face, Eva," she said with a little laugh.

"My face don't lie," retorted Eva. She swept regally out of the room.

SIXTY-NINE

"The Greeks say there is a river in Hades called the Lethe and once the shades of the dead drink from it, they forget their earthly life," said Uncle Harlan, pointing a spoon at Alice. "Perhaps she is not a sprite but a spirit. Pass me the gravy, would you, niece?"

"Alice merely bumped her head, Uncle," replied Tamsin. "But she's improving. This morning she remembered she likes poached eggs on toast because she ate four. Would you hand Uncle Harlan the gravy, Alice?"

Alice carefully picked up the heavy silver gravy boat and handed it to the old man. "Thank you, dear. Ah! Was that just a hint of a smile?"

"I think it was, Uncle, I think it was," beamed Tamsin. She patted Alice's hand. "At last."

"Has Freddy shown you her plants yet, Alice?"

"Aunt Freddy is gone now, Uncle Harlan."

His face fell a moment. He looked at his plate and back at his niece. "Of course." He turned to Alice. "Would you pass the gravy, dear?"

Uncle Harlan was seventy-eight and sometimes called Tamsin Freddy. Tamsin told Alice he confused her with his sister, Frederica, who died thirty years earlier from a fall from her horse. She had been an amateur botanist and Uncle Harlan had been very close to her.

After dinner Uncle Harlan read the newspaper aloud in a voice that would have reached the last row in a large theater. Tamsin, used to these readings, embroidered or sometimes took a secret nap behind a magazine, but Alice listened intently.

In the days following what the Richmond paper called "The High Hope Massacre," columns had been filled with editorial prophecy. For some reason, the fact that Hale Talbot's dog was also killed seemed to evoke a sort of special horror. "No pity for even an innocent beast."

The terror the "massacre" inspired was illustrated by a Mrs. B of _________ Street in a letter to the paper as read by Uncle Harlan:

> So the insurrectionist is still running free. How many others are there? Our trusted servants, our Uncle Samuel and Mammy Bess, who bore us formerly in joy as well as sorrow with all good grace, now look at us with eyes that do not conceal absence of any affection. It turns me cold to think it may well be that affection was but a sham, that our Negroes only pretended to love us. And those we believed to be harmless as a basket of kittens have been transformed into a nest of vipers by Northern lies. If this is true, may God have mercy on their Yankee souls, for just as the creature Frankenstein could not be made fully human, neither will the monsters created with a promise of freedom. This monster is turned loose on us all.

There followed predictions of slaves armed with stolen muskets and bloody axes burning their way to Richmond. This seemed, at least from the writers' perspectives, a prospect even more dire than a successful invasion by Yankees. "Now let us move on to the Amusements section," said Uncle Harlan. "Then we'll go to Lost Articles. What is it, Alice dear? You are positively twitching, I believe. Are you unwell?"

Alice had been trying to interrupt Uncle Harlan as he read by waving a hand in his direction. "Back a bit. Before what you jist read. You said somethin' 'bout a monster? Not bein' found? That means they ain't found him?"

"Him who, dear?"

"I think she means the slave who murdered that man and his dog, Uncle."

Uncle Harlan looked at Alice. "Don't worry. There's no need to be frightened. We'll not dwell on any more morbidity." He rattled the paper. "I think we'll pass over the lost articles this evening, but here, there's this about those Yankee guns":

> A correspondent of the *New York Commercial,* who witnessed the experiments at Fortress Monroe with the big gun "Union," says:
>
> There seems to have been two objections suggested by this experiment. First, that it requires too much time and too many men to load and fire the gun. Second, that the projectile used is defective. The men who handled the gun on this occasion were mostly inexperienced, being nearly all of the "contraband" persuasion. It may be that regularly drilled gunners, with constant practice, can load and fire more rapidly, and

> without employing so much force. It may be, also, that a projectile of a different and much improved character can be used—ensuring more precision of aim, more directness of motion, and a still longer range.

Fort Monroe. And the magical word. Contraband.

"How far is it?"

"How far is what, Alice?" asked Tamsin.

"Fort Monroe."

"Uncle?"

"Twenty-five, thirty miles." Uncle Harlan looked at Alice over the newspaper. "The Yankees will never get this far up, my dear. Never fear. Our boys are stationed all around the property here, around all the great houses. The roads are covered. No Yankees will get past. In fact, my dears, I meant to mention to you to take care in walking too far afield. Soldiers can sometimes be a bit trigger-happy."

"What? Are we not to walk on our own land, Uncle?"

"Oh no, I'm just saying take care. But you see how we are guarded by our brave boys. Now, the Yankees might have the bay blockaded at Point Comfort, but they'll never get upriver to Richmond. And even if, *if*, mind you, they did get past us here, they'd never get past the fortifications at Drewry's Bluff outside Richmond. So don't you worry your dear little head, child. But if they dare come around Bell's Bliss?" He rang the little bell beside him on the table.

Attis appeared. "Fetch me the Mantons," commanded Uncle Harlan.

Attis opened a cabinet and pulled out a large mahogany box inlaid with ivory.

"Show our little mermaid the contents within."

Attis opened the box and displayed two long barreled dueling pistols resting in a nest of faded purple velvet.

"These beauties were made by Joseph Manton in 1814. I once shot a snifter of Calvados right off Attis's black head, did I not?"

"Yes, Marster, you surely did," replied Attis, closing the box with a snap and putting it back in the cabinet.

"What a bang that made! And, my dears, I pour my own shot," declared Uncle Harlan proudly. "Oh, you have all your modern revolvers, your Colts, those Walkers the Texans love, but you'll never find anything superior for one deadly shot than those pistols. It's the hidden rifling in the barrel does it. Adds spin to the ball. Maybe not as sporting, but then, we're not going to be using them for duels any longer. Attis keeps them cleaned and loaded. So you girls can rest assured you are safe from any marauding Yankees."

Alice was barely listening. *Contraband.* Fort Monroe. If that was where he was, there were only twenty-five miles between them. But how could she possibly get to him? She was going to ask if a person could walk there, but Uncle Harlan's head had fallen to his chest. Anyway, what difference would it make even if she could walk? He said they were surrounded by Rebel soldiers. They weren't likely to let her just walk her way to the enemy.

Attis scooped Uncle Harlan from his chair as if he were light as leaves. The old man murmured in his sleep and wrapped his arms around the servant's neck as he was carried off to bed.

SEVENTY

"I know you a liar," said Eva. Alice tried to turn her head to deny it, but Eva had hold of her hair.

She cried out. "What you mean? Let go!"

Eva dangled something on a long piece of string in front of Alice's eyes. "What's this?"

"Oh Lord! I thought it was lost forever," breathed Alice. "Give it to me!"

"This here witch dolly, you mean?"

"It ain't that. It's mine! Let go a me, damn you! Give it!"

Eva yanked Alice's hair harder, forcing her head back. "I knowed you wasn't a proper lady minute I seen you. How you fool Miss Tam, I don't know, but she ain't gonna be fooled no more." She abruptly released Alice and put the little carved willow stick in the pocket of her apron and went to the door of the bedroom.

Alice ran after and grabbed her before she could open the door. "Give me it!"

"Let go. I'm gonna burn it."

"No!" She shoved Eva against the bedroom wall and tried to get her hand in Eva's pocket.

"What's going on in here?" Tamsin came into the bedroom, her silk skirt billowing around her. "What on earth? Alice? What are you doing to Eva?"

Alice had Eva by the wrist. She wrenched it now and Eva howled with pain. "She stole somethin' of mine and won't give it back."

Eva turned a furious face to Tamsin. "She ain't what you think, Miss Tam. This one been lyin' to y'all, you and Mister Harlan."

Alice's face was red; she was nearly panting with rage as she snarled, "Give it to me."

"Eva has never stolen anything, Alice. I'm sure you're mistaken. Let her go."

Eva ripped her wrist loose from Alice's grip and pulled the willow woman from her pocket. "See this, Miss Tam? This here ain't no regular dolly. This be a conjure charm. I found it out by the wood pile this mornin', starin' right up at me with them dead li'l eyes. Attis tole me it was round her neck when he fished her out the river. It fell off a her when he brung her inside and he forgot about it 'cause he doan know what it is, but I do, I know."

She pointed at Alice. "She a liar, Miss Tam. She ain't nothin' but po' white, common as pig tracks. She doan even know how to git her underbritches on right less I help her. This here poppet be used for cursin' folks. She be up to no good, I tell you."

Alice grabbed the doll from Eva. "*He* made it for me! It's mine." She was crying now and she didn't care. She felt her heart might snap in two. She clutched the willow woman to her breast. "It's all I got of him."

"Eva, leave us now please." Tamsin put her arm around Alice's shaking shoulders.

"I'm tellin' you, can't trust . . ."

"Go on," said Tamsin.

"Oh, I'll go. I'll go but you be sorry."

"That's enough. Get out," snapped Tamsin. Eva slammed the door after herself so hard a painting jumped half a foot from the wall.

Alice hung the willow woman around her neck and wiped her eyes. Tamsin lifted it from where it lay on Alice's breast. "That face. It's uncanny. It's the eyes, I think, the way they're worked in the wood there. Oh, don't worry. I don't believe any of that slave mumbo jumbo. Curses, soul catchers, all that." She looked into Alice's eyes. "But who is this *he*? The one you said made it?"

Alice turned away.

"Won't you tell me?"

Alice sank onto a velvet-covered chaise longue. "Oh woe," she sighed. "He's gone." She covered her face with her hands. "I think I might die of it."

"Oh, true love!" Tamsin sank down beside Alice and held her while she sobbed, smoothing her hair, saying "shush, shush, that's all right," over and over until at last Alice said, "He might even be dead by now, though I think I'd feel it. Oh!" she cried, burying her head on Tamsin's shoulder.

"Oh now, there, there, honey, it's all right. You tell me whatever you want, you poor puss. Here's my hanky." Alice dabbed her eyes and blew her nose. She peered up at Tamsin through long, wet eyelashes. Tamsin clucked and hugged her again.

Alice pulled away and slowly composed herself. She wiped her face with her sleeve, sniffled some more, and then looking at her lap as she fiddled with her fingers, she said softly, "You gotta understand what happened."

Tamsin nodded encouragingly.

"See, 'twas like this. My aunt." Alice paused a moment. "Green. Aunt Green. That's my name. Alice Green."

"Green! Alice Green. Do we know any Greens? No, I can't think of any."

"You wouldn't know us anyhow," said Alice. "This was up near Norfolk and we was poor. Folks like you Bells wouldn't know us Greens. Anyway. Aunt Green died. Sudden like. Her heart. It plumb give out on her one night. Yes it did. And we lived all alone. And I'm an orphan. Been one always. Not always, but you know, *always*."

"Oh!" said Tamsin. "Yes. I do know. Our parents died when we were babies. Like my brother and I! I knew it, I somehow knew it!"

Alice smiled thinly and continued. "And she raised me. My aunt, I mean. But there she was! All a sudden keeled over like this." Alice clutched her chest and rolled her eyes. "Dead as a boiled tater. What was I to do? I didn't have two pennies to rub together, for we was poor folks." She looked sadly at Tamsin. "I'm jist a poor orphan, you see. We was too poor for me to even git any schoolin'. I can't even write my name and I ain't never had pretty things like this here dress afore now. Y'all have been so kind to me." Alice squeezed her eyelids together to wring out a last tear or two. "Well"—she sighed dramatically—"I reckon I better git goin'."

"Oh!" said Tamsin, grabbing hold of one of Alice's hands. "No! Of course not. You poor, poor thing. You will stay with us, why forever if you want to! But who is this man? The one you love?"

"Well," sniffled Alice, grasping at half-truths and whole lies. *Best leave that out but tell this.* "It was late at night when she died. I was so afear'd. We lived miles from town. Where to go? Who to tell? What will happen to me? Then"—she leaned to Tamsin—"the most awful thing!"

"What? What could be more awful?" asked Tamsin, already horrified by the image of poor Alice alone in a house with a dead body. "What?"

"The place ketched fire. It were lightnin' what done it. Hit the roof and whoosh!" Alice raised her arms toward the ceiling. "Jist like that! I couldn't even see the door no more in all that smoke and flames. I'm tellin' you there was mountains of fire. Flames from here to the moon! It were all I could do to scream and I thought I was done for. Then. All a sudden. The door, well, the door fell in! And there he was! Standing in a ring of firelight. He lifted me up like I was a little baby and carried me right out of that burnin' hell."

"How marvelous, how brave," whispered Tamsin, her face alight. "Like a knight."

"Yes, in the night. Oh, I can't tell you what happened then for it's jist too—Why, it's jist too . . ."

"You can!" said Tamsin. "You can tell me anything, Alice. Don't be afraid. And don't you worry." She patted her hand. "You can stay with Uncle Harlan and I just as long as you want. Oh! You know? Maybe Uncle Harlan can adopt you and you'll be my real sister!" She kissed her unscarred cheek softly. Surprised and confused, Alice pulled her face away.

"I always wanted a sister," said Tamsin. "Now, you are good as mine. So go on, tell me everything."

Alice eyed the blond girl. "All right," she said. "What happened was . . ."

The sun was sinking and the light in the room had faded when Tamsin rang for Eva to light the lamps. "So you volunteered to nurse with General Jackson's men? And you were at Manassas! Oh, my. I am"—Tamsin shook her head—"I am just in awe of you. How brave you are, Alice! And then for your dear Henry to be wounded and captured by the Yankees. What company did you say he was in?"

"Um, Alabama it was," replied Alice. "The Fourth Alabama."

"You really think they're holding him a prisoner at Fort Monroe?"

Alice nodded. "I heard that's where they took 'em."

"But how did you end up in the river?"

"I jumped in to keep that Yankee from—oh! I can't tell you that!" She broke off with a sob. "It's jist too awful."

"Oh Lord God Almighty," replied Tamsin with horror, and gathered Alice into her arms. She pulled back a moment and smoothed the hair away from Alice's cheek. "Is that how . . . I mean . . ."

"He had a big knife," whispered Alice, and she pulled the hair over her scar. Beneath her gown, Alice felt the willow carving press into her flesh as Tamsin held her.

"Oh you poor, poor child. I'll ask you no more, not another word about it," said Tamsin, as Alice did her best to tremble in her arms. She apparently didn't notice the scar was years old.

The French doors were open to the last of the afternoon sun. A hummingbird hung perpendicular in the doorway, green headed and ruby throated. Alice could hear the whir of its wings. It almost seemed to be contemplating whether to come inside. *It's too late in the year,* she thought. *It ought to be gone by now.*

"You're safe now," said Tamsin, hugging Alice fiercely. "Nobody will hurt you here, no they won't, you're safe now."

SEVENTY-ONE

They had to stop halfway up the peninsula. It was too far to go without changing horses or letting the gelding rest for the night. They'd stopped in a village, more of a hamlet. There were no more than six or seven buildings lining the gravel turnpike. One was an inn or really a tavern with two small rooms to let and a stable. While the artist ate a hearty meal by the fire and fell asleep on a goosefeather mattress, Bledsoe was given a bowl of fatty stew by a thick-armed colored woman in the clay-floored kitchen. He ate beside the horse in the stable. It was also where he slept, and badly. His shoulder ached from the still-healing wound. The floor of the stable was damp through the straw.

Near dawn he woke up, went out into the stableyard, and ducked his head in the horse trough. The sky was just beginning to lighten. There was no wind. He heard a mourning dove's ghostly hoo-hoo and the answer of its lover. The flap of wings sounded like buckshot when it took off. The back of his neck prickled and he turned to see a cat, the type Reecie had called a tortie, watching him dispassionately from atop a fence post. "Kit-kit," he whispered, holding out a hand. "Kit-kitty." The cat arched its back and ran off.

He started back into the stable but stopped right before crossing the threshold. Every cell of his body seemed to freeze. The air was filled with the scent of mint and clover. *Sweet potato vine says you're mine.*

The fragrance settled around him like a robe. "Alice?" He peered across the threshold into the gloom of the stable, holding out his hands like a blind man. "Alice?"

Behind him a donkey tied to a post hiccupped a nasal bray and a rooster started up. A moment later hens were clucking around his ankles. In the inn yard, a little boy, maybe six or seven, began pumping water in a bucket while a big collie barked at the stream of water. The sun was painting pink streaks across newborn clouds when the back door of the inn opened and shut with a bang. But Bledsoe didn't turn around. He remained pasted in the doorway of the stable. Then the gelding neighed and stamped its hooves impatiently. It was light enough now for him to see there was nothing but old stalls of rotting wood and dirty straw. Manure stink filled his nostrils.

"Joe!"

He wiped his eyes.

"Joe, come on," yelled the artist. "Time to go."

He pushed down the lump and knocked the dust and straw from the gray trousers and pulled on the jacket. Then he harnessed the gelding to the buggy and rolled it to the back of the inn.

"Here you go," said the artist, climbing into the landau. He shoved a half loaf of bread and a hunk of cheese at Bledsoe. "We want to get a good start; we've still got a lot of road to cover. We'll stop again for supper, but we'll go on to Richmond tonight."

Three hours later, the artist had climbed in the back of the buggy and was lounging on the thickly upholstered passenger seat. "Tell me then, what have you read beside the encyclopedia and that awful novel? Any John Stuart Mill?"

On the driver's bench Bledsoe shook his head.

"Hobbes? Voltaire?"

"I read *Last of the Mohicans*," replied Bledsoe shyly.

"Rot!" replied the artist. "Silly novel."

Bledsoe almost said, *No it ain't,* but didn't. No matter what, the man behind him in the elegant landau was white. But when the artist added, "Romanticized claptrap," he couldn't help himself.

"But Hawkeye was like an Indian!"

"Indians? What? Ah, I see. You mean you find that natural man nonsense appealing? Listen here, my friend. I spent time with a band of Paiutes and let me tell you, all that noble savage stuff is a load of bull. They were dirty, smelly, and if you got them drunk, murderous." The artist's silver flask flashed in the sun as he tipped it back and drank. "Noble savage, my ass. Those Indians had nothing more than animal intellect. In fact, they claimed they could *talk* to animals. They smeared themselves with bear grease and ate grubs like beasts. Nothing noble about it. Just plain savages. Now forget that. Read yourself some Hegel. Or better yet, Schiller."

He took another swallow from the flask. "None of that lovey-dovey nonsense," he went on. The artist was sprawled in the passenger seat like a pasha. "*Die schöne Seele.* Know what that means? No, I see you don't. Well, not your fault. It's German. It means the beautiful soul, or the shining soul. One of Schiller's philosophical theories; a man can be lifted up through reason and beauty to pure goodness. Now, maybe that's as much rot as Rousseau came up with but it's worth a try anyway, I think. But listen here, you couldn't lift one of those damn Paiutes higher than my ankle. I tried to help 'em out with their treaty. Ungrateful brutes. Just shot at us. Read something worthwhile, not silly girl books. Love. Women always want some Sir Galahad to come save the day. As if we have time. As if we don't have more important things to attend to."

A coach was approaching just then at high speed, forcing Bledsoe to pull off the road. When he pulled back on, Bledsoe turned around. "But *Last of the Mohicans* isn't a lovey-dovey story, it's . . ." He turned to see the artist no longer sprawled like a pasha. His mouth was open and he was snoring.

SEVENTY-TWO

Alice cradled the willow woman in the palm of her hand. It was past midnight and Bell's Bliss was asleep. She was alone in the bedroom. The velvet drapes were pulled across the window and the room was a black box. The only light came from the beeswax candle burning on the floor. She looked down into the tiny face. What made something a charm? *Believing.* That was the biggest part of it. You could take someone's hair or their clipped fingernails and use them as a charm. It had to be something that belonged to the person you wanted to work on.

Maybe Eva was right. Maybe the tiny carved doll was magic. What made something magic? *Believing.* She'd heard of people who'd endured the worst tortures without a scream because they believed in Heaven. Those thrown in with lions without being afraid because they believed in the Lord. She stroked the miniature woman. *He made you for me, so it's some of him and some of me.* She kneeled in the candle's halo, her white nightdress pillowing around her.

She was not a conjure woman. The only things she knew were from spying on the old woman. Church people said it wasn't right to meddle like that. God had a plan for the world. Anyone who tampered with it was asking for it, according to every preacher she'd ever heard preach. But look at all the people who came to Granny Guthrie. Came all the way to the Deep Dismal—church people too. They came for love, for hate. For revenge, for money. They came, high and low, not caring in the end how they got what they desired. *You kin git 'em to believe they're bein' eaten up with worms, git 'em to believe they kin fly. Or you can make a handsome woman love a old ugly man—spell 'em, that's what I do. Git 'em to believe.*

But binding was different. It was darker. Binding one person to another could be dangerous. It could come back on you. She thought of Keenan Wheeler devoured by his own dogs. The thought of him just blood, bones, and a scrap of wedding shirt sent a worm crawling down her spine. But she went on and did it.

She wound the string tied to the willow woman around and around, until the little figure was bound like a mummy. She looked up from her work, hearing something behind the pulled velvet drapes. A whirring. Like a big bug, beating against the window glass. She ignored it and pulled off her nightdress. To do this work you had to wear only the skin you were born in. Naked, she stood in the little circle of light and called out to the dark. She called him to come. Bind with her. She used the words the old woman used—guttural ancient words, memorized generation upon generation until the meaning was lost. Alice didn't understand a one of them. But she put all her heart into it. All her believing. All of her love, all her soul. She bound him to her like she'd bound what he'd made for her. *She believed.*

When it was done she was overcome with exhaustion. She unwound the little willow doll and hung it once more around her neck, feeling the wood prick her skin where it lay between her breasts. She lay down on the carpet, naked as the day she was born. She immediately fell into a deep sleep with no dreams.

She woke in the morning before the house was up. Stood and stretched. She felt wonderfully energized, full of hope. She pulled the curtains open to let in the light. She stifled a scream when she saw the little thing at her feet. Tiny as an emerald fairy. The hummingbird was dead.

SEVENTY-THREE

They arrived in Richmond just as the sun was setting. "Stop there." The artist pointed to a shop with "TAILOR" in the window. Although his breath smelled sour and his eyes were bloodshot, the artist walked ahead of Bledsoe into the shop. He told Bledsoe to stand by the window where he could keep an eye on the horse outside. He soon had outfitted himself in a stylish walking suit, vest, and a top hat boasting a cashmere underbrim. He also purchased full evening dress, including maroon leather gloves. The shopkeeper showed him a new coat called a billiard jacket.

"Lord yes. We need that, don't we? As well as a dressing gown, that walking stick, some of those vest buttons." He held up a gold watch chain. "And this."

"Yes, sir," said the shop man for the fifth time, as the artist pulled bill after bill from a leather wallet. "Anything else, sir?"

"I need something for my boy, here. None of that cheap stuff either. I have a reputation to uphold."

"Yes, sir," said the shopkeeper. "Baltimore you say you're from?"

"That's right. I like that black coat over there for him."

"That's the finest wool, sir, and I don't know that your negro . . ."

The artist picked up a silk handkerchief and stuffed it in his new jacket pocket. "You don't know is correct. I'll take it."

Bledsoe put on the immaculately tailored black frock coat, dove trousers, an emerald-green vest. The artist purchased two soft linen shirts for him and a pair of kid leather boots. They were a deep rich ocher. He'd never dreamed of wearing anything so fine, even if he were free and rich. He couldn't help but rub his hand over the soft weave of the pants. They were even better than the ones he'd snatched from the laundry when he ran from Our Joy.

"Ah," said the artist when he emerged from where he'd changed in the back, limping slightly from the pinch of the new boots. "Excellent, Joe. Now. He needs a hat."

A type called a melon was found and set on Bledsoe's head. The artist smiled and smoothed his goatee. "Well, look at us. I do believe we are ready for Richmond, though I wonder if Richmond is ready for us!"

Having settled the bill, he walked out of the shop, with a twirl of his gold-topped cane. Bledsoe, following, glanced at a large standing mirror. He was startled to stillness by the dark gentleman who looked back with the same surprised expression. He lifted his chin and pulled on the gray leather gloves the artist had bought for him, pushing the leather down between each finger. He flexed his hands. The gloves were like a second skin. Though the new boots were rubbing his ankles raw, he turned and walked head high to the landau. The artist was already in the passenger seat. After Bledsoe lifted the reins, the artist tapped his shoulder with the gold knob of his cane. "Onward, boy, don't dawdle."

He doesn't mean it like that. But still some air whooshed out of his soul as the gelding trotted into the new capital of the South.

There's a war? Tell Richmond, thought Bledsoe as they drove through the city that evening. The only sign was the hundreds of Confederate flags. They hung from every official building and many residences as well. Though it was past nine o'clock, the city was lit up bright as day with gaslights. As the red-spoked buggy wheeled down the pavement, a snatch of someone singing gaily—*listen to the mockingbird, listen to the mockingbird, the mockingbird still singing o'er her grave*—streamed through a window. Hansom cabs for hire passed left and right. Ladies in gowns and men in elegant suits and top hats strolled the sidewalk on Broad Street. Up ahead a wonderful smell reminded him of Reecie's delicate almond macaroons. If she was in a good mood, he'd get one or two just out of the oven before they went to the table. The scent emanated from a place called Pizzini's Confectionery. Through the window a richly dressed crowd was enjoying ice cream.

Carriages and their colored drivers were lined up in front of the Richmond Theater waiting for the program to let out. A large gaily painted signboard advertised that the entertainment was *Orfeo and Euridice*. The artist waved a dismissive hand as they passed. "Oh, Gluck. I've always found him wooden. Hopefully the program will change while we're in town."

Bledsoe looked at the gloriously lit opera house. *We.* Was he going to take him to the opera? Through the great windows open to the stifling late August heat came a voice that Bledsoe was certain could not possibly be human. A woman's voice that wound upward toward the night sky above Richmond.

"Turn up here, Joe," said the artist, tapping him once more with the gold knob of his cane. Bledsoe turned the buggy and the last long-held notes faded away. They stopped at Eighth and Main in front of an imposing five-story building. "The Spotswood Hotel," said the artist. "Wait here. I'll book a room."

Bledsoe climbed down from the buggy and held the gelding, smoothing his coat, talking to the high-spirited young horse softly to settle him. A colored man in elegant livery held the door and bowed as two men emerged from the Spotswood. "Here, boy," called one to Bledsoe. "Come on, Fred," he said. Both men climbed into the landau before Bledsoe could say a word.

"Cary Street, driver."

"I ain't a driver," said Bledsoe.

"What you mean, you ain't a driver? You're in front of the hotel, aren't you?"

"Sorry, Massa, I'm waitin' on someone."

"That would be us," said the other man cheerfully. "Take us to Cary and Second. Wait till you see her, you won't be sorry," he said to the other man in the buggy.

When Bledsoe didn't move, he said, "Let's go, boy."

"No," replied Bledsoe.

"No?" replied the other. "Did I hear you? What do you mean no? Are you telling us no, you won't drive us?"

"No," replied Bledsoe. "I mean yes. But it's not because—"

Before he could finish the man jumped out of the landau and grabbed him by his new lapel. "How dare you, you smart-mouthed monkey. Now you drive us or I'll have you taken down to the Bottom and your hide—"

"Let go of him."

The man turned to the artist standing behind him on the sidewalk but didn't release Bledsoe.

"Take your hands off him this instant."

"What? Go away."

"Unhand my man or I'll have *your* hide."

The man dropped Bledsoe's lapel. He held up his hands. "Now see here, I didn't know he was yours. He's standing out here with all the other hacks, and for your information, he was unbearably insolent, never told us he belonged to anybody. Acted free as the wind. Gussied up like he's some sort of—"

The artist lifted his cane and poked the man in the chest with the tip. "I think," he said between gritted teeth, "that we're finished here, don't you?"

"What?" The man batted away the cane and turned to his companion. "Can you believe this?" And back to the artist. "Are you threatening me?"

"Do you wish to be threatened?" replied the artist, twirling the cane with a mean little smile.

A crowd was beginning to grow around the two. Bledsoe held the horse by the bridle as it danced nervously. Too many people were pressed too close. Someone in the crowd said, "Will they fight?" A young soldier threw a coin to the sidewalk. "A nickel on the fancy-pants with the cane."

The artist took off his hat, set it on the sidewalk, and began to take off his jacket. The crowd rumbled with eager anticipation. Even the liveried doorman had joined the ring around the men. Somewhere a gun went off and the gelding reared up with a scream, nearly crashing back down on top of the soldier who'd bet a nickel. The crowd drew back. The man threw up his hands, backing away from the artist. "Well, see here. Forget it then. I was only . . . Dammit. Oh, come on, Fred. Look, there's another hack." The two men quickly disappeared into a closed carriage and the crowd broke up.

"Let's go," said the artist. "The hotel's full. Doesn't really matter now that the president has moved to Clay Street. Let's try the Exchange. Keep going up there and turn right."

Bledsoe clucked the gelding forward. The artist had stood up for him, had even been willing to fight. No one had ever done that. No one. It was on the tip of his tongue to thank him, but the silver-haired man pulled his silver flask from the inner pocket of his elegant new frock coat. He sucked on it and smacked his lips loudly as he recapped it. "Ambrosia," he said. It was as if nothing had happened a few minutes before. "Yes. The entire South has come up to Richmond," he said as they pulled up behind a long line of carriages in front of the Exchange Hotel. "Every Southern politician, every socialite, every newspaper reporter, wants to be here now that the war has started. And Richmond's got it good, considering there's a blockade. It's surrounded by farmland, you know. Rich farmland. They have plenty of the best meat and produce, don't have to rely on imports. And plenty of free slave labor to build fortifications, run the ironworks, whatever else you need. It's one huge party. Look around. Yes indeed! Richmond is the place to be."

The artist climbed out of the landau and walked in the great brass front doors of the hotel. Bledsoe went around back.

SEVENTY-FOUR

There was a crush in the lobby of the hotel. One hoopskirted lady in a broad-brimmed hat pushed through the crowd, recklessly knocking a much smaller man nearly onto the carpet. She didn't stop. Either she didn't notice or didn't care, but she continued onward like a ship at sea, the skirt a tossing froth of sapphire brocade.

"The place is a madhouse. I had to offer double the rate," grumbled thc artist.

Gaslit chandeliers illuminated the guests, who despite the late hour seemed far from bed. A string quartet played amid enormous urns of flowers. Women in gowns sculptured into giant bells by crinolines and hoops swished by. Men in evening dress and others in uniform flowed around any ladies who had paused for conversation.

The artist said, "Wait over by that statue there. I'll be back in a moment." He was soon swallowed by the throng. Bledsoe wedged himself between an exotic fern and a life-size statue of Hera holding a marble pomegranate. The marble folds of Hera's tunic stabbed his midsection and the fern tickled his neck, but he was grateful to be out of the crush, where he was frowned at, pushed aside, or commanded to do something. Between the statue and the fern he was almost hidden and could observe the crowd unnoticed. That is, until a pudgy woman in a grass-green gown was so busy talking to another woman she backed smack into him.

"How dare you," she exclaimed, turning to Bledsoe with a furious glare.

He pushed himself farther against the wall behind him and mumbled, "My fault, Mistress. Sorry."

She brushed the skirt of her gown furiously as if it were somehow now dirtied but forgot about it when another woman said, "Oh look, Lou Lou. Who's that tall officer with the long sandy beard? Such eyes, such a handsome face."

"Where?" replied the woman in green, craning her neck. "Oh bother, if that man would only take off his hat . . . oh! That's the Texan everyone's been talking about. Colonel Hood. John Bell Hood is his name. I met him at the Bollings' last Sunday. They say Texans have no manners, but I've never met such a gentleman. Oh look! There's General Lee coming over to speak with him. Wouldn't you love to be a fly on that wall?"

Bledsoe stood behind them, pinned in place. Though the women's huge skirts were only fabric, they might as well be giant boulders at the mouth of a cave. He could not touch them or ask them to move. He closed his eyes and forced himself to breathe evenly. When he opened them, the woman in green was ogling another man across the crowded room. "I must say, General Lee *is* every bit as imposing as they say, isn't he?"

"No fun, though," said the other. "We had him with the president and his wife and he said about three words the entire night. Just sat there looking regal."

"I heard he's a bit deaf."

"A bit *dull* is more like it."

"Mary Agnes!" laughed the woman in green, playfully smacking her friend's arm with her fan.

By now Bledsoe felt he might faint. It was suffocatingly hot. The combined odors in the room, flowers, sweat, perfume, made him feel nauseous. He sidled a bit to the right, trying to get some air. This set the huge fern in motion. The woman in green was smacked on the back of the head by one of the giant fronds. She slowly turned her head to Bledsoe. "Did you just touch my hair?"

"Oh no, Mistress. I never! It were dis here plant what did it."

The agitated plant was still furiously waving the offending frond. She eyed Bledsoe suspiciously while patting the back of her elaborate upsweep. "Well? Why are you standing there then? Are you spying on us?"

By now his blood was boiling. The muscles in his face were rigid as brick and he clenched his teeth to keep from blurting out what he was thinking. He shook his head.

"Answer me. What are you doing there?"

"I don't have to tell . . ." he began through pursed lips.

"Ah, how delightful," said the artist, who had appeared at the woman's side. He looked over her shoulder and winked. Bledsoe let out his breath as she turned away. The artist bowed. "If it isn't the Rose of Richmond. How are you?"

The woman's face turned a blotchy tomato color and Bledsoe realized she was blushing. She fluttered her pale eyelashes at the artist. "Mr. Capello! Why do you always call me that? So silly of you. Are you staying here? When did you get back to town?"

The artist took one of her gloved hands and brought his lips within close proximity. "Not soon enough, Mrs. Canty. Away from your bloom, the world is a dull place."

"Oh now," she beamed, and tapped him on the shoulder playfully with her fan.

"And yes. I've put up here The Spotswood is full. I hope my man here has offered you any assistance you may require?"

Mrs. Canty turned to Bledsoe. "Oh. He's yours. He's been, well. Just standing there like some sort of, well, I don't know what."

"Is there something you need?"

She looked Bledsoe up and down. "You certainly dress him up fine."

"Why not?" The artist smiled. "He's a reflection on his master, isn't he? I told him to wait there for me. I hope it didn't inconvenience you."

"Oh, anyway," she replied, waving a chunky pale hand, with what Bledsoe imagined she fancied was a charming smile. "Do you know Mrs. Pettigruel?" She indicated the other woman, who was eyeing the artist with barely concealed hauteur. She was younger than Mrs. Canty and would have been pretty if only her big eyes weren't set so close. *Like a spook owl,* thought Bledsoe, glancing at her.

The artist, bowing in turn to her, said, "Do I have the pleasure of meeting Senator Percy Pettigruel's wife?"

Mrs. Pettigruel did not offer her hand to be breathed over but affirmed she was the same.

"Mary Agnes, this is Mr. Capello. Mr. Quincy Capello. The painter I told you about from Baltimore?"

The artist nodded to the woman in green. "Simply Quint will do, dear. We're after all old friends, aren't we?"

The senator's wife smiled thinly. "You're the one who did that big picture of Lou Lou in their drawing room at Merry Meadow."

The artist bowed again. "Guilty."

"Well," said the senator's wife, fanning herself briskly. "I must say it is a *miraculous* likeness."

"Why thank you, Mary Agnes honey," beamed Mrs. Canty.

Seeing the senator's wife's expression, Bledsoe was fairly certain she hadn't meant it as quite the compliment Mrs. Canty assumed it was.

"My duty is to put truth to canvas," said the artist.

The string quartet began playing a waltz from *La fille du régiment*. Bledsoe shifted from foot to foot. The new boots had raised blisters. They burned. He was exhausted and hungry. It was now past midnight. In a corner a card game had attracted a ring of spectators. The lobby was so crowded that usual manners had been discarded. Ladies were exposed to smoking, earnest drinking, and gambling. A few feet away an elderly woman had fallen asleep with her head on a marble side table and no one seemed the least concerned. Slaves fetched and carried refreshment. Bells tinged constantly for service at the front desk and somewhere a baby was crying piteously.

Bledsoe became aware of hot breath on his pant leg. He looked down at a shiny-coated spaniel with a blue ribbon tied around its neck sniffing his boot. Bledsoe nudged it toward the statue and the dog lifted its leg against the marble base. It snuck past the two women, both now leaning toward the artist as he spoke, and padded away, unnoticed by anyone else. Bledsoe sidled closer to the potted fern and away from the yellow stream running in a clear line to the green satin hem of Mrs. Canty's skirt. When it made contact he restrained himself from clapping.

"The whole world seems to be in Richmond," the artist said then. "Who's that over there talking to the mayor? Didn't I see his picture in the *Times-Picayune?*"

"Folks are sleeping in the hallways; no one can get a room," replied the Rose. "However did you?"

"Money has a remarkable ability to find space even when there is none to be had. But who *is* that man with the mayor? He looks so familiar."

"That's Lord Winterham. It's quite certain that the English are going to throw in with us. There's a rumor John Slidell is to go talk to the French too. Imagine that. Both the English and the French with us!"

"Really? Slidell? Wonderful news," said the artist. "Now I must beg you ladies to excuse me. I've had such a time getting down from Baltimore and I'm afraid I'm all in. May I call on you tomorrow?"

The Rose of Richmond bloomed with a new patch of blotches. "We're in number two seventy-seven. We've been here for a month, so my husband managed to get us a suite. Lucky Mary Agnes and the senator keep a town house here."

The artist bowed again to the senator's wife. "I hope you might give me the opportunity to paint you also, Mrs. Pettigruel."

"Oh, I don't think so," she replied with a grim smile.

"What a pity. Such beauty should not be kept from future view."

"You lay it on thick as butter, don't you?" The artist laughed and the senator's wife turned her back to him.

"Come along, Joe," said the artist. As they walked away he muttered to Bledsoe, "And butter wouldn't *melt* in *her* mouth."

He followed the artist as he wove his way toward the grand staircase, stopping now and then to exchange a word, a laugh, or shake a hand. Two men in uniform were bumping clumsily through the crowd. One smacked into the artist, spilling some of his drink. "Watch where you're going," the soldier slurred.

"Watch it yourself, Lieutenant." The artist angrily began blotting the wine from his coat with a handkerchief.

The drunk lieutenant started to reply, but his friend grabbed him by the arm. "Come on, Bell. He's sorry, sir," yelled the other soldier, steering the lieutenant away from the artist and Bledsoe. "Send the bill to Lieutenant Bell. Bowdeen's Rangers. We're in the park." They vanished in the crowd.

The Rose of Richmond had not been exaggerating. When they'd climbed to the top floor, they passed a man stretched out on a sofa in the hallway. Another had made a bed of a line of chairs and still another simply was passed out on the floor.

The room was in the back of the hotel. The window faced an alley. "Probably meant for the help," groused the artist. A bed, washstand, chair, and a table. There was also a small closet where a broom had fallen to the floor. Above the bed was a painting browned by years of tobacco of a stag surveying a landscape. The wall was papered with a pattern of flowers that seemed to have died long ago. The artist took off his coat and threw it angrily on the bed. "This won't do. It won't do at all, dammit."

Bledsoe just wanted to sit down on the chair and take off his boots. Climbing the stairs had been agony. He felt one of the blisters pop and ooze as he carried the artist's carpetbag and leather satchel into the room.

The artist sat down on the edge of the bed. "But we can't do anything about it tonight, I suppose. At least back here it's quiet. Ah, give me a drink there, won't you, Joe? Hand me the bottle. That's rich," said the artist, "sending Slidell to the French." He untied his cravat and pulled a heavy revolver out of the inner pocket of his coat. He laid it on the table. The barrel looked nearly blue in the light. He glanced at Bledsoe, who was studying the gun. "Pretty thing. It's a LeMat. Made in New Orleans. Unusual in that it has a nine-shot cylinder."

"It's yours?"

"Why wouldn't I? There's a war on, my friend. Even if there weren't, a gun is always handy."

"You ever shoot anyone?"

The artist smiled. "There are some things you just don't ask a man. Now. That senator's wife looks like a tasty little morsel. Or would be if you could get her to shut those spook-like eyes. What do you think?"

Though he noted the artist had avoided answering his question, he let it go and gratefully sank down on the chair, not minding the hard seat one bit. He bent to take off a boot. "She got owl eyes," said Bledsoe. "Will the French send soldiers to the Rebels?"

"I don't think so. They want to stay neutral like the British right now—that is, until they know which way the wind blows. That's how it always is, you know. You get into a war for what you think you'll get out of it. All the rest is hot air to stir up the masses. And you need to stir them up since they're the ones who're going to be doing all the dying."

He unbuttoned his shirt. "Tomorrow I'll send you with a note to that senator's wife. She can't be more than twenty-five. Married to old Pettigruel. The senator's sixty if he's a day. Oh yes, butter wouldn't melt in her mouth. What I need is to get invited over there. Do her portrait. She said no, but you'll see. Listen, Joe, fetch me some whiskey from downstairs, will you? And see if you can rustle up some food while you're down there."

Bledsoe looked over at the bed. It was past two in the morning. The artist tossed him a couple of coins, which clattered to the wood floor. "Go down to the kitchen. It's late, so something cold is all right." Bledsoe picked up the money and wedged the boot back over his swollen foot. "Good man," mumbled the artist as Bledsoe left the room.

By the time he returned with the whiskey and a plate of fried chicken, the artist had tucked himself in bed and was softly snoring. Ready to drop down dead with weariness, he surveyed the little room. The chair was too uncomfortable and he wasn't about to sleep beside the bed as he did at Our Joy. There was nowhere else except the closet. It wasn't big enough to stretch out fully, but he tucked himself up into a ball. He was so tired he fell asleep the minute he closed his eyes.

At some point in the night he drowsily opened his eyes. The closet was so dark he might have been wrapped in black velvet. He realized he'd woken up because he'd heard someone whispering in his ear, a persistent muted stream of indecipherable words. He listened, tensed and ready to spring. The only sound now was the whistling snore of the artist. *Just dreaming.* He slowly relaxed and sank back into a deep sleep. As daylight began sneaking into the closet, he became aware of an odor. At first it was faint, but it grew stronger—almost a fog of skin, sun browned, and rain-wet hair with an undertone of salt. And mint. Fresh-picked mint. He peered in the dim light at the blank walls in the cramped closet. He'd burst into a sweat; his heart thumped. "Alice?" he said in a shaking voice. "That you?"

Sweet potato vine says you're mine.

"Where are you?"

"Who are you talking to, Joe?" The artist was standing in the doorway, looking down at him. Bledsoe sat up, startled, and glanced nervously around the blank walls of the closet. "And what the hell are you doing in here? Didn't you see I had them put down a pallet for you outside the door?"

SEVENTY-FIVE

The garden was dying. Summer was over. Though days had continued hot and humid, the asters were brown and the hollyhocks skeletal stalks. A circular hedge maze wound around and around, but its geometry was lost in untrimmed wild growth. At the center of the maze stood a laughing boy and a marble bench to contemplate his happiness. Alice sat on the bench staring at the statue. "What you so dang glad about?" She kicked a piece of gravel toward the marble boy and bent back to the primer in her lap. "What's she say that bird's called? Ain't got no color, how you supposed to tell?"

She wrinkled her forehead and stuck her finger on the picture. The bird was almost at the end of the illustrated alphabet. "Abcdefgjlmnyz," she whispered. She'd forgotten some of them. She always did. She sighed and started over, slower this time. "UVW! Damn me. It's a what? Wren, ain't it?"

The marble boy was laughing at her but she wouldn't cry. She was going to learn to read these words if it killed her. Which was not unlikely. Reading was much more difficult than she had ever imagined. Just getting to *Wren* had taken her most of the morning. But she would know how to read when she saw him again. If she saw him again. *Stop that.* She pulled the little willow woman free from her blouse and clutched it in her hand. *He'll come.*

RED BALL BLUE BIRD GREEN TREE

She'd wanted to go to Fort Monroe, but Uncle Harlan said, "Oh no, my dear. The Yankees have foraging parties on the peninsula. The damn thieves. We're lucky to be so out of the way they don't even notice us. Cadan says there've been skirmishes, but they've held them back. A band of Yankees stole Kendall Simpson's carriage horses a week ago and nearly all his winter corn. Our boys pursued, but two of them were killed and the Yankees got away. Even if you did manage to get to the fort, what good would that do, dear? Your Henry is a prisoner of war. I doubt they'd even let you see him. They might even take you prisoner. Oh no. You couldn't possibly go. You'll be safe here and besides, look at Tamsin's face. Why, just the thought of you leaving has broken her heart in two."

Alice had to agree that Uncle Harlan's logic made sense, if Henry and his capture weren't complete lies. She was trapped at Bell's Bliss. There was nothing she could do about it for now. She might as well use the time wise as waste it. She flipped through the pages of the workbook. *DOG. CAT. RAT.* A little boy and a little girl. What were they doing? It looked to Alice like they were poking something with a stick. Poking at something dead on the ground. She shook her head. *No, it's a hoop. A stick and a hoop, you dumb girl.* She was seeing things.

She tried to concentrate on her copy work, but she couldn't shake a feeling of something wrong. It crawled along her skin, like a tiny insect. Something bad was coming. She looked up. The sky was brooding, the sun orange as a pumpkin. It was already getting dark earlier. She tried to shake off her feeling of dread. It was fall now. That was all it was. The sense that things were dying. But they came back again, didn't they? She nodded to herself. It was the circle of life. Winter was just a time for sleep. Not death. Soon it would be spring again. She sighed. That was when they'd found each other. Spring. *When things are blooming.*

She opened her workbook and slowly copied the letters Tamsin had printed for her.

A L I C E. She turned a page. There was a *BROWN COW.* Carefully, she copied the letters. *ALICE BROWN. Me.* She grinned, admiring her work. Then slowly and painstakingly she picked out letters. *B L E D.* She traced each one slowly. A thick rumbling filled the air as if something enormous were being rolled through the clouds. She looked up. The sound continued. Guns? There was a bright flash on the skyline. No. Only thunder. *Where are you?* She sighed and rubbed her hands together. It was growing cold.

"Alice. Alice! Hurry!"

She jumped at the panic in Tamsin's voice, and the paper she'd worked on so carefully all afternoon blew away in the wind.

"Alice! Where are you? Come quick."

"What's the danged hurry?" she muttered nervously. She shivered as she wove her way through the overgrown maze, through the garden and back to the house.

Even before she opened the back door she heard Uncle Harlan hollering, "Find her! She can't have gotten far."

When she got to the library she found him shaking his cane at Attis. "Saddle Helios. Why are you standing there? Find her!"

"Uncle, calm down, please calm down. Helios died years ago."

The old man turned to Tamsin, his cane still raised. "How can I calm down? Why would she say such a fool thing? Let go of me, boy!"

"Sit down, Marster. You gonna fall down if'n you don't." Attis tried to take the cane from the old man, but Uncle Harlan whacked him with it on the leg so hard the old servant yelped with pain.

"Get going! Find that damned slave or I'll skin you!"

"Uncle Harlan! Please, you're only making it worse. Sit down, please sit down and have a sip of this brandy."

"What's wrong?" asked Alice from the doorway.

"Eva," Tamsin whispered to her, as Uncle Harlan continued yelling for the long-dead horse. "I told Uncle that she refused to wait on you."

"But I don't want her to anyhow."

"She disobeyed me, don't you see, Alice? I couldn't let it go. You can't do that even once or they'll think they can do it again. Eva heard Uncle tell Attis to whip her for punishment. Eva's never been corrected. She ran off. And, it seems she took Aunt Freddy's jewel box with her too."

"Ran off! Thief!" shrieked Uncle Harlan. "After all these years. I should've sold that sneaky half-breed when Freddy died. I'll hide her, the damn black bitch! I'll hang her skin on my wall, the whore!"

"Uncle Harlan!" cried Tamsin, covering her ears. "Stop that right this minute!"

"Petted and spoiled like a dog. And look what happens! Goddamned bitch."

"But she weren't a dog, she was a people." Alice didn't even realize she'd opened her mouth. Uncle Harlan rushed to Alice, cane raised, but Attis grabbed it before he could strike her.

"Give that back, you insolent monkey!" he screeched, reaching for the cane. Suddenly his mouth twisted in a horrible grimace. "Arrrhhhhhhh," he gurgled. He crashed to his knees.

"Marster!" Attis sank to his knees beside him.

"Uncle!" Tamsin dropped on the other side as the old man pitched forward onto his face.

SEVENTY-SIX

Sometimes it seemed as if the artist thought he really was his slave. But it had to seem that way, reasoned Bledsoe, in order to fool these people. It was all a game of cat and mouse and he had to be certain to be the cat, said the artist. Except for these uncomfortable moments, the silver-haired man seemed to take an interest in him. Sometimes he seemed almost . . . Bledsoe hesitated as the thought grew. What was it he seemed? Fatherly? He called Bledsoe *my friend*, called him *son*, called him *Joe*. Well, Joe wasn't his name, but this was necessary and he generally said Joe nicely, except when ordering him to do something. Had to keep up appearances for these southerners. Of course Bledsoe's idea of fatherly was based on stories he'd read, certainly not on his own experience. For instance, today the artist had given him a small amount of pocket money. "There you go. Buy yourself a—? What would you buy?"

Bledsoe felt the coins rattling in his pocket and it felt good. His very first *own* money.

"A book," he replied without hesitation. "But I ain't supposed to know how to read."

"Say it's for me then," said the artist.

And the artist talked to him about books, about ideas. That is, when he wasn't at a luncheon or a dinner, or losing money at a card game. He'd admitted he wasn't very good at cards. He only frequented the tables, he said, because it was a way of getting the type of news that didn't make it into the outer world. And when he wasn't with some woman. That girl—what was her name? Barbara? No, Belva, this week it was Belva, last one was Eleanor. The artist met her at some party after the opera. Bledsoe was confounded by all the parties these white Richmonders had going on despite a war. It troubled him too. Because if the South was able to throw balls and go to operas, then it didn't look like Lincoln and his army were making a bit of difference. He'd said so to the artist.

"The whole thing will be over soon, Joe."

"You mean they're gonna win?"

The artist had looked at him intently a moment. "I didn't say that. Don't worry. President Lincoln and his generals have things in hand. Plans. But let's enjoy while we can. Life's short."

Later when the artist mentioned to Bledsoe how much he'd spent on feeding Belva oysters and champagne at a restaurant with a private room, Bledsoe was astonished. That was enough money to live in New York for a year, he reckoned. It sure seemed a lot of money to spend on a girl who it turned out was engaged to be married to some boy in the Henrico Mounted Rangers.

"There's nothing that'll set a woman to chattering like a set of wood teeth than thinking a man thinks she's pretty and that he wants her," replied the artist when Bledsoe asked why he bothered with these women. "I get information any way I can." He smiled and patted Bledsoe on the back. "But I have to admit some ways are nicer than others."

No. He wasn't exactly fatherly, thought Bledsoe. Not in a Bob Cratchit and Tiny Tim sort of way, remembering a story snuck to him by his half sister once long ago. But still. The artist spoke to him as an equal. When they were alone, anyway.

One evening the artist was on his second whiskey, leafing through a newspaper. Bledsoe was polishing the man's shoes. He didn't mind, he told himself. He was really polishing them for Lincoln.

"How old are you, Joe?"

"Seventeen."

"Heavens. I thought you were older—twenty or so. You have such a serious way about you. And so quiet. So. Melancholy. Yes, I've seen that in you. Seventeen. My my. So young. Why'd you run away?"

Bledsoe looked at him, surprised. "Because I was a slave."

"There have always been, you know. Gone on from antiquity onward. Did you know that, Joe? Look at the Bible. The Jews were slaves in Egypt; the Greeks were slaves to the Romans. Slaves were nearly always spoils of war."

"That was other places and other times. This is America," replied Bledsoe. "Everybody supposed to be free here."

"Who told you that?"

"Nobody told me. I read it," said Bledsoe.

"In the encyclopedia? Well." The artist drank deep.

"America was built by us," said Bledsoe. "There wouldn't be America without us. White people don't pick cotton, plant tobacco. They brought us here to do all the work and thought we would just stay quiet about it."

"Remember how we talked about Schiller and his concept of the shining soul? Man's ability to rise from the basest to the highest by using reason? Sadly, as much as I've clung to the notion that it might be possible, in the end I think you'll find that Schiller's ideal is pure romantic nonsense. Lovely, but impossible. There are certain individuals, sure, that might reach that lofty height, but the average man? Or should I say, average mankind? No. They'll steal, rape, enslave, murder." He smiled at Bledsoe. "Do whatever needs doing to stay the ones that are up, not the ones that are down."

The artist picked up the bottle of Old Crow from the table. "Now"—he walked toward the door unsteadily—"think I'll mosey downstairs."

SEVENTY-SEVEN

Tamsin had been crying for ages. At first Alice didn't do anything except sit beside her on the sofa, but the blond girl's tears about broke her heart. So she awkwardly put her arms around her. "Hush now," she said. "There, that's all right now."

Tamsin sobbed into Alice's shoulder. "I'm sorry, I'm sorry, it's just I'm so frightened. I mean, Uncle Harlan? He's all we've ever had for mother and father, Cadan and I. Did you hear him? Oh, Alice, he's done more than lose his mind. What is happening? I never heard him say a coarse word in all my life. He was always a gentleman. He would've whipped any man who spoke like that in my presence. Bell's Bliss was always such a happy place. Now Eva's run off. I thought she loved me. She used to call me her baby. I thought she loved me, Alice. What if he dies? What if Uncle dies and the Yankees come?"

"He ain't gonna die," said Alice soothingly. "Not right now. I gave him the hawthorn tea and the color come back to his face. He's sleepin' now. Something jist went in his brain for a little while. He'll be all right. Your brother says the Yankees can't git up this far, so don't worry about that neither."

Tamsin sat up and blew her nose into her handkerchief. She looked at Alice through tear-glistening eyes. "You must think I'm so selfish."

"I never," assured Alice.

"You with your poor Henry locked up in the prison at the fort and not knowing if they're treating him right. You must be out of your head with worry."

The drum of rain on the window reminded Alice of the bloody dining room. For a second she thought she heard the awful sound of Dr. Loveall's bone saw. She shook it out of her mind. "Yes, I do worry," she said softly. "Can't help it."

Tamsin patted her hand and gave her a sweet smile. "Thank you, Alice dear, for being such a kind and loving friend," she said.

How I been a kind and loving friend? Now she was sorely tempted to tell the truth. The real one. The tall blond girl looked at her with eyes guileless as a rabbit caught in a snare. She opened her mouth—why she'd snap that rabbit's neck because that's what you had to do to stay alive—and closed it again. She smiled at Tamsin and gave her a reassuring squeeze. Tamsin would never understand if she told her she loved a man who wasn't white. A slave. A runaway slave. Never. Ever. Those rabbit eyes would turn hard as bone.

SEVENTY-EIGHT

Bledsoe was driving the landau down Franklin Street. When they'd entered Richmond the first night, the only obvious signs of the war were all the flags and men who thronged the streets in brand-new uniforms. But now he knew different. There were so many wounded from the battle at Manassas the hospitals were overflowing. Also, typhoid was rampant. Hundreds of soldiers had died from it since July. Children were especially vulnerable. Funeral processions of tiny caskets were an everyday occurrence. Buildings had become hospitals. They passed the almshouse for the poor where, the artist told Bledsoe, the Sisters of Mercy treated hundreds who had fallen ill. Even schoolhouses and private homes were being used to care for the sick.

They drove past the new fairgrounds, now used as an army training camp. It was filled with white tents, a few set up like Indian tepees. The sounds of drilling filled the air as raw recruits were taught by former instructors at the military academy how to march smart. Despite losing many men to battle wounds and even more to sickness, there were still plenty of soldiers spending their free time singing, drinking, and doing their best to impress the local ladies. The artist told Bledsoe that women often brought baskets of homemade goods to the men, to cheer them up and help cure homesickness. Sometimes romance grew out of these visits.

Smoke from so many cook fires in the park turned the air gray. The smell of roasting meat wafted across the city for blocks on many evenings, but during the day drums beat for endless drilling. Even in the stifling heat, the officers kept the men at it. "Keeps them from running amok," said the artist to Bledsoe as they watched a company drill in tight formation.

Runny muck. Runny muck among our southern flowers. He saw her in his mind, that wild hair, innocent eyes wide in that dirty face. She rose up through the water, and into his consciousness. He saw her so clear, right there in front of him, that the street melted away. He wasn't even conscious that he'd let the reins go slack in his hands and the gelding was beginning to break into a trot.

"Slow down, Joe. What's the hurry? Stop here at the corner so I can get a sketch of the camp."

Alice receded beneath the green water of his memory and Franklin Street was abruptly in front of him again. "Whoa," Bledsoe called to the gelding, reining him to a halt.

After the artist finished his sketch, they drove on toward the James River. "Out there is Belle Isle prison camp," said the artist, pointing. "That's where they've dumped Yankees they took at Manassas that they couldn't fit in Libby." Bledsoe looked out at the island. There were some tents visible, but he couldn't see any of the prisoners.

They were in an area the artist called Shockoe Bottom. "Over there is what the blacks call the Devil's Half Acre, Lumpkin's Jail. You've heard of it? No? Be glad. I was there once. It's the biggest negro jail and auction house north of New Orleans. Has a special room just for flogging with drains for the blood to run out. Lumpkin. I saw the man once. Fat little man with a warty nose. Lumpkin. Pumpkin. Bumpkin. But he's rich. Rich man, that Lumpkin Bumpkin." He leaned from the passenger seat toward Bledsoe. "I hear he keeps a pretty negress like a wife and has had umpteen little mulattoes with her. Sends his own little pickaninnies to school up north."

Bledsoe eyed a tall brick wall topped with metal spikes. All he could see of Lumpkin's jail was the second story of a brick building with bars over the windows. He'd heard stories all his life of slaves being sold at auction but had never seen a place where it happened. He felt cold even though it was hovering near ninety that afternoon. He was glad to pass the place.

There was a burnt smell in the air. "That's charcoal from the Tredegar ironworks," the artist told him. "That's where they manufacture munitions. If the Yankees got a hold of it, the South wouldn't last a year."

They paused so the artist could also do a sketch of the great ironworks factory and the docks on the James. Before Virginia's succession, the artist told Bledsoe, ships would dock here with goods from all over the world. Now the ships rocked empty at anchor. A clink and heavy clank of chains made Bledsoe look over his shoulder. A coffle of manacled slaves were approaching the landau, urged on by a driver. They passed single file on the narrow street. He flicked the whip over the gelding's ears and the landau shot ahead. He didn't want to see a single one of their faces because he knew he wouldn't be able to stand it. The artist put his handkerchief to his nose. "That's right, drive faster. Stinks here."

When they got to Broad Street they were forced to stop for a funeral procession. People lined both sides of the street, faces drawn; some women were weeping. A band played the most mournful tune Bledsoe had ever heard. It sounded as if Heaven itself were crying. An ebony horse with an empty saddle was led by a soldier. They were followed by the dead man's regiment, swords in scabbards swinging at their sides as they marched in slow stately unison. Behind the regiment came four more soldiers balancing a coffin draped in the Confederate Stars and Bars on their shoulders. A woman, head to toe in mourning, was supported by an older man. Two black-clad children, pale and clearly frightened, clung to one another's hands.

The spectators pressed handkerchiefs to their eyes. Even Bledsoe felt something twinge inside. After the last of the procession had passed, he noticed a woman directly across the street. Her face was at first shadowed by the large brim of her hat. Then she turned her head and the light fell across her face. "Oh," he gasped. He stepped down from the buggy, into the street, paying no attention to the traffic, which had resumed after the funeral cortege had moved on.

"What the hell are you doing?" The artist yanked Bledsoe back to the safety of the sidewalk. Bledsoe scanned the faces across the street.

"What's wrong with you, Joe?" The artist was holding on to the reins of the nervous horse.

"Nothing," gasped Bledsoe. *It was just a trick of the light.* "Thought I saw someone, that's all."

"Then let's go," said the artist. "All this death is depressing. I need a drink."

❧

It was past eleven. A crescent moon hung like a scythe above Richmond. The wind was surprisingly cold for only the end of September. Sitting in the landau he scrunched down farther on the seat and pulled his coat closer. The neighborhood was dismal. The street was filled with ramshackle taverns and derelict buildings, some with the audacity to call themselves hotels. Women strolling by the buggy made eyes at him. Some called out or blew kisses. One tall, gangly colored girl had exposed her breasts and licked her lips. Bledsoe looked away. Another woman threw an empty bottle at the buggy, causing the horse to rear in its traces. She staggered backward from the explosion of glass and collapsed in a drunken heap on the sidewalk. People stepped around or over her without a glance. *What were they doing here?*

The landau wasn't the only buggy waiting. Some of the men who went inside the house he was standing in front of were very well dressed. Though the curtains in the window were closed, Bledsoe saw silhouettes moving about inside. A piano was playing something fast and dancey. The artist had called this area Locust Alley, though it wasn't an alley but a dingy, ill-lit stretch of street, smelling of piss and bad liquor.

A big-boned white woman, face grotesquely whitened with powder, lips and cheeks red as blood, wove spasmodic figure eights down the street. She was wearing a bright yellow ball gown. Bledsoe gripped the reins tighter. The horse nickered nervously, shifted from hoof to hoof. The gas lamp beside the buggy revealed a pelt of dark curly hair above the plunging neckline of her gown. She was singing, *"A tickle and bounce, a tickle and bounce, give me a nickel for a tickle and bounce,"* in a rousing baritone.

She lifted her skirts and daintily minced up to the landau. "Hello, handsome," she said, pulling up the side of her yellow skirt to display a thick hairy leg. She grinned at Bledsoe and sang out, *"A tickle and bounce, come on and pounce, cost you but a nickel for a tickle and bounce."*

"Go away," said Bledsoe, seeing her up close. It was a man. "Go on. Get off!"

"I ain't on yet!" replied the man, grinning. He whirled and his yellow skirt ringed away from his thick muscular legs. He stopped and staggered dizzily for a moment, then took a gulp from a bottle and winked. "Free for you, handsome."

Bledsoe pulled his hat lower on his head and sunk deeper into the seat. Out of the corner of his eye he saw the yellow dress flounce drunkenly away. He shifted uncomfortably on the padded leather seat. A girl walked by slowly and stopped. She turned to him. She was young, pretty if you ignored the oozing sore on her lip. She looked up at him. Her eyes were dead. The dress she had on was nothing but a rag. Bledsoe felt in his pocket for some money—just to see a flicker in her eyes. But by the time he pulled out the coins, she'd trudged by. He watched her until she disappeared in the shadows at the end of the street.

A door opened and light flooded the sidewalk. A crowd of men emerged from the house. Most were dressed in formal evening clothes. They were roaring with laughter. The artist and a tall blond man in uniform staggered toward the street, arms around each other's shoulders. The artist said something to the tall blond man and he laughed loudly.

The artist climbed into the buggy behind Bledsoe. "Good night, Bell!" he called. "Drive on," he barked to Bledsoe with a grand wave of his hand.

Like he's the king or something. What kind of intelligence could he gather in a whorehouse?

"Home, Joe."

"That's not my name," said Bledsoe. But the artist wasn't listening.

SEVENTY-NINE

"He et some soup, Miss Tam."

"Thank you, Attis."

"I give him some of that trifle left over from yesterday too."

"It was delicious. You are such a good cook, Attis. Thank you, and thank you, Alice, for all you've done for Uncle Harlan."

"Oh, it weren't much," said Alice, blushing. Secretly she was quite proud. The heart attack hadn't killed him, but it had looked like he might not last through the night. The only doctor in the county had joined the army, so they were on their own. She'd made up a tonic of hawthorn berries and other herbs. He'd taken it for the past week. Gradually his color grew better, though he was weak as a kitten. Oddly, he had no memory of what had brought it on. Didn't remember Eva running away. They told him that she'd gone to visit her sick sister in Charlotte and he'd merely grumbled about who would keep things up around the house now.

"You be wantin' anything special for supper, Miss Tam?"

"You decide, Attis."

"All right. Don't be surprised if there's a duck in it somewheres." He left the parlor.

"I feel bad for him having all the work of the house on his shoulders," said Tamsin. "I don't know where we'd be without him. Oh! You know what? I heard a while back they were starting a ladies' auxiliary up in Charles City. I ought to join, I guess. I don't socialize much anymore. I suppose you could use an outing even if it is only to that little puddle of a place. Maybe we should have Attis drive us up; that is if those Yankees aren't still lurking about."

Alice was barely listening. She could care less about ladies' auxiliaries. She stared at the paper in front of her. "Bababa. Bat. Bed," she muttered. "Blab, bless." All she'd managed so far with the help of the primer was a blobby *B* and seasick *L*. "Will you spell somethin' out for me?" she said at last, pushing the paper away with exasperation.

Tamsin put aside her embroidery and went to the desk where Alice sat. Alice felt completely dejected. Her right hand was smeared with ink, and the paper she'd been writing on was covered with drops and drips like thick, black blood.

"Oh, you've split the quill again, honey," said Tamsin. "Don't press so hard."

"Sorry," replied Alice. "I try not to, but guess since they won't come easy, I gotta smash them words out."

"It's all right. You'll get accustomed to it. Be patient."

"I won't," said Alice, throwing the quill down on the desk. "I jist can't do it. I ain't meant to learn it. I guess I'm dumb is all."

"Stop, Alice, you're being silly. Of course you're not dumb. Stop being hard on yourself. You're trying to learn in a month what takes years. Now. What is it you would like to write?"

Alice stared at the ink-blobbed paper and muttered, "Bledsoe."

"Did you say Bledsoe? That's not a word."

What was she thinking? Now Tamsin would ask questions and Alice wasn't sure she could lie so well any longer. Not with all her heart anyway. It gave her a sick stomach just thinking about how the blond girl would hate her if she knew the real truth. *That I wanna write to him. The real him, not some made-up white boy in a made-up prison.* She sighed. Tamsin clapped her hands, startling Alice.

"What?" Alice asked, jumping up from the desk. "Whatcha clappin' for?"

"Why, I know!" said Tamsin. "Of course."

"Know what?" asked Alice fearfully. "What you know, Tam?"

"Why, it's his name!"

Alice turned to the door, prepared to dash out of the room, to where, she hadn't the foggiest notion, but away. Anywhere away from the girl who was beaming at her.

"His *last* name. It is, isn't it? Bledsoe. Henry Bledsoe. You want to write him a letter, don't you?"

Alice found her head bobbing. "Um-hum. Yes. That's it. That's it, Tam."

"Then come back and sit down. Oh, this is wonderful, Alice. Why didn't you ask me sooner? That poor man just wasting away and you too. I see it in your face every day. Wasting away for love. Don't be embarrassed. I think it's beautiful. Your knight is in prison but we will light the darkness of his captivity. You will, I mean. Me? I will merely serve as your amanuensis."

Alice was suddenly terrified. "What you mean, my amhooenthis? Sounds like some kinda poison plant."

"Oh, you silly. No. Think of me as your personal scribe, Alice honey. I will just transcribe what you wish." Tamsin settled herself in the chair, her skirt of eggplant silk fanning around in a purple flood. "Now we will write him a letter and send it to Fort Monroe. And if his captors are not inhuman Yankee monsters . . ." She put a hand on her shoulder as Alice sank beside her on a stool. "You must be strong, sweetheart, for they may indeed be horrid brutes. But if they are obeying the rules of *civilized* warfare, he will be allowed to receive it. Now let us get a fresh quill—we'll use my gold nib—and the French paper that Uncle gave me for my birthday."

She bustled about as Alice watched in consternation. Henry Bledsoe. Fort Monroe. If he really was at the fort, he would never get the letter now. *It ain't his right name.* The letter would be worthless unless she told Tamsin the truth.

"Ready!" declared Tamsin, her sleeves tucked up to keep away from ink. "The beginning is simple. *Dear*—or should I say *Dearest?*" She didn't wait for Alice. "*Dearest Henry, I am with my friends at Bell's Bliss.* Is that all right? That I say you are with us? Well, you are, of course, and that should reassure him that you are being cared for while he is in prison."

Alice closed her eyes.

"What's the matter? You look white as milk."

"Nothin'," said Alice. "I ain't got nothin' wrong."

"I don't," replied Tamsin, "have anything wrong."

"What? I never said you did."

"Remember? We're trying not to use *ain't* and other things like that quite so much."

"I *don't* got nothin' wrong. How's that? Go on and keep writin'."

EIGHTY

The senator's wife had agreed to sit for "a picture." She only sat when the old senator was away on war business, meetings, or fund-raisings in other cities. Bledsoe wondered if the artist had gotten around to actually painting those big, too close-set eyes yet but kept his mouth shut and didn't ask. How the artist got Rebel information was his own business. It wasn't up to Bledsoe to determine what was the right way or the wrong way to go about it.

He generally waited in the kitchen during these sittings, where the senator's cook, a black man named Renard, ran the kitchen like a battlefield. He made certain Bledsoe knew he'd trained under a protégé of Marie-Antoine Carême in New Orleans. As if Bledsoe knew who that was or would care if he did.

But this evening there was no sitting. The senator was in town and the artist was attending a large dinner party. The chef was in a good mood. He'd been called out to the dining room where the guests had applauded him. He returned with head high. In a display of unusual generosity he let the kitchen help sit down and eat the leftovers, which included a peacock stuffed with oysters. The bird's iridescent head still arched proudly above its picked-clean bones. The shiny black eyes stared at Bledsoe. He had just decided against the oysters, taking a big slab of ham instead, when a slave in fancy livery came into the kitchen. "You Joe, ain't you?"

Bledsoe nodded slowly. He felt his stomach shrivel up.

"They wants you in de dinin' room. Come wif me."

"What for?"

"I doan know, but you marster dat tall silber hair one wid a little pointy beard?"

Bledsoe stood. "I 'spect that's him."

"Well. You best come on, den."

Bledsoe followed the footman down a long narrow hallway. Through a closed door he heard a scream and realized it was a woman laughing. She was joined by others. The footman leaned to Bledsoe just before he pushed open the door for him. "Dey happy at least." He gave him a little nudge on the back and Bledsoe found himself staring at the back of the senator's head.

A woman to his right continued to laugh like the drawn-out whine of a squeezebox. Her face was pink. It was obvious that just about everyone was drunk or nearly so. The artist was farther down the table, between the woman he'd called the Rose of Richmond and an older woman with white hair. The senator's wife sat at the foot. Her too-big eyes studied Bledsoe as dispassionately as the bird of prey she resembled.

"Ah, here he is, ladies and gentlemen. My Joe."

All heads turned to Bledsoe.

"Can we just shout out a request?" asked a bald man in a lavender cravat.

"No, no, he picked things up at random. But it's still amazing. Joe, recite something."

Bledsoe stood behind the host, his hands sweating. He felt ill. "What you mean, Massa?"

"You know. From the encyclopedia. No! Wait. Shakespeare." He leaned toward the senator. "He can do most of a scene from *As You Like It*."

"I doan know, Massa," said Bledsoe, voice soft to cover his trembling.

"Yes, you do. *Hath not old custom made this life more sweet than that of painted pomp?* That part. Go on now."

A lady in blue satin giggled and the man next to her said, "Hush, Nora Rose. I want to hear this."

The senator turned in his chair to Bledsoe. "Stand over there by the sideboard, boy, where everyone can see you."

Bledsoe walked slowly over to the designated spot. He stood in front of a great cheese and fruit platter, the savory that followed dessert. The artist was signaling him to start. Every eye was on him. *"If you prick us, do we not bleed?"* he whispered.

"What?" said an old man. "What's he saying?"

"Louder, boy," called someone.

". . . if you tickle us, do we not laugh? If you poison us, do we not die?"

"That's not *As You Like It*," said giggly Nora Rose. "I know it's not."

"Shhhh," hushed someone else.

"Go on, Joe," encouraged the artist, with a smile. "You continually surprise me."

Bledsoe stared over the heads of the guests. *"And if you wrong us, shall we not revenge?"*

"What's that?" asked the woman with the white hair. "What's he saying?"

"If we are like you in the rest, we will resemble you in that. If a Jew wrong a Christian, what is his humility? Revenge—"

"He's doing Shylock on purpose," interrupted the white-haired lady next to the artist.

"Like a parrot," said the blond man in uniform. Bledsoe recognized him as the lieutenant at the whorehouse with the artist. "It's only mimicry."

"What about that one up north? Frederick Douglass? I have to say I've read a bit of his writing and though what he writes is nonsense, he does something of a good job of it," said a short man in spectacles at the farther end of the table.

"That nigger Douglass doesn't write those things," said the blond lieutenant. "Everybody with an ounce of sense knows that. It's one of those abolitionists. They write their drivel and slap his name on it. Everybody knows you can put a hat and coat on a monkey, but a monkey ain't ever gonna dress itself."

"Oh bless me, look what I've done!" exclaimed the man next to Nora Rose. He had knocked over a glass of wine, causing the white-haired woman to jump up to avoid her gown being stained. Servants rushed to right the mess. The dinner party began talking and laughing while the floor was mopped with a napkin and wine refilled.

"I think that was enough," said the artist to no one in particular, "anyway."

Bledsoe felt himself become invisible. Since no one dismissed him, he continued to stand by the sideboard long after the fruit and cheese were served. The party broke up about an hour or so later.

He drove the landau in stony silence back to the hotel. He was seething, furious with the artist, furious with himself. He should have stayed at the fort and dug ditches. *Fool.*

"You did real well tonight," said the artist behind him in the buggy. "You saved the day, Joe."

"That's not my name."

"Here now," said the artist as if he hadn't heard him. He leaned over Bledsoe's shoulder. "Listen, my friend. I sensed there was some suspicion growing about me. I've been asked a few too many questions lately. I had to do something, you understand, to throw them off. What Yankee would stick their slave up in front of them and have him recite Shakespeare? Though Shylock? I mean, really, that was a bit heavy-handed. Rather obvious choice. You might have opted to be somewhat more subtle. Well, doesn't matter. They bought the horse, as they say. Suspicions were put to bed. Here, have yourself a drink, Joe."

That's not my name.

EIGHTY-ONE

Now that Eva was gone, they got dressed together in the morning. Tying each other's stays, helping with all the fluffery required in getting, as Tamsin said, "dressed proper."

"What for? No one here but us."

"We've got to make the effort, Alice," she replied. "Else we'll become common savages."

"Them savages can breathe at least. Lord have mercy, Tam, you're gonna pop me like a blister." Alice made a face in the mirror and both girls erupted in laughter.

"What would I do without you, Alice?" said Tamsin. "You're the sister I never had, I swear. Now I'll tell you a secret."

It was all she could do not to bust out laughing at the "shocking secret" that Tamsin whispered to her. She'd kissed Deal Phillips behind a tree after church last summer! She listened carefully to the way Tamsin spoke, the words she used, the words she didn't. When Tamsin said, "I just about adore you to death," Alice answered, "Me too."

She had such beautiful things. Dresses and cashmere shawls and silks and satins and hats and shoes and gloves of the finest kid. Alice had never in her life seen anything like it. Uncle Harlan was a rich man, Tamsin told her. It was only in the past two or three years that his mind and health had declined to such an extent that he was no longer able to make annual trips to New York and, when she was younger, to London and Paris.

Despite her earlier grumbling, Alice loved every bit of flounce and frill now. She was astonished at the girl she saw reflected back in the mirror. *A young lady.* No one would guess she'd been a filthy thing in a swamp. Wouldn't dream she'd lived with an old woman who everyone called a witch. Sometimes when she and Tamsin were together it was as if they really were sisters.

After they were both dressed, Alice did Tamsin's hair. She liked doing it. Tucking ivory pins into the blond hair. Soft as silk. Opposite of her own. Today, she'd looped it around Tamsin's ears with a border of braids on either side. They framed Tamsin's face like yellow lacework. "There. Looks jist like the picture," declared Alice proudly.

Tamsin turned her head right and left in the mirror, then looked down at the picture in *Godey's Lady's Book*. A dimple appeared in her left cheek as she smiled. "Lord, Alice, that's as good as Eva ever did it. Now you sit and I'll do yours."

They switched places and Tamsin took the brush to Alice's cloud of unruly black. She hummed as she brushed, something sweet and low. The window was wide open in Tamsin's bedroom and the air, unseasonably balmy for the first week of October, smelled lush. "The pear tree is blooming again. The bees are hunting for clover but it's long past, poor bees. Everything's confused by the weather."

"Um-hum," agreed Alice dreamily. A warm breeze ruffled the hem of her green taffeta skirt and tickled her ankles. She absentmindedly twirled the silk tassel of a button on her blouse as the brush shush-shushed through her hair. She closed her eyes. No one had ever brushed her hair before. *This must be how a dog feels getting petted,* she thought. She felt herself falling into a blissful state just short of sleep.

"Did you hear me?"

Without opening her eyes, Alice murmured, "I heard you." Which wasn't a complete lie. She'd known Tamsin was saying something. She just hadn't cared what.

"He's coming."

"Who?" asked Alice, feeling a bit cross. The lovely golden half dream was dissolving. Why couldn't she just hum that pretty tune and keep brushing?

"He said today in the letter."

Alice opened her eyes. She turned to Tamsin, grabbing hold of the brush. "Letter?"

"Not Henry, dear heart," she said, softly. "Cadan. My brother." Tamsin whacked her gently on the shoulder with the back of the brush. "For heaven's sake, Alice, don't tell me you weren't listening to a single word I said."

"He's comin' here?"

"Why, of course. This is his home. He's been ordered to Yorktown, but once he got word about Uncle Harlan he asked for a month's leave to make sure he'll be all right."

She began to brush Alice's hair again, but Alice took the brush. "I kin do it."

"What's wrong?"

Alice yanked her hair back into a big knot and secured it with a comb. "Nothin'."

"I know he was awful to you last time, but he won't get away with it again, I promise."

Alice stood up and shook out her skirt. "I'll stay in my room when he's here. Or, I mean, *your* room. Don't worry none."

Tamsin grabbed both her hands. "Don't be a ninny, Alice." Alice tried to pull her hands away, but Tamsin held them tighter. "My brother can be a devil, but he doesn't mean it. I know him to the core, Alice. We *are* twins, after all, and I love him with all my heart. But even he can't come between me and my dearest friend in all the world." She pulled Alice to her and hugged her tight. "Nobody ever could."

❧

At dinner that night, Tamsin's brother said, "You've worked a miracle. Why, she's pinned up pretty as a picture."

"Cadan, hush your mouth. You are being a complete and total beast."

Alice looked up from her plate and directly at the blond young man in his immaculate uniform. "Yes, you're right," she replied. "Yes, Mr. Bell, I'm a miracle. All 'cause your sister there, for she's a angel."

Cadan glanced at his twin. "At least that's true."

"What is wrong with you?" asked Tamsin, leaning to Alice and taking her hand. "If you say another mean word to her, I will not speak another word *to you* before you leave."

Cadan Bell leaned back lazily in his dining chair, eyeing Alice. "I mean it, Tammy, why she's almost pretty as you, which is as good as saying almost as pretty as me." He winked at Alice. "Who do you think is prettier, me or my sister?"

Alice buttered the biscuit she'd taken from the silver tray, concentrating on keeping her hand from shaking. She bit into it delicately. "You got the same eyes, same nose, even got the same ears, but she's the only one got a heart."

"Oh, Alice, he's only trying to get your goat, honey."

Cadan leaned across the table and looked at Alice imploringly. "Do you find me heartless, Miss Alice? Oh, I declare. I am mightily wounded. Why, what's this?" He looked down at his chest where he'd stuck his hand under his jacket. "Look here. Boom-boom. Boom-boom. It's close to running straight across the dinner table and jumping in your lap."

Tamsin threw her napkin at him. "Ignore him. He's horrible."

Cadan laughed. "I am, I am truly. Oh, you know me so well, sis."

"He's even more stuck up now that somebody gave him a promotion. At least he says it's a promotion, though he's still only a lieutenant."

"A *first* lieutenant, sister dear, is a higher grade than a second."

"Lyle Deal is a captain. You both went to the Institute. How come you aren't a captain too?"

"Because Lyle Deal's daddy kisses Robert Toombs's behind." The question had obviously irked him. He threw his fork down on the table. "Take this away, Attis. That meat is overdone. I could scarcely get my teeth through it."

"Sorry, Massa Cade, you want somethin' else?"

"Just bring me the scotch off the sideboard there."

Alice had finished eating and, copying Tamsin, patted her lips with her napkin. She knew Cadan was looking at her, but she pretended not to notice.

"Well, I'd say Alice and I would retire, but what's the use? With Uncle upstairs in bed all the time, it's only the three of us. Go ahead and smoke your smelly old cigar—that is if Alice doesn't mind."

"Do you mind, *Miss* Alice?"

Alice smiled at him, just barely. *Go away go away.* "Please smoke and smoke and smoke, *Mr.* Bell. It's your house, ain't it?"

Cadan smiled back so thinly it could have easily been mistaken for a grimace. "That's right." He struck a match on the sole of his boot and lit a fat cigar. As he puffed, it filled the air with a scent not entirely disagreeable. He leaned toward his sister. "Tammy, I've got a surprise for you."

"Oh no. Your surprises are sometimes too surprising. What is it this time, Cade?"

When he smiled at Tamsin it was different, observed Alice. It changed his features entirely. *They do look so much alike.* His hazel eyes twinkled. A dimple appeared in his right cheek. *Why, he truly loves her.*

"I know how lonesome you've been way out here."

"Not so much since Alice has been here," she said with a smile at Alice.

"I mean for the type of company you're accustomed to, sister dear. So. I've had the Richmond house turned out for you and Uncle Harlan."

"Richmond?" Tamsin clapped her hands and let out a happy little squeal, then stopped sudden. Her hands fluttered into her lap as if they'd been buckshot out of the sky. "Oh, but no, Cade. Uncle will never allow it."

"He'll have to. Just about everyone down here has packed up and left. Can't sit here waiting for the Yankees any longer. Oh, we'll stop them, of course, but in the meantime they're sending out surveying parties. The bastards are getting more brash every day, looking for ways to sneak up to Richmond. Joe Banks's boys caught fourteen of 'em just four miles from here. Scouting and foraging here on the south neck bold as brass. Shot two, but the rest got away. We've got men posted and there's the Home Guard, but it's too isolated here. Uncle Harlan will have to listen to reason. If he doesn't, well, then I'll simply have to drag him to Richmond. I've got Attis already packing up his things." He pointed. "Look. You can take Alice here with you"—he paused, looking over Tamsin's head at Alice—"to do your hair and such since we've lost Eva." His eyes appraised her coldly.

Tamsin took Alice's hand. She felt the blond girl's excitement in the way she squeezed it. "Richmond, Alice!" She said something else but Alice wasn't listening. She stared back at Cadan as he smoked his cigar. Blank eyes. *Like silver coins.* Could he read her mind? *I hope you die.* She smiled. He looked away and blew out a ring of smoke. Alice watched it until it disappeared into the air.

EIGHTY-TWO

The crowd had grown so large that people lined the streets on the border of the new fairgrounds. Men with boys on their shoulders, wide-hatted ladies with lunch baskets, children, and dogs. The artist shouldered his way through. "Keep close," he barked to Bledsoe. "Coming through," said the artist. "Pardon, please. Excuse me, ma'am, I'm with Mayor Mayo." Or he'd shout, "Official business!" to get through the throng. Ladies clutched their skirts to avoid the hems being stepped on; men eyed him curiously. Bledsoe heard someone behind him ask, "That the mayor?" The artist, chin held high, pushed, elbowed, and 'scuse me'd through bodies until they reached a long line of gray-suited soldiers, backs stiff, shoulders straight. They formed a barricade to whatever lay beyond. Behind him Bledsoe heard the rise and fall of hundreds of voices. The excitement was so palpable it seemed he could almost hold it in his hands. Yet what they were all doing here, what was beyond the tautly drawn line of soldiers, was a mystery.

"Climb up there," said the artist to Bledsoe, indicating an oak tree.

"What?"

"Get up on that branch there. I need you to be my eyes and tell me exactly what you see." The artist had his notepad and pencil ready. "Describe everything in detail." The silvery piping of fifes and snap of snare drums was approaching. The crowd swung their heads toward the sound. "Come on, Joe," begged the artist. "Help me out here." He knitted his fingers together to make a step. By now, Bledsoe was so curious he no longer questioned the artist. He stepped onto the artist's upturned palms. With an oomph the artist gave him the necessary boost to grab hold of a stout lower branch. Bledsoe swung himself upright and sat, legs dangling. Now he could see past the line of gray uniforms. "Tell me what's happening," shouted the artist.

The drums and fifes were louder now. The music was stiff—formal, somber. "There's a line of drummers and pipers," yelled Bledsoe, "and a black horse and a black wagon coming."

"Is the wagon open?" asked the artist, pencil to his pad.

"No, closed like a big box." Bledsoe glanced down and saw that the artist had already quickly sketched a horse and now was adding a box of a wagon. He'd already sketched in drummers and two pipers with fifes to their lips. "I see a couple men out front look important," said Bledsoe. "One fancy uniform, like a general or something. Other one ain't a soldier. He's got on all black." The procession was much closer now and Bledsoe had a clear view beyond the line of soldiers standing at stiff attention. "He's got on a black coat and knee britches and got two big guns, black revolvers, one set on each hip."

"Ah." The artist nodded. "The provost marshal."

"And looks like a preacher coming behind." Bledsoe looked down a moment and saw the artist had sketched a man in black and was quickly, so fast it was a blur, producing another wearing a clerical collar. A boy in a straw hat was craning his head over the artist's shoulder, watching him sketch. From his perch Bledsoe saw that the black horse and wagon had now stopped beside a phalanx of soldiers. The man in all black opened the door of the wagon.

"There they are!" yelled a man perched in another tree. "There's the yellow bellies!" The crowd jostled, stood on tiptoe to peer over shoulders, straining to see over men's high toppers. "Take off your hat!" was shouted again and again.

"Well?" hollered the artist. The drums' measured roll-tat-tat, roll-tat-tat increased. "What do you see now?"

"Two men getting out of the wagon and that man in black is fastening them in irons, hands and legs." Bledsoe leaned down from his branch. "What's going on?"

The artist looked up at him. "Making an example."

The phalanx of soldiers had now formed a V. Two wooden stakes had been driven into the ground before them. He watched as the two hobbled men were led shuffling slowly and painfully toward the stakes by the provost marshal.

The crowd pushed forward but the line of soldiers held firm. "What's happening now?" yelled the artist.

"The men have kneeled in front of the posts. Lord God. What did they do?"

"Deserters!" hollered the boy in the straw hat behind the artist. "Damn cowards run from Manassas. They caught 'em, though!"

Bledsoe drew a breath as the kneeling men were blindfolded. The preacher was saying something but he was too far away to hear. A single drummer now continued the same ominous roll-tat-tat, roll-tat-tat. Then the provost marshal raised his arm. There was a jangle of metal as rifles were raised. "Ready," shouted the provost marshal. "Aim." The crowd sucked in breath. Then the drum shattered the air with a terrifying rapid roll. The provost marshal lowered his arm and the drum ceased abruptly. "Fire."

The sound of the twelve muskets firing could be heard clear across the city. An echo nearly as loud as the original hung in the air for what seemed a full minute. Then a woman screamed and crumpled to the ground. A little girl began to cry. Men laughed. Cigars were lit. Bledsoe clung to the branch with both hands. All he could think was the last sound those men had heard had been that drum and then the guns. He still heard them. He didn't hear the artist now—"What do you see?"—until he felt the man grab hold and pull on his leg.

"What do you think I see? They're dead." A man picked up one of the men's wrists and looked at a watch, then nodded. The other deserter lay collapsed like a sack of flour. A wagon with two plain pine coffins pulled up and the two men were loaded into them.

Beneath the tree a woman and her companion were lunching on boiled eggs and fried chicken. The artist licked a finger and smeared a corner of his drawing, creating a shadow, and crosshatched a woman's shawl. He had drawn her peering over a soldier's shoulder. In the artist's sketch, two men lay on bare dirt, faces to the sky. A woman kneeled beside one, anguished face in tears. Beside her stood a preacher, hands folded in prayer. In the corner a banner declared somberly: "THE COWARDS' DEATH BY MUSKETRY."

Later at the Lafayette Saloon, the artist sold the picture to a man from a South Carolina newspaper. "But there wasn't a woman there," said Bledsoe. "And the preacher didn't pray after those men were shot. They just put them in boxes."

"That's not what people want to see, my friend," said the artist. "They don't want just any old death. They want drama." He jingled the coins in his pocket, tilting to the right—the effect of several rum toddies. He climbed into the buggy and plopped heavily in the back. "Go round to the senator's house. Let's see if he'll pay up for what I've done so far with that wife of his." Then the artist tilted so sharply to the left, he nearly fell out the low-slung side of the landau.

Bledsoe glanced back from the driver's seat. "Sure you want to do that right now?"

"Why not?"

"'Cause I think you're drunk."

The artist righted himself. "What? Me? Drunk? Hogwash. And who are you anyway? Just drive. Go. Go on." He flapped a gloved hand. "I once sold a battle scene to a newspaper in New York for fifty dollars. Did I ever tell you that? This one today was only worth five. Battles. That's the big money. Lots of death, lots of blood and guts. Ka-boom. If you're good enough you can almost hear the artillery. That's what they want to see. War in all its glory!"

Bledsoe was barely listening. The roll of the drum vibrated inside his head. *We ain't desertin', we're just restin'.* The other boy throwing a rock in Bull Run creek. Then dead. All dead. Just like that. Alive, then nothing. Unconsciously, he rubbed his shoulder. *Shot me too. For nothing.*

They passed along the river. A gang of slaves in leg manacles were building an enormous stone barricade. Every day there was a new demand in the Richmond papers for slaves, manpower to continue the digging down and the building up against a Yankee invasion. *Donate your property to the Cause!* Or, *We buy strong hands.* The day was cold yet the men were sweating in their rags. Bledsoe's hands tightened on the reins. Behind him he heard the artist unscrew the top of his silver flask. "Look at them there. How about that, Joe? Why, you're young and strong. Someone'd make a small fortune selling a boy like you to the fine City of Richmond."

Bledsoe pulled the gelding up and turned to the grinning man. "What?"

The man saluted him with the flask. "Lucky for you I'm not someone. Now knock that frown off your face. Can't you take a joke? You know I wasn't serious. Drive on. A lady awaits my artistic touch." Bledsoe pulled up in front of the ornate Italianate house. "Now wait here. Oh please, cheer up. It was only a joke." The artist had put on his new beaver top hat. "I'm not going to sell you."

"Then why'd you say that?"

"Oh please, Joe. I'm sorry. All right? Stop the sulking."

You said it because you can. Because you can do it too. What am I doing here? In Bledsoe's head Boaz lifted the bottle. *This war? White man's war.*

The artist said something as he got out of the buggy, but Bledsoe ignored him. He watched him walk up the drive to the senator's house. *I'll get out of here. I'll go back to the fort. Damn him, damn them all, I'll—*

The artist was climbing back into the buggy. The brim of his stovepipe was pulled as low as it would go on his forehead. After a minute or so he let out a great sigh. "The senator's wife has gone to visit her mother in Macon."

Bledsoe didn't reply, just shook the reins loose and clicked his tongue. The horse started up the street. The artist said loudly, "In Georgia, Joe. Macon is in Georgia. She won't be back until January."

Bledsoe didn't care, so he didn't say a word.

"Joe, we've got a problem, don't you see? The senator won't pay me until I get those terrible eyes and the rest of her immortalized on canvas. Not a farthing. A shilling, a penny. Oh damn it all to hell. I've lost her, my goose," he moaned. "She's flown, she's gone.

Bledsoe looked at the artist. His hat was off and his head hung low. "Didn't know you loved her," he said.

The artist glared at him. "Loved her! Her? Are you joking? I can't stand that spooky-eyed bitch. It's the money that's the problem. Funds are low, Joe, low low low."

Bledsoe remembered the pile of banknotes that the artist had shown him at the beginning of their trip. He thought about the women and the restaurants and the new cashmere cape the artist bought a week ago, the flowers sent, the cigars, steak dinners, champagne, the late night and early morning card games. *Gathering information,* the artist would assure Bledsoe as he staggered up the stairs to spend an entire day in bed. *Hard work.*

"Love is for fools, Joe," said the artist. Behind him, Bledsoe could hear the artist unscrewing the cap of his flask. "Fools. Who needs it? I don't. Never did. Well, once. Don't ask me about that," murmured the artist, though Bledsoe hadn't said a word. "I was a fool then too. Some of them get their teeth into you, you know? I don't wanna talk about it," mumbled the artist. "I hate love."

Later that evening there was a determined knocking at the door of the hotel room. The artist hid in the closet and whispered to Bledsoe to see who it was.

The man at the door was perspiring, though it was so cold Bledsoe had on his outdoor coat. He had clearly been strenuously exerted by the long climb to the uppermost floor of the hotel.

"Where is he?" demanded the man. He was in his fifties, most likely, and pudgy in the middle. He tried to poke his head around the door.

"Who are you?" replied Bledsoe, blocking the doorway.

"I'm the night manager is who, not that you need to know. Is he here?"

"Who?"

"Don't you give me any lip. You know who. Where's your master, boy?"

"'Fraid he's out," replied Bledsoe. "Sorry," he said, inching the door closed.

The man stuck a shoe against the doorjamb. "Well, when he's *in* give him this. And tell him if he doesn't pay up soon he's going to be *really out*. Get my drift, boy?"

Bledsoe took the paper, nodded, closed the door, and handed the bill to the artist.

The artist glanced at it. "What? I never had champagne sent to my room! Who knows what else these crooks tacked on here?"

"What about that there?" Bledsoe pointed to three bottles on the table.

"They call that monkey juice champagne?" replied the artist. He sat down on the bed. "Pull off my boots, will you? I need to lie down. Got to think. Clearly, we're going to need to find a more accommodating base to operate from." He lay down. "Hey, Joe, be a good sport and see if you can rustle me up a sandwich and a beer, won't you?"

❧

The artist had put a feather pillow over his face, which barely muffled the rumbling and occasional startled snorts. Bledsoe picked up one of the wine bottles. It was nearly full. He poured himself a glass and looked out the window. It was past midnight. The room smelled of liquor and sweat. The sheets hadn't been changed since they'd arrived—extra for clean linen. He raised the window. Cool air cleared his head a bit. The tavern across the alley from the hotel was emptying out. Three soldiers, arms around each other's shoulders, sang:

Her name was Lil and she was a beauty,
She came from a house of ill reputy,
But she drank too deep of the demon rum;
She smoked hashish and opium.

Day by day her form grew thinner,
From insufficient protein in her.
She grew two hollows on her chest.
Why, she had to go around completely dressed.

As Lillian lay in her dishonor,
She felt the hand of the Lord upon her.
She said, "Me sins I now repents,
But Lord, that'll cost you fifty cents."

This is the story of Lillian;
She was one girl in a million.

Bledsoe took another swallow as the soldiers' song faded away. A few minutes later there was the sound of breaking glass—a bottle dropped or thrown. The light in the tavern winked out. In the distance a horse trotted; voices occasionally drifted on the air, but the words were unintelligible. The street below was quiet and dark. Then somewhere someone else began to sing. At first he couldn't make out the words; it was too far away. He strained to hear it, holding his breath as a chill ran through him. *"Grasshopper sitting on a sweet potato vine."* He clutched the glass tighter.

"Along comes a chicken . . ."

Shoving his head through the open window, he looked down at the dark street far below. Something too small to make out distinctly scurried across the cobblestones. "Rat or cat or somethin'," he mumbled. "Stop it. In your head's all." He closed the window. He tipped the glass back and finished the wine in one swallow. Then through the closed window—*"Along comes a chicken says you're mine."*

He no longer bothered with a glass. He drank from the bottle and heard nothing else.

EIGHTY-THREE

They left Bell's Bliss early. The morning sun was a cold disk through heavy clouds. The light was sickly. Everything was oddly tinted as if dipped in dull sepia. The autumn landscape was alien to Alice's eyes, naked tree branches like forlorn bones and flat land shorn of corn and wheat. In the Dismal the underbrush was thick even in winter and if the air froze, the swamp stayed alive, winding its way around mangroves under the ice. As she looked out the coach window's glass, everything looked dead to her. They hadn't seen another soul for miles.

When the door of the elegant black carriage had been closed and locked, Uncle Harlan had been confused and then angry. He threw the lap blanket off his knees and rapped on the roof of the carriage with his cane, bellowing, "Stop, goddamn you." But when Attis didn't stop and Tamsin began to cry, the old man began to tremble. Then to sob. "My Mantons, at least, niece, give me my Mantons."

Tamsin pulled the box from beneath the seat and spoke to him in a soft voice. Alice could barely hear her but after a while he fell asleep, head back, mouth open, the ivory inlaid box with his dueling pistols in his lap. Tamsin looked across at Alice and dabbed her eyes. Alice half formed a smile in return, but she also felt like crying. She was going to Richmond. Now she would be even farther from Fort Monroe. All possibility seemed to have evaporated.

The carriage was expensive, large, and sturdy. It rocked gently and she barely felt the bumps in the road. She was sitting on smooth red velvet. The walls of the coach were padded with soft leather. Glass vases were set in gilt holders beside each window, though they were empty this time of year. Out the window she saw Cadan dash by on his gray hunter, scouting the road ahead. *Looking for trouble where ain't none to find,* thought Alice scornfully. *Showin' off is all.*

Across from her, Tamsin whispered, "Poor Uncle. He's afraid he'll never see Bell's Bliss again." She looked at the old man sadly. "Oh, I hope it will be all right in Richmond."

Alice looked out at the lonely landscape. The light had gone from yellowish to a woolly gray.

"I fear it's about to rain," said Tamsin. "That will slow us down. I know Cadan is hoping we'll make it to Charles City by evening. We'll stay overnight at the White Dove. That's where we always stayed when we traveled down from Richmond in the summers. It's been so long since I've been there. Oh, I can't wait to show you Richmond. We'll have some fun at last, though my gowns are all completely ancient now. Well, I can hire a seamstress when we get there. Alice? Hello? You're walking in dreamland, I swear. Why, you look downright miserable, what's the matter?"

Alice turned away from the window and murmured, "He's back there."

"Oh Lord, honey, I'm such a selfish beast," said Tamsin. "I didn't think about that." She was quiet a moment, then leaned across to Alice and said softly, "But you're no farther away from Henry than you were before. You're linked by hearts." She put her hand over her own and said,

Maid of Athens, ere we part
Give, oh give, back my heart!
Or, since that has left my breast
Keep it now, and take the rest!
Hear my vow before I go,
Zoë mou sas agapo.

Uncle Harlan stirred and Tamsin looked at him alarmed. But the old man let out a loud snort and sunk deeper into the soft upholstery.

"Lord Byron. The last part was Greek," whispered Tamsin. "*My life, I love you.* That's what it means. So beautiful. You're so lucky."

"Lucky? How the"—she gulped back the *hell*—"am I lucky?"

"You have someone who loves you."

Rain popped against the glass beside Alice. *Loves me. Does he? Is he even alive?* The window became a streaked blur; water pinged fast and heavy on the canvas roof. The coach came to a stop. There was a rap at the window and Tamsin let the glass down a crack.

"We best stay under de trees, Miss Tam. Can't do much more'n splash till rain let up."

"That's right, Attis. We'll wait until it lets up. Do you see Cadan?"

"He stop back at the Fogel place, said he'd catch up. Probably he stay there till rain's over."

Tamsin pulled the window glass up with a purple silk cord. Alice pointed at the umbrella leaning beside the velvet seat. "Pass that out to Attis, why doncha?"

Tamsin shook her head with a tiny smile. "Oh, Attis doesn't need that, Alice."

"But he'll git soaked and it's cold out."

"He doesn't mind. They're not like us, you know."

Alice looked out the steamy window. Attis stood miserably under the tree, rain running off the brim of his hat, coat and pants wet through. *Not like us.* Was that what she'd say about Bledsoe? Alice turned away from the window. "What do—"

"Why not rest a bit now, dear," said Tamsin softly. She sat with gloved hands clasped neatly in her lap, eyes closed. Uncle Harlan was sound asleep beside her. "Might as well. Can't do much else until the rain lets up."

After a quarter hour, the air inside the elegant coach had become stagnant and humid. The wool in Alice's high collar chafed her neck and she pulled at it with a finger. Tamsin breathed rhythmically in and out while her uncle sputtered beside her. A thin line of drool had spilled down his chin. Alice felt a tear start down her cheek and brushed it away. There was a rap on the window. She smeared the steam with the palm of her glove, expecting to see Attis looking through the glass. But it was a stranger. His face, wet with rain, was thin and lined. He motioned to lower the glass. Bewildered, she hesitated a moment. He rapped on the window again, only this time it was with the butt of a revolver. "Open the damn window," yelled the man. Across from Alice, Tamsin screamed.

Glass flew into the coach; a shard embedded itself in the back of Alice's hand, piercing through the fabric of her glove. But she didn't feel it, didn't notice the spreading red stain on the pale kid leather. The man was reaching through the shattered glass and unlocking the carriage door. The door flew open. Beyond the stranger Attis lay on the ground.

The man grabbed Alice roughly by the arm. "Your money," he yelled, holding up the gun. She pulled back with all her might, flailing at him with her free hand. The next thing she knew she'd fallen backward onto the velvet seat and the man had disappeared. Tamsin was screaming. Alice recognized the acrid odor in the air.

Gunpowder. Tamsin continued screaming as Alice managed to pull herself upright.

"Got the bastard," shouted Uncle Harlan. The Manton dueling pistol in his hand was leaking curls of white smoke. "Got 'im!"

Cadan stuck his head inside the carriage. His hat was gone and his wet hair, pressed tight to his skull, looked black. He waved his revolver. "Tam, you all right? Uncle Harlan?"

Tamsin was hugging her uncle, who had dropped the dueling pistol on the floor. Tamsin nodded, but her face was bloodless, her eyes wide with shock. Cadan looked at Alice but said nothing.

Behind Cadan, Attis was sitting up, blood running from his temple. He mopped it with his sleeve.

"Close the door," Cadan ordered Alice. But before she was able, the wind blew her hair into her face. As she pulled the hair from her eyes she saw that the man Uncle Harlan had shot was still alive. He moaned on the muddy ground beside the coach.

Without a glance at Alice, Cadan lowered the barrel of his Colt at the man's forehead. The man looked back with terrified eyes. "Oh please, mister, I'm sorry, I . . ." And Cadan pulled the trigger.

"Oh, oh," cried Tamsin, putting her hands over her ears. "Stop it, stop it!"

Cadan holstered his gun. "Don't worry, sister. He got what was coming. Get on up there, Attis. Wipe your face with this here. You can drive, can't you?"

"Yes, Marster Cade, I kin."

The coach rolled back onto the road. The rain lightened to a patter. Alice pulled the shard of glass from the back of her glove, dyed red now from blood. Across from her Tamsin whimpered. Her eyes were tightly shut. Uncle Harlan looked at Alice. "I finally got that damn deer been eating all your flowers, Freddie. Tell Attis bring me a tall bourbon."

"Oh, Uncle," said Tamsin, her eyes still tightly closed.

"Where are we going, Freddie?"

"Home, Uncle Harlan."

Alice pulled off her glove. The cut on the back of her hand was already coagulating. Cadan and three other soldiers escorted them on to Richmond. Attis drove without sleep. So did Alice. *The man was a thief, maybe a murderer. He got what was comin'. But him?* She looked out the window at Tamsin's twin. He cut quite the figure on the tall stallion. He knew it too. *There's law against jist shootin' people in cold blood, ain't there? But him? Why, he liked it.*

EIGHTY-FOUR

The Bells' massive house on Clay Street was built of red brick. Box hedges bordered the yard, which extended nearly half a city block. In springtime, Tamsin said, it was filled with yellow jonquils, snowdrops, forget-me-nots, and purple violets. She told Alice that cherry blossoms snowed pink on the green grass, so lovely. In June, the yard was filled with the delicate scent of malmaison and a hundred other roses. There were apple, pear, and plum trees. But it was fall when they arrived. Tree limbs were naked tangles; the grass was a sad yellow brown. The heavy black iron fence that surrounded the yard reminded Alice of the iron gate surrounding the graveyard at High Hope. So it was with a twinge of foreboding that she stepped through the great front door behind Tamsin.

Once the door closed, it was as if Tamsin also closed her memory of the events on the way. She laughed and grabbed Alice by the hand. "What fun we'll have now!" She pulled her from lavish room to room. "I'm so happy to have you to share it with."

Each room in the mansion took Alice's breath away. In one she walked across a floor of polished marble, so deep blue it was as if she were gliding on a lake of glass. There was a room just for music inhabited by an ebony piano and a harp with a golden ram's head with curled horns at its top. Tamsin plucked a string—oh! the note quivered inside Alice, then floated right through her. "You like it? We can get you a teacher," said Tamsin. "You can learn to play. Would you like that?"

Alice looked at Tamsin wonderingly. "Me? Play that thing? You mean I could?"

"Of course. You'll probably be better than I am."

The ceilings were at least twelve feet, some higher. Alice got a crick in her neck from staring up at one of these ceilings. She'd never seen the like. There was a painting up there. A most handsome man—no, not a man, an angel because he had wings—bent in a kiss to a just as beautiful girl with lips lifted to meet his. On the girl's raised finger rested a golden butterfly. In the dome of the ceiling behind this miraculous pair puffed perfect clouds in a perfect blue sky. She could almost hear the bright birds singing, the silver harps the little baby angels in the background played. Tamsin told her the painting illustrated the story of two lovers.

"Is it a happy one?" asked Alice.

Tamsin said at first it wasn't because somebody or other was jealous but that in the end it turned out well. "Which is unusual, you know, because those old myths hardly ever turn out for lovers."

Lovers. Tamsin was smiling and telling her something but Alice didn't hear. She felt very alone in the magnificent room. Suddenly she was frightened. All along, despite everything, she had told herself that somehow, some way, she would find him. She hadn't thought of it in terms of being a miracle exactly, more like things just slipping into their proper place. What Alice believed was their proper place. She was his and he was hers. She had faith. Faith that he was still alive and that somehow they'd find each other. Now as she followed Tamsin to another room, with more paintings and rugs and sparkling things, it felt as if something were crumbling inside her. She felt it viscerally so deep inside her that she clutched her stomach.

"Do you feel ill?"

Alice shook her head and Tamsin pointed to a painting. Alice watched her mouth moving as inside a dark hollowness spread, as if she were being filled up with nothingness. It was all she could do not to shriek, *What if I never see him again? What if he is truly dead?*

She reached instinctively for the little wooden carving under the neck of her dress but dropped her hand when Tamsin looked at her curiously.

Late that night after everyone was asleep, Alice crept down the great winding staircase and opened the door. Holding a candle aloft, she looked up at the painting. But it was too dark and too far away to make out more than shadowy shapes. In the flicker of the candlelight, they seemed to bend down to grab her.

She ran out of the room and started up the great winding staircase. Her hand was on the graceful mahogany banister when the hair on her neck rose. She turned, expecting to see someone, or something, on the staircase behind her. There was nothing. The solemn tock and stately tick of the brass pendulum in the long case clock at the bottom of the stairs was the only sound.

When she got to the landing and all the closed doors, she couldn't remember which one was hers. One, two, three doors to the right. Three doors to the left. Was hers the third on the right? No. Yes. When she put her hand on the doorknob she dropped the candle in shock. Someone opened it from the inside, then picked up the still-lit candle.

Cadan said, "Trying to set the house on fire?" He was wearing a nightshirt and his blond hair shimmered. He looked down at her. His eyes were almost black in the shivery light of the candle. "Or maybe you wanted to come in?" Then he blew the candle out.

Alice ran to the other side of the landing and pulled open the correct door. She could hear him laughing as she closed it.

EIGHTY-FIVE

Attis's duties were solely to tend to Uncle Harlan now. The first few days in Richmond he carried him from the dining room to his bedroom. The old man had aged even further since the incident on the way to Richmond. Wrapped in blankets, he resembled a mummified child with a wizened face. Attis spoon-fed him at the table and wiped his face. He didn't recognize Tamsin or Cadan but called Alice Freddie whenever he caught sight of her, though lately he didn't come out of his room at all. Once Alice heard the sound of a gun going off and saw Attis a few minutes later carrying the inlaid box with the dueling pistols out of Uncle Harlan's room. Then he went back into the bedroom and closed the door. She only saw Attis from time to time carrying a tray to or from the bedroom. Had Uncle Harlan tried to shoot a glass off Attis's head again? Or, wondered Alice, had he maybe tried to shoot himself?

She spent the first few days wandering the rooms of the house. It was big enough to lose your way until you got the hang of it. The Richmond house was far larger than the house by the river. Tamsin told her Bell's Bliss had been built as a summer home on the James away from the outbreaks of malaria and yellow fever that came with the heat and humidity.

Cadan had bought new servants. Even if Uncle Harlan had been in good health, it would have been impossible for Attis to keep the big house in good order alone.

One of the maids had freckles sprinkled across her nose and cheeks. Bits of red hair escaped her kerchief. Her name was Hannah. But when the woman began to unpack the trunk in Alice's room, Alice told her to stop and sent her away. No more Evas. She would take care of herself.

But this afternoon was different. An old friend of the twins' mother was coming to call, and Tamsin insisted Alice join her in the front parlor—the grandest of three. She was mortified. Callers? What would she say? How was a person supposed to act? The closest thing to a caller she'd ever known was somebody knocking on the witch's door for a cure. They skedaddled as fast as possible. It wasn't as if folks in Gates County wanted to sit and visit with ol' Granny Guthrie. And certainly nobody in the Dismal had ever come calling on *her*.

The only thing Alice knew was she ought to look her best. She'd look as good as she possibly could and keep her mouth shut. Hannah tied bone stays, helped her into crinolines, camisole, and bodice. The red-haired woman was quick. Her hands were soft. She had far prettier hands than Alice. She looked at the red-haired woman and wondered where she'd come from. She was going to ask, but there was something about her, a studied blankness. Her face was as unknowable as a mask sewn right onto her skin, though she was perfectly polite—nothing like Eva. She worked efficiently, smoothing Alice's hair with sweet oil, skillfully arranging it so the scar barely showed. She tied pink ribbons behind Alice's ears. Hannah patted the intricate knot at the back of Alice's head, making certain it was pinned securely.

When Alice looked at herself in the tall pier glass, she stared in wonder. Why what? That girl there was just about pretty.

Alice was drinking a third cup of tea. If she was drinking tea, she couldn't be expected to talk. She sipped and bit into another shortbread cookie. Mrs. Dollar and Tamsin's mother had grown up practically as sisters, Alice learned. They had been born on the same day in the same year and only separated by a few hours. They had shared the same French tutor and the same dancing master. Mrs. Dollar had brown hair that was wound around each of her ears like two cinnamon buns. She wore a sateen blouse and matching skirt in a green and blue tartan plaid. She had a high color and her skin was good. The other Dollar sat beside his mother, one arm carelessly slung over the back of the fancy parlor chair. He glanced at Alice from time to time and she pretended not to notice.

James Dollar ("Jamie," whispered Tamsin, while the maid was busy taking Mrs. Dollar's wrap and her son's hat, "doesn't he look like Lord Byron?") was a tall, colorless, large-eyed young man. His dark hair gleamed like the fur of an otter. When he pulled off his gloves, his fingers looked pale and delicate. *Like white worms,* thought Alice. He wore a black frock coat, a green vest, a peach cravat artfully arranged to look careless, and checkered pantaloons that fit snugly over highly polished lace-up boots.

Mrs. Dollar had been talking a blue streak ever since she sat down, which was a relief to Alice. Once introduced, she'd focused entirely on Tamsin. "Don't you think so, dear?" she said to the blond girl beside Alice.

The son was now staring directly at her, so Alice took another bite of a cookie and concentrated on the crumbs falling into her lap.

"You must have been terrified. I heard about that Yankee on your way up!"

"Oh yes," replied Tamsin. "But we were saved, thank the Lord."

He wasn't a Yankee, he was jist a thief. Looked poor too. Alice took a sip of tea.

"They're a plague," said Mrs. Dollar. "They want to invade our hearths and homes like the locusts of Egypt. Tear us from all that is dear and make us worship at the feet of that ape Lincoln. That's what Mr. Dollar says. They want to subdue us. Subjugate us to Federal policy. Take away our states' rights, force us to drink at the well of humiliation claiming it is in the cause of destroying our peculiar institution. They want to own us is what it is, isn't that right, Jamie?"

James Dollar looked at his pocket watch and said, "It's nearly four."

"A plague. Like locusts, says Mr. Dollar," continued Mrs. Dollar. "My friends, the Worths, you remember Jemimah Worth, don't you, Tammy? She's just two years older than you and married Levalon Bother. They live in Petersburg now. You don't? Oh, surely you do? I'll ask them over for luncheon; they have a new baby, cross-eyed, poor thing. What was I saying?"

"Locusts, Mother," said Jamie Dollar. "And Lincoln."

"Yes. Well. Listen to this. The Worths had four of their negroes stolen by Yankees just days ago. In Petersburg! Lured them somehow. Can you believe it? That's close enough to throw a rock. My kitchen girl is scared to death of them. She heard what they do to the females. Nor do those brutes have any sense of decency for white women either. I've got a cousin over in Newport News. They're camped out there, thousands of them. She wants to leave, but where will she go? They grabbed a young white girl on her way back from church, broad daylight. And"—she lowered her voice and leaned across the table—"you know what they did to *that* poor thing."

Tamsin fanned herself rapidly. Alice poured herself yet another cup of tea. Mrs. Dollar continued, "She killed herself, of course. Drank rat poison. As for me, I had rather die too. But that's what they do. Did you know we have a new cook? Trained in London. Cost the world."

Sleek otter-haired Jamie Dollar picked up the plate of cookies and held it out to Alice. She felt herself go hot.

Mrs. Dollar turned her pink-cheeked face to Alice. The woman's eyes seemed to want to swallow her. Alice nervously stirred her tea. "A friend of Tammy's, are you? Where is it you say you're from, dear?" asked Mrs. Dollar.

"Carolina," mumbled Alice, trying to mop up some tea that had sloshed on her lap with a napkin.

"North or South?"

"Huh?" Alice looked up at the woman, startled.

"Here, please. Use mine," said Jamie Dollar, flourishing a bright silk handkerchief.

"That's all right," mumbled Alice, flushing a deeper red.

Happily the maid entered with a white cake sprinkled with coconut and Mrs. Dollar oohed. "I see you've got a decent cook also. They're rare as hen's teeth these days." Mrs. Dollar surveyed the freckled maid as she handed a clean napkin to Alice and quietly gathered any dirty plates. "This one of them your brother bought from Lumpkin down in the Bottom?"

"Why, yes," said Tamsin. "We were lucky to get her. Thank you, Hannah; please tell Cook to look out for some fish for dinner."

"Yes, Missus," she said.

As Hannah left the room, Mrs. Dollar said, "You heard about Mrs. Chesnut's cousin, did you not? You know her husband, Mr. James Chesnut, was the one ordered them to fire on Fort Sumter? Hero. They're just down the end of Clay Street. You must meet Mary, Tamsin, dear; she knows *everyone*. Her husband is in the president's cabinet. You must invite them to your ball."

"Well, I said perhaps a little party. I don't know if I can throw a *ball*, Mrs. Dollar. I doubt it would be proper. I mean, Uncle is ill and there is a war on. Would that be right? And there are so few young men. Even Cadan is leaving for Yorktown in a few days."

"Oh, just a little dance then," replied Mrs. Dollar, "but as I was saying, Mrs. Chesnut's cousin was murdered down in Dinwiddie, you know."

"You didn't tell her she was murdered, Mother."

"Didn't I? Well, she was."

Alice, relieved to once more be ignored, wondered how it was possible to get from dancing to murder so quickly.

"Murdered!" exclaimed Tamsin. "How awful."

"Murder is usually awful," said Jamie Dollar. "For the murdered, that is."

Alice could feel his big eyes on her as he said this. Was he trying to be funny? Or did he know something? He couldn't. How could he? She brushed crumbs from her lap and readjusted her hair over her scar. She sank lower in her chair and kept her head turned toward her lap.

"*And* by her own people. *Trusted servants.* Been with her for years and years. She was old, you know, near ninety. They smothered her with a pillow, hoping it would look natural, but of course it didn't because she was blue in the face when they found her. They'd stolen all her jewelry but had second thoughts and tried to put it back. That's when they caught them. They confessed. They're to be lashed, then hanged. Mr. Dollar wants to drive down to see it. Says everyone should go and bring their servants so they can see what happens."

"Devils," said her son, wiping his long white fingers one by one. "Hanging is too good."

Maybe they had a good reason to murder the old lady. Alice found a loose thread in her shawl and began to try to weave it back in to keep her hand from shaking.

"We don't know *who* any of these servants are anymore, do we? I mean, murder you in your bed as you sleep, the *trusted ones*. How do you feel safe at all?"

Tamsin said, "Oh, don't worry, Mrs. Dollar. Attis is with us. He's our majordomo. He'd never hurt a fly. And I'm quite certain my brother wouldn't have bought any murderous negroes. Besides, this is Richmond. Practically the whole Army of Virginia is camped over in the fairgrounds, aren't they? And then *you* are right down the street from us." She smiled shyly at Jamie Dollar.

He bowed his otter-haired head gracefully to her. "Though I'm not worth much these days, I'm afraid."

"That simply isn't true," exclaimed Tamsin. "Not every man is meant to fight. Some have higher callings. Why, you're a poet!"

"He is so talented. That is how my dear Jamie makes up for his infirmity. He's written a whole new book of poems celebrating the noble Confederate soldiers. Warriors, he calls them. Well, come along, Jamie, we should be leaving. You must come tomorrow for luncheon, Tammy. We're having a little soirée to benefit the Chimborazo Hospital. Have you been yet? No? Mr. Dollar will be happy to escort you, though you must wear a veil over your face. Diseases, you know. But you can take them something to eat. I took six jars of the nicest apricot jelly."

At the door as Mrs. Dollar was putting on her wrap, she said, "Did you know the Shaw girl? Oh, you must remember her, Tammy dear, father shot himself?"

"Oh yes. I do remember her. That was horrid. Margaret, wasn't that her name?"

"That's right," said Mrs. Dollar, pulling on her gloves. "Wrap that scarf around your neck, Jamie. Yes. The mother went mad and the girl was left to run wild." She leaned to Tamsin. "She's in jail!"

"Whatever for?"

"Consorting with negroes." Hannah handed Mrs. Dollar her rabbit fur cape, then held the door open for the visitors. "Can you imagine? Have you ever? We shall see you tomorrow then."

James Dollar tipped his top hat to Alice and bowed to Tamsin. She blushed and smiled. After the door closed, Tamsin sighed. "Isn't he beautiful?"

Consorting with negroes. A girl was in jail. For consorting, whatever that was. "I never thought of boys bein' beautiful. How come he ain . . . I mean, *isn't,* in the army?"

"He has a bad chest. It's so very sad. He was born like that. His lungs are weak. Oh, but his mind isn't and he writes poetry. Just like Byron. Come and help me decide what to wear tomorrow. He has such a noble nose, don't you think?"

They can put me in jail all they like. I won't just consort, damn them. I'll marry him right proper.

"What's the matter, Alice? Why do you look so glum? I know Mrs. Dollar is a pill, but it's all right to laugh to yourself. Just smile sweet and nod now and then. That's what I do."

If he's still alive.

"Alice? Are you on the moon? Come with me. Let's walk out a bit in the garden before it gets dark. He's got the most heavenly eyes, don't you think?"

EIGHTY-SIX

Very early. Knocking on the door again. Rabid, staccato, like the rat-tat-tat of a drum. It folded into Bledsoe's dream. Bull Run. But the soldiers from the 4th Alabama weren't there. He was outside his body watching as he kneeled in front of a tree. Saw himself staring at lowered Yankee rifles across the creek. Funny thing. He could only see the silver barrels, not anyone attached to the rifles. Then, somehow, he was back in his body because he could feel himself rolling, rolling toward the water. *Am I dead?*

"Wake up."

He opened his eyes. The artist was shaking him by the shoulder. "If it's that damn manager again tell him I'm out," he whispered.

Bledsoe pulled his suspenders over his shoulders and rubbed his face blearily. He hadn't had a good night's sleep since he could remember. With his hand on the doorknob he turned to the artist. "He's gonna see you there behind me the minute I open the door."

"Excellent point." The artist crawled under the bed.

Bledsoe opened the door. "Sorry, Marster," he began. There was no one there. He was speaking to empty space. He felt a tug on his pant leg. He looked down. A little boy, five or six, held out an envelope. Bledsoe reached for it.

"You ain't the right one," said the child, snatching it back.

"Who is?"

"The white man with the pointy beard."

"Well, I work for him, so give it here." He grabbed the envelope.

"You gotta least give me a penny," said the child.

"I ain't got a penny. But how 'bout this?" He pulled something from his pocket.

"What it?" asked the boy, staring at it suspiciously.

"A pencil."

"Don't want no pencils."

"Someday you might," replied Bledsoe. He shut the door.

"Is it safe?" asked the artist from under the bed.

"Letter." Bledsoe slid it under the bed and sat down at the table with the empty wine bottles and rubbed his temples. His head hurt.

"Excellent!" exclaimed the artist a moment later. He scrambled from beneath the bed and waved a piece of paper. "Good news."

"Only good news would be that I wasn't here anymore."

"One thing I admire about you, Joe, is your unbounded enthusiasm. Come on, no long faces. We'll have oysters and champagne tonight. *Real* champagne. Let's go. Pack up, pack up. Well? Make haste, my friend, away we fly from this hellish hole."

As much as he wanted to simply walk down the stairs and out the door, Bledsoe knew it was impossible. He would never get away. He'd be recaptured within moments and this time he'd most likely be jailed, or even worse, sold. As far as Richmond was concerned, he was a slave and if he left, he was a runaway. He might even be sent back to the Rebel army. So he packed. But all he thought was, *There will be a chance and I'll take it.*

Despite the early hour the lobby was filled with coffee drinkers and newspaper readers. The artist and Bledsoe managed to wend their way past potted plants, waiters, and early risers without detection by the front desk.

"But what about the horse and buggy?" asked Bledsoe, panting down the sidewalk behind the artist. "Ain't we going to get them?" He was carrying a large suitcase in one hand, a big wooden box containing paints and brushes in the other, and the artist's easel was strapped to his back. "Wait," he said, shifting the easel. "What about the horse and buggy?"

"Come on," said the artist, walking in front so fast he was just short of breaking into a run.

"What about them? Why're we walking?"

"Forfeited," barked the artist over his shoulder.

"Forfeited? What you mean?" Bledsoe sped up until he was shoulder to shoulder with the artist.

"Let's just say," said the artist, lips drawn tight, "a certain gentleman had a very negative opinion of IOUs."

Bledsoe dropped the easel. "You lost *again*? The whole horse and buggy?"

The artist turned around and said softly, "Pick it up. Those people across the street there are staring." He whispered, "The US government can afford a loss. Don't look at me like that. What would happen to you if I was to end up in a box six feet under down here? You'd be in chains digging for the Confederate army." He glanced down the street. "Come on! Hurry! I think that's the man from the hotel back there." He turned down a side street. Bledsoe followed. What else could he do? But in his head the guard at Fort Monroe said, *I mean, boy, he* saw *they were about to be blown to pieces, but did he warn them? No. Just drew fucking pictures. Oh, and his nigger ran off from there and never came back . . . 'Cause maybe he oughta know what a shitty yellow belly that man is.*

Soon. I'll get out of here. Somehow. I will.

EIGHTY-SEVEN

Tamsin pulled off her gloves, handing them to Hannah.

"Would you want anything, Missus? Tea? Coffee?"

"No," replied Tamsin. "And in the future I prefer you address me as Mistress, not Missus."

Alice glanced at Tamsin as she untied her bonnet. It wasn't like her to sound so cross. Alice followed her into the music room. "Is it because of this here? Why, Tam, I don't even want it."

Tamsin plunked three or four notes on the piano. "I don't know what you mean." She banged out four more notes that made little sense. They were not musical.

"Here. You take it," said Alice, holding out the little red leather-bound book.

"He gave it to you," said Tamsin coldly, sitting down on the bench, her hooped skirt belling brightly behind her. She played something fast with a lot of black keys and vigorous pedaling. Alice fanned the pages of the little red leather-bound book of poetry. The print was tiny. There were no pictures. A piece of paper fell to the rug. She picked it up and unfolded it. *Dear. Miss. Green.* He called her dear. Miss. Yes, she supposed she was as she wasn't married. Green was her supposed-to-be name. She could read almost all colors now, though complex mixes of them like *vermilion* and *chartreuse* eluded her. She puzzled over the next word. *Eh eh eh nuh ch,* she mouthed softly. That was as far as she got when the note was snatched out of her hands.

"Enchanting to see you this afternoon," read Tamsin. *"Please accept this humble effort as a token of my esteem. However, I am not talented enough to convey your singular charms in verse. They are far beyond my modest talents. Respectfully, James Dollar.* Ugh!" exclaimed Tamsin, dropping the note as if it were covered in spiders.

"But I never wanted the dumb ol' thing. I—" began Alice. But Tamsin had run out of the room, her gown billowing in her wake. "—don't know why he give it to me," finished Alice. And she didn't. She had done nothing at all to encourage him. Every time he approached her, she'd gone the other way. Finally, worn out from ducking here and there, she'd sat down in what looked like a quiet corner away from all the punch-drinking cheer in the middle of the Dollars' great room only to find him at her elbow saying something about a place called Venice, Italy, where men sang as they rowed you on canals and had she been to Europe? Alice had muttered something in such a low voice that James Dollar had to bend down low beside her face. "I'm sorry, what was that?"

"No!" she'd exclaimed.

Two older women turned disapproving faces. Alice had looked out the window beside her chair, feigning fascination with a leafless cherry tree, but not before catching a glimpse of Tamsin, one of a gaggle of enormous-skirted girls. The look on her face roiled Alice's stomach. Jamie Dollar said something else, but Alice didn't turn from the window, so at last he walked away. Moments later Tamsin announced to Alice it was time to leave.

As the Dollars' maid was handing Tamsin her wrap, Jamie Dollar had pressed the little red leather book into Alice's hand. Tamsin stared at her hard, even as the sleek-haired young man bent low over Tamsin's hand and spit out all manner of sweet compliments. Tamsin had pulled her hand away from Jamie Dollar with such a face that Alice wanted to shrivel up and blow away, though it wasn't her fault that paste-faced Jamie Dollar gave it to her and not Tamsin. She hadn't spoken a word to Alice on the ride home.

Now Alice looked around the room: the silk draperies, wainscotted walls, gilded urns, a mandolin on a turned-leg table, the harp with the golden ram's head. Her feet hurt. Her head hurt. The stays in her corset were digging into her flesh. *Can't breathe.*

Tamsin stomped back into the room. "Wouldn't he be surprised to learn *you're so low you can't even read!*" She turned and flounced out once again.

"Reckon so," whispered Alice to the empty room, giving the little book on the rug a kick with her shoe. "So tell him, why doncha!" she yelled to the ceiling.

The second maid, whose name she didn't know, looked in the doorway. "You all right, miss?"

Alice nodded and ran past the maid and up the stairs to the third bedroom on the left side of the landing and closed the door behind her.

Upstairs Alice unbuttoned her dress as fast as the buttons would allow, pulled off her bodice, ripped off the petticoats, and tugged and pulled furiously until she had gotten out of the stifling corset. She sat on the bed in her chemise. *I hate it here, what am I doin' here? What is this place? I—*

There was a knock at the door. "May I come in?" said Tamsin.

Alice wiped her eyes. Tamsin opened the door, holding her hands out to Alice. She said, "I am so very sorry." She sat down on the bed beside Alice. "I am ashamed. I am beside myself with it. After all you've endured. I was just jealous. Which is a sin and God will write it in my book and on my day I will be judged for it. Oh, I may be plunged below for my wickedness and I accept that, but will *you* forgive me ever?" She reached a hand to Alice. After a moment's hesitation Alice took it. "Oh, thank you, honey," she said. "I am a horrible thing. It's not your fault that the Lord made you the way you are."

Alice opened her mouth, but Tamsin went, "Shhhh. Listen, honey. There's something about you. You're not like me or any of the girls I've ever known. You're almost out of a storybook, aren't you? Like Uncle said, a mermaid washed up from another world. It's not your fault you have no idea about etiquette or were never taught proper things or that you're a bit slow—oh, I didn't mean that—I mean no wonder you can't read, being a mermaid and all. Land's sake! Under all that water how could you read a book?" Tamsin dimpled and patted Alice's hand. "The pages would be just ruined, wouldn't they?" She lifted the little willow woman from Alice's breast. "You still wear this dirty old stick? Why, it's just heathen, Alice." She dropped it. "But never mind."

Alice searched Tamsin's face as she went on about how it wasn't Alice's fault she was this and she was that, trying to fathom the real meaning hiding in the blond girl's words. Though Tamsin was speaking sweet as new butter, beneath was something bile bitter. "No wonder Jamie's fascinated by you, you mysterious thing. Well, you go on ahead and like him if you wish—"

"But I don't! Not a little bit," replied Alice, pulling her hand away. "I love—"

"I don't care," continued Tamsin. "But just don't like him too much. Seriously, honey, I don't know why I was wasting my time. He's consumptive, you know." Tamsin stood and shook out her billowing skirt. Looking into the tall pier glass mirror, she rearranged a loose blond curl. "So he's bound to die soon." She smiled at her reflection and the dimple in her cheek reappeared. "Now Captain Merryman Wheeler is another matter entirely. Oh, you know what?" She bent and picked up Alice's discarded skirt and bodice from the floor. "I'm not entirely certain this blue really suits you. Why not wear my gray instead to dinner? I'll have the maid bring it to you."

Alice sat on the bed without moving for a long time after Tamsin left. She was perfectly aware that the blue *did* suit her while the gray did not. But she no longer cared. Whatever had kept her going was leaking out of her. She almost believed she could see it rising out of the pores of her skin—a wispy hopeless smoke. Here in this big city, a drip here, a drop there, every day, hour, minute. She didn't feel him. Not in this house. Not in this city filled with fancy dresses and gray uniformed soldiers. It was all foreign. Before, everything new had been different. Because, she realized now, it had been shared with Bledsoe. Her memories, once real enough to feel and smell, light on their secret pool of clear, clean water, honeysuckle—a curtain of yellow perfume. The powdery scent of the cool floor of the rock cave. Kisses she never wanted to end because then they would be apart—all of these were fading. Without these memories she had no more substance than a ghost. Soon she would collapse into a pile of empty clothes like an unstuffed scarecrow.

She took the willow woman from around her neck. The salt and sweat of her body had stained the wood, made the features difficult to make out. She dropped it in a drawer of the dressing table. After she'd closed the drawer, she touched the space between her breasts where the carving had rested beneath her clothes. Between her breasts and near her heart. The skin was cool and smooth and, now, naked. She opened the drawer and pulled it out. Clenched it in her hand and closed her eyes. *Please.* But there was nothing. Still, she put it back on. Otherwise there was no hope left.

Later she changed into the high-necked gray silk. Without looking in the mirror she parted her hair in the center and pulled it into a severe chignon and covered it with a plain crocheted snood. The scar, an angry red crisscross from ear to chin, seemed to pulse. When the bell rang for dinner she went down.

EIGHTY-EIGHT

Bledsoe set up the easel. The light here was perfect, the artist had said. The blond lieutenant, Bell was his name, had shown the artist all around the lower floor of his big brick house so he could select the room he wanted to paint in. Bledsoe had followed silently behind. The room he chose was large and windowed on two sides, both south and west. The furniture was very good, noted Bledsoe. Finer even than at Our Joy. He looked up at the ceiling. "Benjamin West," the artist said, standing behind him. "*Cupid and Psyche*. Of course it's a copy. I saw the original only once in New York. Not my thing, but it is pretty, I'll admit."

Psyche, with a butterfly, which is placed on the left hand and held by the wings with the right, remembered Bledsoe from the encyclopedia. He took in the painting. The girl with mouth upturned and winged boy bending in a kiss. Something fluttered inside him.

"Are you familiar with the myth?"

Bledsoe shook his head.

"Didn't read that in your encyclopedia? Well." The artist picked up a small vase and turned it around. "Venetian glass. Early on too, I think. These Bells are doing very well. We'll see how that plays out if the Confederate winning streak breaks." He glanced at the ceiling and set the vase down carefully. "Of course, if they do manage to get either the French or the English into it, they just might continue that winning streak and then we'll all have to see which way to land, hum? But I digress. Yes. Cupid and Psyche. Love story. Gods, monsters, goddesses. All that. Mythology is rarely what you'd call logical." He walked around the room, stopping occasionally to study some piece of furniture or object in detail. He looked up at the painted ceiling again. "Pretty good, I suppose, if you like that sort of thing."

"What sort?" asked Bledsoe, looking up at the ceiling. To him it was amazing. He'd never seen a painted ceiling before. He was trying to imagine how the artist had managed it.

"All that carefully draped nudity and parted ruby lips sort of thing. Breathless yearning. All. That." He turned to Bledsoe. "Love. I paint the truth. I paint what is visible and real. Now then, Joe. Stretch some canvas for me and set out my paints. Do it neatly, Joe, neatly. I've got to change now. Dinner with these Bells tonight. Get to see whatever fright I'm supposed to somehow make palatable."

After the artist left, Bledsoe opened the wooden box and pulled out the trays. The artist's paints came from England and France. He took out the palette, the brushes of hog bristle, fitch hair, and most prized of all, Siberian mink. This last brush was very fine and for delicate work, while the hog bristle was for broad strokes. He set the linseed oil on a table that he had covered with an oilcloth. One by one he laid out the metal tubes of paint. Vert Véronèse. The rich emerald green was derived from copper. It was very poisonous. It was rumored to have led to the death of Napoleon, said the artist. (The walls on Elba were painted with it and once they became damp, toxic fumes were released.) Then Naples Yellow. A pigment so ancient it was used in glazes in Babylon as well as on glass found in Egyptian tombs. Carmine Lake. Deep red. Made from the crushed bodies of beetles. When mixed with oil it was beautifully translucent.

The artist had taught Bledsoe how to stretch the linen to the frames he built himself. On nights when he wasn't too drunk he'd given Bledsoe blank paper and a pencil and told him to draw whatever was set in front of him—a dented pewter vase, a half-eaten apple, a wine bottle, a hat. At first the wine bottle and the hat were scarcely indistinguishable, but with practice, he improved quickly.

"Not terrible," the artist had said one evening, looking over his shoulder. He pointed at the drawing. "You drew the book well. But look. The chair looks sad. See how flat it looks? Who could sit in a chair like that unless they lived on the walls of an Egyptian tomb? Don't draw the outlines of things. No no no. What you need to understand is chiaroscuro. We don't see lines around objects or people; we see light and shadow. Draw only the light and shadow and you create three dimensions."

A few days later he looked over Bledsoe's shoulder again. He'd drawn the artist's LeMat revolver. "Hmm. Let's see. You have shaded this well and left it bare where it should be to stand as light and it's convincing."

Even though he'd tried not to show it, he was secretly proud anytime the artist gave him a compliment. When he was drawing he lost himself. Anything he wanted could be drawn on paper with a pencil. The better he drew it, the more real it seemed. Now he unrolled a sketch he'd made several nights ago. It didn't look like the portraits the artist did. The artist's paintings of people, though extremely lifelike in every detail, seemed to Bledsoe strangely life*less*. He unrolled a canvas from the artist's bag of a woman with a black cat on her lap. Every detail was right. The texture of the woman's hair and the cat's silky fur seemed real enough to stroke. Her hands, even her fingernails—were perfect. Each eye looked just like a human eye. But that was where it ended, thought Bledsoe. The woman and the cat didn't breathe and they would never move. It seemed to Bledsoe that they had frozen to death on the linen.

This drawing of Bledsoe's was rendered in black charcoal. At first glance it was just a riotous mass of black strands and wild tendrils that at first looked to have no rhyme or reason. But looking longer a pair of eyes peeped through the wild black tangles. A nose. A laughing open mouth. It wasn't really a picture, thought Bledsoe. It was more of a moment. A thought grabbed out of the air. A refracted memory. He'd caught a fragment of her. A spark. He traced the crazy soot-black swirls with his finger. *Only on paper. It ain't real. She's dead.* He looked up at the ceiling. In that moment, maybe it was the light and shadow in the room. It was dusk. The girl and winged boy looked real enough to believe that when he left the room they'd whisper. Laugh. Kiss. Her mouth upturned to his.

He looked back down at his drawing and tore it in half. *She's gone.* But why wouldn't she get out of his head?

EIGHTY-NINE

In the dining room Tamsin said, "What kept you fellows so late? I sent Cook out to find you just as you were coming in." She turned to the artist across the table. "Now, sir, you'll have to watch these two boys. My brother and Captain Wheeler have been troublemakers since they were children. You never know where to find them when you need them."

"I do apologize, Tam, you may blame me entirely," said the captain. "Your brother was not on duty when they brought through the Federal prisoners from the battle at Leesburg. He insisted on accompanying my squadron as we escorted them down to the prison."

"I would never blame you for doing your duty, Captain. I didn't know about the prisoners."

Cadan said, "The Yankees snuck over the Potomac and thought they'd discovered one of our camps at Ball's Bluff, except it was nighttime and what they thought were tents were only trees. Our boys routed them, drove them over the bluff into the river. A lot of them drowned and the rest surrendered. How many you got there at the prison, Merry?"

"Over five hundred," replied Captain Merryman Wheeler. "We made quite a parade of them down Broad this afternoon. People lined the street. Some threw perfectly good fruits and vegetables. The enlisted men were a ragged bunch, wholly undisciplined, but the officers looked fine enough, seemed well brought up. Too bad for them, I guess."

"It's their own fault for starting this war," said Tamsin. "They ought to stay north where they belong. You don't start fights if you're well brought up. You do, however, defend yourself."

"That's right, Tam," agreed Captain Wheeler. "We will defend our near and dear." He smiled wide at her. "Especially our dear. And of course you also, Miss Green, it's just I've known Tammy since she was nine. She was knock-kneed and snaggletoothed back then. I haven't seen her for what, Tam? Ten years? You've straightened out very nicely. Very."

Tamsin smiled back at the captain. "And aren't you just fine in that uniform, Merry?"

"*Damn* right, we'll defend ourselves," said Cadan. "Wine." He held up his glass and the maid refilled it and returned to stand by the sideboard. "You need to train these girls, sis. They just stand around like donkeys. I never would have to ask Attis for more wine."

Tamsin said something but Alice didn't listen. Then Cadan was going on—she heard *Ball's Bluff, look how we're whipping 'em,* but then the rest faded as if she'd been transported three rooms distant. She ferried the green beans and lamb on her plate past the fried potatoes, then back again. Captain Wheeler was a tall young man with a cheerful smile under a thick brown mustache and muttonchop sideburns. Alice had avoided looking at him or the other guest, a silver-haired man with a sharp goatee and equally sharp eyes. He was an artist here to paint Tamsin. She was aware he studied her when he thought no one else noticed. She felt his eyes on her again. She began to build a wall of her potatoes, separating the lamb from the green beans.

"Now what I want to see is those spies hanged over at Castle Thunder tomorrow. Unfortunately, I'll be on duty. I'd like to see those traitors' necks stretched. They say one is from right here in Richmond, can you figure it? Turning like that on your own?" asked Captain Wheeler. "I declare it's a fact. Spies are the lowest. Spineless cowards. Sell their own mothers."

Had it been her imagination or had the man with the goatee looked uncomfortable at that moment? He'd cut his lamb into pieces but hadn't eaten a bite. Maybe he didn't like lamb. Though he seemed to like wine just fine. His glass had been refilled twice. She pushed her green beans to the right and then the left. Why should she care? She didn't give a damn if they hanged spies or if this artist didn't like the food on the Bells' table. He glanced up and Alice glanced down. *Mind your own damn business.*

"I saw a mention of it in the paper. Castle Thunder?" asked Tamsin. "I never knew there was a castle in Richmond. I'd love to see it. Is it pretty?"

"It's not really a castle, Tammy. Just three old warehouses down on tobacco row. We've run out of hospitals and now we're running out of prisons. Thunder is where they put the worst. Deserters, Union prisoners they couldn't fit in Libby, spies. They have one building just for negroes and women. It's run by a Captain Alexander and they say he's the one who named it Thunder in order to strike fear in the inmates. I've heard he personally does a lot of the lashing and keeps the prisoners, even the women, in chains. Humiliates them. There are some sorry stories about his brutality. Once—" Captain Wheeler looked at Tamsin. "I apologize, ladies. Hardly something to discuss in front of y'all."

"No need," replied Tamsin. "These people are only getting their just desserts. Speaking of desserts, I believe we have an apple charlotte."

As the final course was served, the artist held up his wineglass in a salute. "I'm delighted to be engaged to preserve such youth and beauty for future generations, Miss Bell."

"Oh," replied Tamsin, a pretty rose spreading from her neck to her cheeks. "I'm hardly that."

"Well, I am," replied Cadan with a grin. "I'd have you paint me too, but I'm leaving for Yorktown day after tomorrow."

"Remarkable resemblance between the two of you. I'd love to paint you both together someday."

"Look around at these old pictures on the wall here," said Cadan. "Bell family goes back to 1740 in Virginia."

Tamsin smiled at the men across the table. "Oh, boring, Cade. No one cares about those old things."

"That's not true, Miss Bell," said the artist. "Who is that fine gentleman over there?"

"Well. That one over the buffet is our grandfather Winn Weston Bell, and next to him is his second wife, Alethia. Our grandmother Mahlia Moxley Bell died from the grippe when we were babies. That's Aunt Freddy—you remember her, don't you, Merry? Didn't you come down to Bell's Bliss one summer before she died? And next to them is our mother and father, Winn Law Bell and Vaudy. Her name was Valentine, you see, but they called her Vaudy, sir. There are more Bells, as well as Blythes and Unwolds scattered about. Other names I can't remember. There's a man in the back parlor who looks to me just like the Devil. Uncle Harlan said he's Great-Great-Uncle Poteous Bell. He invented some sort of currycomb, I believe. As for me, I'll be content to hang in a broom closet."

"When you see my painting, Miss Bell, I promise you will not want to hide it in a closet. I may be somewhat immodest, but that is only because I am so inspired by my subject."

Alice gazed at the paintings. So that was Freddy. The young woman wore a riding habit and stood holding the harness of a very tall chestnut horse. She looked like she was holding back a laugh. Beside her a nearly bald man and a steel-haired woman stared out of their respective gilt frames. Next to them were the twins' parents, Winn Law and Vaudy

Bell. They appeared to be as young as their now-grown children. Tamsin had told her they'd been on a train and it had collided with another when the twins were only a year old. She wondered why Tamsin hadn't shown her the pictures before. She wondered, in fact, why Tamsin seemed almost another person since they'd arrived in Richmond. She turned to Tamsin beside her. "They're real handsome, your folks, Tam. I'm sorry for your loss."

"What about your family, Miss Green? I'm certain they're every bit as handsome," asked the artist.

"They're gone," she said softly to her wall of potatoes.

"You know, I'd be delighted to paint you also." He looked at Cadan. "I would love to do it for my portfolio. No charge at all to you, Lieutenant."

"No," said Alice to her plate.

"Can't I change your mind, Miss Green? May I show you some of my work? Perhaps that might sway you."

"Alice is shy, sir. I'm sure she'd rather not." Tamsin smiled too hard at Alice and she felt herself flushing. She really didn't want to be painted. Well, not so much, although it might be nice to be able to look out on the world from a gold frame after she was dead. She speared a green bean.

"Alice isn't the type for that sort of thing."

The artist signaled for a refill of his wineglass. "Is there a type? Do you mean some people should be painted and others not, Miss Bell?" He smiled at her warmly. "Miss Green has the most arresting face."

"You mean this?" Alice touched the scar with the speared green bean. "That why you want to paint me?"

The artist blanched and set down his wineglass. "Heavens! Of course not, I—"

"Alice isn't," began Tamsin, "well, you see—"

"Oh, Miss Green here is our mystery woman," interrupted Cadan. "Floated down the James River to our summer home. Apparently fell in or was perhaps pushed. We never really got the story straight, did we, Miss Green? My uncle claims she is a Nereid."

"Naiad," corrected Tamsin. "Nereids are in the sea. Naiads in rivers."

Alice unspeared the bean and buried the lamb with the potatoes.

"You get the idea," said Cadan. "Our uncle pronounced her something mythological. She is certainly *something*. Has trouble remembering things. Like her name, we only got to Alice Green through weeks of waiting. And still?" He looked at Alice with a smile though his eyes remained flat. "We're not even sure about that. Or her background. Apparently, as I've recently learned, she even forgot how to read—"

"She was never taught," interjected Tamsin. "She grew up in unfortunate circumstances."

"I'm sorry," said the artist. "You lost your memory?"

Alice felt herself melting into her chair. She was growing smaller and smaller and soon, with any luck, she'd disappear entirely.

The captain spoke up. "Amnesia? Had a field hand out at our place got hit in the head with the dull end of an axe. Couldn't even remember to swallow afterward. Man died. Amnesia. That's too bad," he said, looking sympathetically at Alice.

"Yes," said Tamsin. "Poor thing. I take care of her, you see. She's a sweet thing."

"She's something. That's for certain," added Cadan.

"Amnesia," repeated the artist. "Tragic." But he didn't take his eyes off her. None of them did. They were all looking at her. She could feel herself catching on fire from the inside out. Her skin was so hot she would surely burst into flames.

Then Captain Wheeler said, "This is surely the best apple cake I've ever had."

Everyone concurred. No one noticed Alice didn't take a bite. Or if they did, no one said a thing about it.

NINETY

That night Bledsoe lay on a straw-filled pallet in a pantry of the Bells' Richmond house. It was after midnight but sleep wouldn't come. His brain kept up a steady argument. Sneak out of the house and make a run for it. *Where the hell to?* He was in the land of the Rebels now. Even if he did manage to figure out how to get out of town, how far would he get before he was caught? The artist was surely right. He'd be enslaved by the Confederate army again. *But I'm as good as his slave right now.* How was he helping the North win the war here in Richmond? The artist was no father figure. Bledsoe was furious at himself for such naïveté. The artist was a con man, a liar, and a coward. All he cared about was liquor and gambling. And why was he so friendly with this Lieutenant Bell? Oh, he knew what the artist would say: "More flies with honey." But he didn't believe it anymore.

He stared at the darkness above him. The next thought took him by surprise. *Maybe he isn't even working for the North. Maybe he's a spy for the South. Traitor! Or even. No. But what if . . . for both? Oh!!* He gnawed on this revelatory idea. What exactly did he know about the man? Nothing really. Not where he was born. Not where he really came from. Hell. He didn't even know his real name! He'd watch him. Watch his every move, every minute. If Bledsoe discovered he *was* a traitor . . . he'd what?

I'll kill him.

The how or what might follow didn't enter his mind. He had reached a satisfying conclusion for the time being. The whirl of debate in his head immediately ceased. He closed his eyes. Sometime in the early hours he dreamed he was back in the Dismal. Hungry, cold, and lost. He heard the forlorn call of a nightjar. On and on it called with no answer. He was afraid to go forward and afraid to turn back. Things splashed in the water behind him. Pawpaws and dogwoods clicked bare branches; buttonbush and sweet alder rustled though there wasn't the slightest breeze. The sky was empty of stars. It was a dead land.

He realized he was sinking and had been all along. Ankles, knees, thighs. Down and down. The more he struggled, the more he was sucked under. In the darkness was a flash of light. Then he realized it was an outstretched hand. He grasped it and it pulled him slowly free. When he reached for her, all he was left with was a strand of black hair. In the darkness of the Great Dismal Swamp she was the only light.

Upstairs Alice huddled beside the bed, a quilt pulled tight around her shoulders. She had finally stopped shaking. *What am I gonna do?* Where could she go? The answer was plain. Nowhere. She had no money and she barely knew where she was. Oh, she knew it was Richmond, but it might as well have been a city in China for all her understanding of geography. *I'm stuck. Stuck like a pig in the mud.* She sighed. But she didn't cry. *Nothing grows from salt.* That was what Jenny had said back at High Hope. Jenny. For the first time Alice let herself think about Jenny's fate. The others. Caught and blamed for what she'd started. She groaned aloud. She'd killed that dog with a shovel and then that man was shot. That horrible man. He should be dead. But she had started it all. And now? *They're all dead.* But what could she have done? Just stand there and wait to be dragged into slavery? That man's slave? It hadn't occurred to her that everyone at High Hope had believed she really *was* a slave. She'd never believed it. But if that man was still alive, she would have found herself truly enslaved. Without him.

She dropped the quilt. Lit by candlelight, she studied herself in the mirror. The dress, though not the most becoming, was of excellent quality. The gray satin was the color of spring rain. The fabric shimmered. She remembered the gown the slave dealer Aubrey had bought for her. She grimaced. She'd thought that cheap thing was beautiful? She knew better now. She knew so much more now.

Downstairs the long case clock gonged three times. *Three's the number of power.* That was what the witch said. *When the clock strikes three, the Devil walks free. That's when dead and living meet.*

Alice unhooked the high-necked bodice and skirt. They fell into a silvery heap around her ankles. She pulled off the snood and let down her hair. Set free, it sprung around her shoulders and snaked down her back. She lay down on the bed. *If you are dead, come to me. I no longer want to live without you. Come and take me with you.*

She lay there naked atop the counterpane, hands clasping the willow woman, eyes shut. She lay like that until her skin prickled with goose bumps. It was cold. *Come,* she begged.

After a while the candle sputtered and the dark fell on her like a blanket. In her sleep the swamp sang to her. Its creatures joined in an orchestra of hums and chirps. She felt herself floating in water warmed by the sun. It cradled her as she looked up at night stars. Which she realized weren't stars at all. They were his eyes looking down into hers.

NINETY-ONE

Inside St. Paul's she was dazzled. She'd never seen such a church. Row upon row of polished pews filled with gorgeously dressed men and women. Graceful fluted columns flanked an altar draped with a white cloth embroidered in gold thread. A crate had served as a pulpit for the circuit rider in Geegomie. The building had smelled like fish and decaying wood. This church smelled like Heaven. There was a great deal of standing up and sitting down. She just followed what Tamsin did. When prayers were uttered, she mumbled softly and hoped no one noticed she didn't know the words. But as the preacher went on and on about war and death and God and righteousness, Alice studied the pictures in colored glass in the line of windows on either side of the church in awe. She recognized Jesus in a robe of glowing crimson immediately. Wasn't that his mother in a robe of cornflower blue? Creamy lambs and alabaster doves. So beautiful.

When she felt Tamsin nudge her, she stood, holding one edge of the hymnal while Tamsin held the other. Tamsin sang,

There is a fountain fill'd with blood
Drawn from Immanuel's veins,
And sinners plung'd beneath that flood
lose all their guilty stains

Alice bent her head to the book. She didn't know this hymn. It was awful bleak and depressing. So much blood and a great deal of drowning in it. In the pew in front of her a woman in an arsenic-hued bonnet sang loudly off-key.

She glanced to her left and found the artist staring at her. He'd accompanied them to church. He wasn't singing either. She blushed and turned back to the hymnal. Thankfully, the song and service soon ended with a final *amen*.

Outside the church, Tamsin was surrounded. Strangers to Alice, but obviously friends of the Bells. Alice had hung back as Tamsin had laughed and chatted. Now, up ahead, she walked arm-in-arm with a pretty girl in an emerald-green cape. She leaned and whispered in Tamsin's ear and Tamsin giggled in reply. Alice followed. *Dumb thing, she's dumb as a rock; listen to her cacklin' like a damn chicken. Oh, I can't breathe.* She tugged at the high, tight neck of her gown.

"May I accompany you?"

Alice turned to the silver-haired man at her side. What was his name? She didn't recall if she'd even heard it spoken. She fumbled a reply, something between *don't* and *oh*, that came out so limply meaningless he took it for acquiescence. He touched the brim of his hat and began to keep pace beside her. "Did you enjoy the sermon?"

She glanced at him. "Suppose so."

"I must confess, I find your story fascinating, Miss Green."

She increased her pace, but the man kept up.

"There are certainly some things *I'd* rather forget myself," he said with a smile.

Alice was walking so quickly now she was in danger of soon running into Tamsin's back.

"I apologize. That was meant to be funny and I see that it wasn't. Please, Miss Green, how can I get you to reconsider? I promise I will do you justice."

She stopped and turned to him. "Go away," she said softly.

He took off his hat. "I shall do as you wish but only for the moment. I will not desist until you surrender." He bowed before her.

"Oh, git!" She realized she'd said this louder than she had intended. Tamsin and her girlfriend swung around. Tamsin gave Alice a reproving look. The girl tittered behind her gloved hand and stared at Alice. Both turned their backs. Tamsin whispered something and the girl glanced over her shoulder at Alice. They walked on, arms again intertwined. Alice, her face on fire, looked right and left. The street was filled with ladies in Sunday finery, men in brushed beaver top hats, officers in fancy uniforms. Children yelled and dashed between adults followed by barking dogs. Carriages rolled past one after another. *I could just walk away. She'd never even notice.* But she didn't even know what street she was on. And she had no money. In the distance she could hear the tinny sound of bugles from the fairgrounds. *Soldiers everywhere.* At least the silver-haired man had disappeared from her side.

"Hurry up, Alice," said Tamsin, turning to her. "I swear. Sometimes I just don't know what to do with you."

"Do nothin'," muttered Alice. "I ain't your damn dog." But she followed the two the rest of the way home because she couldn't think of anything else to do.

Later that afternoon she dropped her needlework in her lap. She couldn't help the dark feeling that rose in her every time she heard the girl's high-pitched giggle. Tamsin and her friend were in the room with the painted ceiling. Alice was next door in the parlor. Tamsin hadn't asked her to join them for tea. *Not that I care.* Now she gnawed her tongue as the girl, blond like Tamsin but a duller straw shade, laughed. *Like a damn wheezin' squeezebox.* Alice jabbed her needle into the cotton pulled tight in her embroidery hoop. *"Ow!"* she exclaimed, dropping the needle. She sucked blood from her thumb. *Damn me. No. Damn* you.

A few minutes later Alice heard the girl saying her goodbyes. Tamsin came into the parlor. She picked up the discarded embroidery hoop. "Dear Lord, was there a murder? Look at the blood on this pillow cover. Let me see your hand. Give it to me. Why, you've poked yourself full of holes." Tamsin wrapped Alice's hand in a handkerchief she pulled from her sash. "Why didn't you join Caroline and me for tea?"

Alice pulled her hand away and shoved the handkerchief back at Tamsin. "'Cause y'all were in there laughin' at me."

"Oh, Alice, that's ridiculous," she replied with a huge sigh. "I swear. I've done all I can. I don't know what to do with you anymore."

Alice looked out the window. After Tamsin left, Alice sniffled and wiped her nose with the blood-spotted pillowcase. *It was this city changed Tam. These folks changed her.* Or was it because here in Richmond, Tamsin no longer needed her? She was back among her own kind. *It's plain as day, ain't . . . I mean, isn't it? Might as well be one of them damn mermaids. Mebbe I ought to just throw myself in the river again. Only this time I'll make sure to do it good. But she wouldn't care none.*

She stopped blowing her nose when she heard voices outside the doorway and strained to hear what was said. *Were they talking about her?* She recognized the voice of the silver-haired artist.

"Miss Bell will sit tomorrow. I wish I could talk her pretty friend into sitting. She's the more interesting. Such a face, almost otherworldly. A wildness in the eyes. Says she doesn't remember her past. She's a clever girl, whoever she really is. Managed to wrangle quite a nice situation out of these people."

Curiosity pulled her from the sofa. He was talking about her. *Says I'm clever.* Who was the artist talking to? She couldn't hear any of the words said in reply, only the timbre of the voice. Something about it.

But both voices were fading away. She heard footsteps receding and she ran to the door. But when she stuck her head out, the artist and whoever he was talking to had disappeared.

A moment later in the distance she heard the piano. She walked swiftly to the music room and opened the door. The artist was at the piano. "Hello there, Miss Green," he said brightly. "Please join me. I'm not very good, but perhaps I could amuse with something. Do you know this one?"

He began to play, but Alice interrupted. "Who were you jist talkin' to?"

He stopped and looked at her curiously. "Talking to? Why, no one. As you can see I'm alone, though I'm delighted with you for company." He began to play again.

"No. Before. In the hallway. I heard you."

He looked at her again, puzzled, but kept playing. "You must mean Miss Bell?"

"No! It was a man! You were talking to a man."

He closed the cover over the keyboard. "A man? Oh. Wait a minute. You must be referring to my servant, Joe. That's who I was speaking to. Why do you ask?"

"Your servant," muttered Alice from the doorway. "Only was your servant?"

The artist was starting toward her. "Who did you think it was? Oh, you look pale, Miss Green. Please. Come sit down."

But Alice closed the door of the music room. *I'm truly goin' crazy.*

NINETY-TWO

"Meet Clarisse, Lieutenant," announced the artist, taking the rolled canvas from Bledsoe. He opened it on the tabletop.

Cadan Bell grinned at the pink and white confection. "Goddammit, I got to give it to you. You're putting me in the mood for a visit to our lady friends in Locust Alley." He poured another tumbler of whiskey and refilled the artist's.

It was very late. Or very early. The clock had struck four a good half hour ago. "You like Clarisse? Wait until you see Alma. Joe, bring me the other portfolio from my room."

Bledsoe went to the door. "Wait, wait," said Bell. "Come back here, boy." The lieutenant was drunk. He pointed at Bledsoe. "Say something. Do one of them Shakespeare speeches." He dropped heavily into a chair.

The artist glanced at Bledsoe. "Sure. Joe'll be happy to oblige." Bledsoe's hand tightened on the doorknob. "When he comes back with my portfolio. Right, Joe?"

"Yussuh," he mumbled. He couldn't kill them both. *Couldn't I?* He breathed deep, unclenched his hand, and left to fetch the watercolors. The artist did them in the evenings. Women draped like sunning cats on beds, sofas, fur rugs. One, naked as a jaybird, riding a horse down a street. The artist sold them in saloons or traded for liquor.

When he reached the landing, a woman was just entering a room to his left. He only glimpsed her for a second before she vanished, her satin skirt disappearing seconds later. He suddenly felt light-headed and leaned a moment against the fancy papered wall. It was all he could do to resist knocking on the just-closed door. *You're seeing things. Stop it.*

When he returned to the library, the artist put a finger to his lips. Lieutenant Bell had passed out in the chair. As they watched, an empty tumbler dropped from his hand, landing noiselessly on the thick rug. The artist pushed Bledsoe out the door and closed it softly. Finger to his lips again, he beckoned Bledsoe down the hall to a darkened parlor.

"Listen to me," he whispered. "I need you to do something very, very important."

Bledsoe could barely see the artist's face in the gloom. He found himself whispering back, "What?"

"How long does it take you to remember what you read?"

Bledsoe shrugged, forgetting the artist couldn't see him in the dark. "I don't know. Usually it sticks in my head right off."

"Amazing, amazing. Good. Perfect. Now stay in this room and wait until you hear Bell go up to bed. Then go back into the study. On that big round table near the window is a stack of papers. Do you know where I mean?"

"Think so," replied Bledsoe. "What about it?"

"There's a map sitting there. I want you to memorize it with that encyclopedic brain of yours, then leave the study, go back to your quarters, and redraw it from memory."

"Draw you that map?"

"No, not me. For Lincoln."

"Draw the map for Lincoln?"

"For Lincoln and the North."

"Then why don't I just take it?"

"If Bell comes down in the morning and finds it missing, I'll be suspect. He's always asking questions, trying to trip me up. He's still suspicious. Be quick. Servants will be up soon after he goes to bed."

The artist was already almost out the door when Bledsoe said, "Wait. What's it a map of?"

"The defenses of Richmond."

NINETY-THREE

The hinges on the door squeaked. In the stillness of the sleeping house, it seemed to Bledsoe loud enough to wake the dead. He paused but it was almost quiet enough to hear a feather fall. He quickly opened the door just enough to squeeze inside. He was sweating though it was cold in the study. A last bit of wood erupted, then collapsed in glowing embers in the fireplace. He lit a candle. He was terrified of being caught, but a strange excitement had risen inside him. He was *doing something*. Something that mattered. This map could change the course of the war and break the South's winning streak. He felt an odd surge of something nearly like affection for the artist. Yes, he was a bad gambler and often a drunk, but he wasn't a traitor. He'd been wrong about him after all.

Maybe, thought Bledsoe, just maybe, after the Yankees took Richmond, the artist might take him to meet President Lincoln if he asked. *Yes, this is the man. Couldn't have done it without him. He's the one you should thank.*

In the hallway the clock's brass workings chimed five. He began to study the map.

Immediately he began to panic. Words mysteriously seemed to glue themselves to the inside of his head. Sometimes he wondered if one day his head would no longer be able to contain them all and swell up big as a fall pumpkin. Or perhaps words would just leak out his ears in a continuous stream of ink. Lines and circles. Pictures. *Stop it. Concentrate. See what the pictures represent. Look at the words beside the symbols.*

Deep Run, Meadow Run, Meadow Bridge, Richmond Hill, Academy Hill. Here a cross-hatching represented the Richmond to Danville Railroad. There was the river: *Rocketts*, read the legend. Drewey's Bluff. *James River Squadron; CSS Richmond, CSS Merrimack.* The little squares, he realized, represented various ships guarding the river entrance to the city. The map was laid out in expanding concentric circles from the center, which read Capitol. That was where the governing power of the Confederacy was located. It was surrounded with hundreds of black lines labeled *rifle pits.* He scanned, taking pictures with his mind: *Iron Works, Cannon. Twenty Pounder Parrots. Barricades.*

He nearly jumped out of his skin when footsteps rang out in the marble hallway. He ducked behind a sofa but the footsteps passed. Another door opened and closed. He put the map back on the table. He looked out the study door. He heard someone singing softly in the parlor, and he ran toward the back of the house and outside to the pantry where his pallet was laid out in the kitchen.

Sitting on his pallet in the milky morning light, he quickly sketched everything he remembered on the pad the artist had given him. But there was a blank space and for the life of him he couldn't remember what was supposed to be there. *What if it's the most important thing on the map?*

He had to go back. Too much depended on getting it right. Next door in the kitchen the cook was clattering pots and pans. The smell of frying bacon sweetened the air. The household would be up soon. Fortunately the cook had her back to him when he snuck through the kitchen and ran back to the mansion. He wound through the service hallways without seeing another soul and was soon back in the study. This time he brought his copied map with him. He was just filling in the section, disappointed to see it was only more rifle pits, when the sun blasted through the window and hit him square in the face, blinding him. He heard the study door open. He thrust the copied map behind his back.

"I jist lookin—" he sputtered, "for somethin' my massa left last night." Bledsoe barely made out the woman in the doorway. He shaded his eyes. A young woman in a high-necked gray dress. Her black-as-night hair was looped around each ear. She was pale as milk. On one side of her face an angry scar zigzagged toward her chin. He dropped the map and stumbled backward. *Ghost.*

She took one tentative step into the study. *This dream is too cruel.* Sunlight radiated in a halo around him like a saint in the window of St. Paul's. She moved slowly toward the vision, afraid if she moved too quickly it would evaporate. But when he looked down into her face, she let out a little mew of wonder. His eyes were so luminous and his skin like living flesh. With a shaking index finger she gently brushed his cheek. "Oh Lord," she barely managed. She didn't notice the tears rolling down her cheek.

"Can a spirit feel true as flesh?" he whispered in return. He took her hand from his face and turned it over so that her palm and wrist faced upward. He held a finger to her wrist where the blue veins showed. "How can a ghost have a beating heart?"

"Oh, my love!" Alice threw her arms around his neck. "My love, oh, I ain't a spirit," she said. "It's me, I'm real, but you? I was dreaming. Dreaming and in my dream I came to this room and opened the door. And in my dream—oh Lord, you ain't a dream, a dream don't feel so—I couldn't sleep, something called me to come."

Their words tumbled over one another, interlapping, interweaving. "My God, I thought you'd drowned. I thought you were dead. I've thought you were dead." He wrapped her in his arms. She couldn't think at all, could only feel his arms, smell his fragrance, feel his lips, and he buried his head in her neck, their words tripping over one another.

❧

"My God! What're you doing! Get away from her!"

Alice turned, still wrapped in Bledsoe's arms. Tamsin was standing in the doorway, her face a mask of shock. Her brother pushed her aside and rushed at Bledsoe. Suddenly it was as if Alice's flesh were ripped from her bones. Cadan tore her away from Bledsoe. "Let me go!" she screamed. "Let me go!" She reached for Bledsoe as Cadan held her by the arms.

"What's going on?" said the artist, coming into the study, looking first at Bledsoe, then at Alice, struggling in Cadan's grip.

"Your boy there," screeched Tamsin, pointing at Bledsoe, "was, oh my God, I can't even say!"

"He wasn't!" screamed Alice. "He wasn't! Let me go!"

"What happened?" The artist turned to Bledsoe.

"Get him out of here," yelled Tamsin. "Dirty brute!"

Cadan's face had gone crimson trying to contain the fury that was Alice. "Appears," he panted, "Miss Green didn't mind his pawing her a bit."

"Let her go," exclaimed Bledsoe. "She ain't done nothing, let her go."

"Let me go, let me go!" Alice delivered a furious kick to Cadan's knee. He let out a howl and Alice broke away and ran to Bledsoe.

"Get back," Bledsoe yelled as Cadan limped toward them.

Tamsin screamed, "He's trying to kidnap her!"

"No, he ain't!" Alice screamed back. "Leave him alone!"

Cadan picked up Bledsoe's map from the rug. He glanced at it. Then looked hard at Alice. She grabbed Bledsoe's hand and held it tight. "You're my friend, Tam," implored Alice. "You say I'm like a sister to you. You wouldn't want your sister to suffer, would you? I been suffering awful all this time. I wanted so to tell you the whole of it, but I was scared. Now you know, so let us go. Please. Tell him to just let us go. Just let us go, Tam."

"Have you lost your senses, Alice? Get away from him! What are you doing? Heaven's sake, Alice, think of Henry!"

Alice smiled weakly, tears pouring down her cheeks. "Oh, this *is* Henry. Only it ain't his real name. This is the one I love. I love him, Tam, jist like you love Lord Byron!"

Tamsin stared at Alice and Bledsoe a moment and then let out a wail. "Oh my God. Brother, do something. I feel ill. Good Lord! Do something!"

"Oh, don't you worry, sister. They'll hang. Funny thing is not only did we not know *who* she is, we didn't even know *what* she is."

"Oh," whimpered Tamsin, dropping her hands from her eyes. "What are you saying? You saying she's a—oh, oh, I can't bear it." She lifted her skirt and ran out of the study. "She wore my clothes," she shrieked. "I'll have to burn everything!"

Cadan looked at Alice coldly. "So. I must admit you're much more clever than I've given you credit for. Acting like an ill-bred cretin when all along . . . I *am* surprised."

"What?" Alice stared at Cadan. "I ain't that."

"I never would have guessed you of all people. A spy."

"Step away from the girl," said the artist, the LeMat revolver pointed at Bledsoe's chest.

"What're you doing?" asked Bledsoe, bewildered. "What the hell?"

"Shut your damn mouth," said the artist. "Shut it or I'll shoot, and step away from her."

Bledsoe unwrapped Alice's unwilling arms and stepped away. "She isn't a spy," said Bledsoe. She started back toward Bledsoe, but the artist pointed the gun at his head. Alice stopped in her tracks.

Cadan waved the copied map under her nose. "You can drop the act now, Miss Whoever You Are, though you'll be much more inclined to talk once you see what's in store for you."

"Let her go," said Bledsoe. "*I* drew the map, I and—"

"No!" screamed Alice. But too late. The artist had already brought the butt of the revolver down on Bledsoe's skull. He crumpled to the rug. Alice dropped beside him with a moan.

"I should have known better, Bell. Can't trust any of them." He smiled coldly at Alice on her knees, Bledsoe's forehead bleeding onto her skirt.

From somewhere came a loud pop-pop and the sound of something heavy crashing. Cadan turned to the doorway. "What was that?"

"Pity," said the artist. "I really would have liked to paint you."

"Massa Cade, come quick." Attis ran into the study. He stopped when he saw Bledsoe on the floor.

"Get up," said Cadan, trying to pull Alice away from Bledsoe. "Help me with her, would you?" he asked the artist.

"He daid?" asked Attis.

"No!" shrieked Alice, as the artist and Cadan managed to pull her off Bledsoe. They pinned her between them.

"Help me get them both out to the wagon," panted Cadan.

A high-pitched scream tore through the house.

"Oh no. Miss Tam musta seen him," said Attis, backing out of the study.

"Seen who? What are you talking about, you old fool?" said Cadan.

"Massa Harlan thought the Yankees come. I doan know how he got hold his guns. I hid 'em good. He shot hisself in the leg."

"Son of a bitch," said Cadan. "All this now? I'm supposed to report for duty at Yorktown this afternoon. Come on then, would you? Let's lock her upstairs and we'll put your boy in the stable for now until I can see what's what with my uncle."

"Bledsoe," pleaded Alice, "can you hear me?"

"Come on," commanded the artist, motioning with his gun. "Quietly or I'll shoot you right now."

"Go on then," yelled Alice. "Shoot me, you damn bastard."

"Him too," the artist replied, aiming the revolver at Bledsoe. "Him first so you can watch." He cocked the hammer on the gun and moved the barrel closer to Bledsoe's head.

Alice went upstairs quiet as a mouse until the door was locked behind her.

NINETY-FOUR

He blinked and with the flutter of his eyelids a heavy weight banged inside his skull with a boom. Groaning, he managed to lift his head and spit out straw. He was facedown, hands bound behind him. With a groan he wriggled over on his back and struggled to sit up, leaning against the stable wall. It seemed his neck was made of rubber. He could scarcely hold up his head. Bursts of colored lightning flashed behind his eyes. Daylight showed gray and dim through the cracks in the wall. It was cold but he barely felt it. The pounding in his head was worse. He licked his lips and tasted blood. He breathed deep and willed himself to concentrate. What had happened? He felt a warm glow of joy. She hadn't drowned. Somehow she'd survived. *She's alive.* Then only a moment later. *The gun at my head, the cold expression on your lying face.* "Ahhhhhh," he yelled. "You fucker! I'll kill you!"

He ignored the burst of sickening light behind his eyes. In their stalls, horses nickered nervously. *Liar. Traitor.* He writhed in dirty straw, struggling to free himself. It only made it worse. At last he forced himself to calm down. He gritted his teeth and began working the rope tying his hands. Slowly it began to grow a little bit looser. Suddenly he stopped. *Alice.* Where was Alice? What had they done with her?

She threw herself against the bedroom door and bounced back again, her teeth clenched in fury. Nursing her bruised shoulder, she went to the window for the hundredth time. It overlooked an enormous back garden that stretched into the distance. Smoke rose from the detached brick kitchen. Chickens pecked around a henhouse. At the rear of the garden behind a pruned hedge was a smokehouse, a pigeon coop, and the stable abutting an alley. She had to get to him before they did. Downstairs she heard Tamsin alternately yelling and wailing. Uncle Harlan was either dead or dying. For the moment at least, everyone seemed too occupied to think about her or Bledsoe.

A colored woman Alice knew to be the new cook emerged from the kitchen carrying a covered tray and disappeared from view as she entered the rear of the Bell house. The sun had disappeared and the sky seemed to have lowered itself only a few feet above the leafless trees. A moment later rain began to pitter-patter against the glass. She pulled on the sash again but the window still wouldn't budge. The wood was swollen. She looked frantically around the room. On the dressing table was a metal comb. She grabbed it and pried at the stubborn sash. At last she was able to wriggle it up, bit by bit. When she stuck her head out the window, the rain stung like needles. It was coming down cold and hard. She looked down. If she jumped she'd likely break her legs.

She pulled her head back inside, wiping her face with her sleeve, scanning the room. She ran to the bed and quickly made a rope of the sheets. It was soon obvious it wasn't going to be long enough. "Damn me!" she muttered. "Damn damn." Frantic again, she once more stuck her head out the window. Just out of reach to the left of the window was a sweet gum tree.

⁂

In the stable, he'd stopped fighting wildly. Only by slow and calculated movements had he managed to loosen the rope binding his hands. A moment later he pulled his hands free. When he got to the stable door, he found it locked from the outside. He banged it with his fists until he felt the skin begin to swell.

⁂

The rain spit at her but she didn't care. She sat on the window ledge trying to get up the courage to make a leap for a branch of the tree. She closed her eyes. She knew it was now or never. She pushed herself from the ledge with all her strength, her arms outstretched to connect with the tree limb. She missed. Her skirt blinded her as it rushed up to meet her face.

Alice lay on her back, her open eyes blinded by the rain. She blinked and water ran down her cheeks. Slowly and cautiously she wiggled her arms, then legs. They worked. She was lying in a muddy puddle. She struggled to stand, her wet skirt tripping her. She fell again but managed to get up. She quickly patted herself. Nothing broken, though she knew it would all ache like hell later. Without a glance at the Bell house, she ran through the brown winter garden toward the stable.

NINETY-FIVE

Alice threw back the iron latch, and without a second's hesitation Bledsoe pulled her to him. "Get inside!" he yelled. "Hurry." Puzzled, she looked over her shoulder as he pulled her into the stable. Racing toward them were Cadan Bell and the artist, both with pistols aimed. A gun was fired just as Bledsoe struggled to close the stable door. He heard the bullet's whistle as it passed and lodged into a post.

"Halt!" Cadan yelled. "Halt! Put your hands up!"

Bledsoe slowly raised his hands. Alice raised hers.

The artist called out behind Cadan, "Bell! Look here!"

Cadan turned and the artist pulled his trigger. Bledsoe and Alice watched astonished as Cadan Bell fell to his knees in the garden. He opened his mouth but all that came out was a waterfall of red. His eyes widened with surprise. Then he fell face-first into the mud.

Speechless, Bledsoe and Alice turned now to the artist. Rain had plastered his silver hair to his skull, and his goatee hung limply. He walked toward them and Bledsoe put his arm protectively around Alice's shoulders, drawing her backward. But the artist turned the revolver around and handed Bledsoe his LeMat.

"Now," he said with a thin smile. "Don't kill me. Aim for the left arm. That way I can still paint."

"What?" breathed Bledsoe, looking at the gun in his hand and then at Cadan Bell, rain splish-splashing off the back of his golden head. "You killed him. Then why'd you hit me back there?"

"Oh, for heaven's sake, Joe, I couldn't risk you exposing me. This way you'll be the one blamed for Bell and I will have survived your murderous attack by a miracle, leaving me free to continue my work."

"You *want* me to shoot you?"

"Better hurry. You and your lady don't have much time. They'll be out looking for us any time now." The artist smiled at Alice. "So this is why you always looked so miserable. I commend you. Now hurry up or we'll all be dead."

Bledsoe shook his head. "I don't understand you."

The artist shrugged. "Honestly? Neither do I sometimes."

"You two are wastin' time. Give it here," said Alice, reaching for the revolver. "I'll do it."

But Bledsoe held the gun out of her reach. "What about the map?"

The artist patted his pocket. "Right here. Good work, not sure if it'll do a damn bit of good, but that's all we can do is try. Now." He looked hard at Bledsoe. "You ever fire a gun? No, of course you haven't. Good Lord, what am I thinking?" He glanced at Bell, crumpled in a pool of his own blood. "But there's no other way," he muttered. He held his target arm out away from his body. "Listen carefully, aim for the flesh at the upper arm," instructed the artist, "so it hopefully doesn't break the bone, Joe, and—"

Bledsoe fired. The artist immediately screamed and clutched his upper arm. "Jesus goddamn in Heaven oh goddamn Joe goddamn Joe!"

Bledsoe looked at the gun in wonder. "That's not my name."

Groaning and cursing, the artist paced in a tight circle of clear anguish. Then stopped abruptly. "All right." He moaned a moment and sucked in air between clenched teeth. His face was nearly the silvery pale of his hair. "All right. Now. Let's give you a fighting chance, shall we? Only fair. Reach in my inner coat pocket. Made Bell pay me in silver, none of that Confederate stuff. Take it."

Bledsoe pulled out a small velvet bag. He shook it. Coins jingled inside.

"So now you're not only a murderer, but a robber, Joe," said the artist with another muffled groan of pain. "Damn, I do believe you nicked the bone."

"His name's not Joe, it's Hawk," said Alice.

"Hawk," repeated the artist. He sat down heavily on the wet ground, a hand pressed to his bleeding arm. He grimaced with pain, then fumbled in his coat and pulled out his flask. He opened it with his teeth and drank deep. "Ah. That's better. You told me another name once. The one she called you by a bit ago. No matter. What we call ourselves is not who we are, is it? Hawk is fine. I take it that's Hawkeye from *Last of the Mohicans*?"

Bledsoe tucked the LeMat into his belt. "Guess so."

"Figures," said the artist. "Always the romantic. Now listen. I don't know how far you'll get. They'll have the whole city out after you very soon for the murder of one of their fair sons of the Confederacy. And rest assured, if you're caught and tell them different, I'll deny it all. Who do you think they'll believe—me or you? Now go on, get out of here. I have a distinct feeling I'm about to faint."

NINETY-SIX

They had made it through back alleys and nearly empty streets to a part of town near the river. Though they'd been looked at more than once, no one had stopped them. Brick warehouses and other mercantile businesses lined the street where they stood beside an abandoned cart. The rain had stopped but the sky was even darker. It was oddly quiet considering it was the middle of the afternoon, but the weather was no doubt the reason. The temperature had dropped suddenly and the air was frigid. A woman in a building across the street opened a second-story window and emptied a chamber pot. Alice glanced at her fearfully, but the woman closed the window and yanked a ragged curtain over it. There was no one else on the street.

"Your head," Alice said, reaching toward it.

"I'm all right." He gently pushed her hand away. "We should split up."

"No!"

He looked at her sadly. "There's no chance if we don't. We've already wasted an hour. Someone has surely found them by now. They'll have our descriptions. Look how we stand out."

Alice threw her arms around him. "I won't. I won't be apart from you ever again."

"But it's impossible," said Bledsoe quietly, untangling himself from her. "You'll be safer this way."

A man came out of a dry goods shop across the street and spat tobacco juice on the wet sidewalk. He either didn't notice them or didn't care. He walked away and disappeared around a corner. "I got an idea," said Alice quietly.

"No," whispered Bledsoe. "No ideas. I'll go now."

But Alice looked up at him with those eyes. Were they gray? Or green? "Please," she said. "Please give me that money and don't go."

He handed her the velvet bag and sighed. "Go ahead then. Guess I'm just going to end up dead no matter what," he muttered.

It seemed like two days but was really only ten minutes before Alice returned. "Come on," she hissed, beckoning him to follow. The rain had stopped but the air was colder, the sky the color of granite. A dog growled as they passed the rear of a tavern, but it was on a chain. "Here," she said. "Wait here for me."

Bledsoe reached out to grab her, but she'd already vanished into a falling-down shed next to the rear of a tavern. "Oh Lord," he sighed, and pressed himself against a wall, hoping no one would come out back and wonder what he was doing. Five minutes, then ten passed. What the hell was she doing? The dog on the chain began to bark. Loud and furious.

A short white man in a bowler hat suddenly appeared a few feet away from Bledsoe. He looked right and left but there was nowhere to run. He put a hand on the revolver at his waist. If they thought he'd killed one white man he might as well shoot another. But before he could pull the gun free the little man was on him. With astonishing strength, he grabbed hold of Bledsoe's collar and yanked his head downward. Then he kissed him with a loud smack right on the lips.

Bledsoe shoved the man away, drawing the revolver.

"Honey!" exclaimed the little man. "Shhh now. Don't you know me? Who else'd kiss you like that?"

❦

It began to snow. Flakes soft as feathers at first. But within moments the flakes were large as popped corn. They could barely make out the opposite street through the veil of white. Alice's breath hung between them as she said, "Sometimes I have good ideas." He saw now that beneath a greatcoat she wore a man's plaid suit. Too big, the trousers hung awkwardly over a pair of muddy boots. She held up a satchel. "I got you clothes too. Now, how we gonna git out of this damn town?"

"The map," replied Bledsoe. "I have in my head where their sentries are."

Alice stuck out her tongue to catch a snowflake. "Snow ought to slow 'em down, I reckon. We could try to git back to the place in the hills."

"Yes," he replied, "but even like this, staying together makes it easier to get caught. You know if that happens, we're bound to swing."

"Then"—Alice smiled up at him through the falling snow—"we'll swing together."

Bledsoe said, "What am I ever going to do with you, Alice Brown?"

"Just take me with you."

AUTHOR'S NOTE

I didn't know I would write this novel. It started as a few exploratory pages. There was a young girl, she spoke in a dialect, she lived in a swamp with an old woman she referred to as "the witch." There was a preacher in those first pages and the girl was digging a grave in the swamp. Then I stopped writing. A swamp? What did I know about swamps? Quicksand, snakes. Stuff gleaned from old B movies. Within a few minutes of Googling, however, I came across a swamp between Virginia and North Carolina named the Great Dismal. I couldn't invent a better name for a place. Or even for the time in which I had set my story. When I also learned it was a hiding place for runaway slaves, Bledsoe was born.

I wrote the first chapter quickly. But now Bledsoe was a runaway slave. I had considered myself not completely ignorant when it came to American history. My father used to teach it and the Civil War was his specialty. But I soon found out I knew very little. Every book I read about slavery in America led to another. Each one more terrible, more horrific. Not only the brutality, but the not uncommon occurrence of children born to their slave masters. One of the most notable examples is Thomas Jefferson's enslaved mistress, Sally Hemings. Not only did she bear six children with Jefferson, she was also half sister to his wife, Martha Wayles Skelton. Sally Hemings was three-quarters white, but slavery was determined through the mother's line and her mother was born a slave. What must have been in Sally Heming's mind as she waited on her half sister, the *wife of her owner and also lover?* And what of those owner fathers? Didn't they care about these enslaved women and the children they fathered? Apparently a few did, but most didn't seem too bothered. I learned this was the mind-set of a society that couldn't bring themselves to call those they kept in bondage *slaves*. The preferred term among the genteel class was *servants*. I began to understand that this charade was how slave owners could pretend they weren't morally reprehensible. They didn't have slaves; they had servants, therefore implying that those enslaved humans didn't really mind that much because look here, they're servants! This is a society that referred to the lifeblood—literally life blood—of Southern economic society not as slavery but as the peculiar institution. They justified enslavement by saying those kept in bondage were not quite as human as they were themselves, even if that slave, that human being, carried half their own DNA.

So it's not a surprise that in *Edenland*, Bledsoe despises the white part of himself, the heritage of his owner/father. Yet as I wrote I realized there must be a yearning, as in any child, to be loved. I realized also that his father did love Bledsoe, yet it teetered on the edge of love for a cherished pet rather than a son. He could not accept that Bledsoe had the capability to be his equal, for that would tumble his flimsy house of cards—the one he'd built to justify owning other human beings.

Though Alice is not a slave, she was treated as one. This has happened to neglected and forgotten children since time out of mind. It was only natural, as I continued to write, that Bledsoe and Alice would form a bond. They had a mutual understanding of the feeling of being all alone in the universe. When they discover each other, the love that grows is fiercer than most. It is all and everything. Because not only their love but even their companionship was illegal, and not only in the South. It was punishable at the very least by imprisonment, though it might also result in being burned alive or hung from a tree. To continue to stay together despite these odds takes a powerful kind of love.

I spent nearly a year researching the book. I studied maps of battles, campaigns by both North and South, and decided to write about only the first battle of the war. There are people who spend their lives studying the Civil War. I can't pretend to a fraction of their depth of knowledge, but I hope I did my homework well enough. This war was hideous. Not just the brutality of the weapons and the carnage they created, but also the disease and infections that doomed hundreds of thousands. Many fell, died, and were buried in unmarked graves never to be remembered for what they thought they were fighting for. The numbers of the dead and horror of this war cannot be understated.

As I wrote the end of this book, I found myself wondering how far we have really come since those days. Sometimes it seems we've made it miles. But others times it's all I can do not to break down and cry when I hear of another tragedy chalked up to race. *Doesn't anyone remember?* I say to myself. *Have we learned nothing?* I can only hope that Bledsoe and Alice make it over the mountains and find Edenland.

ACKNOWLEDGMENTS

To Jodi Warshaw, the most excellent of editors, my gratitude is boundless. Deepest thanks to my amazing and tireless agent, Paul Lucas, who found *Edenland* such a wonderful home. Jenna Free, thanks for your splendid eye, and also thanks to the entire team at Lake Union, who made this such a great experience. To my early readers—if I were rich I'd fly you to some Edenic resort where you'd be pampered within an inch of your lives. In the meantime, and maybe forever, I can only offer my deepest thanks. To Debra Eve, who read so many drafts I believe she had to get new glasses, thank you. To my friend across the pond, Rose Kingsland, thanks for always nudging me back on the path when I wandered off picking daisies. To Gayla Terzian, Rebecca Weir, John McInnis, Larry Wells, thank you for reading early and helping me flesh out Bledsoe and Alice's journey. To Elizabeth Few, who traveled the haunted Virginia Peninsula with me, thank you for patiently listening to my historical rants. You didn't even laugh when I stood enraptured inside Fort Monroe and exclaimed, "The walls really *are* that thick!" To Cathie Pelletier and Rachel Samuels, boundless gratitude for your continual support. Libby Flores and Katherine Easer, thank you both for proving me right. A special thanks to Seth McCormack-Goodhart at Washington and Lee University for the unpublished copy of Mary Randolph Blaine's personal diary. This young southern woman opened a window into a world I'd never have seen without your help. And very special thanks to my husband, Nicholas. The words *thank you* here look too thin and puny for all you've made possible. I can honestly say I could never have done it without you. To those departed and once enslaved in this country, you will never be forgotten. There are not enough apologies in this world for the suffering you endured.

SUGGESTED READING FOR A DEEPER UNDERSTANDING OF THE WORLD OF *EDENLAND*

The Internet is an amazing tool, and I bookmarked hundreds of links researching this novel. I once spent an entire day finding a certain type of rifle. I watched videos to see and hear what the rifle sounded like being fired. All of that time for what ended up as something like, "The rifle fired." But you never know what you'll discover when you seek to step into another time and place. Below are some books that gave early bones to *Edenland.* They provide a glimpse into a time not so long past, a time that should never be forgotten.

Johnson, Walter. *Soul by Soul: Life inside the Antebellum Slave Market.* Cambridge, MA: Harvard University Press, 1999.

Baptist, Edward E. *The Half Has Never Been Told: Slavery and the Making of American Capitalism.* New York: Basic Books, 2014.

Yetman, Norman R. *When I Was a Slave: Memoirs from the Slave Narrative Collection.* Mineola, NY: Dover, 2002.

Foner, Eric. *The Fiery Trial: Abraham Lincoln and American Slavery.* New York: Norton, 2010.

Jacobs, Harriet A., Lydia Maria Child, and Jean Fagan Yellen. *Incidents in the Life of a Slave Girl: Written by Herself.* Cambridge, MA: Harvard University Press, 1987.

Douglass, Frederick. *My Bondage and My Freedom.* United States: Bottom of the Hill, 2010.

Litwack, Leon F. *Been in the Storm So Long: The Aftermath of Slavery.* New York: Knopf, 1979.

Gates, Henry Louis. *The Classic Slave Narratives.* New York: Penguin, 1987.

Ball, Edward. *Slaves in the Family.* New York: Farrar, Straus, and Giroux, 1998.

Faust, Drew Gilpin. *This Republic of Suffering: Death and the American Civil War.* New York: Knopf, 2008.

Wiley, William, and Terrence J. Winschel. *The Civil War Diary of a Common Soldier: William Wiley of the 77th Illinois Infantry.* Baton Rouge: Louisiana State University Press, 2001.

Watkins, Samuel R., and M. Thomas Inge, ed. *Co. Aytch, or, a Side Show of the Big Show and Other Sketches.* New York: Plume, 1999.

Chesnut, Mary Boykin Miller, *Mary Chesnut's Diary.* New York: Penguin, 2011.

Hunt Rhodes, Elisha, and Robert Hunt Rhodes. *All for the Union: The Civil War Diary and Letters of Elisha Hunt Rhodes.* New York: Orion, 1991.

Elizabeth Keckley. *Behind the Scenes: Or, Thirty Years a Slave and Four Years in the White House.* New York: Oxford University Press, 1988.

Kelly, John. *The Graves Are Walking: The Great Famine and the Saga of the Irish People.* New York: Holt, 2012.

Herndon, Ruth Wallis, and John E. Murray. *Children Bound to Labor: The Pauper Apprentice System in Early America.* Ithaca, NY: Cornell University Press, 2009.

Hurston, Zora Neale, and Cheryl A. Wall. *Folklore, Memoirs, and Other Writings.* New York: Library Classics of the United States, 1995.

Chesnutt, Charles W., and William L. Andrews. *Conjure Tales and Stories of the Color Line.* New York: Penguin, 2000.

Gordon-Reed, Annette. *The Hemingses of Monticello: An American Family.* New York: Norton, 2008.

ABOUT THE AUTHOR

photo © 2015 by Kate Turning

Wallace King is the author of two previous novels, *The True Life Story of Isobel Roundtree* and *Maybelleen*. After moving from New York to Los Angeles, she became a screenwriter; *Edenland* marks her return to fiction.